The Shrunken Dream

Jane

Tapsubei

Creider

women's
PRESS

CANADIAN CATALOGUING IN PUBLICATION DATA
Creider, Jane Tapsubei.
    The shrunken dream

ISBN 0-88961-175-0

I. Title.

PS8555.R44S5 1992   C813' .54   C92-095538-X
PR9199.3.C74S5 1992

Editor: Mwĩkali Kĩeti
Copy editor: Ramabai Espinet
Cover illustration: Clover Clarke
Cover and Series Design: Denise Maxwell

This book was produced by the collective effort of Women's Press.
Women's Press gratefully acknowledges the financial support of the Canada Council and the Ontario Arts Council.

Printed and bound in Canada
1 2 3 4 5 1996 1995 1994 1993 1992

ACKNOWLEDGEMENTS

To:

Heather Erksine for your uplifting encouragement for my writing.

Joan Barfoot and Ros de Lanerolle for suggesting publication with Women's Press.

Imke Jorgensen, you said after reading my manuscript that you wished anthropologists would learn to write like this. You were generous to give me such a compliment.

Friends who listened and consoled me when my father passed away while I was editing the book: Jean Dollar and her husband John, Jean Spence, Regna Darnell, Jane and Jean-Marc Philibert.

My children: Julia, you tried to let me work; Sarah, the keen interest you took in the work energized me; and Colin, I know you are proud of me.

Chet and Vera, in-laws, and John Hammond, friend, for your enthusiasm for my writing.

Chet, my husband, for your help with text processing.

Mwĩkali Kĩeti and Ann Decter for your editorial suggestions.

I owe thanks to all of you for the many conversations which helped to keep me going as I finished the book.

To the memory of my father,
Suswa Kipserem Arap Busienei Kabelio

NOTES ON NANDI NAMES

Men and women have names with distinct prefixes. Men's first names begin with the prefix Kip– (sometimes Ki–). After initiation, men are usually referred to by the first names of their fathers, preceded by the word Arap "son of." For example, Arap Walei, Mary's husband, was the son of a man named Walei. Women have names which either begin with the prefix Chep– (sometimes Che–) or the prefix Tap– (sometimes Ta–). A family is sometimes referred to as an entity with the prefix Kap–, which literally means "place of or house of." For example, the family of Arap Walei would be Kapwalei. Ka(p)– is also a common prefix in place names. For example, Kamasai literally means "place of the Masai" To avoid confusing families and place names, I have tried to write the family prefix as a separate word — Kap Walei (JTC).

FAMILY TREE

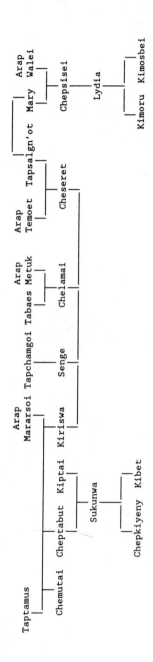

PROLOGUE: 1990

*L*ike their forebears, Sukunwa's parents were proud to live under the bondage of the dreams and hopes they held for their child. Sukunwa was a beautiful daughter, and her beauty lessened the pain of all they had gone through before she was born. "May she be respected by her husband and his family. May she have numerous children. May anything she touches multiply. May the sun shine on her and her livestock — the cattle, the sheep and the goats." The elders had blessed her with these wishes throughout her childhood. As Sukunwa grew up, the neighbours in Mt. Kamasai agreed that she was beautiful. They remarked about her looks, her delicate body, and golden eyes. "She looks as though she has been fashioned by hand," they said. By the age of fifteen she appeared serene and self-possessed, and only one friend and one member of her family had any hint of the turmoil she had endured. Sukunwa had run from that turmoil, she had disappeared from her homeland alone in the prime of her youth. Today, decades later, she was returning to Kenya, dropping from the sky, a woman with two Canadian children and a husband.

At first, Sukunwa had been impressed with North American progress. But after living there for many years, listening to whites brag about their superiority over Blacks while they raped the world of its natural wealth, she was no longer impressed. She saw more white greed than advancement and felt the world would be destroyed by their greed unless their civilization tumbled down like those in Africa thousands of years ago. She thought the word 'progress' had blinded them to what they were doing.

Though people were polite, Sukunwa never made any real friends in North America. Living in a white suburb, she found her presence stimulated talk about that aspect of Blacks which was uppermost in

13

her neighbours' minds — the problems they were having with them. They said nothing good about Black people in general, which made her very self-conscious and defensive. She also found it exhausting to talk to them. Sukunwa had seen white people's faults, too, but could not discuss them and ruin their belief that their culture was perfect. She hated having to listen to how normal, middle-class suburbanites were innocent of everything evil, how evil came from the inner cities, where she knew Blacks lived. The only innocent thing about whites was the way they thought they were innocent. They had their faults. What wouldn't white people do for money, Sukunwa wondered. They had even gone so far as selling plots to the dead who only rotted and turned to soil while the living pocketed the money.

Sukunwa's husband worked as a troubleshooter for the international division of a large computer company which sent him all over the world. They called him Speedo because he was always on the go. Speedo had travelled to Kenya for his company before, but always on short notice. This time he knew in advance. Kenya was the first stop on a three month trip covering Africa and South America. When he called Sukunwa to relay the news, Sukunwa jumped at the chance to accompany him to Nairobi.

"Why not?" he said.

"Yes, I'll remain in Kenya with the children while you are in South America." Sukunwa hadn't told anyone in Kenya that she was coming.

The family spent two weeks in Nairobi sorting out visas for their Canadian-born children. Until then, it hadn't occurred to Sukunwa as a Kenyan that her own children needed special permission to remain in the country. She went from one immigration office to another to be told in the end that only the children of Kenyan men were automatically citizens, not women's children. Eventually, Speedo obtained the children's visas. That evening, Sukunwa and the children saw him off at the airport. A quick hug from the children, a quick kiss from Sukunwa, and they watched him disappear behind the barriers of the customs officers on his way to Sao Paolo, Brazil. They would meet next at home in Canada.

The following day, Sukunwa and the children left Nairobi in their rented car and drove west. The children huddled at the windows, their eyes riveted on the new countryside.

"Did you see those orange and blue birds?" asked her son, Kibet.

"Yes, they're a beautiful, iridescent blue, and they're only found in Africa," said Sukunwa. "They're called *kuliosinik* in Nandi."

"Oh, look at those two ostriches. Those are in Canada. I remember seeing them in the Toronto Zoo," said Chepkiyeny, his twin sister.

Set back from the road on the outskirts of Nairobi stood grey cement-block houses with beautiful red clay tile roofs. The grass, trees and bushes on the edge of the road were brown, and cursed any car that kicked more dust upon them.

Before long they had left Nairobi city and faced the 3,000-foot drop of the Great Rift Valley Escarpment. It was frightening to drive alongside it. The immensity of the view left them breathless. The flowers peeping through the trees from the bottom of the valley were stunningly beautiful. It was the time of year when all the trees and bushes were in bloom. Mt. Longonot rose gently from the valley floor below like a cradle. A long white, muslin sheet of morning fog nestled at the bottom of the cradle. On the other side of the road, black and white sheepskins were hung together with a variety of coloured baskets. As Sukunwa slowed down to allow the children to look at the spectacular view, vendors rushed across the highway, their arms laden with goods.

"*Mama, nunua ngozi, nunua kikapu! Hii ngozi ni nzuri sana!* — Ma'am, buy a sheepskin, buy a basket! This skin is a better quality one!"

"Not now. Another day," said Sukunwa.

The car started rolling on the road again and the children started begging.

"Please, mother, we want to see the animals," they said. Sukunwa promised to take them to see the flamingos on Lake Nakuru. Africa's positive image in the eyes of North Americans consisted of animals, and Sukunwa's children were no exception. "Mom, people say there are huge spiders in Africa. Where are they?" Their constant refrain of

15

"Mom," irritated Sukunwa. "We are not on a hunt for wild animals. I miss my family now that I'm driving home, and I'm rushing to get there."

At eleven o'clock they left the rim of the Escarpment and made their descent. Down the valley in the distance lay the dying Lake Nakuru — a white ribbon of soda surrounding its shrinking waters. A few flamingos could be seen hopping around. It looked close, but it took an hour to drive across the plain. Lake Nakuru seemed to move away as they drove.

At midday, they stopped for a snack in Nakuru. Clouds moved in the sky like billowing, black smoke from a factory. It was almost dark when the rain closed in as they finished eating.

"The rain in Kenya has its own mind," Sukunwa told the children. "It can go on until tomorrow or end in ten minutes. We have to drive on. I'll take you tomorrow to see the giraffes at Kamagut, outside of Eldoret, the next big city on our way."

They drove through heavy rain for miles and miles before it lessened to large, intermittent drops. "Is that person Nandi, mother?" the children asked.

"How can I tell in the rain?" replied Sukunwa. She had taught them that not everyone in Kenya was Nandi. There were shepherds standing in the rain along the road guarding their cattle and the children asked why they stayed in the rain without umbrellas.

They saw children coming home from school, with their books inside their shirts to protect them from the rain.

"Why are they walking in the rain? Don't their parents go and pick them up?"

They saw women walking, little children strapped to their backs and firewood balanced on their heads. At Tegat they saw women shielding themselves from the rain with empty gunnysacks over their heads, hauling the potatoes they were selling away from the roadside. And these, too, gave rise to questions.

Late in the afternoon, they reached Eldoret, 200 miles from Nairobi, and drove on, Sukunwa worrying whether the road ahead was still not paved. Thirty miles later, the pavement ended in the muddy city of Kapsabet. After wallowing in mud for ten minutes, Sukunwa got out to go for help. She ran and knocked on a bar door near the road where old men were drinking in the afternoon. The men reaffirmed her faith in the kindness of Africans. Even the ones who were unsteady on their feet came to lend a hand. Sukunwa gave each of them two shillings after they had lifted the car out and drove on about a hundred yards to where the pavement resumed.

At dusk they reached Chemobo Valley where Sukunwa's childhood friend, Lydia, lived. Sukunwa and Lydia had been friends ever since they had been aware that they were human. They were born in the 1950s in western Kenya in a location which is now called the Nandi Escarpment, the steep edge of a mountain range stretching from Lake Nyanza to Mt. Elgon, on the border between the Luyia and the Nandi. The friendship of their families extended back five generations. Prior to the British occupation, the families were considered the wealthiest and most politically powerful in Nandi history. The men of their lineages led the Nandi in successful resistance efforts against the first two British expeditions in the 1890s. After the defeat of the Nandi in the third and final expedition, the families lost their eminence, but their names still echoed in legends.

Lydia now worked as a housekeeper for Tapsirorei, a rich widow who had been married to an English settler. She went to work for her after Sukunwa left Kenya, and over the years had become Tapsirorei's right hand woman. Standing in the doorway of her house, Lydia couldn't believe it was Sukunwa stepping out of the car. They ran to each other.

"*Asai* Lydia!"

"*Asai* Sukunwa!" They hugged and cried.

"You've come back at last!" Lydia said through tears, "you've come back at last."

"You haven't changed in all these years, Lydia. You look the same," Sukunwa smiled.

Lydia looked at her carefully, "You look like Sukunwa, but...." She stopped.

"You can't imagine me with grey hair?" asked Sukunwa. She had a patch of grey hair on the right side of her head and wore glasses.

"Not that," said Lydia. "You look very distinguished, and more beautiful than before."

Lydia's oldest son advanced to shake Sukunwa's hand, but Sukunwa pulled him to her and hugged him instead, tears running down her cheeks.

Lydia tapped her on the shoulder. "Sukunwa, Kimosbei is waiting for you. Kimoru, you were a baby when Sukunwa left. That's why she hugged you for a long time. You are like an old friend."

"This is Kimosbei, of course," said Sukunwa. "Has your mother told you I am your second mother?"

"No, but she has talked about you very much," said Kimosbei.

"Can I hug your children, too?" asked Lydia, unsure if Canadian children hugged.

"Of course," answered Sukunwa.

"Let me guess — this is Chepkiyeny, and this is Kibet." She hugged them.

"Yes, you are psychic," said Sukunwa laughing. She turned to her children. "She is joking. Lydia knows your names because 'Kip-' in Nandi is always a boy, and 'Chep-' is always a girl."

Lydia took Sukunwa's hand and led her into the house. The children followed them in. Sukunwa's children stood dumbly in the middle of the room. Chepkiyeny was embarrassed to see her mother cry in front of strangers.

"Have the children sit down, Kimoru. Why do they look so cold? Tell them their aunt's house is their house," said Lydia.

"Give them time, they've never seen me excited like this," Sukunwa answered.

The children went to the next room beside the kitchen. The fire in the kitchen made the house cozy and warm. "What I have missed in Canada is sitting around a real fireplace in the winter," Sukunwa said.

"Don't you have fireplaces in Canada?" Lydia asked.

"We do, but we don't sit around them. We sit in front of them since they are built against the wall."

"How do you sit to get warm?"

"Fireplaces are mostly built for show, not for daily use. The houses are heated by gas," Sukunwa said.

"Mother?"

"Yes, Chepkiyeny, what is it?"

"Did we leave Canada on Friday the 13th?

"Why?"

"Kibet almost burned the house down."

"Watch how you walk in the kitchen. The wood sticks out of the fireplace here, and you might kick it."

"Mother, that's exactly what Kibet did. The embers spread all over the floor."

"Has Kimoru swept them?" asked Lydia.

"Yes, but mother," Chepkiyeny walked to her mother and whispered in her ear, "I'm afraid we will be burned here. The fire is in the middle of the house with no screen over it."

"No, Chepkiyeny, we have always had a fire like that — the house won't burn. Stay here with us if you are afraid," Sukunwa said.

"What is she talking about? Did she say she was afraid of the fire?" Lydia asked.

"Yes, it started when we arrived in Nairobi. Twice the hotel where we stayed almost caught fire," replied Sukunwa.

"Poor children! Sweetheart don't worry. I will look after the fire myself," Lydia said.

For the first week after their arrival, Sukunwa was visited every day by old friends and curious neighbours. Life in the country was still serene. Nobody ever seemed to be in a hurry. They came and made themselves feel at home. They made tea, drank it, and brought Sukunwa up to date about themselves and their mutual childhood friends — who married whom, who had how many children, whose husband didn't have a job, whose husband had become alcoholic. This was the daily routine in the country, one piece of gossip after another.

Afterwards, the women hurried home for their evening chores, some gathering firewood on their way. If it was very late, they went straight home, took a container and went to the dairy to milk the cattle.

The preparation of dinner began very late — around eight o'clock when all the livestock were in the kraal.

Lydia's children arrived home from school, put their books away and went to bring Sukunwa's children home from a little adult literacy school in the community where Lydia had taken them to learn Nandi. They played with friends on their way home.

Whenever Sukunwa had a moment alone, memories came flooding back. Tropical east Africa had no twilight, and every day she watched the sun sink swiftly below the horizon. By six-thirty, a fleeting, rosy afterglow touched Kesenge mountain, while the valley below was already covered with a black blanket of darkness from Kapchorwa mountain looming above it. Before she had finished admiring the dying, pale pink and orange rays, the stars had appeared, hanging in the sky like faceted diamonds floating in a sea above her. The dim, fluttering light of the stars gently caressed the ground. No place in the world that Sukunwa had seen had sunsets like the Kenya highlands.

It took Sukunwa a week to get used to the arrival of darkness at seven. She had dinner on the table when Lydia arrived. The children sat on a mat laid on the kitchen floor. They all ate from a common dish, and Chepkiyeny grumbled about having to use her hand. Lydia's children were polite enough to let themselves be her victims. They said, "Take the corn bread, roll it round in your hand, press a little hole in it, and scoop the stew up with it." But instead of learning, Chepkiyeny complained, "Ouch, the corn bread is steaming hot and the stew is boiling. I'm burning my hand. They expect me to put my hand in this boiling hot stew. Couldn't these people think of something as simple as a spoon!"

Sukunwa replied, "What could be simpler than an edible spoon — one you don't even have to wash up afterwards?"

Tonight, Lydia seemed more cheerful than usual, which was a relief, thought Sukunwa, considering the gloomy, suicidal weather they'd had that day and Chepkiyeny's complaining.

"Oh, did you remember to go to the Women's Cooperative today?

Kopsilei's house was being plastered," Lydia asked after Chepkiyeny had stopped.

"No, I didn't. By the time I finished the housework, I felt it was too late," Sukunwa replied.

"You have disappointed them. There were some women who wanted to meet you more than have your help plastering the house."

"Why didn't you tell me that yesterday? I could have dropped everything and gone, although I think I have seen them all. I would have plastered the house, too!" exclaimed Sukunwa.

"Would you have?"

"Of course I would have. A woman doesn't remain a guest for long."

"If I had married a white man, I would sit like a white woman," Lydia said.

"You think the old-fashioned way — white women just sit on their fannies. You should go to their country and see them work. They may not put their hands in mud, but they work as hard as you do."

"Sukunwa, no one will believe you. What do they do with all that money?" asked Lydia. "We still see them around. They look elegant, with fingernail polish and lipstick. They don't look rough like us."

"I don't have anything to gain by saying they work when they don't. Caring for children is women's work over there. If they work outside, they still come home and do housework. If you looked closely at those hands with fingernail polish, you would see they were dry and cracked from household chores like yours. We have something a little bit like women's cooperatives, but not quite. It is called car pooling — where some women help each other driving the children to school. When I first arrived in North America, I felt as though I had jumped 200 years into the future because everything was available inside. I didn't go out to look for firewood, to gather wild vegetables, to garden. But the longer I stayed there, the more I came to realize there was work. You could be inside all day long washing, cleaning, making beds, cooking and not have anything to show for it."

"You can give me that any day — to be able to use a car to go anywhere you want and sit and clean the house and cook," said Lydia.

21

We finished building the school last month after months and months of asking the men to build it, and now we have decided to do things for ourselves whenever we can."

"Women did things for themselves anyway until Christianity came and told us we should wait for men to do things for us."

"We should make arrangements with Senge to have her set a day for us to make up for our absence today."

"We were not the only ones who weren't present."

"Kopsilei's house didn't get plastered then? I have no luck. I had hoped with my heart they would have done it without me," said Lydia.

"Can't you stop going to this Cooperative if it's such a burden to you?"

"I can't. No one wants to be the first to break the solidarity."

"Well, this will be good news for you. The house got plastered anyway without us."

"Who helped them to carry water from the stream to mix the clay?"

"They channeled the water from the eavestroughs into the clay-mixing area. Your co-worker Tamara told me this."

"What was Tamara here for?"

"To chat, as usual, and to bring the list of those who were absent. Chepchirchir, Chepkoech, and Chepkosgei Kimunai weren't there either."

"I should have known that Tamara, the neighbourhood newscarrier, would be here."

"No news is too small for that woman," Sukunwa said.

"What else did she say?"

"Nothing." There was a long silence. "Was she supposed to say something else?"

"I thought she might have heard about Kimunai and his wife," said Lydia. Kimunai was the son of Tapsirorei, Lydia's employer.

"What happened to them? She didn't talk about that."

"She ran away, and you can guess the rest."

"Chepkosgei ran away. Kimunai hasn't changed from the day I

first set eyes on him. I know years back there was talk about him and you. Is it still true?" asked Sukunwa.

"It was never true, but Tamara hangs on to the belief. Anytime Chepkosgei runs away, she wishes I was involved."

"I know him so well. Kimunai makes my blood chill. He's crazy, and he's made his mother crazy like him. Why haven't you told Tamara to mind her own business?"

"She can't even if she's told to. She thrives on other people's misfortunes. I don't find talking about her very entertaining. Let's talk about your day apart from her."

"My day was not exciting. Chepkiyeny is beginning to get under my skin."

"It's part of growing up. I've heard girls have a hard time at her age," Lydia said.

"Being miserable is part of her nature. She's been like that ever since she was born. I hope you will go in and talk to her. I've just yelled at her."

"And now you're feeling guilty, aren't you? I'm like that."

"More or less."

"Do you think she is missing her father?"

"I have no idea. She and Kibet are picking on each other more than usual. This afternoon I heard her crying in her room. I went in and asked them what was happening. Chepkiyeny said, 'Kibet has put his smelly shoes beside my bed. When I sprayed them with air-freshener, he slapped me.'"

"'Maybe you should have asked for permission before you sprayed. And where did you get the spray?' I asked. 'Don't you remember, Mommy, we brought it with us from Canada?'"

"I told Kibet to remove his shoes from his sister's bedside and left, but I suspect that before he removed them he slapped Chepkiyeny again. The last thing I heard was a scream and a door slamming. I saw Kibet's shadow passing the window outside. I asked Tamara if she had seen Kibet when she came. But I didn't finish asking her. Chepkiyeny ran in from the other room and said, 'Mother, Kibet would not kill himself — he took his coat. Someone who is going to kill himself is not going to worry about the cold, is he?' I was embarrassed," Sukunwa said.

"Children are children."

"I remember getting along with my brother when I was that age."

"All children fight, but you have raised the child to speak to you in front of other people like that."

"What should I have done? Every child in North America is raised that way. It's called 'freedom of speech'."

"I couldn't care less what gets said in front of Tamara," said Lydia. "She would invent something if you didn't say anything anyway," she added. "I'm going to have a talk with Chepkiyeny as soon as we finish eating."

Later, Chepkiyeny and Lydia came out of the other room, their faces beaming. Sukunwa didn't know what Lydia had told Chepkiyeny, but it worked. Chepkiyeny came up and apologized to her.

Lydia was heading for the water pot to fetch herself a glass of water. The children were in their room with Lydia's older son, Kimoru, and his friends. Sukunwa had just gone and sat with her back against the wall between Kimoru's room and the fireplace when Lydia suddenly turned around.

"What was that?"

"I didn't hear anything."

"You didn't hear that? There was an enormous bang at the front door."

"Kimoru and his friend are making too much noise; I can't hear. In fact, they are getting out of control," Sukunwa said.

They fixed their eyes on the door. Sukunwa turned to Lydia. She stood still with her water glass in her hand. She peered at Sukunwa and shrugged her shoulders, "Maybe I didn't hear anything."

"Were you expecting him?" inquired Sukunwa.

"Him who?" asked Lydia. She knew or at least suspected that Sukunwa thought it was Kimunai, but she couldn't believe it because she had just finished telling her nothing was going on between herself and Kimunai. "You don't believe it, like Tamara. I wouldn't be going around looking surprised if I was expecting Kimunai," she snapped.

24

"I didn't think Kimunai was coming for you. I thought he might come to see me if he knew I was here."

"Do you have a friend coming tonight?" Lydia called to Kimoru.

"No, I don't," said Kimoru.

"Someone knocked at the door and stopped and then knocked again," said Lydia.

"It must be Tamara. She always knocks and eavesdrops for half an hour. You want me to go out and drag her in, mother?" Kimoru asked.

They laughed. "Heavens no. Let her be. She will come in eventually."

"We know it is you, Tamara. Come in!" Chepkiyeny yelled out.

Kimosbei heard his brother talking to their mother and thought that this was the time to get into the arena. He ignored Chepkiyeny altogether. He emerged from the bedroom he shared with his brother and came to stand in front of his mother, half-naked, his blanket dragging on the floor behind him held up between his collarbone and his chin like a violin. He had to work hard to fit into the social group. Whenever his brother said something, he made sure he undid it.

"Mother, did I hear Kimoru saying Tamara was knocking at the door?" he asked with self-assurance.

"Yes, Kimosbei, but go to bed. You are supposed to be asleep."

"Yes, mother, I know, but Kimoru was wrong! It can't be Tamara at the door. She eats with...," he stopped. "I mean, Sukunwa said that Tamara eats with hyenas, and that means she eats late. She must be at home eating."

"Go to bed Kimosbei! Sukunwa, you don't know Kimosbei. He repeats everything you say," Lydia said.

Sukunwa got up and led Kimosbei back to his bed.

"You must never repeat what you hear grown-ups saying, Kimosbei. It was only a joke."

"Aren't you going to find out who is outside, mother?" called Chepkiyeny from her room.

"Yes. Go to bed too!" said Sukunwa.

"Kimoru is right, you know. She is eavesdropping now," said Lydia.

"I would have thought she would eavesdrop before knocking," said Sukunwa.

"Oh no! She knocks first. Since I don't have a man, Tamara assumes I have men visitors. She knocks and listens to hear if I call out for one of them by name."

"She was here about three hours ago. One would think she wouldn't have had time to eat, wash the dishes and come back," said Sukunwa.

"She wouldn't have to do all those. Her grandchildren do everything for her, but what she might be coming back for is beyond me," said Lydia.

"The name Tamara doesn't suit her. In North America she would be called a busybody," said Sukunwa.

Sukunwa went to open the window beside her bed to check if the moon was out. The darkness was alarming, and she slammed the window shut with apprehension. As she turned to Lydia, a voice at the door called out.

"Lydia, are you in bed yet?"

"Who is it?" Lydia asked.

"Tonti!"

"Who did he say he was?" asked Chepkiyeny.

"Not he, she! Chepkiyeny! Go to bed! You will be told your punishment tomorrow morning."

"What did I do?" asked Chepkiyeny.

"It is called 'mental abuse of a parent', and enough is enough," said Sukunwa.

Lydia sighed with relief as Sukunwa went to shut her daughter's door. Mmm. So she found it better to have Tonti than Tamara, Sukunwa thought to herself.

"Oh, come on in Tonti." The hardness on Lydia's face softened. Now she was smiling and listening to Tonti boast about her car falling in the ditch and how she had knocked on the door and gone back to help push the car out.

"Sukunwa, how nice to see you."

"Same here too, Tonti."

"Why did it take you so long to open the door? Were you frightened?" Tonti asked.

"No, you knocked once, and we were trying to figure out who could be outside in this darkness," said Lydia.

"My driver had a torch, and why do you close the door this early? We don't close the doors in Asurur until ten o'clock."

"That's why that woman was murdered there two weeks ago," said Lydia as she walked to the kitchen.

"Not by anyone from Asurur. Her murderer followed her there from Nairobi. How long has it been since I last saw you?" she asked Sukunwa.

She hasn't changed. Her mind still wanders away from the subject, Sukunwa thought.

"It was Christmas Day of 1967. I wouldn't have thought you'd have forgotten. It was a night to remember," Sukunwa said.

"We don't live reminiscing about what has happened in the past," Tonti said. "Kimibei is married. I've heard from Tamara that they have three children." Kimibei was her son.

"Why did Tamara have to tell you? He is your own son," Sukunwa asked.

"Tamara is closer to them than me. He married someone from her people. I haven't bothered to interfere with his precious life with his woman. I've told him never to bring the children to my house. I may not greet them, and who knows what the spirits will do to them if I don't?"

"Do I detect unhappy feelings about their marriage? What kind of girl is married to him? Did they meet at the bank where he works?" Sukunwa asked.

"No, she doesn't work, but she has brought all of her family to my son's house to spend his money."

"Where did they meet?"

"In a whorehouse. I've given him up. Let's talk about you now," Tonti turned around in feigned astonishment.

"Where is Lydia?" she asked.

"In the kitchen, I suppose."

"What is she doing in there alone?"

"I don't know," Sukunwa replied.

"I have the feeling that she is uncomfortable around me," said Tonti.

"I don't know," Sukunwa said again.

Just then, Lydia came in from the kitchen with a pot of tea.

"Oh, you were making tea," said Sukunwa.

"Yes, would anyone care for a cup of tea at nine o'clock at night, or have I made it for nothing?"

"Oh, thank you! I feel rather chilled," Sukunwa said.

"You shouldn't have gone to so much hard work for me," said Tonti. "I ate just before I left. I went to Eldoret first, and you know how people like me there, Sukunwa. I was invited to eat at five different places."

Oh gag me, Sukunwa thought.

"That was nice, but you can still have a cup here." Lydia smiled at Tonti. "It was not a big effort. You don't come to my house often."

Here Lydia goes again. Couldn't she stop? She's going to make her go on and on, Sukunwa thought as she poured the tea for herself. "Lydia, it is old-fashioned to make people eat when they don't want to. If Tonti doesn't wish to drink tea, it's all right. We don't make people eat in North America if they don't want to," she said.

"I know whites are like that. Did you know that, Lydia?" Tonti asked.

"No," answered Lydia.

"How is your mother doing, Lydia?"

"She is doing splendidly, thank you. She was here three weeks ago."

"Who is looking after her now in Mt. Kamasai?"

"I still have relatives there. She is with my aunt and her family. Kitoi has just built a bigger house for them, and they like it immensely, though it took my aunt weeks to get accustomed to the banging on the aluminum roof when it rained," said Lydia.

28

"I hope they know not to make a fire in that kind of house. Everyone wants possessions of their own nowadays. What did Tapsirorei or his wife think when her son built you a house? I don't think it is right for someone in your situation to depend on a married man. Sukunwa, don't you think it is about time for Lydia to be on her own?"

"I work for the Kitois also. Don't forget that part," said Lydia before Sukunwa opened her mouth.

"Yes, Lydia works for what she gets here, Tonti." Sukunwa echoed Lydia's statement.

"I know, but it doesn't hurt to think ahead. People get old. You can't work until you are 90. You should heed advice from those of us who are more experienced in life," Tonti said and looked around. "I can see you have beautiful chairs."

"Yes, she bought them herself," Sukunwa said before Lydia could answer. Sukunwa had grown up in the same neighbourhood as Tonti and knew her nosiness and vanity. She put up with her because Tonti was the same age as her mother. It was nothing for Tonti to proclaim that something was beautiful to praise her own possessions in the process. At the same time she might get Lydia to say the Kitois had bought the chairs for her. She was as predictable as a cuckoo clock. She flushed dark black when Sukunwa jumped ahead and asked her, "Do you think these chairs are good enough to be used in your house?"

"Oh, yes," she said. "I could use them in the patio."

"Why use them outside? Do you want more people to see their beauty?" Sukunwa asked.

"Nothing like that. I have very expensive ones there now, and I'm apprehensive the children may destroy them."

Sukunwa seems to be enjoying this, Lydia thought. She wished them both good night, and went to bed.

Sukunwa was at a loss. I wish I had been the first one to go to bed, she thought. She and Tonti sat observing each other for a few minutes. "We should go to bed," Sukunwa said.

"I have my car with me. I must go home," said Tonti.

They embraced. Sukunwa searched for something nice to tell her before she left. At last she remembered Tonti's housekeeper, an old, deaf lady named Chemotwek. "My greetings to Mary Chemotwek, and your children."

When Sukunwa awoke the next morning, the sun was blazing. The house was situated part way up the hillside, giving a spectacular view of the slopes of the Chemobo River valley. From the window a waterfall could be seen. The water above glistened, racing along with trees of the forest towering on either side of new-green banks. It crashed over the edge, pounding down on the rocks below. A fine, mushroom-like cloud of mist formed above the pool, and between mist and water the sun's reflection formed a rainbow. Just below the mist, the colour was light green. Then red and yellow. Finally blue, faintly visible. Around the mist a flock of butterflies fluttered, moistening and refreshing themselves. It was twelve o'clock, the time in the valley when all of the animals went in groups, both large and small, but never alone.

For a fraction of a second Sukunwa forgot everything. Lydia's hand on her shoulder brought her back to the present.

"You are trembling," Lydia said solicitously.

"I have been on my knees for a while looking out there."

"Tea or lunch?" Lydia had made tea for the family in the morning, set Sukunwa's aside, and left for work. Back for lunch, Sukunwa's tea was still standing.

"I wonder if this means bad luck. I wonder why, of all people I know in Asurur, Tonti had to be the first one to visit me."

"I came back because I know you are a late sleeper."

"It's not true," Sukunwa protested.

"I'll tell you what happened. I decided to finish work early today. Since you have arrived, we haven't spent time together — there is a lot of gossip to catch up with."

The children finished their lunch and returned to school. "The coast is clear. Let me hear this gossip," said Sukunwa.

"Would you like some tea?" Lydia asked.

"Let's hear the gossip."

"Let me say the sun rose from a different direction today for Tapsirorei. She was excited, full of aspirations. When I arrived at her house, it wasn't long before she blurted out to me why Tonti was here in the valley."

"She was happy because of Tonti?"

"Yes."

"I didn't think Tapsirorei was as much a hypocrite as a compulsive liar. She hated Tonti so much she even hated seeing her shadow passing by," said Sukunwa.

"People say that since Tapsirorei's husband and then her sister died, she has changed, and I've seen that during the last few years too, though I didn't know her when her husband was alive. Since her sister's death, she looks dazed sometimes. When talking to her, I have to repeat myself before she answers. Maybe this has caused her to be susceptible to people like Tonti."

"Has she changed that drastically? Or is old age part of it? They are not matched. Tapsirorei is unfriendly, but she is kind-hearted and helpful to other women. Tonti is cruel, arrogant, and contemptuous of everyone else."

"I know. No woman from the reserve can stand her. She speaks down to them, telling them about cars, about colour-matching in clothing, and what kind of shoes she wears on Saturday for the market and Sunday for church, even though she knows they will never have such luxuries. The country women call both of them women who live at the edge of society."

"That old feeling — the city women think the women in the country are not intellectual enough to understand when they are being patronized," said Sukunwa.

"The women in the country think the women from the city are crazy."

"Yes, I can understand Tapsirorei saying, 'Tonti is better than nothing.'"

"More or less. But that is not what's keeping their relationship going. When Cheptepkeny, Tapsirorei's niece, arrived from Canada after her mother's death, her father thought she needed the company of a woman and sent her to live with Tapsirorei. Cheptepkeny was neither charming nor rude, and Tapsirorei felt she couldn't communicate with her. She sat and read in her room. When Tapsirorei tried to talk to her, she only said, 'yes' and 'thank you' and 'please would you.'"

"They didn't get along?"

"It's hard to know. Cheptepkeny is not much of a talker, but she's extremely polite. From the little she said, Tapsirorei concluded she was bored with her because she was old. Ng'aing'ailem, the son of a farmer in the neighbourhood, had just arrived from school himself," Lydia said.

"Was he in Canada?"

"No, in Mauritius, but Tapsirorei thought he and Cheptepkeny might know each other. After all, both had been abroad. She had no idea Mauritius was in the middle of the Indian Ocean!"

"Would it have made any difference if she had known Mauritius and Canada were not the same?"

"Maybe not, but maybe she wouldn't have thought of him. In any case, Tapsirorei had no way of knowing the introduction would lead afterwards to their spending night and day together. Arap Ng'aing'ailem is a good-looking man. No doubt about that. His innocent charm is effective with women, but he did not charm Tapsirorei for long. She was sure he was using his charm to wheel Cheptepkeny to bed."

"Setting aside what Tapsirorei thought of Arap Ng'aing'ailem, did he love Cheptepkeny?" asked Sukunwa.

"I don't know. He didn't get a chance to prove it. On the other hand, he loves anything in a skirt. I can say that much because by the time Cheptepkeny arrived, he had slept with every woman there was to sleep with in this neighbourhood. But Tapsirorei didn't know this until later when people started seeing Cheptepkeny with him, and the gossip reached her. I knew about him, but I didn't worry. Cheptepkeny was better educated than the rest of the women Ng'aing'ailem had gone with."

"Tapsirorei learned about his reputation from the gossip?"

"More or less, but she told me not to talk about it. She was frightened to think Cheptepkeny would turn out to be another victim of his. 'Romance without sex is no longer appreciated. This generation believes relationships improve by lying down, but it isn't true. They deteriorate instead,' she said. 'Doesn't this education they take all the way overseas teach girls self-respect?' she continued. The Nandi elders still don't know no one teaches morals in the educated world. You must understand that up to now this conversation was taking place behind Cheptepkeny's back. Tapsirorei was raging when Cheptepkeny arrived from what Tapsirorei presumed was one of her visits with Ng'aing'ailem, and she could not restrain herself any longer.

"'Cheptepkeny! Come here!' she commanded. 'I think I have made a mistake introducing you to that young man. Because of you and him, I haven't slept a wink for two days. The neighbourhood is buzzing about what he did to Tarkwen, the daughter of Kap Chemiron from Kipsigak, and I am sure it's buzzing about you and him as well. Oh! I'm too old for this! You'd better not see him again. The women say he told Tarkwen that if she refused to sleep with him, he would get someone else. He wasn't going to play cat and mouse while he waited for her initiation. Oh, can you imagine? He said this only three days ago. You can ask Lydia! She heard it when I was told he was heard bragging to her of other girls who would go to bed with him if he only snapped his fingers. Oh! I shudder at the thought that he meant you!'"

"Cheptepkeny just sat through all of this without a word?" Sukunwa asked in disbelief.

"What would you have done? Tapsirorei exploded before Cheptepkeny's feet were in the door."

"Walk back out until Tapsirorei had stopped shouting."

"It is easy to say, but you would not have done it either. Tapsirorei immobilized her with words, bitter words. With Cheptepkeny's character, it was hard to know what she was feeling. She stood there appearing cool and unshaken. She passed by Tapsirorei looking as though what she had just heard was no more consequential than the mice scampering around in the loft eating bread crumbs. Tapsirorei

33

was so flustered and embarrassed to be ignored in front of me that she broke down and cried. She was sick for two days."

"It's too bad Tapsirorei only had sons. She doesn't know how to deal with daughters, especially of this generation."

"This was a severe blow to her. She told everyone about her wounded heart."

"Eventually, Cheptepkeny told her rather jubilantly that, 'Ng'aing'ailem is not using me. We have both decided to get married.'"

"This was like pouring paraffin on the flame to Tapsirorei. 'Over my dead sister's grave! You have decided to do what?' she raised herself up in bed and fell back down, 'No one knows Ng'aing'ailem's family, for heaven's sake! You don't know them yourself,' she said."

"'I don't have to know his family. I know him,' said Cheptepkeny."

"'One week of going to bed with him gives you his entire life history? What about your initiation? In normal circumstances your family arranges the ceremonies a year ahead of time. You know that,' she said."

"'I'm not going to be mutilated. Do you hear?' Cheptepkeny said. 'Not for you, not for my father!'"

"It would be an understatement to say Tapsirorei was upset," Lydia continued. "She threw the bedding off and walked up to Cheptepkeny. I thought she was going to slap her."

"'You what?' she shouted. 'You are going to carry a clitoris around the rest of your life? You are in for a surprise. I can list some of the things that are wrong with it for you. It will strip you of self-respect. You won't be able to admire a man in silence. Any time a good-looking man stands beside you, it will itch wanting to be tickled! You won't have any say over your own body because you will be driven by it,' she said."

"What in heaven's name made Cheptepkeny sit through this?"

"Tapsirorei shouted it out practically in one breath," said Lydia.

"'I won't let this happen. I promised my sister on the day she died that I would look after her children, and I will.'"

34

"This generation wants exactly what Tapsirorei's didn't, and she doesn't understand. They can't be told not to show they are enjoying sex. I wish I was here when this happened. I would let her know the world has changed. Every young woman is trying to know how to do it better than the next one. In North America where Cheptepkeny was, nobody is too old when it comes to knowing about how to do better sex. Women Tapsirorei's age are being asked on television if they still enjoy sex, and they say yes."

"They talk about sex on television?"

"Yes, with the whole world watching, young and old," said Sukunwa.

"Oh my! Men must be wanting women over there all the time with all the stimulation they get," said Lydia who preferred hearing about North America to talking about Tapsirorei.

"I didn't say the men were interested in women. I said sex is not bad to talk about. One watches it when it is shown on television to learn how to do it, or reads about it. Even though they look provoca-tive to traditional people like Africans, it's part of their society for women to look inviting. They actually look awkward, too. Although they think they are sexual experts, they make big swinging moves. I would take Tapsirorei's generation anytime where women were taught not to move when they were in bed with a man," said Sukunwa.

"Are the men any better?" asked Lydia.

"They are better in the sense that they don't advertise themselves on television."

"But if the women are awkward, then the men must be awkward too," said Lydia.

"Lydia, forget I used the word 'awkward.' The movements are too wild to be enticing."

"You married a white man," said Lydia.

"We're not talking about me," said Sukunwa.

"What you're saying is that women were more restricted in Tapsirorei's generation."

"Yes," said Sukunwa, "because Nandi law was based then on the idea that men and women lived in different worlds. Women were not allowed to do work such as warfare, raiding and hunting, and they had no say in these matters. However, in areas that concerned them, women made laws to be followed by each generation of women. In sexual matters, since their own bodies were involved they made the laws to be followed. After the honeymoon, a woman had the right to say no to her husband, and that was the law. She was not obliged to have intercourse with her husband if she felt unable to. She also could never be made to sleep in any position other than what the law of women permitted — sideways.''

"Today many young men celebrate the death of Nandi women's rituals. They prefer uncircumcised women who have not received instruction in women's laws," said Lydia. "But I'm sure women's laws have been broken at times, even in the past. When a man has several wives and likes one of them more than the others, haven't you heard what the other wives say?" she asked. "They say that she knows how to feed the man."

"Yes, I have."

"Do you think they are really talking about food?"

"What would Tapsirorei say if someone told her she was wrong to say an uncircumcised woman is not capable of controlling herself."

"I know she would die. Or if she didn't, she would look as though she hadn't heard. But who would have the courage to tell her a thing like that?"

"Me! I would!"

"Would you?" Lydia asked, surprised.

"She needs to be told that the clitoris has been studied by scientists in the English-speaking world. It's a good thing to have."

"You're joking! How do they know when they don't...," Lydia stopped herself.

"Circumcise? There are books to be read which have been written by other women who have come to Africa to study circumcision and other customs," said Sukunwa.

"How do these women know what it feels like not to have it when they are not circumcised?" wondered Lydia.

"Circumcision is practiced by people in other parts of Africa.

36

Women talk about it and how they feel without it. Half the world doesn't think that to say 'sex feels good' is bad like the Nandi do. Tapsirorei should know a little bit. She married a European and lived in the city. Women in the city always admit that sex is good. The studies even show that it gives women more choices."

"Are you thinking of..." Lydia was sitting on the edge of her chair ready to beg Sukunwa not to tell Tapsirorei things like this, even as a joke. Lydia felt Sukunwa had lost her sense of propriety in Canada, that she had to watch out for her not to speak so freely that she used language which would be considered offensive by older women like Tapsirorei. But she became sidetracked when she heard about having more choices. "Having a clitoris gives women more choices?" she asked.

"I've heard that uncircumcised women can live happily with other women."

"They don't say a woman becomes destructive to other women if she is circumcised, do they?" asked Lydia.

"No, living together in a relationship, like a man and a woman. If you don't understand, let's leave it at that."

"I would like to know more, but I don't know what to ask first. Have you ever felt that you have missed out on excitement without it?" asked Lydia.

"Of course not."

"Is that the only answer you can give? What I mean is does knowing that it brings excitement make you miss it?"

"What is this? Am I supposed to confess something here? No, I've never felt deprived of sexual excitement because I didn't have it. Nandi circumcision also is not as brutal as the kind I have read about that is done in some parts of Africa. There are books on the subject," said Sukunwa.

"Aren't the people objecting in those places? Here the President has passed a law telling the Nandi not to circumcise women."

"Yes, they must be objecting. I'm sure the reason these books are being written is to make people like Tapsirorei, who are insisting that girls should be circumcised, understand that it is not good any more.

I don't believe Tapsirorei will give up. Did Tapsirorei regain her lost ground? What happened to Cheptepkeny?" asked Sukunwa.

"She hasn't lost any ground yet. The marriage never took place."

"I can't believe it. She used the Nandi initiation ceremonies to defeat Cheptepkeny and Arap Ng'aing'ailem?"

"With eloquence. She said that she must protect the interests of Nandi women. To teach girls to obey circumcision and the customs of senior Nandi women. And to teach them what the initiation ceremonies of the Nandi mean. She also feels that women who don't want to be circumcised shouldn't be told how the circumcision is performed. They should just respect the ceremonies without acquiring knowledge of them, and if they want to know about them, they should be circumcised first," said Lydia.

"How can you respect something you've never seen? I agree that Nandi girls should know about women's ceremonies and customs, but not in exchange for circumsion. Poor Cheptepkeny," added Sukunwa.

"She's not poor," interrupted Lydia. "She's very happy now in Canada. Don't the two of you talk about home?" Lydia asked.

"No, she lives in Guelph, 100 miles away. We don't see each other very often. But where was Cheptepkeny's father while this went on?" asked Sukunwa.

"He was in it. All the women who live on the edge of society including Tonti were brought in to run the show and the father came to listen. He said he didn't know what was going on with young people. He knew only when girls were initiated and the parents looked for husbands for them.

"'I've heard that nowadays girls look for their own husbands,' he told Cheptepkeny's half-brothers. 'Why don't you young men deal with this matter; you are more up to date than I am."

Cheptepkeny's brothers told her, 'Come home with us. If this man wants you, he will follow you, and we will talk the matter over with both of you.' In the meantime, Tapsirorei was doing everything she could to discredit Arap Ng'aing'ailem. Cheptepkeny accepted her brothers' suggestion and left Tapsirorei's house three days later. Arap

Ng'aing'ailem never came, and Cheptepkeny left Kenya altogether in two weeks," said Lydia.

"I called her before coming to Kenya. After our phone conversation, she came to London to visit me. I learned then she had been back to Kenya for the second time after her mother's funeral, but she didn't say anything about almost getting married," said Sukunwa.

"I should think not. It was nothing to be proud of. After Tapsirorei had made it public concern number one," said Lydia.

"Yes, having Tonti in it guaranteed its status as a public concern too."

"Now they are trying to organize where the next meeting will be held to decide what should be taught to girls about the old initiation ceremonies and customs, and Tonti is only too glad to be part of the discussion, for the reason you and I both know — it gives her a chance to take over the proceedings. She'd never be able to do that to women in the city."

"She is going to lobby now until everything is done her way," said Sukunwa.

"Yes, this is what keeps us going in Chemobo — city women's politics."

"Tonti angers me. She doesn't know anything about Nandi rituals! She left Nandi traditions long ago while other Nandi were still observing them strictly. Now she wants others to keep the traditions for her? None of her older children are circumcised — I grew up with them in Eldoret," Sukunwa said.

"None of her sons are married to Nandi women. She told you only about Kimibei last night, not the middle son who married a Swahili girl from Mombasa. You also told her to say hello to Chemotwek."

"Yes."

"She didn't tell you she murdered her, did she?"

"What? How? She is not capable of murder?"

"Yes, she is. Poor Chemotwek! She was a nice woman. She took over the family when Tonti became alcoholic and stayed out drinking until dawn. When moonshine became illegal — one went to jail for possessing even a bottle of it — Tonti decided to drink at home and made Chemotwek go out to buy it for her. One night when Tonti couldn't get enough, she sent her out in the dead of the night with a flashlight for more. Chemotwek didn't return. The next day she was found dead on the road, a broken bottle beside her. She had been hit by a car. The worst thing of all is that Tonti didn't even go to claim the body. The municipality buried Chemotwek in a pauper's grave!"

"That is so dreadful! Why did Tapsirorei ask a sinner like her to deal with an important matter like this? There are women like Tabarbuch and Tabletkoi to ask if she wanted her ideas to be taken seriously? Those are the women who would be listened to here, not people like Tonti with her sin or Tapsirorei herself who married an Englishman." Sukunwa said.

"Tapsirorei hasn't left anyone out."

"The whole affair is a comedy — to mix city women and home women," Sukunwa declared.

"I didn't say people were not laughing. The meeting will be held next week in Chemobo Church. You are invited as well." Lydia was saving the best for the last. "Tapsirorei told me to tell you. Tonti was absolutely excited you were here."

"No doubt she was. But it won't last — I will be leaving for my uncle's any day now, and I hope you will have time to come with me too," said Sukunwa.

"Yes, I haven't been to Mt. Kamasai for a long time. Too bad for Tonti. She told Tapsirorei that she couldn't imagine anything so 'positively thrilling' as to have you on their side in this matter. 'It was fate,' she said. You have lived abroad: people will listen closely to what you have to say."

"What makes them believe now I was in Canada? I remember in your letters to me you said they thought I was hiding somewhere in Africa," said Sukunwa.

"That was at first. Now they know because your children don't speak Swahili or Nandi. Tonti said your position in the meeting should be 'coordinated sufficiently' for you to convey some idea of North American culture. That might help, she said, and she added that she had heard that some Europeans circumcise."

"Won't she ever leave me? She was on the list of the people I worked hard to forget during the years I was absent. I don't want to appear to be on her side in any discussion whatsoever, even if she is right," said Sukunwa.

"It sounds as though Tapsirorei is having second thoughts too, although she doesn't come out and say so. Tonti was waving her arms and laughing with a shimmering vision of self-congratulation for her brilliant idea of bringing you in. Tapsirorei was livid later, after she had gone. She said it was so irritable and shameful to see a grown woman exciting herself like a Chelendo preacher having convulsions and claiming the idea to bring you in was hers when Tapsirorei had mentioned it to her first."

"Well, it is irrelevant. I don't see any connection between what is going on in Canada and circumcision here. They don't circumcise there," Sukunwa said.

"Oh no! Tapsirorei says English people circumcise. Her husband did."

"It's not part of their religion, it's done in the hospital for cosmetic reasons. And women are never circumcised."

"They are in for a surprise, then."

"Well, let them be excited now. They won't be excited when I tell them I don't think circumcision is important myself."

"Are you refusing because you hate Tonti, or do you really think it's not important?"

"Both, but I think girls should be taught women's law and go through the entire initiation, including seclusion, without circumcision."

"No one will go for that," said Lydia.

For a reason Lydia had never understood, after many years, Sukunwa still couldn't stand the sight of Tonti. The tension between them was said to have started when Tonti borrowed twenty shillings from her. When Sukunwa went to ask for the money, Tonti had said, "I won't pay it. You want to sue me, you sue me! And I will tell the judge how many times your aunt has eaten in my house. The judge will understand. He knows food is expensive in the city."

Lydia thought the matter had been dealt with long ago. "Why do you go on hating Tonti when she's not saying anything bad about you?"

"That's a strange question. I don't know if it requires an answer — you know what kind of person she is. As soon as I join them, something is bound to start. I don't care for her. Her presence is like a dry season where everyone hopes it will rain so they may see some green on the ground and forget the parched grass," said Sukunwa.

"I hope you forgive her soon," said Lydia. "You can't hate people forever, and what will you say if they come themselves and ask you to be in it?"

"'Get out of my life!' That's what I will say."

Somehow, Sukunwa regretted the time she had spent in Canada. Although she had friends, her heart was never won. She knew she was considered inferior because of her colour in the society at large, and she always felt empty and lonely. But now, seeing what was in store for her here, she almost preferred being in Canada on her own. There everyone was out for themselves. One did not have to put up with a person one didn't get along with.

She realized she didn't have any home. She loved being with Lydia, but it no longer felt like home in Africa. And Canada didn't feel like home either. In part Sukunwa knew she was being selfish for not wanting to meet with the women in the church to discuss North America. She knew all humans liked sensationalism, especially these women, who had lived in the city and the educated women who knew white hatred for Black, but she would not be the one to feed their hungry minds with it.

She knew what kind of subject would get people's attention. She had read the books of English explorers and missionaries in Africa, and had learned from them. They had to paint a picture of Africa in such a way that the reader felt sorry for them as though they were the only humans on the entire jungle-continent. The only time Africans appeared was when witchcraft and savagery were being mentioned to add "primitive colour." The rest of the time they complained and complained of suffering as though to assure their readers they were indeed in a barren land. It did not matter that millions of kind-hearted Africans were there and found it a pleasant and happy place to make their home and live harmoniously. No, they didn't say that. They didn't say, "They were happy until we arrived to cause them grief." They didn't dare to mention anything good about these unselfish people from the "dark" continent, because it would have lessened their heroism, eliminating the courage that it took for them to be "alone in a land of savages."

Sukunwa was sure that Tonti and the other educated Nandi women who were aware of how Africans had been put down by Europeans would be at the church meeting, expecting a similar dramatized and sensationalized version of her experiences abroad, in which Westerners were portrayed as having the most disgusting customs a civilized Nandi could imagine. While Sukunwa knew that in fact this was partly true — some North American and European customs were nothing less than revolting, and life there was characterized by a never-ending competition which reduced everything to economics — she had no wish to lower herself to the same level as European writers who wrote about Africa because she knew better. Every society had its good and bad points.

But there was also another side to all of this. Sukunwa had an innate sense of privacy that made it almost impossible for her to describe to anyone how she actually felt. She kept everything to herself. Even Lydia, her closest friend, knew only a fraction of Sukunwa's life. To speak about North America here was to bring her two worlds together, and that frightened Sukunwa. It made her feel that she had never escaped, it made her remember Taptamus and Mary and Lydia all those years ago, when Mt. Kamasai was the whole world.

She's stubborn like her grandfather, Lydia thought, remembering how her own grandfather used to say Sukunwa's grandfather was notorious for his stubbornnness during the British occupation, always doing exactly the opposite of what the settlers wanted him to do. Maybe it's genetic — Lydia was sure Sukunwa was going to do the opposite of what Tonti and Tapsirorei wanted. She wondered if when people became older, they came to resemble their parents, because when she and Sukunwa were little children, she, Lydia, was the one who was the leader. "Sukunwa, I like the idea of this meeting, and I want you to be part of it, too," Lydia said.

"Why didn't you tell me right out that you wanted me in it? Although if you had told me, I would not have participated anyway. I have to go to Mt. Kamasai now. I've been here too long, and my family will be upset that I've been in Kenya without rushing to greet them. I really wanted to spend time with you because I didn't know if there would be time to spend together before I leave Kenya."

The next day Sukunwa left for Mt. Kamasai, their childhood home. Lydia was disappointed. Talking about the meeting had probably hastened Sukunwa's departure. Sukunwa hadn't even waited for her to get time off from work. "I'm going to take the children and come back for you later," Sukunwa promised before leaving, and though she meant it, they both couldn't help feeling that this parting had happened before, a long time before, when the world changed too fast for two girls who meant the world to each other.

MT. KAMASAI: 1950

CHAPTER ONE

*S*ukunwa had been born to two lovely people in Mt. Kamasai. Cheptabut, her mother, was a kind-hearted and generous woman, and her father, Kiptai, a gentle and devoted husband. Even in those times, when it was disgraceful for a Nandi man to do or say anything that might seem to show weakness towards his wife, Kiptai always endeavoured to include his wife and her opinion in whatever he said. On occasions when elders met to recount and relive their struggles and achievements, it was not the custom for a husband to ask his wife directly for corroboration of what he was saying, yet Kiptai invariably would.

"My ox! My white ox with white horns! The horns that shine at night like the moonlight! I went raiding across the River Nile under cover of the darkness at midnight. Coming back with my white ox, I was shot with an arrow. I dove into the water and hung on to the ox's tail. I crossed, wounded, and made it home to my wife Cheptabut. Isn't that true Cheptabut?" When a man spoke in that manner, he was considered to be under the shadow of a woman.

It was likewise for Cheptabut. "I don't care for fresh milk that is still warm, and Kiptai doesn't like it either. Isn't that right Father Sukunwa?" she would say, referring to Kiptai by his daughter's name.

Despite the unusual love between Cheptabut and Kiptai, they were apprehensive for their daughter, Sukunwa. The first three children born to Cheptabut had died. Sukunwa was the first to survive. While she was carrying Sukunwa, Cheptabut was emotionally torn. She wanted her baby very badly, yet she was afraid her touch would mean the child's death. During labour, she said, "I won't keep this baby if it lives. Let anyone who wants it have it."

Her mother, Taptamus, said that she would raise the child, and she did. As soon as the child was born and the umbilical cord severed, the women present laughed ceremonially four times to let the men outside know the birth was successful. After the laughter, Taptamus received the baby from the midwife.

"If she lives, her name is Sukunwa," said Cheptabut. Sukunwa is gold and pure beauty, and so that became her name.

When she was three weeks old, she was brought back to receive the name of the spirit who was reincarnated in her, Chemigok, Kiptai's mother. Kiptai was overjoyed. "The baby's name is Sukunwa Chemigok Kapchamtany, my mother," he said with great delight on his face.

Taptamus, Cheptabut's mother, was a hard-working woman who had lost her husband in the fighting between the European newcomers and the Nandi. Living with her five children on land that the British had seized had taught her to work hard to survive. She had one boy and four girls. Cheptabut was the baby and had a wonderful marriage in spite of burying a child every year. Taptamus didn't want anything to ruin the marriage while she was alive.

Although she wanted to send for her oldest daughter, Chemutai, — whom she always called on when she needed help, Taptamus thought Chemutai would be too harsh for Cheptabut. She would interfere with Cheptabut's life thinking she was helping her but doing her more harm than good. Chemutai had left her real Nandi husband and had gone to the city of Eldoret to work for Europeans. Taptamus couldn't recall having seen her with the same man on any two of the occasions when she had visited her. She thought that the last man she had seen her with was the worst of them all. He knew how to do three things — drink, sleep, and ask Chemutai when she came home from work what he was going to eat. Taptamus dismissed from her mind the thought of calling Chemutai to come. She might invite Cheptabut to visit her in the city, and then Cheptabut would learn the unpleasantness of her sister's life. Worse yet, Cheptabut might be persuaded to join her sister in that disgusting way of life.

It was late when Taptamus finished with the cooking and cleaning in Cheptabut's house. She was finally ready to go home with baby

Sukunwa. Outside, a newly-ploughed field stood between her and her house. The deeply-rutted path which had previously connected the two houses had been ploughed over. The sun, low on the horizon, was redder than usual, and after the rain, its reflection off the furrows of the soil made walking across the field an onerous task.

The land was rocky at the foot of Mt. Kamasai on the plateau overlooking the Cheboiywa River. The rain made the view stand out in three dimensions and left Kimugei Forest steaming. The big boulders on the mountain shimmered when the sun hit their wet surfaces. The monkeys were swinging from tree to tree, calling their children, and the birds were beginning to twitter as they readied themselves and their infants for the night. Smoke was already visible from the houses in the neighbourhood showing that all of the families were home.

Taptamus stumbled over the furrows trying to get home before the sun set. It was bad luck to be out with the baby when the sun went down unless you had ashes to put across its forehead. She realized that she might not make it and covered the baby's face. Finally, she staggered into her house and laid the baby on the bed. Kibet, her nephew, dashed in laughing enthusiastically.

"Where is the baby? I want to see it." He rushed into Taptamus' bedroom, going right by Taptamus without realizing she hadn't said a thing. Taptamus called him harshly.

"Kibeeet! You didn't tell the man who came to plough the field not to plough the path along with it the way I told you to. What's the matter with you? Are you stupid?"

"Oh, but I did! I did, but he said that the tractor was not made to stop and start again in such short distances."

All of a sudden, Taptamus felt empty. She thought of her husband. If he were alive, no one would have dared to plough the path! He would have been able to stop that tractor at any distance he wanted. How, Taptamus didn't know, but her husband had been a uniquely courageous person. No one measured up to him. At least that was Taptamus' view. She had been married at thirteen, her husband being quite a bit older than she was. Like all Nandi girls, no matter how young they were, she was nevertheless ready to take on the duties of running a household and to receive all of her husband's friends with grace and dignity. At the time of circumcision, the initiates' special instructors taught them the responsibilities of being a woman. Above all else, Nandi law required them to be sweet and gentle towards their new families. Taptamus was all this, and in her, it was genuine, sweet and beautiful. Her husband was her glory and her happiness. She was younger, but he treated her as though she were his age.

And yet he made everything so easy for her. He never once came home late because he knew his wife was too young to be awakened to work at night. When Taptamus was pregnant with their first child, her husband told her, "Taptamus, don't carry too much firewood and be sure to rest often." She liked that.

Taptamus sat back day-dreaming out loud and recalled the first time she brewed beer for her husband and his friends. Kibet sat listening by the fire.

"The men drank until they were really drunk, and they ended up arguing about who was richer. One man said, 'I had more oxen than you, but the white man has taken them. Now I have a lot of money.'

"'What is money?' my husband asked. 'What do you do with it? How much is a lot? I have enough to boil a tea-kettle full of water.'

"'Mine can boil enough water to make another pot of beer,' said the other. Money had no value in those days to the Nandi, and the two men challenged each other until they burned all their paper money boiling the water. Oohh, I wish I had known then that money was so valuable — that in the end everyone would be chasing it.

"In Kamagut, where my husband had refused to work for British settlers, he became a squatter on his own land with his wealth scattered all over. After the railroad line was laid through the farm, sheep, goats and cattle were run over. Furiously, my husband ran to the settler's house.

"'Your train has killed my cattle, and I want you to stop it.'

"'Who are you?' the settler said.

"'I am Arap Mararsoi. I've come to tell you to stop your train from killing my cattle.'

50

"'It's not my train, but the government's,' said the settler.

"'But I want you to tell them to stop!'

"'Go to Eldoret and tell them there. I don't want to see you on my farm.'

"He went to Eldoret and was told that the train couldn't stop. He would have to look after his livestock himself. He went home and after a sleepless night, he woke up and went down and dug up the railroad track. The train came along at noon, and had no difficulty stopping. My husband went back to the government office in Eldoret and said, 'You told me the train couldn't stop. Come and see it! It stopped this time.' The government sent railway officials to go to check.

"When the government learned what had happened, they assigned four policemen to arrest him the next day. There was one European, one Nandi named Arap Walei and two Nubians. When Arap Walei found out who was to be arrested, he went to the nearest farm to find some Nandi warriors to inform Arap Mararsoi that the police were coming to arrest him. They would arrive at his farm early in the morning, arrest him and confiscate his cattle.

"'Urge him to leave as soon as possible. There is no place nearby which is safe. Tell him to take the children to Mt. Kamasai, to my home. If he agrees, take the children straight away, but take the cattle in the opposite direction at the same time. Go east with them to Chebororwa. The next day head southwest all the way to Terem. There are many caves there where you can hide easily for awhile. Then divide all the livestock into three groups. Bring the livestock in these three batches with at least two weeks separation between each batch. Be sure to come at night. The adults in the neighbourhood are no problem, but you never know what can slip out of the mouth of a child if the police should ever come snooping around.'

"Just as it was getting dark, I heard a murmur, almost a whisper outside. Of course my husband was still outside by the fire with the children, and warriors from the neighbourhood might drop by at any time. I didn't bother to listen to what was going on out there, and shortly my husband came in with the children.

"'I'll be at my mother's house,' he told me, and left.

"About three hours later my mother-in-law came over. She spoke gently to me and the children. She said that a message had arrived saying that the enemy might strike this neighbourhood tonight, and the children must be removed at once.

"'There are two warriors outside. They are well-armed and ready to take you with the children. Your husband will tell you more about where you will be taken,' she said to me.

"I knew that she was trying desperately to be calm, but I could see right through the mask. Her red eyes were ringed with a deep black shadow. She had no spirit, a premonition of impending grief had overpowered her. I didn't ask any questions, and I had no words with which to comfort her.

"I turned around to a pair of eyes looking up to me questioningly: 'What now, mother?' Their searching looks hit me like hailstones. Their silence froze my heart, and I became uneasy and apprehensive. The children were ready in a few minutes, and my husband came in.

"'Are you ready?' he asked.

"'Yes we are,' I said.

"'You'll be taken with the children to Arap Walei's home, and you will wait there until you receive word from me of what to do next.'

"'Where are you going?' I asked.

"'I'm staying. I want to meet the enemy,' he said.

"'I'm staying with you, too, then. The children and the babysitter can go,' I said. So they left without me.

"His family told him to run but he refused, and prepared to die, and I prayed for the impossible to happen. He was waiting with his sword at the door of the house when the police came. His mother, because she couldn't understand Swahili, poured her heart out to the police. She pulled out her breast and showed it to them, saying, 'This is my baby. Don't kill him. He sucked this breast.' But to no avail. The harshness in the voices of the policemen caused her son to swing at one of them, wounding his arm. The others fired at him immediately. He rolled down the hill in front of the house and spoke his last words.

"'I have no debts,' he told us. 'I die for my cattle. The white man's face will always mean bloodshed for us.'

"Left-handed Arap Walei took his hat off, turned around and knelt on one knee. Firing three times in rapid succession, he brought down the other three policemen. 'I no longer respect the crown of the white man,' he said and trampled on his police hat. The others quickly took him away from the sight of the tragedy. They hid him in the forest until after he went through the purification ceremonies. Then he was taken west to Bungoma out of Nandi country. He stayed away about a year until the British had given up looking for him.

"My husband was buried thinking that the Europeans were only a curse for the Nandi nation. He didn't live long enough to witness the fulfilment of his prediction and then some: indescribable crimes were being done to the Black race by the new settlers all over the African continent.

"I hope the children never have to know how their father died. Otherwise they will always live with bitter thoughts of revenge in their hearts. It was a painful death to stand by and watch, but for him it was an honourable death. He died proudly defending what was rightfully his. Oh Kibet! I mustn't go to pieces after all these years. I should go to milk the cows before the baby cries," Taptamus said.

Kibet never talked very much, but today he was especially silent. Wordlessly, he stared at Taptamus while she talked. Now that she had finished there wasn't even the smallest flicker of movement on his face. He sat mute as though frozen. Taptamus walked across the room to the fireplace to where Kibet was and knelt beside him. She shook him. His hands were clasped together between his legs cold as ice. His narrow eyes gazed outwards unblinkingly. She felt a chill of terror. A shadow of death ran across her mind. Oh no! He's not dead is he?

Taptamus ran to the waterpot, dipped up some water, ran back and poured it over Kibet. He sprang up into the air with a little jerk.

"Are you all right?" Taptamus asked.

"Yes I am. Is it morning already?" Kibet's mind was in complete disarray. He had no memory of what Taptamus had just been talking about. "Did you finish the story?" he asked.

"Yes I did," Taptamus answered. "Would you look after the baby while I milk the cows? Be a good boy and don't let the cat go near her. It will lick her face."

Sukunwa was born in 1950 just at the time when a few things that had been introduced by Europeans were certified by Nandi for use by humans. Some mothers were using baby bottles to feed their children and soap to bathe them, but Taptamus felt that these things were too risky. She was going to cup her hand to the child's mouth the way she had done with her own children even though it was harder that way. She had heard only horror stories about the bottles and other "gifts" of the white man from her friend Mary. If the baby should ever swallow the nipple, she would die unless she could be taken to the hospital for an operation. But to say "hospital" in those days in Nandi was itself synonymous with saying "death." If the nipple was left in the sun, it would melt and become poisonous. The bottle might break and cut the baby. And soap was just simply dangerous. It was a poison, caused a rash, and if it slipped into someone's eyes, it would blind her forever. Mary knew far more about these things than anyone else because her husband Arap Walei had been a policeman and worked for the white man.

Taptamus had finished milking her cows now. She waited for the calves to suck the two teats which she had left on each cow for them. When they were finished, she would separate them from their mothers and take them to their own separate accommodation. By the time all of this was accomplished, it would be pitch dark. If it weren't for the baby, Taptamus would never milk in the dark. Kibet would have gone and milked them, but now, she didn't want anyone touching the baby's food except herself. With her teeth chattering from the cold of Mt. Kamasai and her skin cloak feeling as though it had been dipped in ice-water, she made her way painfully back to the house through the intense darkness created by the big green leaves of the castor trees. When the wind touched the leaves, it sounded like an invisible congregation of people clapping steadily and deliberately. On both sides of the path, crickets chirped and twittered, leaving a ringing in her ears. The huge-winged African bats flitted in front of her with a mighty wind, which felt as though if a wing hit your face a piece might be gouged out. The frogs sounded as though they were croaking right in her footsteps. What next?

Taptamus' life was neither easy nor happy, but she had not expected life to be easy from the day she stood in the dark and watched her husband being buried. In spite of what she thought of her condition, she knew that women weren't made to be happy or for their lives to be easy. "You are the one always left picking up the pieces behind the family," her mother had said when giving her last advice to her daughter before Taptamus was married.

Taptamus had thought that her mother would tell her what she had already learned during the three years of her seclusion after initiation when she studied Nandi women's law and Nandi law in general. She had started to lose interest even before her mother had begun talking to her, but her mother had caught her attention with her eye and said, "You had better pay attention to what I'm about to tell you because it's the truth. What you have been told by your teachers is the truth, too. I know, because I was told the same thing when I was in seclusion like you. I was told that when I got married to your father, I would be grown up. Everything in your father's home would be mine to look after and mine to pass on to my children so that I would have security in the future. That was true, but no one emphasized the tremendous price one had to pay to earn all these things. The criticism of a man always saying to you, 'Woman, what do you have in life? Without a man to provide all these things for you to own, where would you be?' All of my life I have wished someone had told me differently, and that is what I'm going to share with you now. I'm going to tell you the way I wish I had been told.

"Now you are about to discover what it means to say a woman is grown up. It is growing backwards. From now on it's tolerance and putting up. You will do your tasks plus, yet sometimes your husband will show no appreciation. He wanted it done differently. Hold your tongue and don't question his motives. That is what is called a good marriage," her mother said.

"A woman is naturally tied to her children. In order to counterbalance this our religion gives a man the power to curse a disobedient wife and children. If the children are disrespectful to the father, the mother must bear the responsibility, and her children will never receive the father's blessing. A man basks in the sympathy and pity of the society. 'What a shame. Marry another woman to wake this one up,' he is told. Or, 'Let her know who the man is! Beat her once in a while!' A man owns the livestock, the property, the children, and the woman glues it all together. If she is successful, the man gets praised. 'You've done well. You deserve another wife.'"

In the beginning, Taptamus didn't try to understand why her mother wanted to tell her differently, but as time went on, and though her own situation was very different, she grew to understand what her mother had meant by saying that a woman paid a price to get a share of what was hers.

Kibet was sitting with Sukunwa as Taptamus returned. He had started sleeping in Taptamus' house since Sukunwa had been born. Taptamus needed him with her to help with fire-making at night. Someone was needed to blow and to put grass into the fire in order to get it started. Kibet did this because Taptamus wanted him to, but he didn't like sleeping in a house with a woman when his friends were in the warriors' hut, a house for young unmarried people in the neighbourhood. Taptamus was an old lady, and the other boys were sure to make fun of him, he thought to himself. Everyone knew that old women scratched themselves a lot because they had lice, and that if they farted on you, you became stupid. And when they woke up in the morning, they shook their clothes out, sending the lice flying. Soon all the boys would think Kibet had lice too. Kibet pitied himself. Soon, he thought, he was going to tell Taptamus that he was not going to sleep in her house any more.

CHAPTER TWO

A week later, Taptamus was sitting in the shade in the back of her house. She watched as Tapchamgoi came up the path towards her. There is something fishy going on in the neighbourhood, she thought. It's too early in the day for Tapchamgoi to come by.

"How is the little one today?" Tapchamgoi asked.

"She is fine. She's so little she can literally slip through my fingers," Taptamus replied.

"Oh my goodness! She is too little even to start thinking about looking for a baby sitter for her," Tapchamgoi said when she saw how little Sukunwa was.

"I wasn't thinking of looking for a babysitter yet. I don't even have anyone in mind."

"Oh! I don't think you will have any problem finding a babysitter, and I'm sure Mary would be willing to help you in the meantime."

"Yes, you are right. I don't know what I would do without Mary."

"Don't feel so grateful. She wouldn't be doing it only for you. I know she is a charming woman, and I'm not trying to criticize her or anything, but I'm sure she would be glad to do it because it would give her a chance to teach her slow-witted daughter Chepsisei how to look after a baby," said Tapchamgoi.

"I don't understand. What the devil are you trying to say? Are you laughing at Mary or at Chepsisei? You know Chepsisei is not even capable of dressing herself. What makes you think she can learn how to look after a baby?" Taptamus asked.

"I didn't mean it the way you've made it sound," Tapchamgoi said, trying to to regain safe ground. She didn't want Taptamus knowing that she really had more in mind. "You know I don't have any evil feelings about Mary or her daughter. It was just a suggestion on my part."

"Tapchamgoi, please! Spare yourself the complexity of detective work and tell me what you want to say or ask me what you want to know! Otherwise we won't get anywhere. For your information by the way, I haven't seen Mary for three weeks," Taptamus said.

Tapchamgoi laughed, wrinkling her nose and leaning back against the tree. Her long, elegant legs stretched towards Taptamus, and the tobacco she was chewing was visible between her teeth. "I had better go. I have nothing to say anyway," she said. And she left.

Taptamus went in to feed and bathe the baby. She always felt bad after a visit from Tapchamgoi because the latter's conversation was never clear. She always manages to leave you frustrated and unhappy, Taptamus thought.

Taptamus had no further time to wonder what Tapchamgoi had really been up to as Kibet arrived with a load of firewood. Looking pleased with himself, he set the firewood on top of the hill beside the house. He arranged the wood so as to make a traditional man's fireplace. Taptamus knew something was wrong with Kibet. The reason a Nandi man made a fire outside was to sit alone and think or to entertain young warriors with good conversation. The general idea was to distance yourself from women, but for Kibet it was to get a message across to Taptamus not to forget that he was a boy, not a girl, and that he should be doing men's things.

"Kibet," Taptamus called him.

"Yes," he answered defiantly.

"Are you coming to look after the baby while I go to milk?"

Kibet cleared his throat and replied with a murmur. "I don't like to smell like a baby. I'm not a woman," he mumbled.

"Speak up Kibet! What did you say?" Taptamus exclaimed.

"Arap Chebinjor said ... I mean ..." he hesitated, realizing it would seem childish to say he was told. "I think looking after the baby is a woman's job. I don't want to smell like the baby," he repeated, this time in a clear voice.

"Is that what Arap Chebinjor told you?" Taptamus asked.

"No! He said a man shouldn't sit indoors with women. He should be out looking after the cattle. When he comes home, he should make a fire outside and sit there thinking," Kibet said.

"Oh, so that's what Arap Chebinjor said! I always see him around drinking. It never seems like he's thinking. But anyway, I'm sure he really didn't mean tonight, Kibet. He meant after you are circumcised and have a wife, then she will do everything for you while you sit and think. And besides, I'm not a woman to you. I'm your aunt, and Cheptabut, Sukunwa's mother, is your cousin. You're the baby's uncle. We're not women to you; we are your family."

Kibet chose not to argue with Taptamus although he felt that Arap Chebinjor had meant a man should stay away from all women, not only from his wife. He had also said that women preferred light conversation because they didn't think big thoughts. They always 'thought' around the fireplace in the kitchen and only talked about children and husbands and cooking. Arap Chebinjor had told him that when a man was talking with a woman he had to master the ability of seeming to listen without really listening.

When Taptamus came back from the cattle kraal, Kibet was ready to go to the warriors' hut.

"Kibet! Where do you think you are going now?" Taptamus didn't wait for Kibet to answer. "You have to sleep at home and help me at night with the fire-making. The baby must eat!" she said.

"You still have a lot of paraffin in the lamp and matches. Would you like to use that?" Kibet suggested.

"Kibet don't be unreasonable! You know the lamp is not safe in a grass house. I might forget it." Taptamus remembered when she used to visit her daughter in town. They used paraffin lamps which let out clouds of dark smoke in all of the houses. Everything around the lamps was black as charcoal, and everyone in the shanty town coughed so vigorously in the morning that Taptamus was sure that it was the smoke from the lamps that had caused them to contract tuberculosis.

Taptamus didn't sleep well that night. She had a mysterious nightmare. She was walking on an open, dry, dusty road. Ahead of her and all around her was a cloud of dust. It was not dark or light, just dusty. The sun's rays came through the dust. The light from the sun fell in a circle around her body as though a spotlight had been shone upon her. The road was peaceful. Everything was still — no wind, no flies, no movement of the dust. Although the dust was motionless, it was not solid. Taptamus could see the particles of dust. As she moved through the dust, the spotlight moved along with her. She didn't turn around. She kept looking ahead. She couldn't feel any movement under her feet even though she thought she had moved.

Ahead of her, the lighted area seemed to expand and the dust seemed to thin. All of a sudden, she felt as though her eyes were opened and she could see for real. She saw a rectangular house through the thin dust. Two women were at the door. One was very plump and brown-skinned. The other, standing behind the first, was very thin and was dark black. The face of the first one peered out through a white headcloth.

Taptamus could see the women, but their faces were indistinct. They beckoned vigorously to her, but her feet felt so heavy that she couldn't move.

All of a sudden she heard a voice telling her, "Run! Run! She's waiting for you." Then the voice pleaded with her, "Please don't make her wait!" Finally she succeeded in willing her legs to move. She stood before the thatched house, and the two women pressed her to enter. The room was dark and smoky inside, and appeared to be a deep hall. She could discern the faces of many women lined up along the sides of the hall. Everyone's eyes were riveted on a sick, bedridden woman. She recognized that it was her sister, Senge, but she felt no emotion of love at seeing her. Rather, she was gripped by fear. Her sister's eyes appeared extremely tired to her, but a faint smile shone in them. A tall, black woman stood up and asked the sick woman, "Who are you waiting for?" She pointed out various women. Finally she pointed to Taptamus. Senge smiled and nodded.

Everyone in the hall told Taptamus, "Shake her hand! Shake her hand!" Taptamus couldn't move, but they dragged her to her sister's bedside. With a horrible feeling, she extended her hand. Her fingertips touched her sister's, and Senge died. Immediately all the other women vanished. Senge was Kibet's mother. She had died five years ago.

The following morning Taptamus consulted her sister's spirit concerning various trivial matters Senge might have died without understanding. Taptamus' sister had lived some 40 miles from Taptamus when she was alive. When she took sick, she was brought to a medicine man nearer to Taptamus and everyone in her family went home, leaving her in the care of Taptamus and the medicine man.

Taptamus did her best to be at the medicine man's house early every morning with tea, a gourd of milk, and sometimes with fresh clothing for her sister.

On the day of Senge's death, she had asked Taptamus to go home to bring milk for her. It was December 25th, late in the morning. Taptamus quickly went home and fed the baby-sitter and Kibet, who was two then. As she was leaving to go back to Senge, Taptamus met her own son, Kiriswa, at the door. He had come to visit from Cheboiywa where he had moved with his wife and one child.

"I don't have time to greet you properly, Kiriswa. My sister is sick and wants some tea. I'm taking it to her now."

"Let me go, mother. You stay home and rest your feet."

"No, I can't. She is waiting for me, and I'm afraid she won't recognize you. She is beyond recognizing many people," Taptamus said.

"Let's go together then," said Kiriswa. As they went the silence was more than usual. Taptamus' mind was on her sister Senge. Kiriswa was saddened by his mother's appearance. She looked lonely and wasted.

"Mother, I'm surprised at Aunt Senge's family. How could they...?" He couldn't find any way to express his feelings without hurting her. "How could they be so inconsiderate as to bring her to the medicine man with her child and then leave them both in your care? You're not getting any younger, you know," he said.

"This is no time to be criticizing one another. Your aunt is exceedingly ill. We are hoping for a miracle, but the chances for one are minute. It is like holding a tiny bead between one's teeth all day long," Taptamus said.

They were only five yards from the house when the medicine man's wife ran toward them. "Please hurry! She is waiting for you! She would have gone an hour ago, but she hung on."

As soon as Taptamus entered the house, a blink registered on her sister's face, and she was gone. Everything stood still in the house as grief made its way into Taptamus' heart. She collapsed, and the milk spilled. No one cleaned it up. It was left for the spirits to drink later. Kiriswa stood beside his aunt's bed and closed her eyes.

"Why haunt me now eight years later?" Taptamus asked. "Senge, it is quite obvious that I have done what I was expected to do and more. I have pulled my weight in doing all the chores of your family and mine. How much nicer can anyone be?" Taptamus demanded of her sister's spirit.

"I think it is time for you to be responsible for your own children. If you want to come back to them as a reincarnated spirit, you come. I think it is about time. You lazy woman! I think you have waited too long!"

Now Taptamus was talking seriously. With complete confidence in her own husband's spirit, she scolded her sister for not being cooperative. She knew her husband would agree with her absolutely.

CHAPTER THREE

*A*s her last-born child was married, Taptamus was an elder. According to Nandi tradition, which was still followed in her generation, she was a 'retired' woman, free from domestic responsibilities, but she still worked. Her five children, one son and four daughters, were all married. By Nandi law, she should have lived with her son, but she chose not to, because she wanted her daughters to be able to come as they pleased to visit her and to stay as long as they wanted. They wouldn't be able to do this if she lived with her son.

She was a tall woman, held her head high, and moved with simple grace. Her beautiful long neck complemented and provided a setting for her large, slanting, light-brown eyes. She was dark black and had wide-spaced teeth. There was no haughtiness in her soft and gentle face. But her gracious spirit was accompanied by a complete lack of humour. She would have been considered a most beautiful woman if only there had been a twinkle in her eyes or a slight warmth in her smile. She spoke with a soft, gentle voice full of kind intentions. It was a voice without force, but she was nevertheless obeyed.

Taptamus remained as the family's holder of wisdom, the one who in the eyes of her family knew the answers to everything. Many times she told her children, "I don't know all of the answers in life. It is a mystery, and I can't give you a prescription to follow to achieve happiness. Nor can I tell you why some people die and others don't. I think life is a gift for every living thing. No one in particular owns it. But death is not a gift, we have it somehow underneath the clothes we wear when we are first born, and all of our lives we will carry it without ever knowing it."

"The advice I can give you children to be happy is not to try to search for the undiscovered because you are afraid of death. Make a song with a beautiful melody. Listen to the children cry and sing them a lullaby. Listen to the new music being sung. Have good morals, be tolerant of others and keep greed out of your lives. Greed is a silent death of the soul. You will always want more and more. I don't know myself why I am alive and my sister and my husband are dead. Death is a thief, and grief is the joy of death. Should we grieve death?"

The only thing that was predictable about the weather in the tropical highland forest on Mt. Kamasai was its unpredictability. Even the animals living in the thickets below the trees were confused by it, and it upset Taptamus' plans for going with the baby to see Mary. Starting in the late morning, the brisk, restless wind blew wet and chilly, forcing every living thing on Mt. Kamasai to take shelter. The three-room thatched house had no real windows. The room which served Taptamus as both bedroom and kitchen had a little peephole in the wall which Taptamus stuffed with rags when she was not using it. She took the rags out when she was cooking to let most of the smoke escape, while the rest leaked through a small chimney in the centre of the thatched roof. She also pulled the rags out when she retired for the night, to give her eyes relief from the burning smoke. The sitting room had two of these holes, one facing east and the other west with the door in the middle. These holes were used in the night if the cattle outside seemed restless, and were in use all day today as Taptamus kept a watch on the outside while trying to avoid opening the door and letting the cold wind in.

By mid-afternoon, a rainbow lay across Mt. Kimugei on the other side of the valley, looking almost like the adornment rimming a warrior's shield. A small, innocent sun shone faintly through the greyish-blue clouds. The wind abated, and Taptamus stood at the door absorbing the changes in the air after the rain. Finally, she stepped out to see if there was any sign of Kibet down at the brook where he often went to listen to the frogs sing after the rain. The air's smell was refreshing. Something beyond the *simotwet* milk tree caught her eyes. A tiny antelope emerged gracefully with her family. She was brownish-grey with a white belly. Her horns were ringed almost to the tips. The male appeared separately, walking gingerly on the wet ground. It walked past the youngsters, brushing them away as it approached the female, smelling and licking her lovingly. But she kicked him and ran to the youngsters.

Across the brook at the foot of the mountain lay a flat stone on which a family of thickset, red-bottomed, olive-brown baboons were lined up basking in the sun. The upper torso of the male was well-developed, like a weightlifter. The female was slimmer, with an infant between her feet, facing her while she picked lice from its fur and popped them into her mouth. The male had detached himself from the group and lay with his head down as though keeping an eye on them. He had a dog-like tail which he carried upright in a loop. It was not unusual for Taptamus to see these animals, they all inhabited this land. The baboons occupied the country stretching from rocky Mt. Kamasai forty miles up to the forests on Mt. Elgon and the open plain of Endebes. Taptamus had grown up with these animals and took them for granted, but that day she was tired and her mind wandered. Are the females tired too? she wondered. Are the male animals the same as human males? Do they think the female and children are their family? Is there a grandmother looking after the grandchildren in the animals' society?

Taptamus was interrupted by a voice from behind. "Where is the baby?" cried Cheseret. "You don't have her with you."

"Oh, Cheseret! When did you arrive?" exclaimed Taptamus with the barest trace of a grin.

"This morning," Cheseret said as she and Taptamus ran to embrace each other.

"I thought your mother told me you were going to be there for a month. Has it been a month yet?" asked Taptamus. She reached out and took Cheseret's hand. "I was on my way to find Kibet to tell him to bring the cattle closer to home. Let's go together, and you can tell me what happened."

"Being in that place for a even a week was too much for me," said Cheseret. "If I'd been in my right mind I would have left in three days."

"Oh dear, you didn't like it there at all, did you?" said Taptamus.
"No, I didn't. After I had decided at the end of the first week I wanted to return home, the days grew longer and the nights dragged on endlessly. Everybody in that place was boring. One of my cousins was exceptionally boring," said Cheseret with a sigh of relief to be back home.

"I thought you went to Muguri to your Aunt Chebii," said Taptamus in disbelief and amazement. She herself had grown up in Kaplamai, which was not even five miles east from Muguri, and all of her happy childhood memories came from there. In Taptamus' generation, Muguri had been the home of the most dazzling warriors and girls of the period, and in fact her own husband had come from there. She remembered that once the girls from Kaplamai had been forbidden to go to see warriors from Muguri because if they did, it would have meant that the warriors of Kaplamai would have been left out in the cold. Taptamus found it hard to understand how someone like Cheseret could have failed to enjoy herself in Muguri when she was so absolutely attractive.

Cheseret was flamboyant, five-foot-six with woolly, thick-matted hair and a bubbly personality. She didn't bother with the Nandi habit of salvaging something from the worst situation. She was natural and expressed her views with forthrightness and directness, holding nothing back. Her mother hated her for this openness and told her repeatedly to keep to herself what she disliked in other people.

"You are going to cause a scandal one of these days, and no one will stand you afterwards," her mother had said. On the contrary, Cheseret was admired by everyone in the neighbourhood for her openness, and along with Mary, she was Taptamus' special favourite.

The routine of women's work was hard, but it was straightforward and never varied. The morning job was sweetening and sterilizing the milk gourds and then taking them to milk the cows. The same job had to be done in the evening, but that particular evening there was a blessed change for Taptamus. That evening, Cheseret took over the baby, and Taptamus got everything done in good time without worrying. Cheseret knew about children; she had babysat some of her sisters and brothers.

They ate just after sunset. The house was warm and friendly — the roaring fire, the baby, Kibet and Cheseret gave it a cozy, comfortable atmosphere.

"It is so wonderful to be back home where I can eat without agonizing about whether I have done something wrong," said Cheseret.

Taptamus could no longer ignore what Cheseret had talked about earlier. "What went wrong that made everything in Muguri so unbearable that even eating was painful?" she asked.

"My cousin Chepkurgat, her god, her church, and her Lawrence!"

"Who is Lawrence?"

"Lawrence is supposedly Chepkurgat's boyfriend, but Chepkurgat follows him around like a puppy dog. Taptamus, do you really want to hear this? My mother certainly didn't."

"I don't mind," said Taptamus, "I have the whole night to listen."

"To start with, almost everyone in Muguri goes to church on Sunday. My Aunt Chebii goes to the Catholic church at Chepterit because you can get drunk after you come home and chew tobacco and still go to it. And if you die, I guess you still go to heaven anyway. Chepkurgat goes to the church at Mugundoi, Chebisas, because Lawrence goes there, and at that one you don't drink. If you drink, you will never see the kingdom of heaven. Of course Chepkurgat drinks like an elephant, but she goes there because Lawrence likes a girl who does not drink."

"Do you mean that all of the girls that what-is-his-name goes with have to be in his religion?" Taptamus couldn't make any sense out of it.

"That's another horrible thing about this religion. They say that a man and a woman should be faithful to one another, and if a man and a woman don't belong to one another, then they shouldn't go together."

"Do they call the girls women too?"

"Precisely. In this new custom called religion they don't differentiate the behaviour of women and girls. Everybody with a man is a woman, and Chepkurgat is acting out the part beautifully with Lawrence loving every minute of it. You see, Taptamus, Chepkurgat is gorgeous. She is fat and smooth as a bottle, and Lawrence says that if you lie between her legs it doesn't hurt the way it does with a skinny woman.

"She sits all day long to save herself for Lawrence and contributes nothing to the household. She has no other interests except Lawrence. My aunt is responsible for preparing the food for the family and winnowing millet, fetching water, firewood and looking for vegetables. When Chepkurgat arrives home in the morning from Lawrence's warriors' house, my aunt has to have tea ready for her. Before Chepkurgat will drink it, she makes everyone close their eyes and say, 'let us give thanks to God for putting this tea in front of us.'

"When it came to eating, there wasn't a day that passed without my making a mistake at that house. No sooner would I take my first bite than Chepkurgat would announce that she was going to pray. That made me really uncomfortable."

"What do her parents think about this?" Taptamus asked.

"My uncle has moved out and lives in the grain storehouse now. For one thing he wants to be able to drink his beer freely, and for another, the house has been turned into a pigsty by Chepkurgat. Her mother has been struck dumb by the devil. I hate Chepkurgat! I couldn't stand her interminable talk about god and Lawrence. The house is a mess, and she herself sits beautifully fat with her skin sparkling like crystal in the morning sun. And you know she is such a hypocrite! She sneaks into the grain store to steal my uncle's beer. She spits the dregs she has sucked up from the beer anywhere she can see that's open, so she is turning the granary into a pigsty, too.

"Her Lawrence is equally boring. Anytime he was over, he would start his incessant preaching about their god. I would get nauseous, and I couldn't do anything to shut him up or say anything to distract him into talking about something else."

"What do the girls do then to be with other warriors?" Taptamus asked, half asleep.

68

"I don't think Chepkurgat is trying to see anyone else. The ones who have trouble are the girls who don't want to be made to behave like married women with only one man. Unfortunately I didn't meet them. Taptamus, are you asleep? It's early."

"Oh no, I hear you."

"How is Sukunwa?" Cheseret asked.

"She is sleeping nicely," answered Taptamus.

"Do you care to hear more about the girls in Muguri?"

"Oh, are we still talking about that?"

"Yes, I was just about to tell you about the embarrassment one runs into if she behaves according to the original Nandi custom of *kesach* and spends every night with a different warrior without having sex."

Now Taptamus was awake again. "What kind of embarrassment would that be I wonder?" she said hoping the story would be a little shorter this time.

"The biggest trouble with this new law," — Cheseret paused and sighed deeply — "is that if a girl goes with any warrior, it is a sin, and the following Sunday she has to go to confess publicly in the middle of the service."

"Confess for what sin? What is the sin? Confess to who?" asked Taptamus not knowing what to think of this puzzling new law.

"Confess to god in the church," said Cheseret not knowing herself who the god was and what the sin was that one had to confess. She knew about the Nandi god, the daughter of Kipkoiyo, but the god she heard people talking about in Muguri was a man. Now she wished she had left that part out of the conversation.

"I'm really sorry I can't tell you who is supposed to be the sinner, the girl or the man. I suppose the girl is the sinner. Oh, I know! You can find this out from Mary! She knows all about these church things. She got the name Mary from that place," said Cheseret a little disappointed that she didn't know as much as she thought.

The roosters' crowing echoed through the neighbourhood in a chain reaction indicating that it was daybreak and time to be up. Taptamus was fortunate that morning. Cheseret was up before her and was prepared to do the morning chores in the house. Since Nandi domestic chores were almost uniform, Cheseret didn't have to ask Taptamus what to do. She knew it all, having been taught since the age of six by her mother. Now, at 16, she was a professional, following instructions that had been handed down from time immemorial. She knew that when an unmarried girl or an old woman first got up from bed in the morning she had to take a bowl of water and go out to wash her hands. She felt lucky she was not a married woman who would have to go to the stream to wash her entire body. Although she only knew Nandi law, Cheseret was somehow uncomfortable with what this law laid down for a married woman, who had to clean herself completely when she woke up in the morning before touching anything else in the house just because she might have had intercourse with her husband.

After Cheseret finished washing her hands, she went directly to the fireplace to sterilize the gourds for milking. One small gourd of milk would be enough until noon when a bigger meal would be prepared. Taptamus was about to hand Sukunwa to Cheseret so she could go to milk when Kibet walked in and asked, "What kind of blood do you want for breakfast, coagulated or uncoagulated?"

"Who is doing the bleeding?" asked Taptamus.

"Arap Walei and I," said Kibet full of excitement. Arap Walei had told him he would teach him how to take blood from a cow.

"I think it's really you and Cheseret who need coagulated blood for strength and protection against the cold, but we can have both kinds," said Taptamus.

"Oh, Taptamus! Speaking of Arap Walei just reminded me of what his wife told me. I forgot to tell you — I'm not going home until this afternoon. Mary and my mother wanted you to be at Mary's by sunrise this morning. I wonder if you are late? It's my fault then," said Cheseret. "I think you should leave the milking for me," she added.

"Do you have any idea why they wanted me to be there that early?" Taptamus asked.

"No," Cheseret replied. "Kibet! Did Arap Walei mention anything about Mary waiting for me?"

"No," Kibet answered.

Taptamus looked concerned.

"I don't think there is anything wrong with Mary. She may just want to see you," said Cheseret trying to reassure her. "You know Tapchamgoi has never been accused of having a rare gift of silence, and I met her yesterday coming from Mary's house. Believe me she would been have flying high if she had had something to say about Mary."

"Young and innocent," murmured Taptamus.

"What?" asked Cheseret.

Taptamus didn't answer her question. "Well *senge*," Taptamus said, using a kinship term to address her affectionately. "Look after everything. I'll be back in a little while," she said.

Taptamus *was* concerned. She had no idea how long she would be away, so she went by her daughter Cheptabut's house to let her know she wouldn't be at home and to ask her if she would keep an eye on the children.

"Cheptabut!" she called into the house. "I'm going to Mary's house. Would you check my place from time to time. I know Cheseret is a capable child, but it's good for you to know I'm away."

"What does Mary want, mother?" asked Cheptabut.

"I don't know. She asked me to be there early in the morning so I'm in a hurry. I can't talk to you now. I'll tell you what it was on my way back."

"Let me walk you half way then," said Cheptabut. They walked in silence for a few minutes.

"Mother, why are you so quiet!" asked Cheptabut. "I haven't seen you for a month. How is the baby?"

"Oh she's fine. She's starting to play, and she follows movements with her eyes. You really should come and see her sometime, Cheptabut."

"Yes of course, mother. So why are you so quiet then. You don't look happy going to Mary's house. Or am I imagining it?"

"I was called there three months ago because something dreadful

71

had happened, but its more than I can talk about now. If anything is wrong again today, I'll tell you the whole story when I return."

CHAPTER FOUR

Mary was at the doorway looking as though she had been waiting since dawn. Her house was the only one in the neighbourhood with no smoke coming out of the chimney. Taptamus followed her in. There was stillness in place of the usual warmth of Mary's greeting, and her large, dark eyes contained a look of despair.

"Chepsisei has been sick for the last week. I thought it might be malaria, but she only gets sick in the very early morning. By the time the sun is warm enough for the monkey families to come out to bask, she begins to smile. Although she can't say, 'I feel better now, mother,' I can see the expression of relief on her little face. Taptamus! I hope that what I suspect is not true. Will you check her for me?"

Dumbfounded, Taptamus stood speechless while Mary went into the kitchen to get the ritual butter in the cow's horn. She handed it to Taptamus. "No, heat it up first. It works best when it's warm," but Taptamus said. Mary went back and set the horn in the still-warm ashes from the previous night's fire. The two of them arranged Chepsisei so that she lay on her back with her head facing straight up and her hands relaxed at her side. They also made sure that her feet were not crossed. Taptamus spit on her own hands as a blessing and then poured the oil into the palm of her hand. She anointed Chepsisei's elbows and knees in blessing and then began gently to massage her stomach. When Chepsisei had relaxed completely, Taptamus carefully explored her abdomen with her sensitive little finger. She quickly established that Chepsisei was about three months pregnant. The baby was about the length of the first two joints of her little finger. Poor Chepsisei had no idea of what was going on, but she was not scared.

She always felt safe beside her mother. She looked from Taptamus to her mother, and her eyes seemed to ask, "What are you doing to me?"

"I wish I could say she's not pregnant, Mary," said Taptamus, "but I can't, she is."

Mary was overwhelmed. She had known her daughter was pregnant, but she hoped for a miracle, for her close friend like Taptamus to say that her daughter was only ill, not pregnant. What was she going to do now? Her daughter was severely limited and completely dependent. She never remembered to dress herself without being told. She couldn't go to the toilet without Mary's saying, "Chepsisei let me take you *sang*." Holding a cup of tea without her mother at hand she would burn herself. Her body was very solid and muscular, but she was not steady when she walked. Her legs seemed too heavy for her, and she wobbled. She wasn't violent, but she was stubborn and strong-willed. No one could move her if she didn't want to be moved. She made noises, but no one could understand her except for her mother. When she wanted something, she could make the same sound all day long. The only skills she had ever mastered after many years of effort by her mother were to fetch water and to sweep the house, and even these she could only do when Mary was there to get her started. At the river, Mary would lift a pot full of water to her daughter's head, but half of it would spill out by the time Chepsisei reached home.

Mary and Taptamus were thunderstruck. They were the only ones who knew the full story that lay behind it. How they would convey what had happened to Mary's husband, Arap Walei, no one knew. Taptamus couldn't pretend she had something to say that would make Mary feel better. She got up and walked to the door. Mary followed her.

"There's nothing to say, is there Taptamus?" she asked. "It just has to come out."

"I'm not walking away from you, Mary. I know how it feels to be desperate. I'll never forget what you and your husband did for me and my family when my husband was killed and you gave us refuge. We'll work something out together, but right now I don't think we should make a decision by ourselves. We should discuss the matter with other women."

"Taptamus, there is nothing to discuss. I have made up my own mind. The baby has to come out."

"Yes, of course. I'm not denying that. However, I think we must discuss this with other women who can contribute their own ideas, like your sister. But right now, the biggest worry on my mind is how we should tell your husband."

"Telling him will just cause more problems. There is no need for him ever to know since the baby is coming out," said Mary. Her eyes imploringly sought her friend's agreement.

After several hours of inconclusive discussion, in which Taptamus tried hard not to push her thoughts too strongly on Mary, she asked her if they could let the matter rest overnight. At her wit's end, Mary agreed. On her way home, Taptamus passed by her daughter's. Hopefully someone other than Mary would have a better perspective. Cheptabut was at home.

"Mother, you're finally back. What kept you there so long?" Cheptabut watched closely as her mother moved toward her, dejection written on her face.

"Did you check Cheseret and the baby?" Taptamus ignored her daughter's question.

"Yes, mother. I just got back from your house now. But mother, what happened? You look dreadful."

"I don't know how to explain," said Taptamus looking blankly at Cheptabut.

Cheptabut couldn't keep the curiosity from her voice any more. "Mother, I'm going to Mary's to find out what is going on there."

"This is a sensitive matter. It's nothing to laugh about," Taptamus replied in her usual dry way to her daughter's impatient questions.

"I told you this morning that I was called three months ago to Mary's house. I had been threshing the finger millet. At about the time the sun warmed the ground, Mary came by on her way to fetch thatching grass. She didn't stop to talk with me. Later in the morning, before I had removed the chaff from the grain, a child came running up breathlessly.

"'Taptamus! Mary is calling you. She says to leave everything and come.'

"I went, and when I got there Mary was sitting beside Chepsisei in the bedroom. Chepsisei was moaning. She was frightened and shivering like a wounded lamb. I stood looking down at Mary and her daughter. Mary turned around, looked up at me and said, 'Taptamus, I think she has been raped. I've checked her in every way I could except that I couldn't bring myself to look down there.'

"Mary left. I didn't have to struggle to open Chepsisei's legs. As I lifted up her skirt, I could see that the child had bled. She had been raped."

"But who would do such a thing! Does Mary know who might have done it?" asked Cheptabut.

"The unbelievable thing about all this is that the man who Mary saw running out of the house was Musimba."

"Oh no! I thought..." Cheptabut stopped herself. She was about to say she thought Musimba's penis was dead, but she realized that she could not use that language in front of her mother. However, Taptamus let Cheptabut know she understood what she was about to say. She continued right where her daughter had left off.

"Of course, you know, it has been said that Musimba is not normal, that he doesn't function like a man. But it is Tapchamgoi who started this story."

"Now I can make some sense out of what Cheseret has been saying about Musimba. You know, mother, nowadays the children won't sleep at Tapchamgoi's house. When I asked Cheseret why, she told me that it wasn't worth losing your virginity to Musimba. Tapchamgoi lets him sleep inside because she says he's *kwong'ot* — just slow — and not dangerous, but the girls say he roams around at night and they can't sleep a wink. I must say that this situation has made me curious about Tapchamgoi. She says she doesn't know where he comes from, but I have the feeling she knows more about him than she lets on," said Cheptabut.

76

"I would say that she is only right about one thing — that Musimba is *kwong'ot*," said Taptamus. "But speculation about where Musimba comes from is not going to help. Mary wants her daughter to have the pregnancy removed and for Arap Walei not to be told."

"Oh mother! How...?" Cheptabut had always obeyed her mother's decisions, and she had wished many times that she was more like, but today she felt she didn't know her mother's mind. How can she entertain the thought of ending the pregnancy without Arap Walei knowing? She looked directly at her mother. Has she gone mad, she wondered. "Mother, I hope you and Mary know you are deluding yourselves if you think that you are going to get rid of a three month pregnancy without anyone knowing. I think that is too much for you to hope for."

"I was there listening and giving her my support," Taptamus said with a little sharpness in her voice. "You must understand that Mary is confused today and is saying whatever comes into her mind," she added.

"Yes of course, mother. I'm not denying her her feelings or what she may say. I'm just trying to tell you that what Mary wants could turn into a disaster and spill over on to us because you are involved.

"Yes, you're right. That is the way I've been thinking myself," Taptamus agreed with her daughter.

"Do you mind if I come with you tomorrow to listen?"

"Of course you can come, but I'm not quite sure what we are going there to say. We can't go and advise her to tell her husband the truth and that her suffering and misery will end. You know that wouldn't be true. Her reputation as a mother has been destroyed for good," Taptamus said.

Taptamus went home to relieve Cheseret. It was late afternoon already. She walked alone down the path. The only sounds she heard were the whispering of the grass she brushed against as she walked and the heavy breathing of the cattle who were grazing greedily in their rush to consume enough for the night. Taptamus pitied Mary. She knew Mary wanted the pregnancy ended so that the whole world wouldn't talk about it.

Their "world" was three miles wide and fifteen miles long, a patch of rugged, rocky land along the upper slopes of Mt. Kamasai. At the foot of the mountain ran the Cheboiywa River which was the boundary between the Nandi and the Luyia. On the other side of the mountain from Kapkeimur onwards there were European settlers and priests. But on the slopes of the mountain, in densest forest, the people of Kamasai lived completely cut off from the rest of the Nandi. The land was rocky and rugged, and the houses were built among the boulders. There were no grassy plains for cattle to graze on. The little grass they could obtain was found in gaps in the forest canopy where the trees allowed the sunlight to filter down. The produce of the women's vegetable gardens had to be shared with the monkeys that came from the forest around them. In this little world everyone knew every detail of everything that happened. The world was round, like the inside of an eggshell. Words would start in the east, travel west, north and south, and then end up in the east again.

Only the men wondered what life was like outside of the shell. The ever-present need to find grass for their cattle and to keep track of the settlers oriented them outwards. The women, on the other hand, were entombed inside. Inside the shell, a woman's job was to keep the family name clean. Her responsibility was to teach the children their differences. She encouraged the boys to get out to be with their father and to do whatever he was doing. In the 1950s, this meant not doing much. Ever since the British had arrived in East Africa, what Nandi men could do was limited. Cattle raiding was no longer feasible because it was against British law. The great game animals of the savannah which Nandi men had formerly hunted were gone. There was little for men to do. They had a few trades to teach their sons — how to build a house, how to bleed a cow, how to stay away from a woman so as to not be a sissy — but that was all.

On the other hand, girls' tasks had not changed. The daily cleaning of the cattle kraal and the *injor* — the sleeping place for the sheep, goats and calves, the preparation of the family's daily food, the daily carrying of water, looking for firewood — these were just some of the things women had to do. All of these things Mary had managed successfully. But most important of all was the preservation of the family name, and this was where she was failing. Now she was faced with a problem that no amount of advice or sympathy from best friends like Taptamus would solve. She would be branded a failure for the rest of her life for not being able to look after her daughter. All the fingers around her would be pointing, "Do you see that woman? She let her *abusanet* daughter be raped, and now the girl is pregnant. She's dragged the family's name in the mud."

CHAPTER FIVE

When Taptamus got home her mind was spinning like a tornado. There was no sign of Cheseret outside. She entered the room and heard the soft murmuring voice of Cheseret floating from the other room and then heard a man's voice. Taptamus took off the heavy animal skin cloak that she had been wearing — her left shoulder was beginning to hurt.

"Kiriswa is here! He arrived just a little while ago," Cheseret said excitedly as she appeared in the doorway connecting the two rooms of the house. She was obviously very happy, and her eyes were melting and full of love. She was so excited that she couldn't bear to look at Taptamus for more than a few seconds out of bashfulness. She was blushing.

"I'm sorry I'm so late," Taptamus said. Her face looked tired and sad. She seemed not to notice Cheseret's excitement.

"I don't think I have to go home now. I can even go tomorrow if that can be any help for you, Taptamus," Cheseret said.

"Oh no. I don't want to sound like I'm ungrateful for your offer, but I have to let you go today," said Taptamus. She actually would have liked it very much if Cheseret had stayed, but with her son Kiriswa being there, it would only create more problems. Cheseret would have spent most of her time on Kiriswa's lap with Kiriswa gazing on her as though nothing else around him mattered.

Kiriswa was 20 years old. Being an only son and with his father dead, he had been given a wife at an early age. He had been married for five years and now had one child with another on the way. But five years ago, at his wedding, he almost hadn't made it through the ceremony. After two days and nights of non-stop activity, he was so tired that he had asked his uncle if he could go to the warrior's house to take a nap. "No," his uncle had told him. "You still have your *kerib segut.* You have to guard the wedding ring. You can't let your wife sleep alone. You have to spend four days with her in your new house. You know you're a married man now, don't you?" His uncle smiled and patted him on the shoulder.

After the wedding, everyone's life went back to normal except that of Taptamus — she had to watch carefully to make sure Kiriswa didn't spend all his nights in the warrior's house. Finally, when his wife was pregnant with the second child, Taptamus had decided that he was old enough to look after himself.

It was not more than two months later when Kiriswa came to his mother with the news that he was in love with Cheseret and that he *must* marry her. Taptamus' mind was in a state of confusion. How could the boy want to get married again so soon? He was still too young to make himself an old man with two wives. And in addition, marrying a girl then had become expensive. The girl's parents now wanted a lot of money. Taptamus thought that Kiriswa's first wife had cost a lot — two goats, two sheep, four cows and about six hundred shillings. Besides all this, the mother of the girl had demanded a big blanket costing thirty shillings. Two sheep had been sold to get the thirty shillings, and she had sold five cows to get the six hundred shillings. It had taken two months of heartaches before all the animals could be sold. Selling them was not easy. One had to go four miles to Chepterwai every Saturday, and if the price was not right there, 30 miles away to Lebao. Taptamus didn't even want to think about it now. She had lost a lot of weight when all this was going on and there was no single event in her life that she could remember that had caused her so much distress. And then there was the never-ending bragging of Tapchamgoi that she had had to listen to day and night.

"The whole neighbourhood is so impressed with me," Tapchamgoi had said. "All the men and women ask how I manage to look after my family so well without a husband. Some pretend to have compassion for me, but in reality, they really want to know how I have managed to give wives to my two sons and to live with them without problems in one household. The older son's wife cost nine hundred

82

shillings, four sheep, four goats and six cows. A bicycle was bought for the girl's father, and a pot, a tea-kettle and a blanket for the mother! The younger one's wife was a little more reasonable except that my son had to build a house for the girl's mother and father. And now my daughter is getting married."

This story had been told again and again, and Taptamus knew it by heart, but she never failed to listen politely to it. For one thing, she had been born with genuine patience which allowed her to put up with someone like Tapchamgoi, and for another, she had allowed her only son to marry Tapchamgoi's daughter. But now she felt that she was not ready to go through something like this again, especially when the marriage in question would involve eloping. Cheseret's family would never agree to hand their daughter over because Kiriswa was too young to have two wives.

"Mother," Kiriswa called out. "Why don't you let Cheseret help you tonight and go home in the morning?" Kiriswa asked this only because Cheseret hadn't said a word since Taptamus had asked her to go home.

Cheseret took a deep breath and came out of the dream she had gone into when Taptamus had told her to go home. She had hesitated to respond when Taptamus asked her to go home for one and only one reason — Kiriswa. She didn't want anyone else to have him that night but herself alone. Now, when she heard Kiriswa speak to his mother, her spirits lifted up. She cast a quick glance at Taptamus.

"Sukunwa is playing nicely. I've given her milk. I'll be back in a little while," Cheseret said. She was delighted. Why didn't I think of this before? she asked herself. Her face opened up and shone like a morning-glory. She had figured out how to keep Kiriswa that night for herself! The misery she had anticipated of going to the warriors' house and sharing Kiriswa with the beautiful Chelamai Kap Metuk was about to be solved.

Now she was going home to ask her parents for permission to stay that night to help Taptamus who had come late from Mary's house, and there was still a lot to be done. The baby also seemed to want someone standing around in the evening because she cried when

Taptamus left her to milk the cows. "Of course when I say that, my mother will say, 'Yes, you shouldn't even have come home. You know Kibet is too young to hold the baby comfortably, and maybe Baby Sukunwa is beginning to notice the hands that hold her. You run back and come tomorrow after the morning chores are done.'"

"I hope. Oh I hope that when I get home my father is not there yet," she said, so delighted everything was going to work out just the way she wanted. "When I get back to Taptamus' house, I'll ask Kibet to help with the baby while Taptamus is out milking, and I will cook. Then we can eat before it gets dark because I have to go to the warriors' house today. Of course when Kiriswa hears that I am rushing to cook because I'm afraid to go to the warriors' house in the dark, he will clear his throat and say, 'Cheseret take your time; I will take you.' And then he will probably look at me to see if I agree with him. I'll simply smile at him and say, 'Oh, thanks.'"

This was the best plan she had ever come up with, she thought. It was simple. After dinner, when Taptamus had taken Sukunwa, she would inform Taptamus that she had to go to the warriors' house that night, and Taptamus would dismiss her. "Kiriswa will immediately say to me, 'Cheseret wait. It is too dark. I will take you.' He will come out and hold my hand. He'll squeeze it and say, 'Don't be afraid; I'm holding on to you tightly.' Then I'll yawn as though I'm terribly sleepy. That way, Kiriswa will ask me, 'Are you tired?'"

She would move fast. She would say, 'Yes.' She thought about the warriors' house. She would point out to Kiriswa that it would be very crowded, with many men and not enough girls. Everyone would be exchanging girls all night long. She admitted to herself that it would not take that much talking. Kiriswa would say she was right and ask where they should go to sleep. She would recommend the house that the Kuikuiot's had recently vacated.

"Oh — " she stopped. She was about to say that she would have him for herself to lie next to, her head on his chest listening to his heart beat. When Kiriswa said to her, 'Cheseret, I have been waiting forever for this day to be alone with you,' or who knows? Better yet, he might say, 'Cheseret, I'm tired of coming all the way from

Kipkarren to see you every month. I want you to be mine. Let's go away to get married.' But Cheseret didn't get to say it all. She had to stop to face reality. Suppose it doesn't work, she asked herself. Finally her house came into view as she reached the top of the hill. She heard her father's voice raised. What she heard as she got nearer to the door was very disturbing.

"How many men jumped all over you today? Heh? Don't tell me! Let me guess! You'll say you went to help Taptamus. Someone was not feeling well there. Or to your sister Mary's where you usually say you go when you disappear."

Cheseret's father was enraged, as usual. He was a short, stocky man with a moustache. His head was so bald and shiny you could see your reflection in it. He was much older than his wife, and she had to pay an immense price for her youth because of his jealousy. He only had sharp and suspicious eyes for her. When he berated her, he asked the questions at the same time as he gave the answers himself.

His wife's face always carried a look of child-like innocence. No one ever knew what dark secrets she carried in her heart. Cheseret could only guess what her mother was going through. She had seen her come home late from running errands, and seen her father waiting at the door to drag her to bed to check in case she had slept with someone while she was out. Her mother never breathed a word.

It was late afternoon. Soon the sun would precipitously descend behind Mt. Kamulubi. Cheseret was not yet certain of how to go about her mission now that her mother was upset. She might be made to stay home. She quickly decided against letting her parents know she was there. If she did that, she would spend an enormous amount of time arguing back and forth. Her mother would say, 'Cheseret, this is not a time to ask for permission to go to help Taptamus.' She would then plead, 'Mother, can't you let me go just this once?' Well, knowing her father, she might not even be able to talk to her mother alone.

Cheseret repositioned herself. She thought it was a good opportunity to leave. That she might have Kiriswa sooner than she had thought. She felt so happy and excited that this thought had come to her mind. She wanted Kiriswa. She had to have him, and she had just this one night.

She remembered once he had asked her if she would elope with him. In her heart she had answered, 'Yes, let us even leave right this minute.' But she had asked him to allow her a little time to think. Now she wished she had agreed with him because she had loved him then and she loved him now. She had only said no then because of what she now thought was a stupid reason that her mother had planted in her mind ever since she was a little girl. Her mother had told her never to let a man think she was desperate about him. 'You know, love is only temporary. It is almost like thirst driving one to take a drink. The drive will end after drinking. When you live with a man more than two years, love will change its colours from the original clear crystal into a foggy gray so that a man won't see anything that you do or say as beautiful the way he used to. Then you will despise yourself forever for making yourself available to him almost for the asking.'

Cheseret thought that she had made the biggest mistake of her life by following her mother's advice. She had asked Kiriswa only to allow her a little time to think about it, but he had let an interminably long time lapse. It was now three months later, and he hadn't asked her again. Today she would make certain that he asked her. It wouldn't matter if she had to resort to tricks to make him do this. She would let him think there were other men who were bothering her by asking her again and again to elope to marry them. She was so tired listening to them that she was going to ask her parents to have her circumcised and married away to any man that they wanted.

She thought that with luck this would work. Maybe by tomorrow she would be circumcised and married to Kiriswa. "Oh, would I like to see my parents' eyes when they discover an engagement vine on their roof in the morning showing them that I've been engaged to someone. I wonder who they would think it was?"

Cheseret turned to head back to Taptamus' house. Before she had taken ten steps, she met her brother, Kiptarus, running and breathing heavily.

"Is anything wrong?" she asked.

"Yes, something really bad is happening in the valley at the Metuk house. Arap Metuk wants my father to to bring all the spears he can get," he said as he ran by Cheseret and went into the house. Shortly after, her father came out with two spears and hurried towards Arap Metuk's house.

"What is it, mother?" Cheseret asked as she went in.

"It sounded as though your brother said 'python.' I don't know. I'm going after your father. You look after the house and the children."

"What is all this about, Kiptarus?" Cheseret asked. There was no answer. Kiptarus went into the kitchen looking for food. With his mouth full he returned to the sitting room.

"Cheseret, how old is this *kimiet*?" he asked.

"Kiptarus, how can you eat at a time like this?"

"Easy. Like this." Kiptarus took another big bite of left-over *kimiet* and made a face as he took a swallow of milk.

"I don't know how old the food is. Why don't you find out by counting the mouldy spots?" Cheseret was upset. She didn't want to talk to Kiptarus any more if he wasn't going to tell her what the running and the spears were all about.

"What's bugging you today? Kiriswa? I hope he doesn't get himself eaten up by the python. I saw him running with a spear toward Arap Metuk's," Kiptarus said. "Oh, and another thing. If he survives the fighting, you know who'll get him tonight."

Kiptarus had moved. He had chosen to stand far from his sister while he was talking. He was well aware that she had never been accused of being fragile. In fact, she was precisely the opposite. She was tough, and when she was upset, it was better to keep one's distance.

"Cheseret, it's a joke. Why are you looking as though you just swallowed a handful of salt?" he exclaimed.

"What is a joke? You mean there is no python?" asked Cheseret.

"No, the joke is about Chelamai Kap Metuk getting Kiriswa. To tell the truth, I think she wouldn't have him even if he wanted her to.

Cheseret, why aren't you talking? Don't you want to ask why she wouldn't want to have him?"

"No. Kiptarus, I don't want to ask you. I wouldn't dream of asking you anything because I know you have an answer for everything." Cheseret had now lost interest in Kiptarus' meddling conversation. She wanted to get her work finished so she could go see for herself what was going on. Here was this senseless and strange, mind-spinning new turn of events for her to deal with. She was never going to get anything done her way today. Kiptarus had brought this evening grief to her, and he wouldn't let it go at that. He went on talking about Kiriswa rather than what was actually happening. She detached herself from him. He was being evil as usual, she thought.

Cheseret was on her way out, and Kiptarus went to the door. "When you get there, say hello to Arap Arbap," said Kiptarus, smiling with self-approval knowing Cheseret would be happy to hear that.

"Who did you say?" asked Cheseret.

"Arap Arbap. That is what I have been trying to tell you. There is nothing to worry about after all. Everyone knows Chelamai is in love with him."

To Kiptarus' disappointment, Cheseret stood at the doorway looking as if she had heard nothing he had said. Kiptarus now rushed to get the words out of his mouth.

"The python is there for real. I'm surprised you don't know. Last week Arap Metuk discovered its den with dozens of little baby pythons squirming around basking in the sun outside. He took a stone and covered the hole, hoping the mother would take her children and move away. But the next day a sheep went missing, and today Arap Metuk has found the snake in the same place all coiled up with a huge bulge in its stomach and with the sheep's hind legs still sticking out of its mouth. Arap Walei told him that now was the time to try to kill it because it would lie around for a couple of days digesting the sheep."

When Cheseret got to the scene, the situation was frantic. Her father and Kiriswa were next in order to thrust their spears at the snake. The main idea was for the men to go two by two so that they wouldn't get tangled up with each other. The left-handed Arap Walei and Arap Metuk had already thrust one spear each. Their spears had gone through the python's coils four times and skewered it to the ground. The pain woke the snake up and made it go wild. With one violent wriggle, it straightened out its coils snapping the spears into pieces and almost hitting Cheseret's father.

"Aim for the tail as soon as it hits the ground," yelled Arap Walei.

But instead of thrusting the spear into the python, Cheseret's father threw it into the air and ran to the top of the hill where the women and girls were standing. He grabbed his wife and disappeared to the bottom of the hill. Anger and shame went through Cheseret's heart like a knife. She felt pity for her father mingled with embarrassment. Kiriswa followed the thrashing tail to the ground with his spear and pinned it there. The other men followed, thrusting in every way they could.

Soon the python was dead, and the excitement subsided. The men stood around talking for some minutes, and then Kiriswa walked toward the women and girls at the top of the hill. Standing beside Cheseret was Arap Metuk's wife and a few other women in between her and Chelamai on the other side. Kiriswa walked past Cheseret to Chelamai and whispered something into her ear. Cheseret felt degraded by his walking past without even acknowledging her presence. Mustering up all the pride she didn't feel, she walked past Kiriswa. She hated that day. She hated Mt. Kamasai and the people who lived on it. She hated Chelamai more than anyone else. What does she do to make men give in just like that when they see her? Even Kiriswa, who had said so many mean things about her, just disappeared into her face as soon as he saw her. Last month he told me that Chelamai was beautiful but empty-headed. That he never knew what to say to her when he was in bed with her. And now he's almost attacking her in front of everybody. She must be giving herself to him like a man and wife, but how? When we were seen together last month by Tapchamgoi, she said we were all virgins. Chelamai must know how to make her vagina look small. Cheseret remembered the time she and Chelamai shared Kiriswa, and she heard her say to Kiriswa when he was in between her that something was painful.

While Cheseret was busy thinking, Kiriswa came to stand beside her. "Cheseret, what are you trying to do? You walked away from me."

Cheseret couldn't restrain herself. She was quivering with so much emotion that she made no attempt to answer nor to hide her feelings. The tears streamed down her face. Kiriswa reached out to her and pulled her close to him to lay her head on his shoulder until the emotion had subsided.

"Cheseret, are you all right?"

"Yes, I am. Can you let me go?" She removed his hand, which was resting on her waist, and backed away from him. "I'm going home now."

"What have I done wrong?" asked Kiriswa.

"Nothing. What makes you think that? I'm just sleepy. I have to go home."

"I have something I want to say to you. Perhaps I had better say it before Chelamai comes," said Kiriswa.

"You mean you managed to persuade her to leave Arap Arbap and come to you? Leave me alone. I'm going home." snapped Cheseret.

"Where did you get this idea? I don't care if Arap Arbap has Chelamai. Don't let me give you the wrong impression about Chelamai. She's a very desirable girl, the kind of girl who it's very flattering for a man to wake up and see lying next to him, but I don't care for her."

Kiriswa was holding Cheseret's hand tightly while he was talking to her. "Let's go!" He pulled her by the hand and led her down the path towards home. They walked silently for a while.

"Cheseret, I think it isn't nice for us to go on pretending you don't know what I'm about to ask you. You know I'm still waiting for the answer to my question. It's been more than two months now."

Cheseret bowed her head. Kiriswa pulled out his handkerchief and handed it to her.

"I'm not crying," she said. "The answer is yes, yes! I've been wanting to say yes for weeks, but you haven't asked."

She was looking down while she spoke. Kiriswa lifted up her chin, "Look at me when you say yes." She looked up. "You won't look back and wish you didn't marry me. I love you," he said.

"When are we leaving?" asked Cheseret.

"I'm going in four days, and I want you to leave two days before I do. I'll come and pick you up. No one will suspect it was me until we are married."

"Why four days?" asked Cheseret.

"My mother wants me here a little longer."

"For what?" Cheseret was curious.

"It's something that really has nothing to do with me personally. Chepsisei is pregnant, and my mother thinks I should be here in case Arap Walei should be told."

"Chepsisei is what?"

"Yes, she is pregnant. And I think you shouldn't breathe a word about it to anyone."

"I wonder if they know who the father is?" asked Cheseret.

"If they don't, they will sooner or later come out with some explanation. Anyhow, I think we should talk about ourselves. Would you like us to go to the warriors' house? I had promised Chelamai I would be there. I hope you don't mind sharing me today with her, Mrs. Kiriswa."

"No, I don't, but I hope by the time we get there, she has gone with Arap Arbap," she laughed.

They walked in silence, holding each other close.

"Has Chelamai, you know, got it?" asked Cheseret.

"Lost her virginity? I don't know. If she has, maybe she lost it to Arap Arbap as you say," Kiriswa answered.

Cheseret got home in the morning and excused herself to go to milk the cows before having breakfast. She spoke very little and appeared to be daydreaming. Her mother stood and sized her up.

"Cheseret, what's making you so jumpy? I don't remember you ever looking like this. Anyway, you're late. You should have been here at seven. You've ruined everything today. Now go to Taptamus' house and help her with whatever needs to be done. Tell her to come by. I'm going to milk the cows here with your sister."

When Cheseret got to Taptamus' house, Cheptabut was there already.

"I hope Cheseret manages to come to look after Sukunwa." Cheseret overheard Taptamus speaking.

"Oh, yes. You have to go to Mary's house, don't you? I was wondering what you were going to do about Sukunwa," asked Cheptabut.

"Yes. Believe me, I'm not looking forward to it. I hope I'm not too late and find that Cheseret's mother has gone," said Taptamus.

"I guess if you don't get there on time, they will know you didn't have anyone to leave Sukunwa with. But if you want, when Cheseret comes, I will go with you," said Cheptabut.

"No, you know Mary won't be comfortable with all of us being there at once."

Cheseret entered. "I'm here," she announced.

"Oh, you came. Thank you. Does your mother know you may be staying here until this afternoon?" asked Taptamus.

"Yes, I think so. She told me to ask you to stop by on your way to Mary's. She wants to go with you."

"Cheseret, did you happen to see Kiriswa outside as you came in?" Taptamus asked without giving much thought to her question.

Cheseret didn't say anything, but Cheptabut answered. "He's over at our place, mother. What do you want from him?"

"I want him to fix that fence around my vegetable garden. The goats have been getting into it and biting the leaves off the vegetables."

"Oh, Cheseret has heard it; she can tell him when he comes."

Taptamus turned around and her eye caught Cheseret. Cheseret looked shy. "What's going on here," Taptamus wondered to herself. She exchanged a glance with Cheptabut, but Cheseret didn't notice them.

When Taptamus got to Cheseret's house, Tapsalng'ot, Cheseret's mother, was ready, and they set off for Mary's.

CHAPTER SIX

*T*he day was sweet. The fragrance of the wildflowers was so strong in the air that one felt one could just sit down and sip it. "How can a beautiful day like this have such a horrible event waiting ahead?" thought Taptamus.

Tebengwet blossoms lay against the fence alongside the path and curved up overhead like the gentle white feathers of a dove in flight. Stretching their eyes beyond the plateau, far below and to the west of them, Taptamus and Tapsalng'ot could see the flowering flame trees shivering in the cold. The strong red the trees would display later in the day now appeared as hues of pale white to deepest pink through the smoky apparition of the morning dew's steam mingled with the sun just arriving at the bottom of Mt. Kamasai.

Taptamus led the way along the narrow path to Mary's house. The two women had walked in silence ever since they had set out from Tapsalng'ot's house. Neither of them was able to act as though she knew what they were going to say or do. Taptamus stopped and turned to Tapsalng'ot.

"Do you have any advice about what to do or what to tell Mary?"

Tapsalng'ot sighed and looked down. She shook her head. "No I don't," she said. "I'm her sister; I'm supposed to help her even if she is in the middle of deep water. I'm expected to struggle and pull her out, but this water is too deep. It's spinning inside a whirlpool, and I can't pull her out without drowning both of us. I only hope that she is calmer today than yesterday."

"I was kept awake myself last night by the way Mary has approached this matter. She told me she wanted the baby to be taken out, but I didn't tell her that it was a bad idea or that it was a good one," Taptamus paused. "I think it is too late now, and if something happens to Chepsisei, I will never...," she stopped.

"Don't misunderstand me, Tapsalng'ot. I have been your sister's friend for a long time, but one has to be careful. A friend is someone you stand beside when she is in need, a person you trust, someone you share the same ideas with, someone with whom you always exchange kindnesses. But in this situation, who can say what is wise and what is immoral? This is a situation which can tear even the closest of friends apart.

"No one knows what is right or wrong, but somehow I think that doing things the wrong way is the right way to enrich a society's knowledge. Half of what one does in life is correcting mistakes because one didn't do it right the first time. Unfortunately the men have made the laws here and they have made them with only their own selfish interests in mind. When it comes to the family, they give us all the responsibility for everything, but no room to move about or to learn from our mistakes. Our hands are tied behind our backs. We have to watch our daughters die trying to *kororok moet*, topple the foetus down, and we have to distance ourselves from them in order to save the family name. We have learned that this is wrong. No mother should have to stand by when an accident happens and let her child take her life in her hands, but we have been painted into a corner. The same mistake gets repeated over and over. No one can think anything new."

Women in Taptamus' generation had not been known to question things, and Taptamus in particular was not someone who wanted to change her culture. But she had thought these matters out yesterday while she lay awake unable to sleep after talking to her daughter. Cheptabut had been against Mary's wishes from the first time she heard what she intended to do. Cheptabut had pointed out to Taptamus that they were the ones who in fact would have to try to take the baby out. Chepsisei would never be able to put pressure on her stomach on her own to squeeze the fetus. Taptamus knew that between the three of them, two would have to hold Chepsisei down, and one would have to press on her stomach to force the baby out. She knew this, and she didn't want to be part of it.

"The baby should be born and then given away or allowed to die outside of its mother's womb. At least that way, if something goes wrong, everyone will know, including the father," she said.

"I agree with you. As much as I hate to say so, I think it would be like committing murder for Mary to insist on having the baby out," said Tapsalng'ot. I think she knows it too. She knows what happened to Tamutwol when she kicked her daughter, Tolony, out the minute she found out she was pregnant. Mary knows as well as we do what Tamutwol went through. Not only did she very nearly destroy her daughter's life, she created a scandal trying to preserve the family's good name. If she could have foreseen what would happen, she would never have thrown her daughter out on her own."

"That's true enough. I think both of us are against this operation. Now if only we can convince Mary," said Taptamus.

"Mary saw it. Hopefully it won't be hard to persuade her."

"Yes, that's what Cheptabut has been telling me since yesterday. She said 'Mother, Mary should remember what happened to Tolony and her mother because they ended up at her house after the father kicked them out.'"

"How Mary could ever forget that, Taptamus," said Tapsalng'ot, "is beyond me."

"Let's hope she hasn't."

"She shouldn't. Every woman, every bird who flew across Mt. Kamasai, and every pair of eyes and ears that was there saw and heard it, and none of them will ever forget it. They saw the humiliation and shame Tamutwol went through. Mary was there too, face to face with it. We all watched Tamutwol come to stand at the door silently when she was told that her daughter had fainted on the river bank trying to wash the blood away from the miscarriage she had induced.

"Tamutwol was devastated by remorse. She realized that her attitude towards her daughter hadn't been just. She looked too ashamed even to cry. The shock and the guilt she felt must have immobilized her. She saw the other women in panic over Tolony and stood motionless while she was brought up and laid down on the lawn in front of her house. Her bloody clothes had been taken off, and she had been wrapped in Cheptabut's blanket, but that too was soaking in blood.

"Cheptabut, whom Tamutwol will always thank for saving Tolony's life, showed no sympathy for her. She asked her, 'should I have left your daughter to die by the river so no one would know that she had taken her baby out? Is the family going to be disappointed that she is alive, because now its name is ruined? What kind of a woman are you? You turned upon your own daughter when you found out she was pregnant. I hope you had a better reason than the family's reputation.'

"While Cheptabut asked this question, Tamutwol was paralysed. She was unable to move. Was she shaking for fear she might lose her daughter or because of the shame of it all? Maybe seeing women struggling to get her daughter's mouth open to pour some medicine in was unbearable for her. She fell backwards into the house with her feet sticking out the door, but nobody noticed because everyone's eyes were on the one who was bleeding. When Tolony's mouth finally was opened, Cheptabut called to Tamutwol to bring some milk to mix with the medicine which Tapchamgoi had hurriedly mashed with a stone. She turned around to see if the milk was being brought, but Tamutwol was down flat on her back.

"It was Mary herself who was holding Tolony's head while Tapchamgoi was straining the medicine into a cup. You were the one who was opening her mouth, and Cheptabut and I were at the other end changing the bloody rags. We tried to squeeze the juice from the medicine that Tapchamgoi had given us into her vagina. When Cheptabut saw that Tamutwol didn't move, she asked Mary if she would set Tolony's head down and go to bring the milk. I'm sure Mary can recall what happened next. It was an experience never to forget. You remember that don't you, Taptamus?" asked Tapsalng'ot.

"All this time," Tapsalng'ot continued, "Tamutwol's husband was inside the house. He didn't seem to care. When Mary went in, he was sitting on the clay stoop near the fireplace with a cup in his hand. He didn't say anything and she proceeded to the milk cooler as he watched her.

"When she reached for the milk, he jumped to his feet and said, 'don't you dare take the milk of my cow to rescue that child with. Tell her mother to go to the man who got her pregnant for milk to save her with. This is unheard of in my clan! No girl in my family ever got pregnant before marriage! This is from Tamutwol's side of the family!'

"Mary walked out empty-handed. We would have left when he started using that bad language to Mary, but without a thought, Cheptabut, who I think has the courage of ten men, stood up to face him. She went in and took the milk by force. We poured the milk in with the medicine and got some of it down Tolony's mouth. We had to hold her nose shut so she would be forced to swallow. Then Tolony's father came out shaking his cane. I was ready to leave, but Tapchamgoi saw that it was just a matter of a minute before everyone ran. She stood up and yelled, 'Help! Help! Are there no men in Mt. Kamasai who can help at a time like this? When they make a baby they enjoy themselves, but in a situation like this they dump everything on a woman!' She took a bloody rag and hit him across the face.

"When Cheptabut saw this, she said to us, 'Let's carry the girl and run. He's going to kill us all!' He slapped Tapchamgoi across the face, knocking her down. When she got up she was so dazed she saw a thousand fire flies flying in front of her. Some of the other women were trying to restrain him from beating his still unconscious wife.

"Luckily, Tapchamgoi got up in time and called him by his name. 'Arap Kilach! Look at me here! I am your cousin!' Then she turned around and lifted her dress exposing her buttocks, the worst curse a Nandi woman can inflict upon a man. 'Look at that! Have you ever seen it before?' When Arap Kilach saw this, he disentangled himself and ran. One thing I've never asked Cheptabut is how she found Tolony at the river. Was it by chance or did someone else see her and tell Cheptabut?" asked Tapsalng'ot.

"It's a long story," said Taptamus. "That particular day Cheptabut's husband was not at home, so all of the girls in the neighbourhood slept in her house. Cheptabut said that night Tolony was awfully quiet. They went to bed early because Tolony didn't keep them up late with her infectious laughter. An hour later Tolony went out, and she stayed out for quite a long time. Cheptabut said that she thought she had gone to the warriors' house, but eventually she came in. I guess she thought everyone was asleep, but Cheptabut was still awake. Cheptabut said that she moaned and it sounded as though she was crying. Cheptabut asked her if she was sick, but she said no, that she just had a little stomach ache.

"Cheptabut didn't suspect anything. She thought maybe Tolony had eaten something which didn't agree with her. She told her that if she wanted to go out again she could wake her up.

"Half an hour later, Cheptabut heard her get up and leave. She was gone for about 20 minutes, and Cheptabut said that she was about to go out to look for her when she saw her coming, holding her stomach and not walking straight. She looked as though she were in pain. She tried to go back to bed, but before she was settled she got up again to go out. 'Again?' Cheptabut asked her. 'Yes, just for a little bit. I'm beginning to feel better,' she told Cheptabut, who then got up herself and lit a fire. It took a long time to get it going, and by the time she did, Cheseret was awake too. 'Cheptabut, one of us must have wet the bed. I'm soaking,' she said. Cheptabut lit a paraffin lamp and went to look. 'My God! someone is bleeding.'

"Cheseret screamed. 'Who is it?' she asked.

"'Shh!' Cheptabut told her not to waken everybody. She knew already who was bleeding. Cheseret was the only one to have blood on her clothing because she was the only one sleeping beside Tolony. There were five girls sleeping together in a line on the floor on Kiptai's animal skin bedding in the other room. Tolony was first, Cheseret second, and then the rest of the girls. Cheptabut pulled Cheseret outside the house with her. The wind was blowing fiercely, and if they had held Cheptabut's small, chimney-less lamp in front of them, it would have been blown out immediately. Cheptabut shielded the lamp from the wind by holding it inside the toga she was wearing.

As luck would have it, it was a moonless night, and the lamp's light didn't carry very far. They couldn't see beyond their feet.

"I think that was when Cheptabut told Cheseret that they should go to my place because it was so dark. It was a little past midnight when they knocked on my door. I asked who it was. 'Us,' they both said. I rushed to open the door. They came in and Cheptabut pulled me into the other room to tell me what had happened. She didn't want Cheseret to know any more than she already knew," Taptamus said.

"Cheseret!" exclaimed Tapsalng'ot. "Knowing as much as a mother knows about her daughter, I assure you she knew everything — even the name of the father of the baby."

What Tapsalng'ot said about her daughter was true, but Cheseret didn't know about the abortion at that moment. However, she knew that Tolony's older step-sister had got pregnant and had a miscarriage, *kochil moet*, induced without telling anyone. Not only had no one known it, but when she was going to be circumcised, the old women had examined her and declared her a virgin. That was confusing, Cheseret thought to herself while she waited for Cheptabut and Taptamus to finish talking. Cheseret wondered how Tolonoy's sister could agree to sit on the chair of honour and flick the milk around in her father's presence announcing to all assembled that she was a virgin while the man she had slept with stood by. He must have laughed to himself knowing that years from then she would be going back to the owner of the golden chair saying, 'I'm sorry. I was not a virgin after all. The women didn't check me carefully, and now I have come to anoint the chair so it won't crack.'

What a family, Cheseret thought, and now this one. She was interrupted by Taptamus and Cheptabut.

"The three of us left my place. Cheptabut had told me that we should take Cheseret back to her house to sleep and at the same time check if Tolony was back," said Taptamus.

"My lamp was not much better than Cheptabut's. We made both from cocoa cans that I had picked up at Mary's place to use for salt. When Cheptabut saw them, she suggested we make lamps out of them. She put holes in the middle of the lids and used a strip from an old blanket as a wick. They worked well inside the house, but not outside. We soon realized we had to concentrate too much on the shielding the lamps from the wind. I suggested we go to Mary's to borrow her hurricane lamp. Mary said she would come with us. We returned to Cheptabut's hoping Tolony would be back. We saw better with Mary's lantern and followed the trail of blood that began on the porch. We thought we weren't going to get anywhere because it wasn't a continuous stream. It was just a dribble, but it did help.

"After we had gone 50 yards, Cheptabut guessed that Tolony had headed for the river. We rushed there and found her lying with her feet in the water. She had become dizzy and fallen in. She tried to rescue herself, but hadn't succeed in getting her whole body out of the river. She was terribly cold but breathing. We lifted her up and saw that she was still bleeding. We couldn't see the foetus, but there were some pieces of the afterbirth in the water."

"Was the baby ever found?" asked Tapsalng'ot.

"No. Nobody ever tried to look for it," said Taptamus.

"Why did Cheptabut go to your place? When she realized that she couldn't find Tolony, she should have just gone to Tolony's parents."

"Going to wake Arap Kilach at midnight? You know Arap Kilach's terrible temper. It would have been sheer madness!"

"The first thing Cheptabut told me when she came in was, 'Mother, you have to come with us to look for Tolony so Cheseret can go back to bed.' I could have gone to the parents, but I couldn't bear to face Arap Kilach at that time of night," said Taptamus.

"He is a frightening man, I..."

"Shh! Enough of that. Arap Walei is coming," Taptamus stopped Tapsalng'ot.

"Oh! What shall we say if he asks where we are going?" asked Tapsalng'ot.

"He won't ask us where we're going. He can see we are heading to his house. He wouldn't be rude, would he?"

"Oh, you don't know him as well as I thought. He can be charming, but at the same time he can be tactless."

Tapsalng'ot was not right, thought Taptamus, who knew Arap

Walei better than her friend thought. "I suppose we'll simply have to tell him that we are going to his house," she said.

"Good morning ladies," Arap Walei said, and then he added quickly, "Isn't it a shame you have arrived when we have just finished breakfast?"

"We'll just have to settle for leftovers then," said Taptamus looking down to avoid contact with Arap Walei's eyes. He was a tall, handsome man with a quiet charm, and Taptamus liked him. Years ago a relationship had almost developed between them, but Mt. Kamasai was small. No one could scratch herself in the night without the neighbours whispering the next day. Knowing the consequences, Taptamus had put a damper on even before it had materialized, but she had never lost a tender feeling for him. Once Mary had watched her husband talking to Taptamus and seen the spark between them. She later asked Taptamus, "Why make my husband suffer? At least let him touch you once to ease his feelings about you."

Arap Walei led the way to the house. He called while he was still outside. "Mary, guess who we have here! Taptamus and your sister! I've told them that they're too late for breakfast, but do we still have anything left to eat?" he asked.

"I guess I'll have to look around to see what I can come up with," said Mary.

"You do that, and, oh Mary, I'm going to leave you ladies. I'm going to see if Kiriswa is home. I didn't talk to him last night. Is he there Taptamus?" asked Arap Walei.

"Cheptabut said that he was at her place. Maybe he is at home by now," said Taptamus.

After Arap Walei had gone, the silence became disturbingly long. Perhaps each woman was waiting for the other to say something. Chepsisei walked into the sitting room from her room. She appeared to be walking more stiffly than usual.

Tapsalng'ot watched her coming and asked Mary, "What has happened to Chepsisei? She looks as if she is dragging her feet more today. Or is it my imagination? Come here, lady," she said, referring to Chepsisei.

Chepsisei went and hugged her aunt. Tapsalng'ot felt something around Chepsisei's waist. It was a wide leather belt which compressed her waist and sandwiched her intestines into her stomach.

"Mary, I'm stupefied! You've already tied her stomach!" said Tapsalng'ot. "What's the matter with you? Why were you so eager to deal with this by yourself after getting us involved in it? Why didn't you wait until we were here to discuss this together?"

Mary turned around and walked toward her sister, her dark brown face looking tightly screwed up with an enormous effort to remain civil. Taptamus could see that she was boiling inside, but instead of replying, she sank down against the wall and broke into tears. She buried her face in her hands, took a deep breath, and wiped her tears away. She forced a smile. She was older than Tapsalng'ot, and she had to take control of herself.

"I can't answer your question. If you were a normal human being, you would have understood what I'm facing and not asked it. I had no option, and you are cruel to say I was eager to tie poor Chepsisei," Mary replied.

"I think you had better pay attention to what you are doing to your child. You haven't given yourself time to recover from the shock of finding out about her pregnancy," said Tapsalng'ot.

"You have dictated to me for long enough, Tapsalng'ot. Why should I listen to you make a speech with no beginning or end? But would you mind satisfying my curiosity? How do *you* propose to handle the situation?"

"Let us not mix this with anger," interrupted Taptamus. "Allow me to tell you what we think. The whole situation is delicate for everyone. We don't have an answer yet because no one knows any longer what is right. But Tapsalng'ot, Cheptabut and I all think Chepsisei should be left alone to have her baby because it is too late for it to come out. You know I told you that she was three months along, but that I couldn't be sure — it could even be more. I think it would be hard for anyone to be exact if you haven't made chalk marks on the rafters every month Chepsisei has missed a period."

"I should have known, my dear Taptamus, what would go on

behind my back. I should have known she wouldn't even begin to understand what I'm going through," said Mary, outraged by the way her sister had manipulated Mary's oldest and best friend to agree with her.

"Excuse me Mary!" shouted Tapsalng'ot. "What is it with you? What are you trying to do to me? Has somebody bewitched you against me? You are twisting every innocent thing I say into this huge crime I am doing to you. If there is any crime, it is what Musimba did to your daughter. How asinine can you be? Do you really believe there is nothing that can go wrong in your house without me being the one making it worse? Listen to what Taptamus is telling you Mary! Stop lying to yourself trying to make me your victim. Taptamus said we thought Chepsisei shouldn't have an abortion because it was too late. She didn't say your sister thought this and told her to think the same thing."

"I have let you talk too long already. Can you get out of my house now? You don't know very much anyhow. I shouldn't expect you to know anything. You have never had an *abusan* child and then had her raped. If you had, you would stand beside me now, instead of against me."

"Untie your child's stomach Mary and let us sit down and talk like grown-ups. She is suffering, and I can't stand seeing her sweating and uncomfortable," cut in Taptamus.

Tapsalng'ot went to the door shouting at Mary on her way out. Chepsisei followed her, crying. The scene between her mother and her aunt made her very unhappy even though she might not have known the fighting was about her. Mary went after Tapsalng'ot.

"Mary and Tapsalng'ot, how can you two stand there shouting at each other while Chepsisei is between you crying? Don't you have any mercy?" Taptamus spoke, but no one seemed to notice. She went over and pulled Chepsisei away from them. Suddenly she realized this was her chance to untie Chepsisei's stomach.

"You say I don't know anything, but I know enough to tell you, sister, the way you are behaving is sheer lunacy. You have no moral shame. In spite of what you saw happen to Arap Kilach's daughter,

you still want your daughter to have the baby out? And even more —
it is unheard of for a mother to use her hands to put pressure on her
own daughter's stomach to squeeze the baby out. Can't you see you
are committing a sin?" said Tapsalng'ot.

"Really, Tapsalng'ot, I can't imagine. I mean I'm scared to think
you have used Arap Kilach's daughter to make everyone take sides
with you."

"No, dear Mary, sister, I didn't. They were there with Tolony. I
thought you were there too. Now I realize it is difficult to deal with
you because you are a vicious woman who is about to do an inhuman
thing to her daughter. I'm leaving. Do whatever you want," said
Tapsalng'ot.

"No you can't leave," said Taptamus. "She is your sister. At least
stay for Chepsisei's sake. We have to come up with some sort of
agreement."

"Don't call her my sister. I'd rather have you say a hyena is my
sister than that unpitying woman. Yes, you may do what you want,
Mary. You may also have those cold eyes of yours forever. The only
things that will ever be close to you are the wild animals of Mt.
Kamasai. Poor Chepsisei! Having you for a mother!"

"Don't you feel sorry for Chepsisei! She can't understand your
feelings anyway, so she can't take sides with you like the rest. So keep
them to yourself," Mary said.

"Mary stop it. I don't feel sorry for you for having Chepsisei. You
have eight beautiful children, and I'm not the one who wished you to
have a child like Chepsisei. And I tell you once again, I didn't make
Cheptabut and Taptamus take sides with me." Tapsalng'ot paused. "In
fact," she said, "I didn't tell them what I actually thought. Now I'm
going to tell the truth. I think you should be glad Chepsisei is pregnant
for her to have something of her own. Maybe that is the only child
she will ever have, and you should think of her pregnancy as fate
because Musimba is like her, too. If you make her have the baby out,
don't think you are helping her. You are doing it for your own selfish
reasons. And believe me, if you win and get that baby out, everyone
will still know — even your own husband — whom you are trying so

106

hard to hide this affair from? Good-bye Mary." Tapsalng'ot rushed out of the house before Mary could reply.

"I hate her as much as she hates me, and she is going to cause me trouble. Mark my words — I'm ruined, Taptamus." Mary turned around, put her hands on top of her head and stared at Taptamus with suspicion.

"Unbend, Mary. Your sister means no harm. She wouldn't say anything to hurt you. You know she loves you very much," said Taptamus.

"It was interesting to hear her use Tolony's misfortune as the biggest thing that she had ever heard of. And she was so sure the same thing was going to happen to Chepsisei. If I had been competing with her, I would have come up with far worse stories — like Mukunywa. I'm actually amazed at her for not thinking of that event, too. She was there and witnessed when the mid-wife ripped open Mukunywa by hand until her vagina met with her anus when she couldn't push the baby out. You know what happened next. Not only did the baby die, but Mukunywa was sick for years. Her vagina wouldn't heal, and no one could enter the house where she stayed except for her sister because of the odour. Can you tell me why my sister didn't think that the same thing might happen to Chepsisei knowing her circumstance?" asked Mary.

"I have no idea, Mary," said Taptamus. "I can't answer that. The only thing I may say is that it was known then as a mistake the midwife made. It shouldn't have been done that way. The mid-wife didn't even bring a knife to cut the baby's umbilical cord. She could have used that if she had had it."

"Taptamus, let's be honest. How can I let Chepsisei carry the baby for nine months before she is initiated? It's unheard of. You were talking about danger. It is just as dangerous to have her circumcised when she is this far along in her pregnancy as it would be for her to get the baby out. In any case, who could accept to perform the ceremony for a child who is both impure and *abusan*? People are reluctant to perform the ceremony with such children anyway because they are afraid they will cry during it and bring them bad luck. And then imagine, she's pregnant too!"

"Mary, don't speak as though you are alone. You have us. Give us the go ahead, and we'll do the rest. You don't need to be afraid about her bleeding after the circumcision. I have done this operation for twenty years, and if I think there will be any risk, I won't do it. The bleeding occurs when a girl dances all day and then the women administer stimulants at night and the girl dances again before the operation. This doesn't apply to Chepsisei. She will be operated on before dawn when it's still cold and her blood is sluggish."

"Taptamus, would you tell my husband for me? You are the only one I trust in Kamasai. I know I should ask my sister, but I can't stand her and her husband. My husband also respects your judgement more than theirs." Mary paused to wait for Taptamus to answer, but Taptamus looked flabbergasted. She had thought that someone else, perhaps Kiriswa or an elder in the neighbourhood, would have done the telling while the men were drinking some millet beer.

"Of course I wouldn't want you to mention Musimba. I would prefer that Musimba didn't even enter the picture. And I think I will have you come here. Then if my husband demands an explanation of how it happened, I can do the explaining," added Mary.

Taptamus felt it was a lot for her. However, she nodded in agreement for the moment and got up to leave. She was still holding the leather belt in her hand wondering whether she should take it.

"Are you going to say anything?" Mary asked.

"There is nothing for me to say now. I'll make all of the arrangements as soon as you tell me the day." Then it occurred to her that she should ask Mary if she could take Chepsisei with her that night.

"Would you let me take Chepsisei with me, Mary?" she asked. "I'll keep her overnight and bring her home tomorrow. She could use the company of some other children. I have Kibet, Cheseret, and little Sukunwa."

Mary's face changed from light brown to dark black as the blood rushed to it. Disbelief that her friend didn't trust her was written on it.

"Ah-ah-hum," coughed Arap Walei to make his presence known to the women. Mary had no chance now to say what she wanted. What luck thought Taptamus. Chepsisei may have a better chance of coming with me now.

"I'd better go now," said Taptamus. She walked past Arap Walei and glanced quickly into Mary's eyes to ask the question, 'can I take Chepsisei with me?'

"Taptamus, don't leave on my account," Arap Walei said. "I just came to fetch my chewing tobacco. I've promised Kiriswa to go back in the evening to chat. Anyhow, I don't think you have to be in a hurry. I'm sure everything is under control at your place. I saw a number of girls doing things there."

"Who?" asked Taptamus. "I only had Cheseret looking after Sukunwa."

"Oh no. I saw Chelamai, Kirorei, Cheseret and Taplambus. Cheptabut also was on her way out there now when I left her place."

"Was Kiriswa home?" asked Taptamus.

"He was there this morning when I went by, and he didn't mention going anywhere. Kiptai and I asked him to come with us to help skin that python we killed last night, but he said he couldn't because he had a fence to fix."

"Oh yes. I told Cheptabut to mention that fence to him. I'm glad he took time to fix it. I was doubtful when I told her because I had complained about it before and no one had done anything. So you went to skin the snake?" Taptamus added, standing at the doorway looking washed-out.

"Taptamus, why don't you grab that chair. Aren't you tired standing at the door?" Arap Walei asked.

Taptamus turned around and sneaked a quick look at him. Their eyes met. She dragged her eyes away from his and glided over to a chair, her body swimming in the traditional animal skin clothes she was wearing. She was as thin as a reed by now, and frail enough for the wind of Mt.Kamasai to blow her away. Mary was sitting with her back leaning against the wall wearing a long khaki skirt, vest and toga. Chepsisei was beside her with her usual life of her own listening to them. No one knew how much she understood. Sometimes she laughed. Sometimes she looked like she was concentrating. Mary looked cold and restless. There was no emotion on her face.

"What's happening, Mary? The house looks sad. There is no fire burning, and you haven't said a word since I came in. It's time for the cows to come home and nothing seems ready. Are you sick?" Mary didn't reply.

"Mary, is Chepsisei sick?" Arap Walei asked and sat silently waiting for an answer. Mary and Taptamus exchanged some quick glances. Mary knew her husband had to have an answer when he asked a question. There would be no way out because he would make Mary sit with him in silence until she finally answered.

"Chepsisei has something. She is pregnant," Mary said nervously.

Arap Walei looked unruffled and twisted his moustache. He had large, gentle, brown eyes. He wore a Colobus-monkey fur cape with a toga underneath, but no trousers. He reached inside his toga and pulled out an ivory container closed with a lid of elaborately beaded cow skin. He shook the container, opened it and put some tobacco in his mouth. He bit on some soda crystals to flavour the tobacco and make it juicier, rolled it around, spat across the room and sat back. The copper earrings dangling from the enlarged loops of his ear lobes swung and danced as he moved. Called *olmermerinik*, they were highly polished and ornamented tetrahedrons. At first he remained silent. Then he put aside what Mary had said and returned to his original conversation with Taptamus as though nothing had been said.

"After Kiriswa said he couldn't come with us to skin the python, we walked to Kap Temoet to ask Cheseret's father to come along. It seemed that he was still afraid of it even after its death. He told Kiptai that no one in his right mind would ever want to see that python again. We were skinning it until noon when half of the women in the neighbourhood poured in. Everyone wanted a piece of python fat. They said it was a kind of medicine, and Ketele, who knows all the medicines, told me what it was for, but I've forgotten. Taptamus, do you know what python fat is used for?"

Taptamus looked at Arap Walei with vacant eyes. She had been wondering if he had heard what Mary had said, and if he hadn't, if she should tell him herself, and if he had, what did it mean? What is he trying to accomplish by talking about the python when his wife had told him their daughter was...? She raised her eyes timidly and looked at Mary with an invitation to her to join the conversation.

"I think python fat shields one from evil eyes. Some say it's good for burns too. I'm sure there are even more uses than that. Do you know some others, Mary?" she asked.

The conversation was considerably confused for a moment. Mary had been brought into the discussion when she wasn't paying attention. She hesitated, then asked, "What did you say, Taptamus?"

Taptamus, for whom the whole conversation was frustrating and acutely discomforting, had to repeat her question over again to Mary.

"Does python fat have any uses other than for evil eyes and burns?"

"Yes, I think it is used for ear infections too," answered Mary and looked at her husband.

"Why didn't you two come to get some? It's always nice to have something like that around the house," said Arap Walei.

Taptamus thought that this was the obvious opportunity to bring in Chepsisei's situation again — for once and for all. She felt relieved she had finally found a little hole in the conversation for it.

"As you heard, Mary said Chepsisei is carrying something, and that is what kept us here, worrying about what to do," said Taptamus trying to get it out in the open so that there would no escape for Arap Walei behind the python fat.

"Heh,heh — you mean you and Mary just learned about Chepsisei today? Everyone in Mt. Kamasai knows and it's still circulating. After we finished skinning the python, we went hunting for a beer party. Arap Metuk suggested we try his place first to see if Tabaes had anything for us. The first thing Tabaes asked was how Chepsisei was doing now that she was 'like that,'" said Arap Walei who then got up leaving Mary without an opportunity to exonerate herself with Taptamus' aid.

"I'll be a little late this evening, Mary," he said.

Taptamus was happy anyway because now she didn't have to worry about leaving Chepsisei with her mother any more.

"Do you have any idea of how this whole thing got all the way to Tabaes' house? My sister, you think?" asked Mary.

"Leave your sister out of this, She is not that kind of person. I think I know who might have got it there — Tapchamgoi — and I must say she knew it ahead of everybody else. She came about a month ago with a fake conversation and told me that I shouldn't worry about a babysitter, that Mary would help quite a bit and that of course it wouldn't be a bad idea if Chepsisei were taught how to take care of a baby. Maybe if I hadn't stopped the conversation she would have told me. But let us wait until we're sure," said Taptamus.

"Yes, of course, Tapchamgoi. She was here when Chepsisei was sick twice — pretending to be a good neighbour. I should have known she was too nervy and cunning for that to be true. You might as well stay and have dinner with us," Mary said to Taptamus.

"No Mary. I've been anxious to get home ever since your husband arrived. You heard him say a lot of children were at my house, and who knows how many things have gone wrong by now? Cheseret alone is one thing, but mix Cheruto's children with Tabaes' youngest daughter, and anything can happen. From going through the whole house to losing things in my sewing kit when they're trying to find a needle to take the thorns out of their feet, to setting the whole house on fire. They can't sit still when they get in. They go through the house like a bad wind."

"Taptamus, Kiriswa was at home. I'm sure he would keep an eye on them."

"Mary, men are not so far from being called children themselves. They can't see. I'll see you tomorrow. Would you bring Chepsisei to see the baby?"

CHAPTER SEVEN

*T*aptamus had to pass two houses to get home, Tapchamgoi's and Cheptabut's. She pulled her animal skins tightly around her knees because they made a lot of noise when she walked, and she wanted to sneak by without anyone hearing her pass, particularly Tapchamgoi, who seemed as though she could always hear the rustling of Taptamus' clothing from a distance and would come to sit at the doorway waiting for her. Taptamus and Tapsalng'ot were the only women who wore animal skin clothing in those five houses which were close together. Cheptabut, Mary and Tapchamgoi wore modern clothing. Mary said that the only reason she didn't wear the indigenous clothes was that the people in the church she belonged to said they were Satan's clothes, but she was not proud of her modern clothing. Cheptabut wore them because they were in fashion for her generation. And besides, they were what was available to her. She wore what her mother had given her after Taptamus received the clothing as a present from her daughter Chemutai, who worked for a European family in Eldoret. Both Mary and Cheptabut wore the new clothes with modesty.

Taptamus had tried wearing the clothes herself for a couple of days when she first got them from her daughter, but they didn't appeal to her. She had told Mary that they made her feel as though she were walking naked. Mary had told her to go on wearing them for a little longer, that they would take more than three days to get used to. She told her that she would like the clothes when she got used to them. They were light to walk in, and they didn't get cold in the evening when the weather got cold, the way the skins did. They didn't have to be oiled all the time, yet they were always soft and warm. Best of all, they could be boiled when lice got into them. Mary had been quite sure that Taptamus would soon have good feelings about the modern clothes because they were so easy to look after, but in the end, Taptamus never did get used to them. She said they were no good to wear on windy days. They clung to your body when the wind blew showing everything and leaving nothing to the imagination. Taptamus once told her daughter Cheptabut not to wear those clothes going to a ceremony where everyone would be watching. She thought the clothes gave one the appearance of a prostitute.

Kiriswa, Kiptai, Kibet and Arap Walei were out in front. They had made a fire and were sitting around it when Taptamus got home. Kiriswa called to his mother. He usually addressed her as 'Cheptabut's mother.'

"Mother Cheptabut, where were you all day long? Don't you think of us any more? We were about to come to look for you," he said laughingly.

"I'm home now," said Taptamus, going into the house. She was glad to be home. The girls and Cheptabut had worked hard. The cows had been milked, and the calves had been separated from the cows and brought in with the goats and the sheep. Cheptabut was dividing food by the fire. Chelamai and Cheseret were playing with Sukunwa. And of course Tapchamgoi was just sitting there waiting for her. She knew what had been going on today.

"Thank you very much Cheseret. Without you things would have been hectic today in this house," said Taptamus.

"Oh, mother Kiriswa, I have done my duty here today, too, haven't I? Don't I deserve a thank you? I told Kiriswa to fix your fence," said Cheptabut. Then she smiled showing her beautiful white teeth.

"Oh, I thank all of you," said Taptamus and went to hug her daughter.

"I did something too today, Taptamus," said Chelamai as a joke. Cheseret turned around and stared at her with amazement.

"What do you want?" asked Cheseret. "Do you want a specific thank you of your own because you babysat Kiriswa yourself?"

Cheptabut was embarrassed by Cheseret's remark. She knew each of the girls wanted her brother Kiriswa, but still it was cruel of

Cheseret to do this to Chelamai in front of Tapchamgoi, Kiriswa's mother-in-law. "Mother did not know you were here helping, too, Chelamai," she said.

"Yes, Chelamai should be given special thanks because without anyone around when Kiriswa was fixing the fence, he would have left without finishing it," said Cheseret.

"I wonder how you got to know that I was baby-sitting him? You must have been there yourself baby-sitting both Kiriswa and me for you to have any idea that I was baby-sitting him," pointed out Chelamai.

What a life, Cheptabut thought. They could still express their feelings out loud. Cheptabut knew they both loved Kiriswa very much, but in the end, it wouldn't matter what happened. For the one who ended up marrying him, all the glory and excitement would be over within three months of setting foot in his house after the marriage. And three months was the outer limit, it would last no more than a month, and then all of the sleepless nights without you that they had told you were so hard for them to endure before the marriage would suddenly vanish, and no one would tell you how much they needed your body next to them. Cheptabut cast a sympathetic glance at them. What a shame, she thought, this wonderful feeling of being in love will be ruined by marriage. No matter that you are married to the man you love. The high value you knew you were held in will take a deep tumble. All of a sudden your face has lost its youthfulness, and no one wants to look at it. She took a deep breath and turned around. Oh, if only other men could be like my Kiptai.

"Girls, can one of you ask the men if they want to eat inside or have food taken to them outside?"

Cheseret and Chelamai looked at one another.

"All right. Why don't you both go then," Cheptabut added.

Cheseret got up. She went out and came back.

"They want to eat outside," she said.

"Who said they want to eat out, Kiriswa or Kiptai?" asked Cheptabut, who always worried about what Kiptai said or thought. Every woman's value went down after she got married, and Cheptabut

115

knew that, but she had never experienced it herself. Kiptai was an orphan. His mother had died when he was eight years old, and his step-mother was a bad woman. She had made Kiptai do everything for himself. The only time she did something for him was when his father was at home. When Kiptai was given Cheptabut, he was already used to doing things for himself. So instead of Cheptabut being his wife, he expected her to behave like his step-mother. So Cheptabut had had to tell him, "Kiptai you are a married man now. I'm your wife, not your step-mother. You don't have to pick up after yourself. That is the wife's job. A man's job is to make resolutions to say to his wife: 'I want my blanket washed today,' or 'I want dinner ready before dark.' I will do all of these things for you." That is what Cheptabut had told her husband, and although he never became completely used to this new way of doing things, Cheptabut always did her best to make sure that she didn't intimidate him. Kiptai loved her so much he called her 'mother.'

"Cheseret, can you go out and ask Sukunwa's father to come in for me?" asked Cheptabut. Cheseret was about to go out when Cheptabut stopped her again. "Cheseret, wait a minute. Let me ask Mother Kiriswa whether she wants the men to eat in or out first. Where is she?"

"She is in the other room with Tapchamgoi."

Taptamus had walked into to the other room hoping she wouldn't have to deal with any more complications after coming back from Mary's house. When Cheseret and Chelamai sounded like they were going to start in on one another, Taptamus thought she was too washed out to be part of their disagreement. But she couldn't stop Tapchamgoi from following her to ask what had taken place in the Walei family. Before Taptamus could sit down, Tapchamgoi was already trying to find out what had gone on.

"Tell me what happened," she asked enthusiastically hoping for the worst. "It took you a long time to come home. I was beginning to worry about the whole affair."

Taptamus gasped. "Tapchamgoi, don't you have any shame being the way you are? Are you aware of it when you are making people hate you? If you are, what advantage do you get out of this? Why do you pretend you are a concerned neighbour? You know in your heart that you don't have even a little sympathy for Mary or her daughter!"

"Oh really Taptamus! You are unbelievable! I'm utterly dismayed at the way you have always managed to change Mary's little problems into big heart-breaking problems for you, and then tried to keep anyone else from asking about them. Like a mother chicken shielding her chicks from a hawk!"

"Tapchamgoi, you hypocrite! Don't you ever get tired of yourself? You know what I'm talking about. You knew a month ago that Chepsisei was carrying a baby, and you told every soul in Mt. Kamasai except Mary and me. And now you want me to tell you more. You want to know what happened today, whether Mary was beaten up. No she wasn't. Thanks to you, Arap Walei had already heard from Tabaes and that was the end of that. Nothing else."

"Mother Kiriswa," Cheptabut called out to her mother. "The men say they want to eat out, but I think I should ask them to come in because Kiptai doesn't usually like to eat out. He says the gnats bother him."

"How many men are there who are supposed to eat out?" asked Taptamus.

"Five," answered Cheptabut.

"We will be too many. Let the men eat out. If they make a big fire, the gnats won't bother them," said Taptamus. "Let Cheseret and Chelamai take the food to them."

Cheptabut went into the kitchen to divide the vegetables into five bowls. She gave these to the girls to take out together with two gourds of milk, five cups and a big plate of *kimiet*, the main course. There were not enough dishes for the *kimiet*, and so Kibet had to be asked to come in to eat with the girls since an uncircumcised boy couldn't eat from the same plate with circumcised men. Kibet didn't come in willingly, and Kiriswa had to order him to go in. Kibet met with Tapchamgoi at the door. She was boiling mad that Taptamus had discovered her intrigues and wanted to leave. Before she got out, she stopped and asked Taptamus how long Kiriswa was going to be in Mt. Kamasai.

"I think he'll be here for a few more days. There are a couple of things I was going to ask him to fix for me."

"Oh no!" Kibet butted in. "I heard Kiriswa tell Arap Walei that he was leaving tomorrow."

"He can't leave before he comes to my house! I haven't asked him how the children are at home. And what would he tell them when they asked how Grandma Tapchamgoi was? Wouldn't that be embarrassing when he was here and didn't find out?" said Tapchamgoi outraged that her son-in-law could think of leaving without seeing her.

"That's his problem, Tapchamgoi. If he's going to be embarrassed, that's no skin off your nose," said Taptamus.

"Tapchamgoi, don't feel so miserable about Kiriswa not coming to see you before he leaves. His own mother hasn't had a word alone with him since he arrived," said Cheptabut.

"Or even spoken to him since our first greeting yesterday," said Taptamus who by now was going out of her mind as Tapchamgoi had evidently decided not to leave.

"Tapchamgoi, are you leaving or are you coming to sit and eat with us," she asked.

"No, I'm going," said Tapchamgoi. "I didn't come for a free meal," she snapped.

"What a disaster!" Cheptabut remarked after Tapchamgoi had left, forgetting she was talking to her mother.

They finished eating and Kibet rose to go out, but Taptamus stopped him.

"Kibet, I would like you, Cheseret and Chelamai to go to Mary's to give her a hand. I promised her I would send you there."

Cheseret wanted to say no because she had heard Kibet say that Kiriswa said he was going to leave the next day. She looked unhappy. Kiriswa had told her he would leave in four days. Had he changed his mind about their plan? Cheseret felt helpless. She would have said no if she had had the power, but as a Nandi custom, a child couldn't say no to a grown-up when asked to do something. The children had been

118

taught to respond to all of the women in the neighbourhood just as they would to their own mothers. The saying was that children were only yours while you were carrying them. After they were born, they contributed to the happiness of the whole neighbourhood and were collectively referred to as "our children."

Chelamai was ready to go, but Cheseret was toying with the idea of asking if Chelamai and Kibet could go and she stay to play with Sukunwa. But she didn't have to say it. Cheptabut, who could read Cheseret's mind as plain as day, was there. When it came to her feelings about Kiriswa, Cheseret's skillfully disguised mien was as transparent as glass to Cheptabut's discerning eye.

"Children, leave as my mother says to help Mary so you can return before dark. I'll send Kiriswa to fetch you if you don't make it in time," said Cheptabut.

Cheseret didn't thank her for throwing in Kiriswa in addition, but Cheptabut could see a trace of a smile on her face. Cheptabut liked Cheseret a lot. She was only six years younger, and they got along well. Six years ago, Cheptabut had experienced the same feelings herself.

"Kibet, where are you going?" Kiriswa asked as the two girls and Kibet walked by the termite mound in front of house where the men were seated. He really wanted to know where Cheseret was going rather than Kibet or Chelamai.

"They're going to Mary's. Mother asked them to help Mary with the evening chores," said Cheptabut who had risen and stood at the door to watch them go.

"What is such a heavy task at Mary's that it needs three people?"

Taptamus happened to hear Kiriswa asking Kibet where he was going, but she was unaware of the real meaning behind his question.

"Let Kibet go with the girls," she said. "It's better to have a little man than none at all."

"Nonsense, mother," said Kiriswa who was ignorant of the plan his sister had just hatched inside the house. "Nowadays it's not the way it was twenty years ago when the cattle were kept at a distance from the house and all the young men in the neighbourhood had to stay to guard them and to protect the women from the wild animals when they were milking. But if you want Kibet to go along, are you going to have Cheseret stay here to help you then? I'm sure Cheptabut will want to go home in a few minutes."

"Yes, yes, wild animals!" said Chelamai who was rarely known to participate in decision-making. When she had heard Kiriswa talk about wild animals, she had imagined the worst was about to happen. "How can he want some people to go and some to stay when he's talking about wild animals?" she asked, forgetting that Kiriswa was talking about twenty years ago when the cattle had been several miles away.

"Oh don't waste time, all of you go! I'm going to be here awhile yet." said Cheptabut who turned around and went back into the house.

"There is no way that we are going by ourselves. If no grown-up is going to come with us, we had better take Peter and James; Kibet is not much," whined Chelamai.

"Why take those dogs? What are you afraid of? It's still light. I'm not scared," said Cheseret.

"Speak for yourself. Maybe you're not, but I am. By the time we milk the cows, put them in the *biut* and close the gate with logs, it'll be dark. Can you visualize what the hyenas might do to us? When we take the sheep and goats into the house in the dark, the wild animals may attack us trying to get at the livestock," said Chelamai.

"You are joking!" said Cheseret. "You think we are going to be attacked and you suggest taking those dogs? They can't even chase the monkeys away from the corn in broad daylight. Where will they obtain the courage to protect us from being attacked by wild animals?"

"Please we have to hurry. I want to come back early before Taptamus finishes her tea," said Kibet.

"Tea! I didn't know Taptamus had any tea," Cheseret exclaimed.

"Oh yes, she has tea, but she only makes it when she is upset. She says it relaxes her, and for sure I want to be there to have a cup too. That's the only way I can get it."

"How can you talk about tea, Kibet, when we are worrying about being attacked tonight?" asked Chelamai.

"Arap Chebinjor said that actually the hyenas are scared of people," said Kibet.

"That's not the way I've heard people talking about the older hyena, *magololut*. It attacks anything it meets," said Chelamai.

"Not Arap Chebinjor. He doesn't believe a really brave man can be attacked," said Kibet.

"Lucky him. Maybe we should go get him to come along to challenge them tonight."

"Yes, he is a very brave man. He says that during his entire life, no animal has ever come near him and stayed alive," said Kibet.

"Kibet, I can imagine that you believe anything Arap Chebinjor says. He brags so much! I must give the hyenas a little credit though. I always thought that they ate anything they came into contact with, but now I see I have to change my mind. However, there is only one reason why even *magololut* the great-grandfather of hyenas hasn't attacked him," said Cheseret.

"He is brave," said Kibet, trying to defend his friend's honour.

"No, it's not that, Kibet. Cross that out of your mind. Arap Chebinjor drinks day and night. There is not a single day that I haven't met him and not tried to stay away from him as far as possible so as not to be suffocated by his breath. Oh, the smell of his breath is so asphyxiating! I think that all of the animals of Mt. Kamasai smell him coming and run in the opposite direction. So I'm impressed by the hyenas. I had thought that if they could eat a dead person, they could also eat — I mean attack — someone smelling like Arap Chebinjor," said Cheseret.

"I wonder how he got to marry those three beautiful...," Chelamai caught herself. She realized that she had broken a rule that her mother had taught her. Tabaes had told her many times never to discuss the affairs of grown-ups. They were none of her business. She had said that if she ever found out that she was talking about other peoples' affairs, she would bite her and chew her and spit her out like chewing tobacco. Or pinch her thighs and then rub hot pepper in them while they were bleeding.

"What did you want to say Chelamai? You were wondering how he got to marry those beautiful women? Maybe they never dated him when they were growing up, or maybe their parents simply beat them into accepting him," said Cheseret.

"No, I guess I was not about to say anything of that sort. Listen, let's get going if we are to go at all."

"Where? To Mary's or back inside?" asked Cheseret.

"To Mary's of course," said Chelamai.

"Have they left yet?" asked Cheptabut who thought she heard murmuring voices and returned to the doorway.

"They have just left. Can you come and take the dishes? I'm leaving," said Kiriswa.

"Did Kiptai go home?" asked Cheptabut.

"No, he went with Arap Walei to his place."

"Anything special going on there?"

"No, not that I know of. Did mother say Mary had any beer?"

"I haven't talked to mother yet. Tapchamgoi was there when mother arrived. You know how they are with each other. The two never find any common ground," said Cheptabut.

"What were they disagreeing about this time?"

"Tapchamgoi wanted mother to tell her how Arap Walei reacted when he found out about Chepsisei's pregnancy. When she wasn't told, you can imagine the rest. She found a new topic, started a brush fire with it and fanned it into a blaze. Kibet mentioned that you had told Arap Walei you were leaving, and Tapchamgoi decided that if you leave without seeing her, it would be a punishment to her and a sin on your family."

"Women! women! They get all excited about nothing. Why didn't mother tell Tapchamgoi what she knew? What knowledge would Tapchamgoi gain from knowing about Arap Walei's reaction?" asked Kiriswa.

"Mother felt that Tapchamgoi knew all about it already."

"She should have told her again."

"Ask mother. But I think she wouldn't be enthusiastic to hear you say 'women's problems'. Can you help me take some of these dishes inside?"

"Yes of course," said Kiriswa. "Oh, Cheptabut, I almost forgot. Would you arrange the granary for me? I want to sleep there tonight. I want to be able to leave early in the morning without delay."

He turned around and looked at his sister. She didn't look the least bit surprised. She had a gentle beauty. Her eyes twinkled, and she smiled reluctantly at her brother.

"What? You know?" asked Kiriswa.

Cheptabut looked up and she nodded her head.

"Yes, I do. Why haven't you told mother or me about your plan? Did it slip your mind?" asked Cheptabut with a mock sigh. "You are undependable, Kiriswa. You know her father is a brutal, ruthless man. He can set mother's house on fire."

"Don't be melodramatic" said Kiriswa. "He wouldn't do anything that drastic. You are imagining too much."

"Why don't you come right out and tell me to stop trying to make you see the truth. You have made up your own mind. It doesn't matter what I say," said Cheptabut. "We both know that, without Tapsalng'ot, that house would have become like a contaminated place. No one would want to go there."

"What do you want us to do? We both want to get married. She wants me, and I want her. Don't think that Cheseret and I haven't tried to find a way out of getting married in order to please everyone. I thought when I moved away we would overcome the need for each other, but that was not true. During the six months I was away, every time I went to the *sigiroina*, the warriors' house, I could only think of her when I was with other girls. I have visited her twice in the past four months, and we have both felt the need to be together more than we even did before I moved. Can you tell me now what you think we should do?" asked Kiriswa. "Before you answer, count out the idea that when she gets circumcised, we can ask for her hand in marriage. That is useless. It wouldn't work. Everyone thinks I'm too young for two wives. I know this because I've tried asking mother."

Cheptabut knew well that if anyone had tried to avoid getting married, it would have been Kiriswa, not Cheseret, but she had to be polite.

"I'm not interested in stopping you from getting married, but I think you should take mother's safety into consideration before you do anything else. I don't believe you when you say that Cheseret's father won't do something bad. What guarantee can you give? Are you going to knock on the door before you leave with Cheseret and tell him you are taking his daughter to marry but not to hurt your mother because you get along with his daughter? Of course you won't. You wouldn't do that," said Cheptabut.

"Listen to me Cheptabut. I must go now; I'm going to Arap Walei's and I have to go by Tapchamgoi's. Don't start worrying mother before there is anything to worry about yet," said Kiriswa.

"Oh no! I won't mention it. It's all up to you. She is your mother too," said Cheptabut.

"I would like to see you and Kiptai when I come back this evening — to talk about the plan I've made before you start worrying. I will come by later. Or I may come with Kiptai whenever he is ready to come home."

Kiriswa was annoyed with his sister for always worrying about what was going to happen before it happened. They went into the house together. Kiriswa set the calabash of milk and the cups on the floor against the wall in the sitting room and left. Taptamus was in the other room, which also served as the kitchen and bedroom. She was basking in the heat from the hearth and watching Sukunwa kicking and playing.

"Cheptabut, is that you?" she asked.

"Yes, mother," answered Cheptabut.

"What are you doing? Washing the dishes?"

"No, mother, I'm just bringing them in right now."

"Don't wash them now. Let them go for tonight. Cheseret will help to wash in the morning. I'm sure you are washed out, too, by now."

Cheptabut went to the room where her mother was.

"Are the men still talking out there?" asked Taptamus.

"No, they have gone to Mary's house."

"To Mary's? Poor her! Really, there are times when I'm convinced men are like little children. What a shame! Even an older one like Arap Walei hasn't learned anything. How can he take people home now. When he left the fire was not even made. I'm sure he's taking them for dinner, and Mary must be panicking now. I don't know if she even has flour to make *kimiet*. I should have asked her."

"Oh mother! They are not starving. If Mary doesn't have food, it won't be a matter of life and death. Mary can say she didn't get around to grinding flour," said Cheptabut.

"I wish that were true, but unfortunately Mary belongs to a generation where a woman wouldn't dream of embarrassing her husband in front of his friends by saying there is no food," said Taptamus.

"She would send the children to come to take some flour if she didn't have any," said Cheptabut.

"I didn't know Arap Walei was coming back so soon. I met him when he was going home and then he was here. He didn't seem upset. Did you talk to him about Chepsisei's situation, mother? Although I was told he knew about it already," said Cheptabut.

"Yes, we managed to make fools of ourselves, and then at last after we had heard his story about the python, he told us that Chepsisei's pregnancy was not news. Everybody in Mt. Kamasai knew about it, and he was surprised we didn't."

"That was a strange. I didn't think it was his character to leave people in suspense."

"I had a feeling that he was trying to distance himself from the situation," said Taptamus.

"Kiptai said that when they got to Tabaes' place, the first thing Tabaes asked was how Chepsisei was now that she was 'like that.' He said that Arap Walei didn't seem the least bit surprised. He didn't ask any questions, although Kiptai said that as soon as Tapchamgoi heard what Tabaes was talking about, there was no dialogue after that. Tapchamgoi jumped at the chance to monopolize the conversation."

"She talked about Chepsisei at a beer-party? What a woman! One of these days someone will knock some sense into her. Did Arap Walei talk to Kiptai about his daughter?" asked Taptamus.

"No, and I think we shouldn't worry about them now, mother," said Cheptabut. She thought her mother was worrying too much about the Waleis when, unknown to her, her own troubles with Kiriswa and Cheseret were just about to begin.

"Well, yes and no. We shouldn't worry about it, but we don't know what is going to happen between now and tomorrow."

"Arap Walei wouldn't want to do anything as obnoxious as beating up Mary, although I wouldn't want to be in her place tonight," said Cheptabut. "The worst thing is how he has concealed his feelings. No one knows what he is thinking," she added.

"That family is like that. They think highly of themselves. They have never been known to display their feelings or emotions. They always manage to look unruffled in any situation," said Taptamus.

The lineage of Arap Walei was a proud, self-made clan. They had earned whatever they possessed, and although it was not Nandi custom to place any individual up on a pedestal, the family was rich in spirits, dignified and conscientious thinkers, and great warriors. People were happy to go to them for advice, and they were always willing to share it, as was the custom. Their name was not new in Nandi society. Nandi country was divided into fifteen districts. Arap Walei's father, Kipwalei, was himself a leader in his district and a great warrior with a deep knowledge of raiding. He earned the respect and confidence of his people, and consequently the title of "leader." When he was replaced in his old age, his son Arap Walei's own record was above his. He had already earned three powerful titles. People called him the greatest warrior of his generation, a gentle man, and the master of the forest. At the age of twenty-five, the men in his generation were gathering day and night to seek advice and wisdom from him. By then he had also earned his nickname *Par-ng' etuny ne kibarei kipchoria leplep pek*, 'the man who killed the lion single-handed in the Kipchoria Warm Water forest.'

The family of Arap Walei were rich and well-loved, but they didn't live in a castle. The houses of people of wealth and of those who had less were the same. They were round houses of two rooms. The *injor*, the larger of the two, was where the sheep, goats and calves slept. The other room was partitioned into a section with a hearth where the wife cooked and slept with the children and a section for the husband which also served as a sitting room for the men. The *injor*, and thus the whole house, was larger in the case of a wealthy man simply because he had more livestock to shelter.

CHAPTER EIGHT

*L*ater that evening, Taptamus and Cheptabut sat talking. Cheptabut stood up suddenly, picked up the lantern and rushed into the sitting room. Her mother stopped talking.

"What is it Cheptabut?" she asked.

"Oh nothing, mother. I thought I heard something in this room, but I don't see anything."

"Is the door closed?" asked Taptamus.

"Yes," answered Cheptabut.

"Maybe your dogs are looking for you," said Taptamus.

"No, I don't think so. I thought I heard voices."

"Yes, I thought I heard some murmuring, too, not long ago. Did you go outside?" asked Taptamus.

"Of course not. An animal could grab my face. It's dark out there, mother. The moon isn't out yet.

"There is nothing out there, Cheptabut. The cattle would have let us know by now."

Taptamus took a piece of firewood from the fireplace and walked into the other room. She opened the door and shook the brand until the glowing embers burst into flame.

"Who are you?" she asked the two bodies standing on the porch.

"Us," answered Kibet's voice.

"What are you doing here in the dark? Aren't you coming in?"

"We're waiting."

"What are you waiting for?"

"Don't ask me. Ask Cheseret."

"Why me? You know we're waiting for Chelamai," said Cheseret.

Taptamus went back in, but left the door unbarred.

"What was it, mother?" asked Cheptabut.

"Cheseret and Kibet."

"I told you it wasn't my dogs. What were they doing?"

"They said they were waiting for Chelamai."

"Strange," murmured Cheptabut, getting up to make her mother tea.

"What do mean by that?" asked Taptamus.

"Nothing. I'm just surprised that they could stand at the door, shivering while knowing that inside would be warm. Did they say where Chelamai was, mother?"

"They are children, Cheptabut. I'm not about to go and ask them every detail of what they do. They have to have their privacy. Maybe Chelamai is talking to a boyfriend, or is just out in the bush urinating."

If only her mother knew what was going on, Cheptabut thought. She would want to know everything that was happening on a minute-to-minute basis. Cheptabut wondered if her brother could be so ruthless as to take these two girls, have them both circumcised, and then marry both of them at once. Of course he would, she thought. He is fearless. He's a man, and the more daring something is, the more a man wants to do it.

At that time, Nandi men, if not all African men in Kenya, were suffering terribly. Not physically, but emotionally, for want of suffi-cient challenge. They didn't know what to do with themselves after the British had taken over and laid down their own self-serving and brutalizing — for African minds — law. Those Africans who didn't mind working for a British family, inside as a cook or outside as a gardener, were treated worse than a doormat. Neither the cook nor the gardener nor any black-skinned men around the premises were al-lowed to have their families there. The houses in which these workers lived were no better than chicken coops. During the day their quarters looked like a chicken coop ghost town. The men who lived in these places had to get up to start work at the first cock crow. The gardener stayed out to wash the car before the high and mighty went to work. He polished it until he could see his face in it. The cook went in to the house to make tea before the family were up. He carried the tea to the bedroom, and knocked on the door to let the husband and wife know it was ready. When the tea was finished, the dirty cups and the teapot were placed outside the door again, and the cook was called to take the tray away. Whenever the cook was called, he had to answer immediately. If it happened to be the husband who called, the answer was "Yes, high and mighty man." If it was the woman, the answer was "Yes, great woman."

Nandi men didn't want to cook for the British. They said they would rather get shot than be found in a British kitchen burning their hands on a stove for a British man and his wife. However, although they didn't do housework, many served in the British army, the police force or as prison guards. With that kind of work, at least they felt they were men. Even there, they couldn't escape calling their officers "master."

For those who remained home, mostly the young and the very old, there were three favourite activities — getting drunk, getting married, and raiding. Even after raiding was a matter of life and death by a British bullet, they continued with it anyway and died for it. When government soldiers caught them with stolen cattle, they were beaten and kicked to death. If they somehow survived to be taken to prison, they would die there. The only thing which was safe out of these three activities was getting married. Women were abundant. The men who were in the army or police only had a short annual leave. The girls were there, but the time was too short. A man was married in his absence to a girl his parents chose for him, and she was kept at home pending his return. While this arrangement might be acceptable for a first wife, it was awkward and embarrassing to have two girls waiting for a man who was never there.

The men who remained at home no longer looked on marrying a second wife as an honour which a man might attain later when he retired from the active life of a warrior and spent the rest of his life with his families. The young men of the Fifties regarded women as trophies. Marrying another wife was like getting a promotion in the army. When young men met, instead of asking how many wives they had, the question was phrased, "How many chevrons are you wearing?" The girls didn't mind being the object of competition. They rather enjoyed watching the men pour their hearts out asking for them.

Within his own age group, Kiriswa was a little late in meeting the competition because of his mother. He should have had two or three wives by the time he was twenty-two. But Taptamus was old-fashioned. She couldn't see how a man in his early twenties could have achieved enough to deserve the honour of taking a second wife. Cheptabut thought that maybe he wanted to catch up by marrying two at a time. Such a thing was certainly done, but Taptamus would be absolutely baffled. What a crazy idea for four virtual children to be living in one household!

"Cheptabut, can you ask Kibet to come in? I don't want him to catch a cold," said Taptamus.

"I'm making you tea, mother, and what are you doing in the *injor* anyway?"

"I'm counting the sheep and goats to make sure they are all there."

Kibet was called in, and Cheseret came in too. She didn't want to stand alone in the dark. She hurried to the fireplace. She looked as though she was about to burst into tears. She turned around to see if Taptamus and Cheptabut were looking at her and looked away. The two older women looked at each other in silence. Cheptabut poured the tea into the cups and handed everyone a cup. Kibet took his with gratitude, but Cheseret said she didn't want any.

"Why not?" asked Taptamus. "We must drink together. Do you think we are going to drink while you watch us? I'm sure you know that would be rude. You drink a little."

Finally, Cheseret took some tea. They sat in silence for a while, and then Cheptabut looked at Cheseret and smiled. She thought her brother had good taste. Cheseret was beautiful and had a lot of character. She would never be tiring to be around as long as she lived. Chelamai, on the other hand, was simply beautiful. Her large, plain brown eyes always appeared lost.

It was mid-evening. Cheptabut got up and put her hand on Cheseret's shoulder.

"Can you come along with me? Even half-way. It's very dark out, and I'm not brave enough to go alone."

Cheseret got up. There was a half-forced smile on her face. They went out together. In the west, the darkness was disappearing on Mt. Kimugei as the moon rose behind Mt. Kamasai. The moon itself looked as though it had been set like a pearl between the twin peaks of Kapkeimur and Kaplemur.

"Oh, those mountains! I could never imagine being anywhere but in this very place where we are now. The elders say these mountains are very important — the mountains of peace. Look how the moon always rises and sets between those two twin mountains. There are many stories about these mountains that are known only by wise old men," said Cheptabut. "Cheseret! I'm speaking to myself. Why aren't you talking, and where is Chelamai?"

Cheseret was desolate and sick in her heart. Cheptabut had no idea what she was thinking, but at that moment maybe she was wishing Chelamai would die and leave Kiriswa for her.

"Chelamai is with Kiriswa. She came to help me this morning although I didn't want her to, and she hasn't done a thing ever since she arrived besides going after him. I almost slapped her this morning after Kiriswa finished fixing the fence. There was Chelamai ready to sit on his lap and gaze at his face. I had to make food for everyone, and it was obvious that Kiriswa was enjoying himself. He just looked back at her in a way that made me sick," said Cheseret.

"On our way back from Mary's place we met Kiriswa, and guess what? They disappeared again and told us to wait for them. We are still waiting, and they aren't back yet," she added.

"I realize I'm not in a position to judge you two, but it's common for two girls who like the same man to be jealous of one another. That has happened to a lot of us, you know," said Cheptabut.

Cheseret turned her eyes away from Cheptabut. After a long silence she began timidly to speak. She felt foolish that she was about to talk about Kiriswa to his own sister.

"We don't like the same man, Chelamai and I, by the way. I like a different man from hers. Chelamai is like a disease to me. She

133

follows me around, and she disgusts me. She makes sure she goes after every man I like. When Kiriswa is away, she sticks to Arap Arbap like glue, and he is someone I don't care for in the slightest. She never changes boyfriends like other girls, but everyone thinks she and Arap Arbap matched — they are both empty-headed and dull. I don't see what she sees in Kiriswa. Kiriswa himself told me once he didn't have a lot to talk to Chelamai about. But where are they now? Are they standing somewhere in silence?" Cheseret spoke with bitterness, her face twisted with disgust.

"Couldn't you both be friends and share the same boyfriend?" Cheptabut tried desperately to patch things up for her brother.

"It's not that we can't be friends or have the same boyfriends. No, it's not that. It's just the way Chelamai does it. She takes over."

"I think Kiriswa...," Cheptabut was about to say she thought Kiriswa liked them both the same amount, but she didn't get to speak. Cheseret unexpectedly began to run ahead in the direction of Cheptabut's house. Apparently she had seen Kiriswa coming along without Chelamai. Cheptabut stood there, startled. Soon she heard them laughing. She walked slowly past them.

"Cheptabut! Kiptai will explain everything!" Kiriswa called out.

When Cheptabut reached her house, two men's bicycles were leaning against it. The smoke was rushing out the chimney, and she realized that Kiptai must be inside with someone. If he had been alone, he wouldn't have bothered to make a fire. Kiptai was in the sitting room which formed a compartment of his bedroom. Cheptabut found him getting ready to leave.

"Ha! You are home. It is about time," he said.

"Yes, I was still helping mother. Who is in the other room?" Cheptabut asked.

"Chelamai," answered Kiptai.

"It looks like you are getting ready for something. What's happening?"

"Yes, that is what I wanted to talk to you about. I presume your brother told you he is going to elope with the girls tonight."

"Shh! Be careful! Chelamai will hear you," whispered Cheptabut.

"She knows. She is part of the trip too." Kiptai realized now that his wife didn't know the whole story.

"I would like to think you are humouring me, but it seems like you are not laughing. What has become of Kiriswa? Has he gone mad? What is he dragging Chelamai along for?," said Cheptabut who was now afraid that her premonition was becoming reality.

"I can't say why Chelamai is coming, but I'm sure they've discussed it. To the best of my knowledge, she is just coming along to keep Cheseret company, but I'm just doing what Kiriswa has told me to do — to carry one of the girls on my bike for him."

"What time are you leaving?"

"Right now," Kiptai said. "I'm hoping to be back before dawn."

It was late in the evening when Kiptai, Kiriswa, and the girls left. No one's suspicions would be aroused because it looked as if the party was simply going to another warriors' house across the river. The nightly wind from Mt. Kamasai was now blowing from north to south howling and whistling. Cheptabut, who was worrying about the outcome of the situation, about her brother and the girls, saw that she now had her husband to worry about too. When she heard the wind's whistling, she realized she had forgotten to tell Kiptai to wear his blanket like a cape over his cloak to protect him from the bitter cold.

She couldn't sleep. She lay down in bed and imagined what Cheseret's father was going to do to them. She wished she could go to her mother's, but she knew Kiriswa hadn't told Taptamus. Cheptabut lay down and stared at the door waiting for the morning to come. When the first bird of the morning twittered, she got up and went to Taptamus' house. It was early, but from a distance Cheptabut could see the illumination of the fire inside through the gaps in the mass of strips of vine which were laced through the uprights of the door. She thought that maybe her mother knew too. She tried to open the door, but it was still locked. She called her mother to come and open it. Taptamus was still wrapped in her blanket. She walked to the door asking Cheptabut on her way back to the fireplace what she was doing at her house so early in the morning. Cheptabut was certain now that Kiriswa hadn't said anything to Taptamus.

135

"Did you talk to Kiriswa last night after I left?" Cheptabut asked. Taptamus was warming up her animal skin clothing before wearing it.

"Yes, I did," she said and turned around. Her face looked frightened. "Is there anything wrong with him?" she asked.

"No, there isn't, but he's done something. He left last night with the girls."

"I felt it coming. I had a premonition something like that would happen. But I don't understand. You said he took both of the girls?"

"Yes, but Kiptai said Chelamai was only going to keep Cheseret company."

"Kiptai went along too?" asked Taptamus.

"Yes, he was asked to by Kiriswa," said Cheseret.

"I guess it doesn't matter anymore. It had to happen. I thought Father Sukunwa would have talked some sense to him."

"Mother, you know how Kiriswa always manipulates Kiptai into doing things his way, and Kiptai doesn't take offense because he is my brother."

"I can feel the burning of tears, but they won't come out. Why does this child go out of his way to humiliate me?" Taptamus sat down and putting her elbows on her knees, raised her hands in the direction of the sun's rays to pray to God and to pray to the spirits of her husband's family not to abandon her now.

"Oh Daughter of Kipkoiyo, the girl who rises, the girl who shines, the daughter of the one who holds everything in his hand, and all of the ancestral spirits. Come and be with me! Supreme being Asis, the Sun, who makes everything blossom every day when you rise. Shine in my home! Daughter of Kipkoiyo, gentle daughter, she who is the creator of all things and the source of everything that is good. Shine into my home with happiness! Watch over the children so that they make no mistakes and guard the cattle! Daughter of Kipkoiyo, I beseech you, watch guard for me. Haven't I approached you morning and evening? Gentle girl who looks after everything, haven't I prayed to you? Don't say, 'I'm getting tired. I'm leaving.' Our spirits, because you died and none of us were responsible for your deaths, guard those

136

of us who are up above; guard us well. Ensure that these children reach where they are going safely, and protect us from the wrath of the spirits of Cheseret's family. Help us to negotiate decently with one another!"

"Mother, I'm going home to wait for Kiptai. Let's hope he'll be coming back with Chelamai so that we'll have only one family to deal with. Although that won't be much help. If Kiriswa has Cheseret circumcised, I tell you, mother, there is no amount of praying that will keep her father from setting your house on fire," said Cheptabut. "I think you'll have to leave for at least two weeks until everything has subsided," she added.

"You don't rush a thing like this. Let us wait for Father Sukunwa first to find out where they took them. I may have to go there," said Taptamus.

"Mother, I realize you don't share my view of the situation, but I suggest you and the baby go to Chebutia's place at Indalat. I'll stay here. Kibet and I will manage, you know."

"Cheptabut, go home! Do your morning chores, and if you have time to spare, come back to help me with the housework. Stop telling me to leave. Things like this can't be solved by running away from them and besides, we're not alone. We have others who are looking after us. You see I couldn't sleep last night. Now I know it was because things were happening and they were waking me up," said Taptamus.

Taptamus was talking about the spirits of departed ancestors when she said they weren't alone. Her soul knew only Nandi religious beliefs. The Nandi believed the spirits of ancestors were responsible for everything in the family — sickness, death, health and happiness. They were appealed to and propitiated with milk, beer and food whenever a new person who shared the spirits with the family came visiting. The human soul is embodied in a person's shadow, and it was firmly believed then that after death the shadows of both good and bad people went underground to continue living there the same kind of life that was lived on the surface of the earth. Those people who had great possessions while on earth were equally blessed as spirits after their deaths. The spirits of poor people had as hard a time after

137

death as they had during their life and were always jealous, causing all kinds of problems. Nandi women spent much time praying silently, telling these poor spirits that they were loved, and asking them not to make the lives of those on earth hard.

It was nearly noon when Kiptai arrived. Cheptabut, who had sat on the stump of a flame tree in front of her house, watched him coming. Her eyes couldn't hide her impatience and curiosity, and they lit up for Kiptai's arrival. Kiptai went and laid his bicycle against the house and went in. Cheptabut followed him in.

"Did you come back with Chelamai?" she asked.

"No, and I don't think you really believed she was coming back. Or was it wishful thinking?"

"No, it wasn't wishful thinking. Just that I never heard Kiriswa mention anything to indicate that he cared about her."

"He may not have said anything, but he has them both now. There, you see for once that you can't know everything about your brother," Kiptai said with a sigh. "What else do men do with girls but marry them?"

"You look unhappy. Were you hoping to marry one of these girls yourself?"

"No, I'm waiting for you to tell me to get a second wife — someone you like. Do you want me to get married?" asked Kiptai laughingly.

"If you are ready, why not? Just tell me who you have in mind, and I'll go to ask for her hand."

"You have to chose the girl you like. Not me. You're the one who is going to be her co-wife."

"I like Chelamai. She's beautiful, isn't she? Too bad it's too late."

They looked at each other and laughed.

"What should we do then?" asked Cheptabut.

"I can go and steal her back from your brother."

"Can you?"

"If you want her badly I would."

"Let me have a good look at you. Oh, I think you are losing your hair. She may not like you!"

"There are some girls who prefer bald men," countered Kiptai. He got up and went out and closed the door.

"What are you doing? Someone may come and find us locked in here like newly-weds. What will people think of us?"

"There is no one out there, and if someone is, we'll just tell her to wait."

Everybody in the neighbourhood had agreed that Cheptabut and her husband had never outgrown each other. They were always at each other's side like lovers. Kiptai's age-mates said that Kiptai should be excommunicated from his age-set or be cursed because he was a disgrace to his generation.

When children travelled, their parents gave them the names of friends who were to be found along the route. These friends would be responsible for dinner and a place to sleep. For adults, the members of each generation were responsible for their age-mates. A traveller always asked people on the way if there was someone belonging to the same age-set section as his where he could sleep. If the visitor was a married man, the man of the house let the visitor take his bed and went himself to the warriors' house to sleep. If the visitor was a woman, she would share a bed with the woman of the house. Or, if this wasn't feasible, then the man of the house would again go to the warriors' house leaving his bed for the guest.

Kiptai never participated in this custom. He let Cheptabut feed the visitor, but then even if the visitor was an age-mate and married like himself, he would tell him that they didn't have space in the house and that the visitor should go himself to the warriors' house. If the visitor was a woman, she would be taken to some old woman's house in the neighbourhood. In that era, Nandi depended very much on one another, but Kiptai and his wife were an exception. They depended only on each other and on Taptamus, and there was no one who didn't talk about them in Mt. Kamasai.

It was mid-afternoon when Kiptai announced that he had to go back. "Do you have anything for me to eat? I have to go back to Soi Mining. Your brother doesn't trust the people there. He is afraid they may snatch one of the girls from him."

139

"He took them to Soi Mining?" asked Cheptabut. "My, that's awfully close. If the girls' parents knew they were there, they would have been there by now to get them back. When are they going to be circumcised?"

"Cheseret's initiation starts tonight. She'll be circumcised at dawn in the morning and then get engaged. Kiriswa will spend the day with her. In the evening Chelamai will be taken to Turbo. Her ceremony will start that night, and she'll be engaged the following morning."

"Who is going to bring *sinendet* for the parents to know their children have been circumcised?"

"I'll bring Cheseret's to her parents' house tomorrow before daybreak. They'll find it hanging on the roof when they get up. Kiriswa will have to worry about Chelamai's *sinendet*. Does your mother have anything to say about all this?"

"Yes, she said a long prayer when I told her what happened this morning."

"Prayers of pride in her son's achievement, I suppose," said Kiptai.

"Small chance. When mother prays for joy, it's usually short. This time it was long — she was praying for the ancestral spirits to take a hold of Cheseret's father and make him understand that he shouldn't hurt her. I told her to go away for a few days, but she was not keen on leaving," said Cheptabut.

"Good for her! I think she shouldn't run away because it isn't her fault that the children eloped. And besides we will be around to help after the families have been notified. I think there is no danger today, but tomorrow she should be a little careful."

After Kiptai had left, Cheptabut went back to her mother's to see if she had heard from the parents of the girls. On her way she decided to go by Tapchamgoi's house. All the gossip in the neighbourhood arrived there first before it spread through the district. But before Cheptabut got to Tapchamgoi's house, she heard her scream and curse saying Cheseret's father's name.

"Ohh! Arap Temoet! May you lose what little honour you have.

May you become poor and a fool. May you shrivel up and vanish into thin air!"

Cheptabut stood outside listening to see if she could learn what had provoked this litany.

"Ohh! Arap Temoet! May you be stripped naked by the wind and your manhood struck dead by lightning while you are naked! May you fall on a sharp stick and it pierce your heart! I command the flies to swarm over you. Yes, and may you also be terrorized by locusts." The curses were becoming more pointed.

"Oh my," Cheptabut thought. "Cheseret's father will surely die this time."

"Tapchamgoi," Cheptabut called from outside the door.

"'Nah, nah, nah! Tapchamgoi, Tapchamgoi!' What are you calling me for? Get out of my door! You have come to laugh at me. Yes, laugh because your brother has eloped with a girl, and I've been hit by her father. My son has married beautiful girls, and I haven't once been beaten up like this. I'm going to take him to court or carry a skull and place it on his doorstep or go and piss in his fireplace, and no matter if the whole world begs me to undo the curse, I won't. I will be circumcised again before I undo it, or I will be struck dead first and my spirit return to undo it," said Tapchamgoi resolutely.

"You are upset, Tapchamgoi. Don't say anything that you will regret tomorrow when you think of it," said Cheptabut, trying to help her.

"Are you still at my door? Go Cheptabut! I don't need you here. I'll come and call you if I want your opinion." Tapchamgoi said.

Cheptabut left without another word. At her mother's, everything was quiet. Taptamus was feeding Sukunwa and taking things easy like always. She watched her daughter coming with a blank face.

"Mother, is anything wrong?" Cheptabut asked.

"No, everything is still peaceful and pleasant here so far," said Taptamus. "Kiptai has come and gone already. He will be back before dawn bringing *sinendet* to the parents. If we're lucky, we can sleep well until the sun rises. I mean until they discover what's happened. Tomorrow anyhow."

The next day Mt. Kamasai was quiet all day long. No word was heard, and Tapchamgoi was not seen around. But both sets of parents knew their daughters were already circumcised, and everyone's eyes and ears were on Taptamus' place.

Three days later, when everybody was beginning to return to normal life, Cheseret's father's voice was heard booming furiously like a thunderclap before the lightning strikes. He was saying to Taptamus that he was going to teach her a lesson, a lesson that her son would never forget. Because by the time he finished with Taptamus, Kiriswa would only be coming to bury her.

Taptamus was not saying anything because Nandi law dictated that if you are being accused and are guilty, you don't say anything. Your silence will bring you peace, and you will be punished according to the law. A situation like Taptamus' was normally resolved harmoniously in the end. Most everyone knew that the same thing could just as easily happen to them, except an unreasoning man like Cheseret's father. For this reason, Taptamus was doing everything according to the law. Tapchamgoi, however, was another story. She was there at once when she heard Cheseret's father's booming voice at Taptamus' place.

The more Cheseret's father raised his voice, the more Tapchamgoi raised hers even higher than his in order to be heard by the neighbourhood and to have them come to hear her tell Cheseret's father what she thought of him. The neighbours heard, and they came. The young ones came for a little chuckle. They stood at a distance and watched the grown-ups speak their minds. The grown-ups came to help Taptamus and to tell Tapchamgoi to stop meddling. Tapchamgoi didn't stop, however, she told Cheseret's father that he should never have raised his voice to Taptamus, because his daughter was not a young girl. She was old, sixteen going on seventeen. He should have remained quiet and thanked Taptamus' son, Kiriswa, in his heart if he didn't want to thank him in front of people, because that would have been understandably embarrassing for him. She told Arap Temoet that she, Tapchamgoi, herself was shocked and stupefied that the people who lived on Mt. Kamasai hadn't heard the new law. The new law said that if your daughter eloped with a man, the girl's parents had no right to go to insult the parents of the man until the girl came home and..."

"Take your white law back with you to Kabiyet where you were kicked away after making a nuisance of yourself. I don't need you here!" interrupted Cheseret's father who was on the brink of striking Tapchamgoi again.

"You didn't wait for me to finish. The law says don't insult the man's parents until your daughter says she was forced to elope with the man. And she has to produce witnesses to support her testimony."

"Take this woman out of my sight! Otherwise I'm going to destroy her," said Cheseret's father who now was concentrating on Tapchamgoi rather than the one he had actually come for, Taptamus. When he first saw Tapchamgoi, he knew she would bring only bad luck.

Cheptabut and Kiptai tried to haul Tapchamgoi away, but she twisted herself loose and shoved her way through the sheep which were milling around the front of the house. She went up to Taptamus and said to her, "Don't let him scare you. In Kabiyet, if someone hits you for nothing, you sue, and he'll pay for it. In Kabiyet, if someone slaps you and your nose bleeds, you take a container and let the blood drip into it and take it to court. If he hits you, I will be your witness."

"Here! Take this with you to Kabiyet!" Arap Temoet ran after Tapchamgoi. He took a swing at her, and she ducked. He tried to hit her again, but Kiptai stopped him.

"The next time I get my hands on you, I'll wring you like the dregs of a pot of beer," Arap Temoet said as he walked away.

"May it be your mother you wring instead of me! Don't come and let your testicles flop over me as though you're something big. If you are a man, why didn't you wring that python instead of running away from it? Hey, don't leave! I'm not through with you yet! You should have been ecstatic because your daughter has done you a big favour. She saved you the expense of laying on the festivities for the ceremony," Tapchamgoi shouted after him.

"Oh dear," cried Taptamus. "I'm sure we haven't seen the end of him."

"Yes, I know that," said Cheptabut. "He didn't get to say what he came to say thanks to Tapchamgoi. What is the matter with you anyway, Tapchamgoi? Are you drunk? This was not your problem! Why didn't you let him do what he came to do even if it meant beating up mother? I hope he wouldn't have gone that far, but at least that would have ended the matter."

"Yes, Tapchamgoi, you have made a mistake. You should have left when we arrived. That way we would have calmed Cheseret's father, acknowledged our fault, and maybe he would have left here with his heart softened a bit. And you wouldn't have been beaten again," said Kiptai.

"Now I have to worry all over again," said Taptamus.

"No, you don't have to worry anymore, mother," Kiptai said to Taptamus. "Now that everybody knows what has happened, they will be talking to him." Kiptai stopped and looked at Cheptabut and then at Tapchamgoi, who was waiting for Kiptai to finish talking so she could have the opportunity to explain why she had done what she did.

"Tapkelelei's child, listen to me," she said to Kiptai. "I'm a mother of very fine men and girls. I'm not a stupid, drunk woman. I wasn't drunk yesterday or today. Do you see this swollen eye and this wound on my head?"

Taptamus turned around to look at her.

"Oh! What in a nightmare happened to your eye?" she asked. Taptamus hadn't been able to see Tapchamgoi's face while she was arguing with Cheseret's father.

"This is not from alcohol or an accident. I was hit by Arap Temoet trying to show me who was wearing a skirt and who was wearing pants. Tabaes was saying that Cheseret and Chelamai hadn't been seen all day. Her husband, Arap Metuk, turned to us and said that maybe they had been kidnapped by young men. Cheseret's father heard, and he said that if some man had his daughter circumcised, he was going to circumcise the mother of the man himself. Everyone was silent, and I asked him why have the mother of the man circumcised? Why not have the man who kidnapped his daughter circumcised?"

Tapchamgoi turned around and noticed that nobody was saying

anything. She then swung about, and her one good eye seemed to question Kiptai. Kiptai didn't say anything. Tapchamgoi spat tobacco juice and began to walk towards her house.

"That is what I said to cause that barbarian to slap me," she said.

"I can't believe it," said Cheptabut who really felt sorry for Tapchamgoi.

"You can't believe it? Look at my eye! I didn't sleep last night either. I thought of taking a skull and depositing it at his door, but then I thought of his innocent wife Tapsalng'ot. What a shame that she married that savage man," said Tapchamgoi.

"Wasn't there anyone to stop him from beating you?" asked Kiptai.

"The whole conversation took no more than a few minutes, and besides, no one could predict he would be upset by what I said. Chelamai's mother and I were just laughing as I spoke."

"I guess you had better come back, Tapchamgoi, and sit down while we tell mother the rest of the story," said Kiptai. He stopped and looked at Cheptabut hoping she would take over now, but Cheptabut was tired of talking about the situation to her mother who instead of discussing the matter with her was uncharacteristically helpless and had turned to prayer instead.

"Kiptai wants all of us to know the rest. I think if Tapchamgoi had known that Cheseret and Kiriswa had eloped, she would have kept a distance from Cheseret's father," said Cheptabut. She looked at Kiptai as a signal for him to start talking.

"There is not much detail to go into. Every one knows Chelamai was missing, too. She was circumcised yesterday," said Kiptai.

"I think you'll guess the rest, mother," said Cheptabut. "Kiriswa is engaged to her, too," she added and then stopped, waiting impatiently for her mother to say something. Taptamus tried to show no panic at all, but it was visible on her face.

Cheptabut looked despairingly at her mother. She had never expected to see her appear so defeated and trying not to look it. Her face looked almost frozen in the daylight. Taptamus looked powerlessly at the empty sky. It was noon, and the sun was hot overhead. The blue sky looked like an endless sea.

"It is a disgrace," she finally said, with the tranquility for which she was well-known. "What will the young men and the people in the neighbourhood think of him marrying two girls from the same place and leaving young men in the neighbourhood who are not married? Can you try to imagine?"

"I wouldn't worry about that," said Tapchamgoi. "The girls were old enough to have been married three years ago. What were the other young men waiting for. Why didn't they marry them then? Let us wish Kiriswa happiness, good health and tremendous luck in dealing with Arap Temoet, Cheseret's father."

"Yes, he needs that luck in a hurry, too," said Cheptabut.

Kiptai had finished telling the story and left like a man, leaving the women to worry about the details. Taptamus acknowledged all of her fears and then blamed herself, saying that things had happened this way because she was a woman raising children alone and she had lost her grip on things.

"Mother, you are the one who has always told us that nowadays the dreams of men have shrunk. Since they can't raid any more, they just get married and get drunk. Why are you blaming yourself now for what Kiriswa did? Why don't you want to think he is just doing what everybody else is doing?" asked Cheptabut.

Taptamus sank down under the shade of a tree in front of her house and was silent. Perhaps the conversation was no longer to her liking even though Cheptabut and Tapchamgoi were proposing a comfortable way for her to think.

"Taptamus, my dear, you feel at a loss today. Things seem a great deal worse than they are. I'm sure tomorrow you will feel a little better. I'm happy for Kiriswa that he has married Chelamai in particular. What a beauty. I can't imagine anything more beautiful on this earth than her," said Tapchamgoi.

They sat in silence for a few minutes.

"Well, Taptamus, you know where I live. If you need any help, call me," Tapchamgoi said and left.

Cheptabut could have left after Kiptai went, but she felt obliged to help Taptamus clean the house and wash the dishes. Just to be there to say "Yes, mother, I think so" and "No, mother, don't worry. I'm here to help you."

CHAPTER NINE

*T*aptamus spent the next three weeks sending word to her husband's brothers. The responsibility was too great to take on by herself. There were things like sacred animals, the family totems, and all the ancestral spirits shared by the relatives. Marriages were regulated not only by rules of exogamy, but also by the knowledge that certain clans were not good to marry into, even if it were theoretically permitted to do so because the individuals weren't related to each other. To investigate this was beyond Taptamus' ability. Cheseret was safe. She belonged to the Moi clan which was numerically the largest in Nandi. It consisted of well-known totem animals like the crowned crane, the bird which children are told brings babies, the elephant, the duiker and others. These animals were simple and innocent, and few complications, if any at all, had resulted from marrying a girl of the Moi clan. Taptamus knew of none.

Chelamai, on the other hand, presented a complicated case for Taptamus. Kap Metuk, Chelamai's family, were descended from a line of blacksmiths and, although the attitude which people formerly had toward blacksmiths — contempt mixed with fear of their powerful curse — was now a thing of the past, Taptamus was still not sure what her own feelings were about them. People said that to be married to the blacksmiths was not a big deal. On the other hand, people were still glad it was not their son who had married a blacksmiths' daughter. No one wanted to be related to them. Taptamus wanted her late husband's relatives to go through the genealogical record of the clan to see if someone from the blacksmiths' clan had once married into the rain clan of her husband. And if they had, had the marriage prospered? Was it worth repeating? And of course, deal with Kiriswa, who had defeated them all.

Another problem was that, like Sukunwa, Chelamai was a "special" child. Tabaes lost the first two children before Chelamai. When Chelamai was born, she was taken early in the morning and placed in a hyena burrow for a few minutes after the hyenas had gone for the day in the hope that the hyenas would mediate with the ancestral spirits so that her life would be spared. The women picked the baby up, pretended they had found a baby hyena, and called it *chemaget* 'hyena's daughter' and *chepkering* 'girl from burrow'. This kind of child is different from other children. She should not elope or be kidnapped for marriage. Although she possesses a human body and human looks, her spirit and her being are intertwined with the spirits of hyenas. Because hyenas cannot be circumcised like humans, a secret ritual had to be performed and the hyena spirits' permission sought before such a girl could be initiated.

Hyenas were the animals Nandi hated most, for they ate human flesh. Yet they were believed to possess a sort of human spirit and talked like human beings at night. They communicated with the dead in the past when Nandi didn't bury people. At night before they ate the corpse in the bushes where it was set, the first hyena to arrive would cry. The followers would ask, 'Is it warm or cold?' If the body was cold, they would eat it, but if it was alive, they would lead it home and set it at the doorway. For this they were given grudging respect.

Taptamus spent three frustrating weeks waiting for answers to her questions and praying her long prayers at the same time. For Cheptabut, however, the same three weeks were not merely frustrating but excruciating. She had worked for both houses and lost so much weight that when she ate, one could see the food passing from her mouth to her stomach. She was at her mother's early every morning to help her milk the cattle as Taptamus was so upset she was almost incapacitated, and she returned in the evening for the same purpose. During the afternoon, she took her hoe and went to the field to tackle the rough work of cultivation. On Mt. Kamasai, one had to hoe around the stones and boulders in order to have some soil to plant in. The roughest and worst work of all was taken by Kiptai with some help from Kibet.

"Thanks to Kiriswa, the thoughtless one, who never thinks of anyone but himself! I wonder what he thinks his mother will eat next year if no one helps her to plough?" Cheptabut said when Kiptai got up in the morning and told her that he thought they might not harvest enough that year to feed the two families because it was so late and they were not getting anywhere. Cheptabut was doing all the hoeing alone, and Kiptai was clearing the bush alone, and it was too late to be doing this. Planting was mostly done during the first week of February, but here it was the middle of February and they were just beginning. By March, all the seed should be in the ground.

In previous years, Kiptai, Cheseret's father Arap Temoet, Chelamai's father Arap Metuk, and Arap Walei had worked together preparing the land for planting. They first did the work of clearing the bush, and then they burned what they had cleared. The ashes of the burnt vegetation made good fertilizer. The women, too, hoed together, and then the men assisted again sowing the seed, helping with the weeding and also at the harvest. That year, however, Kiriswa had ruined it for everybody. There wouldn't be much to harvest for any of the families because each family was doing all the work on its own and not getting anywhere.

That evening, Cheptabut again helped Taptamus with all of the work.

"Mother!"

"Yes," answered Taptamus.

"What are you thinking now?"

"What is there to think? There is no bigger mess to be in than this one."

"You're not joking," said Cheptabut. "How thoughtless Kiriswa has been. It is an embarrassment to kidnap girls and leave without coming back to tell his own mother where he has gone. The words I could use to express his thoughtlessness haven't been invented. Perhaps he has gone mad," Cheptabut said in a very agitated manner.

Taptamus turned away, upset. "If he can't come back and deal with the situation, how is he going to deal with three wives?" she said.

"That's going to be his problem. He wanted three wives, and now he's got them," said Cheptabut.

151

Cheptabut was not the only one upset. The neighbourhood people were beginning to talk, but Taptamus only heard what they were saying when she talked to Mary. Mary told her to send Kiptai to have the girls brought back, at least to Taptamus' house. That way, although the families of the girls would be upset with what Kiriswa had done, they would know where their children were. Mary told Taptamus that everyone was concerned that she and Cheptabut hadn't done more because the longer they waited, the more tense the situation would become. And no one would blame the parents of the girls now because it appeared to the people that Kiriswa was utterly lacking in respect both for the girls and their parents. Taptamus silently put both her hands on her cheeks and let the tears stream down. Helplessly, Taptamus told Mary that since Kiriswa had kidnapped the girls, the sun had not risen for her.

Nandi people tried very hard not to do something other Nandi did not approve of, and that was what was hurting Taptamus. What Kiriswa had done had been done a thousand times before, except that he had not brought the girls back home on time. Taptamus was crying now because of the criticism and embarrassment he had caused.

Taptamus' brother-in-law, Kilel, arrived from Mugundoi unexpectedly late in the evening of the day Taptamus had talked to Mary. They did not speak in detail that night because, when a guest arrived in the evening, custom dictated that formal business be put off until the next morning.

Kilel told Taptamus the route he had taken from Mugundoi to Mt. Kamasai. On his way he had visited some of Taptamus' uncles in Baraton, and they had insisted on his staying over for the night. He left before it was light and had had lunch at Lolkerinket. Taptamus was silent, as she could not believe her good fortune. She was overtaken with surprise and relief. Only that afternoon she had not known whether the sun had been out for the last three weeks.

Taptamus was not a helpless woman. She had managed her children on her own, but in her generation, women were not allowed to be smart. Part of the most important and sacred ritual that women were taught after their initiation was that to have a successful marriage, you had to appear stupid. If someone asked you a difficult question, even if you knew the answer, you would say, "Ask my husband." The women who lived happily in their marriages practiced this custom and, soon, pretending not to know much caught up with them. Even women whose husbands had passed away did not know much in order to stay happy in the family they were married to, because as soon as a woman's man passed away, a brother of her husband was appointed to look after his wife and have children for her and her dead husband. Kilel, the brother-in-law who arrived this night at Taptamus' place was the man who was supposed to take care of Taptamus after her husband's death. Taptamus had spent only two nights with him three years after her husband's death, and that was the end of that. His home and his wife now were in Mugundoi, about 40 miles away.

Kilel finished eating. Taptamus had fixed him something to eat, and at the same time she had sent Kibet to fetch Tapchamgoi to come so she could help her with the sleeping arrangements. Taptamus did not want her brother-in-law to have any strange ideas about the sleeping arrangements that night. Kilel had never stopped trying, even though she had made it clear she wasn't having anything to do with any man.

"I'm tired. I would like to talk while I'm lying down," he said.

"I've sent Kibet to let Tapchamgoi know you've arrived. I thought you might like to go to sleep there. Sukunwa is not sleeping through the night. Sometimes she wakes me up in the night and babbles for hours and hours."

"Oh I don't think Tapchamgoi wants me. I came by her place, and she didn't invite me. She made tea for me, and after we finished, she made it clear that she had some place to go."

"What do you mean?" Taptamus could not imagine. Her brother-in-law was the only man Tapchamgoi ever drooled over when she saw him. "Of course I'll make a bed for you." She took a cow-skin and laid it out on a bed of raised clay in the sitting room.

"Sweetheart, open the door. It's me." Tapchamgoi called out to Taptamus.

"Wait a minute. I'm coming," said Taptamus.

Tapchamgoi came in and pushed a bottle of moonshine into Taptamus' hand. "Look for glasses, Taptamus. Where is he? I didn't tell him I was going out for this."

"Why did you bring that here? Take it to your place and drink with him there. I thought you should put him up because of the baby," Taptamus whispered in Tapchamgoi's ear.

"You don't have to tell me to put him up. My place is his place. He can come anytime," said Tapchamgoi. "What is it anyway, Taptamus? Are you kicking your brother-in-law out? What's the matter? Don't you have it?" she added laughingly.

"Watch your language," said Taptamus.

"Cheer up. At least for now your problems are over. A man is here," said Tapchamgoi. "He will deal with the parents."

"Should I come to lie down?" Kilel called from the other room where he was sitting by the fireplace.

"Yes, of course," said Taptamus and handed the bottle of moonshine back to Tapchamgoi.

Kilel came into the room and went past the women to the bed. "Sukunwa hasn't made a sound," he said.

"She has her time. She will be up at midnight exactly," said Taptamus.

"You must be worn out. Where did you start from this morning?" asked Tapchamgoi.

"He started from Baraton," said Taptamus.

"It was a long journey, and the sun was hot," said Tapchamgoi and swung the bottle of moonshine in front of him although Taptamus had asked her not to drink there. "Here! I've brought something to relax you! Taptamus, may we have some glasses?" asked Tapchamgoi.

"I'll never understand you, Tapchamgoi," mumbled Taptamus shaking her head. Tapchamgoi heard her.

"What is it, Taptamus? Are the glasses dirty?" she asked and sat the moonshine down and followed Taptamus into the other room.

"Let it wait until tomorrow," called Kilel from the other room.

"No, I went far away to get it for you to drink. I know you'll feel better after a glass," said Tapchamgoi.

"Why do you insist this *warigi* must be drunk tonight? I don't have any glasses — Tabaes borrowed them last month. You'll have to use a bottle or a bowl if you want to drink here," said Taptamus.

"We will use the bowl."

"I don't understand you."

"You have said the same thing three times, you are becoming monotonous. Are you afraid he will get drunk and then sleep here? Don't worry. If he doesn't come with me to my place, I'll sleep here to look after you," said Tapchamgoi.

Tapchamgoi thought Taptamus was going to explode at this but, surprisingly, she only stared into the fireplace and said, "Take the bowl to him before he goes to sleep."

"You want some?" Tapchamgoi asked holding three enamel mugs in her hand. She had not taken the bowl as Taptamus had requested.

"No, I'm going to bed."

"You should drink. It may help you. I know some women our age who say that if they drink it helps them to rain when they are with a man they like."

"Oh no!" cried Taptamus. "I don't know who told you that, and take the bowl. Those cups are for tea in the morning. I don't have water to wash them in the morning before drinking tea."

They drank. Past midnight they were sure Taptamus was asleep. But Taptamus, who had closed the middle door to try to keep out the sound, could not fall asleep completely. They did it three times, and she heard it all. Tapchamgoi had a strange habit of laughing sobbingly each time she finished. She did this three times in all during the night, the last time just before the cattle began to smell dawn. Taptamus thought that she wouldn't be able to move that morning. At her age, she's overdone it, she concluded to herself. But she had underestimated Tapchamgoi, who got up and left at sunrise. Taptamus got up herself to make a fire, sweeten the milk gourds and make tea, but there were no cups to drink from. She left the tea to simmer and waited for

Kibet to come to sit with Sukunwa while she went to bring water to wash the cups.

Kilel got up very late, and it was almost time for lunch, but his breakfast tea was placed on a hot stone by the fire to stay warm. Kiptai and Arap Walei waited outside, while Cheptabut and her mother waited eagerly inside to ask him what they should do next. From now on, Kiriswa's problems would be in Kilel's hands.

"My dear child," Taptamus said to her daughter, "it is going to be quite embarrassing if the day passes, and the neighbours find out that no one has done anything. You know he has not greeted the children yet. He arrived late last night. Let us hope he remembers to come in to greet them so we can get ahold of him then."

It was past noon when Kilel finally came in to greet everybody. Taptamus quickly brought up the subject. Kilel yawned and stretched with every sentence he said.

"Should I get you cold milk?" Taptamus asked as their eyes met laughingly.

When she saw this look, Cheptabut thought erroneously, so mother can do it after all.

A decision was made that afternoon. Cheptabut was told to leave for Sarura, where they had last heard the girls were staying at her sister's place. Naturally, Kiptai said he was going with Cheptabut. It was only a one night trip, and Taptamus was tempted to ask him to stay behind, but she didn't because she knew he was only comfortable knowing where Cheptabut was. Kiptai took a bicycle even though they would be climbing from the start to the summit. Cheptabut carried two oiled animal-skin garments worn by initiated girls. Kiptai pushed his bike along, mile after mile, just so he would be able to carry Cheptabut on it for the short distance from the summit to Sarura. He looked disturbed and, halfway up the slope, he turned around and paused for a moment.

"This trip is unpleasant for both of us. It was absolutely unnecessary! Taptamus has other daughters who could share some of the responsibility. There was no need to send you to bring the girls. This

156

is exploitation. I'm not going to accept this kind of behaviour from your family any more, mother," said Kiptai.

"It's not mother's behaviour, or the family's. It is my brother's problem," said Cheptabut. You know my sister can't bring them without being asked, she thought to reply, but instead murmured: "I had no idea you would hate for us to help them." She looked down to avoid Kiptai's eyes.

"What did you say?" asked Kiptai. Cheptabut managed a vague smile in reply. Part of a woman's study of how to deal with a husband stated clearly that you do not murmur when your husband asks you a question, and now she had done just that. She rephrased her reply now.

"To tell the truth, I do not think mother...Perhaps if mother had known this would make you unhappy, she wouldn't have asked us to do it. She knows we have our own life to lead."

"I would hope they know we have our own lives to lead, because I have the feeling they would not have asked my permission for you to go if I hadn't been there. Really, I don't think your family knows you are my wife. They don't know I have a right to say no if I don't want you to go." Kiptai grinned, looking down on Cheptabut. This was something that had not happened to them before, and Cheptabut could not tell whether Kiptai was blaming her in part. She looked up, and her eyes met Kiptai's laughing, soothing eyes. She turned away and smiled, unable to look up at him again. Every time in their lives when their eyes met, they looked as though they were falling in love for the first time. People who were jealous of them said that Kiptai was not a man but a sissy. Cheptabut was the one who wore the pants in the family. A man in those days was only called a man if he made his wife cry at least twice a month so that people knew he wasn't taking any nonsense from a woman. He was respected if he spent most of his time with other men discussing intelligent things. The people who knew them well said Cheptabut was such a wonderful wife. She did everything Kiptai asked and, as a result, Kiptai never needed to lay a hand on her.

They arrived at her sister's at dusk.

"Did you say you heard the sound of a bicycle outside?" a voice inside asked.

"Yes," answered another voice from inside.

"Don't rush to the window so fast. You may break your neck for nothing. Maybe it's someone else, not Uncle Kiriswa anyway," said the first voice. The window was opened and then quickly shut. By now, it was obvious to Cheptabut that Kiriswa was not there because his wives-to-be apparently had rushed to the window hoping to see him coming. When they saw the shadow of a woman, they simply shut the window.

The sitting room was dark. Cheptabut called her sister from the door entrance — "Chemengech! The sitting-room is extremely dark. Don't you have an extra lamp?"

"Who is that?" asked Tilinkwai, Chemengech's fourteen-year old daughter. "Chemengech is not in. She's out milking the cows. Is it you, Cheptabut?"

"Tilinkwai, bring the lamp to the doorway connecting the sitting-room and the kitchen so we can see both rooms," said Cheptabut.

"Who is it?" said a voice which sounded like Chelamai.

"Cheptabut! Cheptabut!" called out Tilinkwai and rushed to the next room with the lamp to hug her aunt.

"Tell the initiates not to come into this room. Kiptai is with me," said Cheptabut.

"Do you want me to ask him to come in?" asked Tilinkwai.

"No, let me go to the room to see the initiates first before Kiptai comes in and makes them shy."

"Yes, go before their eyes pop out of their heads staring at the door. My mother is out milking the cows, and the initiates have been gazing out the window while the sun was still out. They were hoping to see some sign of Kiriswa. You see, he has been away, and the wives are beginning to worry. You didn't happen to meet him on your way here, did you?" asked Tilinkwai in a whisper. "Cheseret stayed until...until, well, mother said she stayed at the window all night."

"No, I did not meet him," whispered Cheptabut. For the first five minutes, communication was hard. The two initiates put Cheptabut in the middle between them, and each held her hand and moved close to her. They both remarked to her that they had forgotten how she resembled Kiriswa.

"You're discovering this now?" asked Cheptabut jokingly. "I've known it for many years. You know he is my brother."

"You make me nervous. I feel as though I'm sitting beside Kiriswa," Chelamai put her face into her hands.

"I'm Cheptabut," said Cheptabut laughing. Since being circumcised, Cheseret and Chelamai had not been out. They got up for breakfast and went back to bed. Up for lunch and back to bed again until dinner time. All the roughness from housework, ploughing the field, and staying in the sun all day was wearing off, and softer skin was emerging. The real beauty that hard work had covered was now apparent. Chelamai's figure looked like a beautiful, hand-carved statue. Her face was breathtakingly resplendent. Cheseret's beauty, on the other hand, was the kind that grew on one. It was a beauty with character.

Tilinkwai finished cooking and went out to invite Kiptai in. She opened the front door and turned around and ran back jumping up and down and squeezing her hands saying, "You can't imagine this, but I tell you, you will thank me."

"What? what?" asked Cheseret.

"Oh my mother is coming. She has finished milking the cows."

"That's all?"

"No, I'm saving the best news for last."

"I'm not going to try hard to find out. If it is news, I'll learn about it in the end," said Cheseret.

"Oh all right. Kiriswa has arrived! He's talking to Kiptai outside," said Tilinkwai.

The initiates both went to the window to see, but they came back disappointed. It was too dark to see anything. They had to wait until he came in, and even if he came in, Cheptabut was still going to be in their way. After the operation, the girls could only be in the company of other women while in seclusion until a final ceremony brought them out to be married. Now, for the length of time they were in seclusion, they must not talk to any man except their fathers and brothers. This was how the custom existed, but these two had not followed it until today when Cheptabut was here. They had waited until Chemengech was not at home, and then they made a deal with Tilinkwai to call Kiriswa for them. He would come in and talk and laugh with them while Tilinkwai stood guard outside. When her mother approached, Tilinkwai would whistle and run to stop them from talking. In return Tilinkwai could have her boyfriend come and spend the day playing with her and the initiates would not tell her parents.

The conversation was sketchy at dinner-time. Cheptabut was restless, waiting to explode and hit Kiriswa. She was extremely unhappy with her brother, but held back. All she said was, "Kiriswa, please, you should pity your mother. Why didn't you come and tell her what to do? Kiptai and I have been asked to come to take the initiates back with us. But on our way, we talked and concluded you are responsible for this. It's up to you now to decide how many years you're going to keep them here."

Cheptabut was angry with her brother and sister. Kiriswa made no attempt to communicate his side of the problem. He sat and listened, as though he didn't care anymore what was said about him.

Before going to bed, he said, "I was sick, and everyone will tell you that was the whole matter."

"I would like to see you early in the morning. If you can make it by sunrise that would be nice," said Cheptabut.

"Yes, of course. How are the initiates today?" Kiriswa managed to ask. He left after he was told they were fine. Kiptai chatted with his sister-in-law for a short while and left, too. Both men slept in the warriors' house.

It took poor Tilinkwai ages to finish feeding the initiates. She had to feed them by hand, and Cheptabut thought her sister Chemengech was pathetic. "This is unnecessary, Chemengech. How could you let this go on for a solid month without asking Kiriswa to speed up the Handwashing Ceremony to allow the initiates to eat with a wooden spoon?" she asked.

"Cheptabut, it was your job and mother's to come here as soon as you learned the parents had received *sinendet*. You knew the girls had been initiated then. It was not Kiriswa's job any longer, and you know it. Don't think I still do it the old way where one has to get up in the morning, take a bath and then cook, rolling the *kimiet* up like a sausage to hold up to the initiates' mouths to eat. Oh no!" exclaimed Chemengech.

"But that's what I saw Tilinkwai doing this evening."

"Not because we were frightened the initiates would get infections if the person feeding them were not clean. That was people's imagination."

"Don't tell mother you didn't do everything right. She will be horrified and think you didn't care what happened to the initiates."

"We made certain everything they used was sterilized. We didn't bathe our whole bodies, and we didn't feed them with leaves, but we washed our hands before cooking, sliced the *kimiet* and put it on a half-calabash shell for them," replied Chemengech. "What else would mother want?" she asked.

Cheptabut was silent.

"However," Chemengech said. "I must tell you we do it the old-fashioned way when we have visitors. You see, not everyone has adopted this new calabash method. Most would react like you. But everyone in Sarura is doing it behind closed doors."

"Have you let the initiates take a bath, so they can touch the calabashes?"

"No, Cheptabut, what do you think people would think if they knew I had let the initiates take a bath without going through the Handwashing Ceremony?"

"I thought maybe that had changed, too. You see we still do everything the old way in Mt. Kamasai."

"No, I still wipe them with *irokwet* leaves and the morning dew. And I soak them with oil every night before they go to bed the old way, too. I have to take an extra blanket to your husband now, or do you want to take it?"

"Did Kiptai say he wants an extra blanket?"

161

"Yes, he asked before we started this conversation."

"Take it to him then."

Chemengech took the blanket to Kiptai. Before she left the warriors' house, Kiptai said, "I want some water. Can you tell Cheptabut to bring some for me." Chemengech came back and whispered in Cheptabut's ear, "Kiptai wants you to take him water." Cheptabut asked her if he was all right.

"Oh yes. He was alone. I don't know where Kiriswa went."

"What are you going to tell the initiates?"

"Go and see. Maybe he really does want some water. If you are gone more than a short while, I'll figure out something to say."

Cheptabut was gone for two hours, and no one asked anything.

Early the next morning, everyone had breakfast. Kiriswa arrived late, even though he knew he and Kiptai were supposed to precede Cheptabut and the initiates. Kiptai called Cheptabut aside, "Make sure Kiriswa comes along personally to face the music from the girls' parents."

"Oh, don't you worry. I'm determined to get him home if I have to look for a few men to drag him down for me. I promise you."

Saying good-bye was never easy for Kiptai. He always panicked when he had to leave Cheptabut behind. Nandi do not kiss, but they use a secret body language that expresses their mutual feelings when they stand beside each other. Kiptai burst with love and desire just standing beside Cheptabut, and Cheptabut took pleasure in it and worshipped Kiptai. Chemengech and the initiates watched them eagerly through the peepholes in the house.

Until now, the initiates had been inside as patients. The longest trip they had made was to the bathroom outside of the house. For this they had worn their original clothing and used a blanket to cover their heads so as not to be seen by men or unrelated women. Custom forbade them to be dressed like initiates until they had gone through another ceremony that changed them from girls into initiates. Today, however, Cheptabut was going to bend the law a little bit with the permission of influential senior women. Cheptabut told them she could not imagine herself along the path with two initiates holding blankets over their heads all the way from here to the bottom of Mt. Kamasai. The powerful guardians of the ceremonies gave her permission. "Dress the girls in the garb of initiates. When you get home have them change to their normal clothing until after the ceremony is done," they said. The initiates were then dressed in long animal-skin garments which reached from their feet to their necks: the hood started at the waist and was laced up the front as it went to shoulder height and then over the head. Everything was covered, including their hands, with the exception of two holes in the front for their eyes. The clothing made them look like monks.

Kiriswa arrived shortly after Kiptai had left. He didn't need to be forced to leave. He drank a cup of tea and hopped onto his bicycle hurrying to catch up with Kiptai. Cheptabut and the initiates left a short time after them. It was hard to know what Chelamai was thinking, but she showed her fear that day.

"I know my mother is very upset now, but she will be glad to see me back. However, father will be a different story. I'm sure he's saying, 'Wait until I get my hands on her! She will wish she had not been born!,'" she said.

"No, I don't think he is saying that, but even if he did, he has to go through Kiriswa first. Kiriswa is the one everyone wants to lay their hands on, not you. I want him to explain a few things to me, too. How long was he going to keep you there?" asked Cheptabut.

"He was not keeping us. For two weeks, he had pneumonia and was in bed. He suffered very much, we were powerless to help him," said Cheseret.

"You cannot imagine how frightened Tilinkwai's mother was, though she didn't show it. She went from one herbalist to another, but Kiriswa did not improve," said Chelamai.

"Yes, today is only the second time Kiriswa has been out all day long," added Cheseret.

"Why didn't he send someone to come to tell us?" asked Cheptabut.

"I think he wanted to, but he said he did not want to do anything that was going to cause Taptamus more worry. But who was there in that house to send anyway? Chemengech's husband is never home," said Chelamai.

Cheptabut felt badly about this. She thought she had acted hastily last night toward Kiriswa. Well, she could not take back what she had said that night, she thought.

"Am I to understand he hasn't even gone to Soi to see his wife and children?" asked Cheptabut.

"She came to see him," said Chelamai.

"How did she know Kiriswa was sick, and who did she leave the children with?"

"She brought the youngest child with her. But I have no idea how she knew Kiriswa was sick," said Cheseret.

"Tilinkwai said Kiriswa sent some people who were going there to let his wife know so she would not worry," said Chelamai.

Cheseret turned around and looked at Chelamai. "Did Kiriswa tell you this himself? You were never alone with Tilinkwai without me," she said.

"Of course not! I wasn't told by Kiriswa. I was also not alone when Tilinkwai said this. You were there. Maybe you were too absorbed at the window watching Kiriswa and his wife talking to each other," said Chelamai.

"Didn't Kiriswa's wife talk to you?" asked Cheptabut. She did not know she was adding another dimension to the story. As far as Cheseret was concerned, the subject should be dropped. She had never felt so humiliated in her entire life. When Kiriswa's wife, Senge, arrived, she had spent all the time she had with Kiriswa outside under the shade of a tree in front of the house where Kiriswa lay when he was sick. When the time came for her to leave, she went in, and for half an hour, all she did while Cheseret tried to talk to her was to stare at Chelamai. Because of her beauty, thought Cheseret.

"She did not stay long. She came and went back the same day," said Chelamai. She did not mention the half-hour she spent with them because she knew Cheseret was already upset and would be even more so if Chelamai continued to talk about her.

"She is a good woman," said Cheptabut.

"Yes, she is, and extremely gentle. It is hard to imagine she is Tapchamgoi's daughter, don't you think so?" asked Chelamai.

"Oh, yes," agreed Cheptabut.

"Chelamai, do you remember this place?" Cheseret was tired of hearing about Kiriswa and his wife. She wanted to talk about herself and Kiriswa.

"Yes, oh yes! This is the path we took the day we left home," said Chelamai.

"I'm surprised at you! We didn't just take this path. We slept here in this very spot," said Cheseret.

"Yes, you slept with Kiriswa on that side of the path, and Kiptai and I slept on the other side," said Chelamai as she leaned forward close to Cheseret nearly whispering in her ear. She knew that the reason Cheseret brought the subject up was to say just this, and Chelamai was embarrassed to have it said out loud because Kiptai was her son-in-law now according to Nandi custom.

"Oh, I wish we didn't have secrets between us," said Cheptabut.

"Yes, Chelamai. I don't understand why you are making this a secret. Kiptai was not your son-in-law then. Or what is Kiptai supposed to be to us now, Cheptabut? Isn't he our son-in-law?" asked Cheseret.

"Yes, you're right," Cheptabut said. "The man who marries your husband's sister is a son-in-law to you because you are going to be taking his mother-in-law's place soon. After you marry Kiriswa, you are going to be taking Taptamus' place. She will become a grandmother, and the wives of the son, that is, you, will inherit her position as our mother. I think you can understand this from the point of view of the ancestor spirits. If a woman is married into a family, she will be a mother of all the children born into the clan. And when the spirits of deceased ancestors go into children conceived by these newly married women, they don't choose mothers," said Cheptabut.

"Another way of saying this is it gives more space to the ancestors' spirits to move about?" asked Cheseret.

"Yes, precisely," Cheptabut replied. "If I die now I would not be reincarnated by Taptamus again. She's too old. I will come to you to

165

be my mother, and my mother Taptamus will be my grandmother in that life. Chelamai, are you tired? You look like you need a little rest. We all could use some." They looked for some shade. "I'm sure if we sit in the shade for a little, we will be able to move faster when we start again," said Cheptabut.

"I suspect Kiptai and Kiriswa are home by now," said Chelamai.

"I believe not, because they have a long way to push their bikes," said Cheptabut.

"We know. We did not make it that night. I had to beg them to let us sit down to rest. It didn't matter that I lay on the ground without a bed. I was determined to stop because I was worn out and sleepy — I couldn't walk a step without stumbling over a stone," said Cheseret.

"Kiriswa wanted us to keep going, but Cheseret said she would scream if she was made to take one more step. She wanted to sit down, but slipped and fell in a mud puddle," said Chelamai.

"Oh dear! Why didn't Kiriswa look for somewhere to sleep. I'm sure many of the families in this neighbourhood have warriors' houses. I hope he looked for one," said Cheptabut.

"No, he did not. We spent the night here. He and I slept on this side of the road and Kiptai slept on the other," said Cheseret.

"Are you kidding? Wasn't it wet on the ground after the rain? I thought Chelamai said you fell in the mud," said Cheptabut.

"Yes I did. The ground was wet and muddy, but Kiriswa broke branches from trees, shook the water off, and made a bed out of them," said Cheseret.

"We'd better get moving again," said Cheptabut. "Did you spend the night here, and then go through the ceremony the next day?" she asked.

"Yes, I had to because Kiriswa had arranged everything beforehand. When we got there the women had everything they needed for the ceremony ready, and the woman who did the operating was there waiting. She had been brought from Eldoret," said Cheseret.

"I didn't know Kiriswa could move that fast," said Cheptabut.

"He can move fast. By that afternoon I was already confused. All of the senior women and the operator were all over me like sugar ants. I was beginning to have second thoughts," said Cheseret.

"What?" asked Cheptabut.

"I mean, somewhere deep inside me I felt I was not ready. But I knew also I could not have Kiriswa with me if I did not go through with the initiation."

"Didn't he tell you what was going to happen to you when you got there?" asked Cheptabut.

"We were told. I mean I was, but I had no idea the time would come so soon. I can only say that being told about it and the time for it actually coming up were entirely unrelated in my mind," said Cheseret. "I wish I could have made time stand still. The nearer time to decide came, the more I panicked. I was allowed to be alone before the ceremony, and I went to the stream at the bottom of the house where we were staying. I sat and dangled my feet in the water and watched the water flow rapidly over the slippery, moss-covered stones. I don't know for how long. My concentration was slipping fast like the water over the slippery stones. I day-dreamed as my eyes followed the movement the water took up and down. I heard a voice call me from behind the water. *Water moves fast in this place. You cannot think.* I thought I was awakened from a dream, and I knew it was Kiriswa who woke me up. My mind snapped, and I made the decision then and there that I could not deny myself that sweetness in his..." she stopped.

She remembered that she was talking to Kiriswa's sister, and there was a limit to how much of her feelings about Kiriswa could be expressed to the sister. She had spoken to Chelamai after they had gone through circumcision together, "Kiriswa is present. Just his being near me weakened my concentration. I lost the ability of knowing what to do next. I said yes to any question he asked me, although if I had been in my right mind, the answer could have been no. Oh Chelamai! What a glorious feeling to know he is ours forever. I am so happy. If I had been a tree, I would have grown tall to touch the sky." She had said this smiling, and put her hands around her chest to hug herself. Now she was talking to Cheptabut, and she had to think before talking.

"Did you dance at all that evening before the women took you in and started the ceremony?" asked Cheptabut.

"We sang and danced with a few girls from the neighbourhood. We had thigh bells, leglets of Colobus monkey skin, ornaments from other girls and whisks made from horsetail. I didn't wear them, but the others did. It was a short dance. The women took me inside for the first ceremonies. Then they sang and we danced together and went to bed. In the dead of the night, they woke me up for another ceremony, and then just before dawn the last. Kiriswa was called in for the engagement ceremony, but by then I was gone. The last thing I remember was falling flat on my face, Kiriswa lifting me up and people pouring cold water on me."

"You fainted?" asked Cheptabut.

"Yes, I still have no memory of how we got engaged" said Cheseret.

"They should have had cold milk. As soon as the operation is done, they pour it over you and give you some to drink. Did they do that?" asked Cheptabut.

"Didn't Chemigok say that the women who ran the ceremonies were not experienced?" asked Chelamai, turning to Cheseret for approval.

"Yes," agreed Cheseret.

"Why on earth didn't Chemigok bring up-to-date things to use when the girls were circumcised? Coca-Cola helps if given to drink immediately after the operation. You know Kiriswa didn't talk to anyone about this. If he had told mother or me, I would have told him what was needed to have ready and waiting before you went through the operation. You must have been frightened to go through with your own initiation after hearing what happened to Cheseret," said Cheptabut as she turned to Chelamai.

"I wasn't told about Cheseret, but I think I did not suffer as much as she did. At least I remember getting engaged. Kiriswa was asking the women and the man who performed our engagement ceremony if they could let me sit down. Maybe he was afraid I would faint too," said Chelamai.

"You got circumcised in Turbo and then were brought to Sarura later, weren't you?" asked Cheptabut.

"Yes, I was," was the answer Chelamai gave. Chelamai didn't say much. She resented telling anyone what she shared with Kiriswa. Everyone had seen Chelamai talking with Kiriswa while she smiled with loving eyes. She loved Kiriswa as much as Cheseret and Kiriswa loved her the same. But her love life was shut inside her. She was silent and and only her beauty spoke for her.

Chelamai had known ever since she was nine that Kiriswa was going to marry her someday. She used to come to Taptamus' place and ask for Kiriswa. Whenever he came in, she would cover her face until he was gone. Cheseret had always hated her for her simplicity and her pureness, but now Kiriswa was engaged to her, and she could not change that. They were both engaged to Kiriswa. Cheseret was going to be the middle wife, and she liked that. Chelamai would be the last wife if Kiriswa didn't marry a fourth wife.

Cheseret also was happy because, for the last month, they had been in the same house and she had not heard Chelamai talk about how she had fallen in love with Kiriswa. Therefore, Cheseret thought, Kiriswa actually never loved her. He had never told her how he loved her. Just as he had told Cheseret, if he married Chelamai, he wouldn't know how to talk to her. Cheseret believed that to be the truth. All Chelamai had done since they had been circumcised was listen to Cheseret talk of how much in love she and Kiriswa were, and Chelamai had been genuinely happy for her. She had laughed as though Cheseret was talking about someone she alone loved. And yet, Chelamai had been engaged to Kiriswa too. Cheptabut had once said to Cheseret that Chelamai kept her feelings deep within her, and she always emphasized that she even looked embarrassed when someone talked about love, but in Cheseret's opinion this was not true. She relished it. She has just never been in love herself, thought Cheseret. Maybe Kiriswa had to have her circumcised and engage her to spare her the embarrassment of people asking why she was returned without being engaged after she had eloped.

CHAPTER TEN

*T*he demarcated, straight portion of the path from Sarura ended on the summit of Mt. Kamasai. Climbing the mountain was hard, but the descent was equally unpleasant. The path that was supposed to run along the river from the top of the mountain never went straight. It zigzagged up and down, and every time a boulder confronted it, the path took off in a new direction. The mountain was a main breeding ground for countless varieties of monkeys and other wild creatures. If the beauty of Africa lay in its animals, then Mt. Kamasai held the real living beauty of Africa.

One feared the danger of animals not only at night; life was not so safe during the day. However, people knew when, and when not, to be out. It was safe until late in the morning, but around midday, the river was left for the deadly snakes who descended from the mountains to cool themselves.

Cheptabut and the initiates arrived at this spot around mid-afternoon when the monkeys were hunting for fruit to eat. They moved in groups by clan, and each species had a different demeanour. Jumping overhead and running back and forth across the river on the intertwined branches was a group of gentle, bushy, black and white Colobus monkeys. The forest echoed with a resounding thump when they landed on a bough after a long leap. They were beautiful to watch. Cheptabut and the *tarusiek* walked half a mile and came to some cultivated fields. Talkative grey vervet monkeys came swinging through the trees carrying ears of stolen corn under their armpits. With thick white eyebrows above black-masked eyes, they came swaying in front of a traveler, talking and calling each other as though expressing absolute astonishment at seeing a human. The deep black Blue monkeys with their red behinds never bothered to look at passersby.

They looked as though they were saying "mind your own business and I'll mind mine."

The thickly built olive baboons were the only ones that required delicate handling. They would lie down on any flat stone they found and were not in a hurry to move when they saw humans. They stayed put and stared at you bravely. Some of them would get up and move in a circle barking like dogs. The expression on their faces seemed to be saying, "We were here first. Find a different path to take because we are not moving." When they became stubborn like that, you had to make them think you had more courage than was actually the case, and that's what Cheptabut did. She continued moving forward and prayed they could not read her mind to see that she was in a state of near-panic.

As she led the way down the slope, Cheptabut could see her mother's house from where she and the girls were standing, although not very distinctly. She left the girls standing in the shade of a *murguiywet* tree and went closer to inspect. As she came nearer, she saw some white objects, which she at first took to be goats. Then she realized they were people, and so she took Cheseret and Chelamai to her place first. The house felt warm when they entered, as though a woman had been there, Cheptabut thought. She led the initiates into an extra room for privacy. She spread the best light-brown animal skin for them to sit on, and then she went to pull out a cloth that was stuffed in a little round peep-hole in the wall.

"There. That will bring a little light in," she said. She went into her bedroom — which was also the kitchen — went to the fireplace, and felt the hearthstones.

"Someone has made a fire here. The stones on the fireplace are warm," she said.

"Who would that be?" asked Chelamai.

"I don't know," said Cheptabut. She was hungry and would have liked to go to her mother's place, but she put the thought out of mind. That house is never empty. Particularly now when everybody thinks they must bring some kind of solution for what Taptamus has done. She walked to a basket that was hanging on a peg and reached in.

"Oh-oh! Taptigisei was here," she said gloomily.

"What happened?" asked Cheseret.

"The thief would be lucky to be alive if you hit him in the face with this *kimiet*," said Cheptabut.

"If there is *kimiet*, I'm hungry enough to eat it anyway, no matter how bad it is," said Cheseret.

"So am I!" added Chelamai.

Each of them took a few bites with a gourd of milk.

"Ouch! It's piercing my gums," said Cheseret.

"You should have listened to me when I told you it was hard as stone," said Cheptabut. "I'm sure mother has some food set aside in case a starving guest passes by," she added, but she was not sure how Taptamus would know they had arrived.

"Taptigisei surely has put a lot of maize meal in this *kimiet*," said Chelamai.

"I wouldn't call that putting a lot of maize meal in. I think she stumbled over the firewood and the whole bag of flour fell into the cooking pot!" said Cheseret.

"She didn't stumble over anything. That's her habit! Kiptai despises her cooking, but she keeps up the aunt and nephew relationship. I don't know how she knew I was not home today," said Cheptabut.

Cheptabut went to another small peephole and looked out. She had been hearing humming noises since they had started to eat, and now they were rising in level. She tried to listen, but could not hear well. Suddenly, she recognized Mary's voice.

"What a shame you cannot wait until tomorrow," Mary was saying.

"It is my child. I can do what I want. I can take her at midnight if I wish," said Tabaes. Now they were nearer, and Cheptabut could hear them distinctly. She realized that Mary was with Chelamai's mother, but she was so caught up with what they were saying that she remained glued to the peephole.

"Be gentle with her. The mother-in-law is supposed to bring her, not the mother. Tell Cheptabut you want her home tomorrow, so she will have a night to prepare her. She just got circumcised a month ago. She's still in shock," Mary begged Tabaes.

"Prepare her for what? Are we animals who are going to eat her up? Chelamai should not be afraid to go home. She is my daughter. How dare you tell me what I should and should not do. I'm the mother, and you can stay away from me! You have your own problems," said Tabaes.

Cheptabut woke out of the trance she had been in, and turned to warn Cheseret and Chelamai, but it was too late. In spite of what Mary had said, Tabaes entered the house and marched straight past Cheptabut into the room where the initiates were. Surprised, Chelamai and Cheseret stood gaping.

"Dress in your own clothing and get out," Tabaes said to her daughter. Chelamai did nothing, hoping Mary or Cheptabut would quiet her mother down. They tried, but could not. Tabaes was about to rip the clothes off Chelamai's body, but Mary went and stood between them.

"Don't do it, Tabaes. It is a sin to undress your daughter. Let her undress herself."

Chelamai did not fight. She could not. She was back home, and from now on it was the parents' right to do whatever they wanted with their children. She searched her mother's eyes perhaps begging forgiveness inside her heart. But her mother made no eye contact with her. She seemed a completely different person. In desperation, Chelamai turned to Cheptabut.

"Please come with me! Don't let her take me alone! I'm scared my father will kill me! Don't you see my mother! I've never seen her like that. I know my father is capable of murdering me. He said that if I ever eloped with someone he would kill me himself," said Chelamai in panic.

"You should have thought of that before you left. Let's go," said her mother. Chelamai grabbed Cheptabut's hand.

"Please come with me," she said again.

"Don't make things worse than they are. Come along," said Tabaes. She took her daughter's hand and marched her to the door.

174

Cheptabut took a step to follow them, but Mary pulled her back. "Don't interfere! You have no authority," she said.

At the door Tabaes spoke loudly to Chelamai. "Forget this family! Forget you have ever met Kiriswa or his mother! Consider this a terrible nightmare you have woken up from and never mention the names of these people again if you want to stay alive."

Cheptabut turned to Mary. She was about to open her mouth, but Mary stopped her, "Leave me out of this. There's nothing I can say. I know it's unusual to take the child this way — poor Chelamai! But you can't blame Tabaes. She is upset!"

"I don't think Tabaes was necessarily punishing Chelamai. Since when do women punish?" said Cheptabut. "Women are punished at the first thing their children do wrong," she added, her eyes searching Mary's mind for her reaction.

"You cannot know ultimately how much her husband had frightened her into reacting this way and how much was her own anger. Don't try to make it sound as though Tabaes would be happy if Kiriswa had kidnapped Chelamai if it were not for her husband."

Cheptabut ignored Mary's remarks, "Will you stand guard for me and keep an eye on Cheseret so I can take the news to mother's place where everybody is?"

"I cannot imagine how you can put me in such a position. You have a lot of nerve! You want me to stand guard for you to watch my sister's daughter whom your brother kidnapped? Anyway, everything is arranged already. We had known all along that this was going to happen. When I saw Tabaes coming this way, I followed her, and I suggested to my husband that it would be helpful if he could go to Kap Metuk, Chelamai's home, to check if her father was there. If it will make you feel better, let me tell you also that I whispered a warning to Taptamus about an hour ago."

"That will just make things worse. Now Chelamai's father will think Tabaes went and called people to help her and her daughter," muttered Cheptabut.

"What?"

"I'm saying a woman has no righteous indignation in her own

175

heart. She is never given a chance to be upset and express her own true feelings. The child makes a mistake; the mother suffers the consequences of violence and alienation along with the daughter."

"Cheptabut! You are repeating yourself! Stop talking about her feelings. You don't know what she is feeling. What you're saying is nothing new anyway. It is the lot of a woman — you don't judge things, you only take abuse."

"I would like to know what Kiriswa is saying about this," said Cheptabut. "Has he been told this was going to happen?"

"I'm sure he knows; he arrived ahead of you. But Kiriswa has no say in this. From now on everything depends on the parents of the girls and Kiriswa's parents. There is little he could accomplish by interfering anyway."

"I hope so."

"He can not do anything even if he wants to. His job is finished, and he has been told so," said Mary.

It would have been customary for Mary to show that she was upset too, because Cheseret was her niece, but her natural reaction was delayed by Tabaes' circumstances. Now, however, she turned to Cheptabut and said, "It is important for you to know I'm not on your side. Don't talk to me as though you need help from me. You haven't seen anything yet. You are still going to have to deal with *us*." She emphasized the word "us," and left without greeting Cheseret.

Cheptabut knew that was coming because Mary didn't want to make Cheseret think her family was happy with what she had done. Mary and Taptamus were best friends, but now that Taptamus' son had kidnapped Mary's sister's daughter, Mary had no choice but to stand by her sister. She also wanted to protect herself so that people wouldn't think she condoned what had happened. Although Mary herself did not know how upset her sister was about her daughter, Cheseret, she reacted this way because it was expected of her. Sometimes you went as far as to slap the man's relative.

Cheptabut stood confused for a moment after Mary left. She felt she should take the news to her mother's house, even though Mary had said she knew already, because she wanted to hear for herself what everyone was saying, but she was afraid to leave Cheseret alone. Her parents might be coming to take her, too.

"What are you going to do now? I feel sorry for Chelamai, and really bad," said Cheseret.

"I don't know what to do. I wish I had something sensible to do, but unfortunately I'm helpless," said Cheptabut. "I can't even go to the other house."

"Someone must have seen Chelamai and her mother leave. Remember, Mary said Taptamus knew Chelamai's parents were coming to take her home."

"Yes, I know. But why is nobody here yet, at least to find out what went on?" asked Cheptabut. She went out to look at the path from her mother's place to see if anyone was coming. There was no sign of anybody, and she went back in to start dinner. She stirred the hot ashes, but the fire was dead. She went back out again to pull some dry grass from under the thatching on the roof to stick in the hot ashes. That might rekindle the fire, she thought. She had done that before.

"Cheptabut, I don't see smoke coming through the chimney yet." Kiptai's aunt called from a distance. She was coming from Taptamus' place.

"Aunt Taptigisei! I'm getting some grass to restart it. Where were you anyway? I just looked down the path to see if anyone was coming," said Cheptabut.

"When I was young people used to fly like butterflies. I came to advise you and Cheseret to stay out of sight and leave everything to me. Don't worry," said Kiptai's aunt.

"Why?" asked Cheptabut with surprise. A concern for her mother now came into her mind. "Is mother all right?" Then she realized that if something were wrong with her mother, she would not have been asked to stay away.

"Yes, Taptamus is fine, thanks to your uncle. A terrible thing almost happened. First, everybody got very drunk, including Kiriswa."

"Tell me about mother! Forget Kiriswa! He has beaten us all. How can he drink under these circumstances?"

"I think it was a mistake for him to do that, but believe me, he's paying — your mother and your uncle are very unhappy with him. Your mother was sitting down facing your uncle. No one saw where Arap Temoet came from. He popped up from nowhere and grabbed her by the throat. I tell you, it took three people to undo his hands from around her neck. Oh, Cheptabut, what do you want to know anyway? The important thing is your mother is alive, and I can tell you that everyone sobered up quickly. Thank god blood has not been spilled yet."

Cheptabut was upset with this. She wished she could go to see her mother, but she had to obey Taptigisei and take Cheseret to hide somewhere before her father got there.

"Has Kiriswa heard Chelamai's been taken — or was he too drunk to know what was going on?" she asked.

"No, he knows."

"Has anyone heard from them then since they left?"

"Arap Walei said Chelamai's father was not home when Chelamai and her mother returned. He had gone out to drink. Someone should be there before he gets back, but everyone else is drunk, so there won't be anyone there. Don't stand there and talk. Get out! I ran over here to save you. Arap Temoet will be here any minute."

It was an evening never to be forgotten. Cheptabut and Cheseret went to hide in the bushes behind the cattle kraal until it was completely dark, and then they went into it hoping the breath of the cattle would warm them. They sat there and watched Arap Temoet, Cheseret's father, parading back and forth in front of Cheptabut's place. It was a night worth being alive for some people, as they watched and listened to Cheseret's father, and they remarked, "Did you hear what he said?" And, "What a shame! He doesn't have any self-respect." For Cheseret and Cheptabut, it was not funny at all. The ammonia from the urine of the cattle tickled their noses, but they couldn't sneeze for fear they would be heard. Shortly after sundown, the temperature dropped markedly, and they snuggled closer to the cattle. They stayed another hour in the kraal while Arap Temoet carried on, talking to himself.

"I know my daughter was sold by her aunt, Mary, and her sister, Cheseret's mother. Mary and Arap Walei, her husband, were at Taptamus' house drinking home-brewed beer and Arap Walei was having an affair with Taptamus in exchange for my daughter. I was the only one who was left in the dark while people swapped my child for beer and sex. My wife went with Kiriswa for many years. Now Kiriswa won't take her, and so she tells him to take her daughter. This is plainly a conspiracy between my wife and my sister-in-law Mary against me to drag the name of the family down. The name of the family is dead, but it is over my dead body that I am going to let it die alone. I'm going to make sure Cheseret and her mother die along with it. I'm going to crush my wife like grain, and then I will curse Cheseret to die before the sun rises tomorrow," he said hitting the ground with a stick.

Cheseret and Cheptabut quivered in the cattle kraal. Their eyes were burning from the ammonia, and tears were dripping down their cheeks like rain-water. They could not slip out of the kraal. Cheseret's father was standing stooped at the doorway talking into the house to make sure Cheseret didn't miss what he was saying. He didn't break Nandi custom and go into the initiates' house as they had feared. If they had only known, they would have stayed in! Cheptabut quivered more as she saw the smoke rising above the chimney and imagined sitting by the fireplace drinking a hot cup of tea warming her hands. They crawled on their hands and knees through the bushes behind Cheptabut's house and walked to Taptamus' house where they entered by the back door used by the sheep and goats. Cheptabut hugged her, turned around, and went back to her own house where she went in by the back door too. Taptamus was home with Sukunwa and Kibet. The rest of the people, including Mary's husband and Taptamus' brother-in-law, Kilel, had gone to Kap Metuk pretending they were having an evening stroll. In fact they were going to follow up on what was happening to Chelamai. Kiriswa was in his mother-in-law, Tapchamgoi's, house for dinner.

For the whole week, nothing changed. Kiriswa's heart pained silently and he sweated cold sweat. Cheseret's father abused Kiriswa's family constantly, and they took it because that was the custom. Chelamai's family wouldn't let them come anywhere near their house. They were a quiet family, almost isolated, and they weren't heard from much. Cheptabut went there a week after Chelamai had been taken home. Arap Metuk sat on a little hill in front of his house and watched her coming. When she got near, he approached her quickly as though he was going to hit her.

"Go back! Did anyone ask you to come here? I never want to see your face at my door again, and may your feet never cross the path in front of my house or step on grass that my cattle eat!"

Cheptabut wanted to ask for forgiveness for what her brother had done, but she was barely able to open her mouth.

"Get out of here! Stop scrutinizing us like a watchdog. What we do is no longer your business. If you come here again, you're going to wish you had never been born!" Cheptabut had to retreat.

A week and a half later, no one from Cheseret's home had come. The children were made to stay away from Taptamus' place. Cheseret's mother was told by her husband that if she ever went anywhere near Taptamus' place, she should just move over there completely and share Kiriswa with her daughter. All of their life together Arap Temoet had accused his wife of carrying on with every young man who seemed to say hello to her, and he had become a disgrace even to his own children. They went to other children's homes, but never brought them to their home because when their father started up, he would swear and carry on without regard for the children's presence. On Monday, Cheseret's father disappeared and did not show up that night. On Tuesday, Tapsalng'ot, Cheseret's mother, who had missed her daughter, sneaked away to Taptamus' house.

She rushed there. She did not see herself entering the house. It was a special morning for Cheseret. When she heard her mother's voice, she sprang up almost kicking the burning logs in the fireplace. She was overcome with happiness to see her mother. She forgot she was the villain, and remembered only that her mother loved her. She embraced her mother.

"Oh, mother! I'm glad to see you. Are you coming to take me home?"

"Why did you do it?" her mother asked with tears in her eyes. "Did you think of anything else but your own happiness? Why do you want to know now if I'm coming to take you? You have left that home." She spoke and then turned around and went out. Taptamus lifted her hand to speak, but Tapsalng'ot was gone before she had a chance to say anything. She did not turn around. Taptamus stood at the doorway and watched her go.

Cheseret was happier that day, in spite of her mother's criticism. She was glad to have seen her, and for Taptamus, the visit was better than nothing. She is the only one who has not called me names, thought Taptamus.

The next evening, Tapchamgoi came to Taptamus' place and called her out. She brought the news that Cheseret's mother had been wounded. Tapsalng'ot had been severely beaten, and no one could get in to help her. Cheseret's father had locked the door yelling that he had a knife, that he was going to circumcise her like her daughter. "If you people try to come in, I will kill you."

"You know Cheseret's father," said Tapchamgoi. "He's crazy and can kill his wife to make people know he's a man in command."

"Did anyone manage to help her?" asked Taptamus.

"Kilel kicked the door open and went in. Without your brother-in-law, tragedy would have struck, although if you could have seen Cheseret's mother, you would have said she was as good as dead already. The knife was held at her throat like a goat ready to be slaughtered. Kilel dove for it. Arap Temoet pulled it away and slashed his wife in the process. I think she has lost her left eye. I'm not sure. And the knife sliced Kilel's hand while he was struggling to take it away from him."

"Please! Don't talk about it any more. It sounds bad. Do you know what's happening now? I told Kiriswa all along to stay away from…" she stopped — she had almost said to stay away from Cheseret — "to stay away from anything that had to do with the Temoet family," said Taptamus.

181

"I left when people were still talking to Arap Temoet," said Tapchamgoi. "And don't blame yourself, or Kiriswa or Cheseret for that matter. The children liked each other."

It was evident Tapchamgoi didn't know very much. She went there, saw blood, and the first thing she thought was to come to tell me, thought Taptamus. Sukunwa was in good hands with Cheseret, but Taptamus could not leave because she would have to explain what had happened to Cheseret, and she did not want to alarm her. She went in and pretended nothing had happened. Sukunwa was not asleep, but was babbling to Cheseret. Although Cheseret knew something had probably happened, she didn't ask because the young should not ask questions of grown-ups.

The next day Taptamus continued her morning work as always. The morning was quiet, not a bird sang in the trees. Her brother-in-law was late in coming. That worried her. Then she remembered that when Kiriswa was not there, he always came late. I wish he would come early today to bring the news, she thought. She went to the cattle kraal to clean it, but kept her eyes on the path leading from Tapchamgoi's place where Kilel would be coming from.

He finally arrived at noon. Not long after, Tapchamgoi followed to tell Taptamus how sick he was and to recount all over again what had happened the previous night. Kilel's hand was swollen, and it was obvious to Taptamus that Tapchamgoi had washed it and put some medicine on it. But Tapchamgoi had come to say how much she had done for him as well.

When Taptamus heard the news, she had assumed that Cheseret's mother had been beaten because her husband had discovered she had gone to Taptamus' house, but she was later told it was not that. Before Kiriswa left Mt. Kamasai, he went by Arap Walei's home to say good-bye to the family. Tapsalng'ot, Cheseret's mother, was there visiting her sister Mary, and when Kiriswa arrived Mary started talking to him while her sister stood there. If she had thought of her husband's habits, she would have left because she knew Kiriswa was their enemy. When Cheseret's father returned later, he asked his children, as was his custom, where their mother had been while he was away, and he was told she had gone to Mary's place.

"Was anyone else there?" he asked. He was told that Kiriswa was there.

"Talking to your mother?"

"No, Mary was talking with Kiriswa, and mother was standing there." Mary discovered this because when Tapsalng'ot's husband was beating Tapsalng'ot, he kept repeating, "Why did you and your sister go behind my back to talk to Kiriswa? Were you telling him I was an idiot and couldn't do anything to them? You're going to pay for it today, and Kiriswa won't help." The next day Tapsalng'ot couldn't get up from bed. After watching the house for any sign of life, Mary went to see how her sister was doing. Although Arap Temoet tried to keep her away, saying "We don't need you here," Mary fought her way in to see her sister. Tapsalng'ot's head was puffed up like a balloon. Mary wanted to talk her sister into going home with her, but there was no way of telling her this in private. Arap Temoet sat there to make sure he heard every word Mary told her sister. Finally, Mary said to him, "I want my sister home with me," but Arap Temoet refused. He got up and showed Mary to the door saying, "You are not looking after her."

That afternoon, he slaughtered a goat and kept everyone away. The children did all of the household chores. They were told that their mother ran into a wall and was hurt. That was the story they should tell everyone who asked, and they did so. Arap Temoet knew his wife had lost a lot of blood, and it was customary for the person who caused the injury to slaughter a goat to provide food to give the injured person energy. In those days, the Nandi had not adopted the Western practice of a penalty for causing bodily injury. However, the slaughtered animal served the religious purpose of purifying the heart of the injured person so that she would not curse the one who had harmed her. A child was sent to Mary's house to ask for a bigger knife and a bigger pot to cook the meat in, and this was a way of telling Mary that Arap Temoet was looking after his wife himself.

Two days later he had to go to Taptamus' place for the same

reason. Kilel's hand had got worse. It was not responding to the medicine, and immediately people thought Arap Temoet should spend time with Kilel and eat with him. It was believed that if enemies ate together this would ameliorate the animosity between them, and if peace was made, the injured person could be cured. Cheseret's father was forced by this custom to go to Taptamus' place which he hated. He would rather be dead than be seen in Taptamus' door offering to make peace with one of her relatives. When a child was sent in the morning to call him to come, he sent it back saying, "Go tell whoever sent you I say he can die if he wants to. I'm not coming."

When the child returned with this message, Arap Walei, who was always obeyed in the neighbourhood, went and spoke to him, "No matter how much you hate him, this is the custom. You have to go to make peace. Don't be like a woman and hold things in forever. They did not kill your child. They married her. So you can't wish them dead." He went with Arap Walei, and they brought along a small gourd of milk that he was to drink with the sick one as a peace offering. No one expected him to come, but he did because Arap Walei was the only person who still listened to him, and he didn't want to lose his friendship.

Arap Temoet drank milk from the same gourd and shook hands with Kilel. The two men sat there silently with nothing to say to each other, and even Arap Walei's presence did not help. Tapchamgoi arrived at last and did them a favour. Arap Temoet now had a good excuse to leave since everyone knew he did not like her.

Taptamus, however, was not grateful. "I was very glad Cheseret's father had come and wished him to stay until I had served them the food I rushed to make," she said. "Why did you have to come now, Tapchamgoi? You knew he was here, and we are trying hard to have him talk to us."

"How could you think of getting along with him? How can you worry about his feelings when your brother-in-law is lying on the floor wounded? I would forget him — he's not human. The human in that household is his wife," said Tapchamgoi who was now facing Kilel and didn't know Taptamus had gone in and left by the back door for

Cheptabut's to send her to look for medicine for her uncle. Taptamus also told her daughter about Tapchamgoi, but Cheptabut did not say much.

"Tapchamgoi has her share of problems too in the neighbourhood. I'm sure she's worrying about my uncle, I've run out of things to say about her," said Cheptabut.

The next few weeks were endless days of silence. Kilel was in pain for a week, and Tapchamgoi went every morning to the river to bring algae to put on his swollen hand to reduce the swelling. After the swelling was down, she looked for *kirundut* leaves to bring the skin together and promote healing. She endlessly chewed the leaf-medicine, sprayed it on his hand, and waited until it dried. Then she went to look for honey beer. When she got home, she warmed it up for him. She was praised up and down by Kilel even though Kilel knew Taptamus would have done the same thing except for the beer part.

"As long as your uncle is waited on hand and foot, day and night, he's never going to get better, and that is selfish and unkind of Tapchamgoi. She knows very well that men are like children. They love you best when you baby them," Taptamus once said to her daughter Cheptabut.

"Mother, that is Tapchamgoi's affair, and I'm staying away from it. We know how she is, but on the other hand, I don't blame her. I can't imagine how Kilel could speed things up when the girls' parents won't even talk to us. Really, mother, what is there Uncle Kilel could do even if he were left alone by Tapchamgoi?"

"Nothing much, but he's being manipulated by her, don't you see?" said Taptamus.

Cheptabut thought for a moment that her mother was jealous, but then she changed her mind. She told herself her mother was suffering emotionally, and she reflected that she would not see her recover until the welfare of her son Kiriswa had been dealt with.

Another day went by. There was no word from Cheseret's family. Cheseret was gloomy like a rainy day and went to bed early. She missed her brothers and sisters, but she could not be taken home until

185

her parents had asked that she be brought. She was half asleep when Mary, her aunt, arrived. It was cold. The wind and rain blew over Mt. Kamasai emptying down to the dark moonlessness of Cheboiywa River. It was a while before Taptamus came to the room to wake Cheseret up. She was awake already, but stayed lying down on the bed with her eyes closed trying to hear what kind of news her Aunt Mary had brought.

"Cheseret, are you awake?" called Taptamus entering her room.

"I'm half-awake. Who is in the sitting room?"

"Mary — she wants to take you home. Is Sukunwa awake too?" asked Taptamus.

"No, she is asleep."

"She will miss you a lot," said Taptamus and went back to bring a basket to put Cheseret's belongings in.

"I want to go home, but why didn't my mother come and take me?" asked Cheseret with fear in her voice. "I know my mother would come to take me if they wanted me. Why didn't she come?" She was afraid that no one at her home but Mary wanted her.

"Mary is going to take you to her place." Taptamus could hear that Cheseret was heart-broken, with sadness caught on her throat and only forcing the words out. She sat down to try to assure Cheseret with her wonderful and kind voice that it was all right.

"I'm certain Mary and your mother have talked about this and come to agreement that your aunt should take you to her place," said Taptamus.

Mary found it strange that it was taking them so long to come out. She had stayed behind when Taptamus had gone into Cheseret's bedroom hoping she would not have to answer questions from Cheseret because no one had told her that her mother was extremely sick. She had also not been told that her mother had escaped death by a narrow margin and that the cut on her left eye which had been intended for her throat was badly infected and she might lose the eye. When Cheseret thought she overheard Tapchamgoi talking to Taptamus about her parents, she had been embarrassed to ask Taptamus directly but later she tried to find out by bringing up Tapchamgoi's name in the hope that the conversation would lead to what Tapchamgoi had said about her mother. "I wonder who does the evening work for Tapchamgoi while she goes out this late?" she asked Taptamus.

Taptamus knew that she had overheard Tapchamgoi talking to her and told her only the tip of the iceberg. That her mother had been slapped around by her father in the family dispute, but people had stopped him before things got out of hand, and Tapchamgoi had come to let them know. Cheseret thought something was wrong because when she asked questions about her mother, the answers sounded fake. But it was custom which caused everyone to be secretive. If a girl was in seclusion, she should not be made to cry. It was considered terribly unlucky, the engagement would be broken, and the girl would be given to an old man or to a woman because she was not pure.

Mary came into the room. "What's taking so long? We have to leave. Chepsisei is alone in the house."

"Why didn't my mother come?"

"Listen young lady! You are in no position to choose who takes you home. You should be glad I came at all. You still have a lot to answer to all of us you know. Let's get going. If you have any more questions, I'll answer them at home."

Cheseret gathered her belongings quietly, and Mary led the way. Taptamus looked at Cheseret smiling gently and went to whisper some secrets in her ear. Cheseret smiled a little. She must have been told to bear up for a little longer. She would be out of seclusion in no time and with her husband, Kiriswa.

187

CHAPTER ELEVEN

*T*he rain had stopped, and the moon shone on Mount Kamasai. It looked like dawn. Cheseret was not beaming when they left. She disliked her Aunt Mary, and was not going to start a conversation if Mary did not, so they travelled in silence. Cheseret had always felt that any punishment she had received from her mother was caused by Mary and by no one else but her. Her mother was gentle and would never punish her, she thought. This was Mary trying to take over as usual, thought Cheseret and hated her. Mary enjoyed Cheseret's and her mother's problems when her own should have sufficed. But her problems always managed to slip away unnoticed. She had let her daughter, Chepsisei, get pregnant by Tapchamgoi's shepherd, and the whole thing had vanished under the rug. No one ever mentioned it. Her husband had never lifted a finger against her because of it. What does she have that nothing can go wrong with her, Cheseret asked herself.

"Would you pull your skirt up over your knees? It will be very stiff when it dries if you drag it in the water," said Mary.

Cheseret pulled her animal skin skirt up and did not say a word. That didn't bother Mary. She knew Cheseret's stubbornness, and she was testing her. It won't take too long before she realizes I'm helping her, she thought. "Don't you have anything to say?" she asked.

"What is there to say?" snapped Cheseret, making it clear that she did not want to make friendly conversation with Mary.

"Don't snap at me. You're the one who should be snapped at, not me. You have a lot of explaining to do. Why did you run away with a man when you were almost ready to be circumcised at home and be married anyway?"

189

"Now that I've done it, I don't want to talk about it," Cheseret shrugged her shoulders.

"All right, if you don't want to talk with me, why don't you at least pretend that you are happy to come home with me then?" Cheseret shrugged her shoulders again.

Chepsisei was waiting behind the doorway when they got home. She heard the front door click, and she rushed to see if it was her mother coming. She did this when Mary was away, and people had learned to open the door gently not to hurt her. Mary pushed the door ajar and stepped aside to let Cheseret enter. Chepsisei was there, and her eyes gleamed when Cheseret removed the hood from her head. Although she could not say so, she was happy to see her. She put her arms around Cheseret and clung to her. Then she took Cheseret's hand and led her to the kitchen. Cheseret was happy to see her, too, and Chepsisei felt it. Cheseret tapped Chepsisei's shoulders to get her to turn around and then leaned over to hug her again. Chepsisei was shorter than Cheseret. She looked up to see what was different with Cheseret. She had not seen her since she had been circumcised and wearing an animal skin. She had been told, but had not understood. Although she could see her appearance had changed, perhaps she had no idea what had changed her. Since she could not talk, no one knew what was going on in her little mind. Cheseret was looking at her, too. She was now very pregnant and had been taught to walk slowly because she had a baby in her, and she could run into things easily if nobody looked after her.

Still holding Cheseret's hand, Chepsisei went to sit down. She looked up at Cheseret with unblinking eyes. When Cheseret returned her gaze, Chepsisei looked away shyly and pointed her stomach out to Cheseret. She took Cheseret's hand and pressed the palm on her growing stomach. This was her explanation that she had something new in her. Cheseret pulled her hand away because she felt that her aunt didn't want anyone to learn that Chepsisei was carrying a baby.

"What are you afraid of?" laughed Mary trying to make Cheseret feel comfortable. "Chepsisei wants you to feel the baby. You see, she likes you. I've never seen her ask anyone else to feel her." Mary squeezed Cheseret's hand, and Cheseret's face lightened a bit.

Mary took some food to her husband's house after cooking, and then came back to feed Cheseret and Chepsisei. Then she went to talk with her husband and bring the dishes back.

Early the next morning, the sky was a clear ocean-blue, almost aquamarine, as Mary slipped away to her sister's house with a potsherd to fetch a burning ember. Her sister was at the fire place rekindling the fire when she arrived.

"Have you brought any news?" asked Cheseret's father springing to his feet.

"Is there trouble anywhere?" she looked at him.

"You tell me. What brings you here this early?" asked Arap Temoet.

"Oh come on. Don't you want anyone at your door? I came for some fire. Don't worry. You are safe from any danger. You can kill my sister and nothing will touch you, but I can tell you, if I was your wife, you would have been dead yourself long ago." Mary looked him straight in the eye.

"So you've come to tell your sister how to massacre me? Tell her, and leave before you are declared dead when you leave here." Arap Temoet stepped outside, his eyes red like fire.

"I have not come to tell her how to kill you, but I pray every day that you'll slip on some cow dung and die on your own!"

"Mary! Think things through before talking. You will regret what you have said forever," said Cheseret's mother.

"Never! I'm totally aware of what I've said, and I'm glad to have said it. I've wanted to say this to your husband for so long, you don't know how long," said Mary.

"Leave if you have any regard for me, Mary. You will increase my trouble if you stay any longer." Cheseret's mother was afraid for her life after her sister left.

"I came here to let you know that I have brought Cheseret home, and she is asking about you a lot. What should I tell her? I remember you did not want her to know you were beaten."

191

"Leave Mary! Go make up anything. Tell her I was drunk and ran into a wall and cut my face." Tapsalng'ot watched the door for her husband, shaking in fear.

"Leave him! He is going to kill you in the end if you don't leave now," said Mary.

"Think of the children, Mary."

"There comes a time when the children mean nothing, when your body has been pounded to a pulp like this. Take the little one and disappear, never coming back," said Mary.

"I can't go, Mary. I have nowhere to go. If I go to your house, he will be there in minutes to destroy us all."

"You don't want to leave. In my house he wouldn't make it through the door before being pulverized by my husband. I've told you what I think; now it is up to you. I can't drag you out of here," said Mary. She picked up her potsherd, scooped up some embers into it and left. She looked around as she went outside to check where her brother-in-law was, but he was not around. He had stormed out in a foul temper kicking the door as he left. He went looking for Mary's husband to bring her behaviour to his attention.

"She arrived at my door at the crack of dawn to pick a fight with me. I stayed away from her because I was in a good mood, but I think she should be told to watch her mouth," he said.

"I wish you had told this to Mary herself because I'm not her shepherd looking after her mouth," Arap Walei said spitting out tobacco juice. Mary walked past them sitting on the hill in front of the house. Half an hour later smoke came out of the chimney, and shortly after, Mary brought the teapot out with a single cup which she set down in front of her husband. Arap Temoet was still there. Arap Walei asked her to bring a second cup. She got it and set it down.

The two men stayed out. After a while, Mary watched them walk away, their shadows disappearing in the meadow. Cheseret was peeping through the kitchen door watching Arap Walei talking with her father and hoping that her uncle would talk him into forgiving her, but when they left and Mary came back to sit with a sigh of frustration, Cheseret despaired.

The morning hours passed. When Mary was done with her work she came to sit down with the two girls, Chepsisei and Cheseret. She thought she had better prepare Cheseret for her mother.

"Oh! I forgot to tell you. Your mother had an accident and almost lost her eye."

"What kind of accident?"

"You know how it is at night when someone needs to help themselves and it is dark?" asked Mary.

"That's what happened to mother?" asked Cheseret.

"Yes. She got up half-asleep to go to the bathroom, and she walked into the wall."

"Ahem." There was a cough outside.

"Who is that? It sounded like Kiriswa." whispered Cheseret.

"I don't know. I don't think it could be him. He can't possibly be back already." Mary got up and went to the door to see.

"Oh, it's your brother, Kiptarus," she said.

Cheseret's mother had told her brother that his sister had been brought to Mary's place. If he wanted to go to see her, he should use his intelligence and not let his father or the other children know. His mother knew he missed Cheseret a lot. Since she had left, he had not said much, but she knew he was hurt hearing his father curse his sister.

"How is mother?" asked Cheseret.

"She's sick. What happened to her anyway? Her face has a big cut."

"You don't know what happened to mother, and you live in the same house with her?" Cheseret found this inconceivable.

"I didn't say I didn't know mother was sick. I just didn't believe the explanation she gave me, or I should say when I asked her I wasn't told in any detail."

"What did she actually tell you?"

"She said, 'What happened to me is something that increases women's knowledge.'"

"I wasn't told much by Mary either. In fact, I have no idea why she even told me at all. I didn't ask her," said Cheseret.

"When did she tell you this?"

"This afternoon."

"There's more to this than we know." Cheseret's brother wrinkled his face. "I mean, we haven't been told what really happened."

"Mary said she ran into a wall."

"Who knows."

"I think that is a reasonable explanation. Don't you think so?"

"No, I don't think so, but, Cheseret, I must go. You should know I'm helping to milk the cows too, because mother can't bend down."

"I hope I will be able soon to help mother even to wash the gourds. Have you heard father say I will be coming home soon?" asked Cheseret with a little hope.

"Not yet," answered her brother.

"Have you heard anything about Chelamai?" asked Cheseret.

"Not much. Her aunt came over yesterday to see mother. I heard her say that she met Kiriswa in a beer parlor. Kiriswa bought her three shillings worth of beer, but she didn't drink any of it because she knew Chelamai's parents would never let Chelamai marry Kiriswa, and she was afraid Kiriswa might think this was a sign of the family accepting him."

"Have you seen Chelamai yourself?"

"No, her father won't let anyone go near her."

Chepsisei came into the room and took her cousin by the hand. "What does she want?" asked Kiptarus.

"She's telling you to come into the sitting room to eat," called Mary. "Come! Chepsisei and I have made you something. Eat and then go home. Your father might have seen you come here. I wouldn't want to bring his madness here. My sister is fortunate — none of the children took after your father," said Mary. "Kiptarus is a duplicate of my father, your grandfather," she said to Cheseret.

"Yes," agreed Cheseret. She was helping her brother who was eating and seemed not to be listening to Mary. "Mother has always said Kiptarus looks like our grandpa."

"My father said I looked like him when he was young," said Kiptarus getting to his feet.

"You must go now. It's awfully late," said Mary. "Tell your mother I may come by tomorrow after lunch to see her."

It was another month before Cheseret's mother was well enough to participate in her daughter's Hand Washing ceremony. Waiting for Cheseret's mother to get better gave Mary time to collect milk for Chepsisei to drink after the operation. She was very pregnant now, and nothing else could be done but have her circumcised to change her from a child to a woman and to eliminate the scandal that would arise if she had the baby before she was circumcised.

Given Chepsisei's circumstances, the ceremony would have to be performed with special concern, and skilful women were needed to do the job. Skilful women there were, but no one was willing to accept the responsibility. The rules for the initiation ceremony were hard. Even doing it for a normal child was like being asked to crawl across an ocean on a sinew rope. There were many details which had to be obeyed. The women's ceremony in those days was so strong that no one could question if it was worthwhile to go through with it. People's belief in it was complete. Moreover, the belief in sin was alive and well. If you made a mistake, the other women would turn around and say, 'If you did this knowingly, may you be haunted the rest of your life by sin, may you never be allowed to carry out another ceremony like this as long as you live, and may you never set your feet in the women's ceremonial house again.'

Despite the fact that she knew the responsibility was very great, Mary decided, with her sister, Cheseret's mother, to hand to Taptamus the arrangement of the whole ceremony for her daughter Chepsisei. Taptamus was reliable, and Mary and Tapsalng'ot knew it. She was a widow, and she was only allowed limited ceremonial duties because widows were considered impure, but other women listened when she talked. Thinking that it might help to speed things up between her family and Cheseret's parents, Taptamus accepted although, under normal circumstances, she would only have done the operation itself. After agreeing to be the mistress of the ceremony, she sent Kibet to call Kiriswa's first wife to come.

"And Kibet, hasten back!" she said.

"Mother, I understand you must do things for Mary because she is your friend, but you must not undertake a task which is completely beyond your power," said Cheptabut.

"Don't talk about it now. We will do it together," said Taptamus.

"My dear mother, I have a house to run, and besides, I've never done any ceremonies before."

"You won't be on your own. Other women will teach you what to do." Taptamus believed it was bad luck to talk about a ritual before doing it.

Senge arrived and accepted Taptamus' proposal with grace, but her mother, Tapchamgoi, was unhappy that her daughter was asked to do a ceremony that no one else wanted.

"Let Kiriswa's wife talk for herself," said Taptamus.

Tapchamgoi said that her daughter couldn't talk for herself because she was trying to help her husband get on good terms with his second wife's relatives, just as Taptamus herself was doing. "I have to talk for her. Mary's daughter is *abusan* and pregnant. That is too much for my daughter. She is too young."

"Your daughter is my daughter-in-law. I would not do anything that would ruin her. She is going to do it with my daughter, Cheptabut," said Taptamus.

"What is this? Is it a ceremony run by children? Cheptabut and my daughter aren't much older than Chepsisei herself," said Tapchamgoi. She grinned, showing a little gladness on her face when Taptamus mentioned that Cheptabut was part of it, too. "I know it's difficult to find senior women, but those two, they haven't stopped laughing when they meet, and they might laugh during the ceremonies," she said.

"I know that, but I think they should start taking on adult responsibilities. Of course, with some help and instruction. We've started talking about Cheptabut and her sister-in-law, but the truth is I've come to you for some assistance with them," said Taptamus.

Tapchamgoi relished helping, for like Taptamus she was a widow. Taptamus divided up the teaching duties. Tapchamgoi would teach her daughter and Cheptabut what kinds of special ingredients were needed for the ceremonies.

"Show them where to go to get these ingredients and which one gets used when."

Taptamus taught Cheptabut and Senge the parts each would play. Cheptabut was made the senior mistress of the ceremony, and her sister-in-law was made the shepherdess. Cheptabut would administer the traditional anaesthetic the night before, and would support Chepsisei on the day of the operation. Acting as a stand-in for Taptamus, who would be doing the real operation, she would instruct Chepsisei as to what was going to happen. Senge would give Chepsisei various ingredients the day before the operation and immediately after the operation would apply the antiseptic. With Taptamus teaching them how to conduct the ceremonies, Cheptabut and Senge worked and learned to be ceremonial mistresses. They started a week ahead of time instead of four days. They went every day for three to four hours to spend time with Chepsisei. They took her out and showed her various ceremonial substances. They rehearsed the ceremonies every day, acting them out in the hope that Chepsisei would get some idea of what was going to happen.

The family didn't want a big circumcision festival, but nothing was skipped. All the necessary people were invited: neighbouring women, intimate friends, Chepsisei's sisters and her maternal and paternal aunts and uncles. The night before the circumcision, the male relatives and a few friends gathered as the sun set to drink honey-beer in the guest house. A big pot was put in the middle of the sitting room, and each of the men had a 10-foot long drinking straw. They sat around the pot, and each put his straw into the pot and sucked millet-beer which had been diluted with hot water. They talked quietly waiting for the women to come and tell them, "You are needed. It's time for your part in the ceremony."

In Mary's house, where the ceremonies were held, all of Chepsisei's cousins were singing and dancing for her. Late in the evening the dancing girls were asked to leave, and the men were called to talk to Chepsisei to cheer her up with speeches of encouragement.

197

After the men left, the women took Chepsisei to get a little sleep. Shortly before dawn she was awakened for more ceremonies inside the house and then taken out.

Taptamus walked to the men's house to remind them to come right away because the operation had to take place at sunrise. Arap Walei arrived, along with his brothers and their sons and Mary's male cousins who were acting as Chepsisei's maternal uncles, because Mary had no brother. The women were standing around a big fire they had made outside while waiting. The main participants lined up to be blessed. Cheptabut stood first, Chepsisei followed, and Senge, Kiriswa's wife, was last. Chepsisei's father, her uncles and her cousins anointed her face, chest and legs with butter, and poured milk on her head and on the heads of Cheptabut and Senge.

When the blessing ceremony ended, the men left, and Taptamus dashed into the house to meditate briefly. She reached inside herself for the strength and courage to perform the operation successfully. She came out in a state of great emotional intensity just as Chepsisei was seated with Cheptabut behind, supporting her. Taptamus was known for her quickness, but she was extraordinary that morning. She performed the operation quicker than the blinking of an eye. Cheptabut was confused. When her sister-in-law applied the antiseptic that she had been instructed to administer only after the circumcision, she yelled, "Senge! Stop! Not yet!"

Cheptabut thought Senge was confused, but everybody was ululating and saying "Thank you, Chepsisei, for your courage." They ran to take the good news of a successful ceremony to the men who were waiting patiently a hundred yards from the circumcision place. On hearing the good news, the men went back in to continue feasting. They would drink honey-wine and beer for two days and tell stories of their youth; stories about who was the most skilful warrior, who was the leader on the most raiding parties in their time, who travelled the farthest to raid, who got the most oxen while he was raiding. All this was said tranquilly, through the songs the men sang to themselves to relive their past.

Chepsisei collapsed half an hour after the circumcision, and that kept the women on the run for the rest of the day, although they could do little but sit beside her with cold water and pat her forehead. No one knew if Chepsisei knew what had happened to her. The children were kept away from her, and every day she was told she was an adult and should not talk to children. Senge, Kiriswa's wife, moved to Mary's because Mary needed help now that two people had to be fed by someone else's hand and not their own. Mary took Chepsisei's calabash to feed her, and Senge took Cheseret's calabash to feed her.

Mary sped up the Hand Washing ceremony. In the Hand Washing ceremony, the girls' hands were washed, and the clothes they had worn before they were initiated were changed into initiates' clothes. After that they were allowed to feed themselves with wooden spoons. They could also help with sweeping the house and with cleaning the milk gourds. Apart from that, they sat and made make-up out of spun clay. They could not do much while in seclusion. They were still considered unclean until additional ceremonies were performed.

Chelamai's parents were invited to let Chelamai join Cheseret and Chepsisei in the Hand Washing ceremony. They said they would do their own. They didn't want to have anything to do with Taptamus' family. The women who had circumcised Cheseret had reported that she was a virgin. When the ceremony of Hand Washing was about to start, her mother requested that she be examined to see if she really was. This was done as she wished. Yes, Cheseret was a virgin, but she had a big infection from the circumcision. A woman was brought to check it and to diagnose it. "This infection has nothing to do with the circumcision," she said, but she didn't know what it was. Home medicine was tried and did not work. Mary went to Kap Temoet. There she suggested to Cheseret's father himself that Cheseret should be taken to a doctor in Chepterit, many miles from home. "I've heard he is good. Many people go to him."

Arap Temoet pretended he had not heard Mary. Although he did not speak, he looked at Mary sideways with disgust.

"He's a good doctor. We used to go to him ages ago when my husband was a policeman," said Mary. She gave the impression that she did not see the hate on Cheseret's father's face.

199

"Who would have thought that you, Mary, would come and talk to me about my daughter," remarked Cheseret's father and laughed. "You know I won't take account of anything you say. Why did you come to me with this?"

"I'm only acting according to custom," said Mary.

"How dare you talk about custom? Go to hell! Tell your sister and leave me alone," he said and walked away a few feet and then came back. "Why do you ask me to take Cheseret to a doctor? Doesn't Kiriswa want her now that she's sick?"

"Stop talking like a child. I was trying to rescue you from people's eyes," said Mary and left. Cheseret's father started to go into his house, but halfway in he turned around and went to Taptamus' place. Taptamus was outside her house, angry with Kibet for letting the cows walk on her vegetables.

"Woman, what do you want from me? You have my daughter. What else do you want to steal from me? Your son has made up his mind to marry her. He has done so. Now she is sick. Doesn't he want her any longer? He wants me to take her to the doctor? Well, I have a message for you. I'm going to make sure your son takes her or you do. He wanted a wife. Now he has to do the job. Have you heard that?" he shouted.

"Yes," Taptamus agreed meekly.

"You'd better do it, and don't send Mary to me again. It will not work."

Taptamus did not say she hadn't sent Mary. She let him leave with his thoughts, but she was glad he had said at last that Cheseret was Kiriswa's wife. That evening she relayed the message to Senge and Cheptabut.

"We should not delay for long. Let one of us take her tomorrow," said Cheptabut.

"The doctor needs money," said Senge.

"Go back to bring money from Kiriswa or have Kiriswa bring the money by himself," said Taptamus. Senge left at dawn, and Kiriswa arrived at his mother's house in the evening the next day. He tried to find out from his mother if the kind of sickness Cheseret had contracted had happened to other circumcised girls. His mother said no, it had been a long time since the operation, and this was the first time she had seen an infection last that long.

"Do you think the women made a mistake when they circumcised her?" Kiriswa asked and scrambled to his feet.

"I could not see the mistake," said Taptamus. "I warn you, you can let yourself be driven insane if you don't deal with one problem at a time. I'm going to send Kibet to let Mary know some one is going to be there at dawn to take Cheseret to the doctor."

"I'm going there. Can I tell them?" asked Kiriswa.

"Yes, of course, but I think it is a good idea to send Kibet too. You may meet someone on your way and then not get there."

Kiriswa walked out of his mother's house helplessly and went straight to Mary's place. Mary saw him first and went in to tell Cheseret.

"Really? Kiriswa?" her eyes melted. Mary could hear her heart beating like a bell on a cow's neck.

"Oh, Chepsisei! I wish you knew who has arrived!" She smiled, and then she remembered Mary was there and pulled herself together again. Mary greeted Kiriswa and asked to be excused. She said she had to go to milk before it got dark.

"I will let Arap Walei know you have arrived," she said.

"I have to give you a message from mother." Kiriswa followed her outside. They talked, and he came back in. He sat and glanced outside. Cheseret was in seclusion. He should not see her. He moved across the room.

"Cheseret, can you show yourself to me? Oh, you know I yearn to see you," said Kiriswa shaking.

"Oh no! Someone may find us," said Cheseret feeling craving, fear, love, and desire simultaneously. Never had she felt like this. She was on her feet. Kiriswa went back to the door. He glanced out once more. He walked across the room and stood in front of Cheseret. He pulled her hood off as though his body was on fire and only seeing her face would save him from burning.

"Oh my! If I die now, I would be so happy," said Cheseret.

"Don't talk like that. Those words cut me like a knife," Kiriswa cleared his throat. "You're beautiful. I like knowing that this tall, skinny tomboy will be mine forever." He pulled her hood back on and rushed back to the sitting room. "I understand you are..." Kiriswa paused, "umm, sick?" he asked.

"Yes, how did you know?"

"My wife. Mother sent her back home to tell me."

"Have you seen Chelamai? Poor her. Her parents never let anyone go near their house."

"No, I have not. I've come here because you are sick, and I think I should deal with you first. Mother and I have talked about taking you to see a doctor tomorrow."

"No, I don't think you will be taking me or your mother, although I would have liked that better. My aunt and my uncle have arranged to take me. They say it is their responsibility," said Cheseret.

"Mary is taking you?"

"No, my uncle."

"I still think it would be better for my mother to take you. I don't like the idea of your uncle taking you when my mother is willing," said Kiriswa.

"You can talk to Mary, but I doubt she will change her mind. She wants to make my parents look as bad as possible, but what is there for me to do but what she says? Did you know my mother was sick too?"

"Yes, I know. Does this sickness keep you awake at night?"

"Not very much. It only hurts when I pass urine."

"It's getting chilly out here," Mary spoke from the door before coming in. The conversation shifted in a different direction when she came in. Cheseret did not want Kiriswa to hear about anything else but her, but that is just what happened. Mary told Kiriswa that she wanted Taptamus' family to be left out of Cheseret's problems because Cheseret's parents were alive, and Mary was going to take care of Cheseret because of Tapsalng'ot, and if it cost her a lot of money, she would go after Cheseret's father herself. She talked about Kap Metuk, Chelamai's family, of how hostile they had become even to the people who talked to Taptamus' family. Kiriswa's only answer to this was that they would come around in the end.

"There is nothing they can do. I have married their daughter. And now I would like to deal with one thing first. I understand you have arranged to have Cheseret taken to Chepterit by Arap Walei?" Kiriswa said.

"We have discussed it. I believe you are not happy with this arrangement because her uncle is going to take her rather than me," said Mary.

"You did what you had to, but under Cheseret's circumstances people will find it odd her uncle has taken her when my mother or my sister are willing to take her, Mary. Would you allow them to? Or at least allow one of them to accompany her?" asked Kiriswa.

"There is no need. Cheseret will be taken to my sister, Chebii's place, and she will take her to see the doctor."

"I must come to the point, Mary. I have come because I want my mother to go with Cheseret. And do not misunderstand me. It's an unfortunate situation that this sickness started after the circumcision," said Kiriswa.

"If they insist on going, then tell Taptamus they must leave at sunrise to catch the bus in Chepterwai," said Mary.

Taptamus had taken the bus once to Eldoret, and hadn't liked it, but she knew also that she could not ask Cheptabut to go. She had overheard Cheptabut telling Senge, "If I had courage, I would have said to mother, excuse me please, I cannot make sacrifices anymore. Look for other people to help you with your son's wives," and Taptamus would not forget that for a long time.

At dawn they waited at the bus stop. Taptamus begged to sit between Arap Walei and Cheseret. Cheseret assured her that she would hold Sukunwa with her right hand and Taptamus herself with her other hand. The bus appeared in the distance. Arap Walei stood on the road and waved his hands up and down in alternating salutes to stop the bus.

Cheseret took Sukunwa on her arm and Arap Walei took Taptamus. The sight of the trees and animals rushing by made Taptamus dizzy. She shielded her eyes with her hands until they reached their destination.

They arrived at noon and went straight to the doctor, instead of going to Chebii's house in Muguri, but were told they could not see him until the next morning. That evening, Taptamus and Chebii had discussed the disease, and Taptamus told her no one knew what it was. Cheseret's aunt said, "Leave this to me. My neighbour is outstanding in diagnosing sickness. She works for the doctor in Chepterwai. She is the one who gives the medicine. I will get her when she comes home."

After everyone had eaten, and gone, except for the three of them, Cheseret's aunt went to her friend. She came with a flashlight. It was getting dark.

"Let us have a look at it," she told Cheseret. She took one look and said, "Oh, women!"

"What?" asked Taptamus.

"Is anyone else in the house?" she asked.

"No one. What is it? Can't you say?" asked Chebii.

"How old are you, child?" she asked Cheseret.

"Sixteen. What is it?" Cheseret said.

"*Taganet.*"

"What?" inquired Cheseret, half wanting to shout at her and half trying to appear composed in front of the three older women. It was the custom for a girl or boy in seclusion to act in a calm and deliberate manner.

"I have seen this sickness before. I would not say you had it if you did not," said the nurse again.

"How dare you insist I have it? Did you give it to me?" Cheseret cried out.

"Cheseret! You should not talk like that. You are in seclusion. Haven't you learned that you cannot shout or argue under any circumstances. I called the nurse to help us," said Chebii.

"This is not help, you big witch! You are a three-legged devil! How dare you call your friend to say I have that sickness?"

"Cheseret! Let us talk about it calmly like grown-ups," said Taptamus. She turned to the nurse. "No, it cannot be true," she said.

"How do you explain this infection then which has been going on for months?" Chebii asked Taptamus.

"Why do you wish me to have this sickness so much?" asked Cheseret.

"I'm wondering, too, Cheseret. Stop maligning me," her aunt said.

The nurse was sure that her diagnosis was correct. "You will be made to feel better in no time," she said.

People knew little about nurses, doctors and Western medicine. The woman who came to see Cheseret was not a real nurse. She was a woman who went to church and worked for the man who called himself a doctor. This man was someone who after finishing primary school had found a job in a hospital as a medical assistant. When he left that job, he returned home and opened his own dispensary as a doctor.

People got better when they went to him. He knew that for a headache, aspirin should be taken; for malaria there was quinine; and penicillin was good for all infections. These were perhaps the only medicines the doctor gave to people in his entire life, but no one knew that. The traditional medicines were different. Each one was for a very specific ailment. There was no single, all-purpose medicine like penicillin, so people assumed that the injections and pills given by the doctor were all different and that each one was for a specific sickness.

Taptamus stood and faced the wall as though it was going to produce an answer to this overwhelming enigma. "Cheseret is a virgin. How can this happen?" she asked after a long silence.

Cheseret was now sitting numb, motionless. She thought about it. *Taganet* was something immoral — a vicious sickness. *Taganet* was syphilis. People say women catch it in the city, and I've never been in the city in my life, she thought.

"Don't let yourself be concerned, really," the nurse called her back to life. "Just go to the doctor tomorrow. In three days this sickness will be history. My sister had it once. Her husband brought it to her. She lost three children, but now she has five healthy children. It doesn't stop one from having children," she said. "When you go to see the doctor, ask for me. I will take you in right away," she added. Taptamus asked her to keep it among themselves because she was still not sure if this was really what it was.

The horror on Chebii's face did not go unnoticed. Shortly after her neighbour left, she listed the things Cheseret should not do around people because she had heard that the sickness could be passed on by drinking from the same cup, by passing raw meat to someone, by sleeping on a bed the sick person had slept on, and by passing a burning stick to someone else's hand.

"Maybe Cheseret got it this way at the place where she was circumcised," Chebii said. She asked Cheseret not to take her clothes off when she went to bed and Taptamus to go into a separate room. Taptamus said this was unnecessary, she had slept with Cheseret in the same room at home.

Taptamus and Cheseret were at the doctor's office at seven. The nurse rushed them into the examination room. In a short time the doctor arrived with a needle. He gave her an injection and said, "Come back tomorrow. You will be fine in three days." The doctor never said whether it was *taganet* or not, but when the infection cleared up, everyone said that was it. Even Taptamus did not know what to say any longer.

Before Taptamus left for home with Cheseret, she told Chebii she saw no reason to talk about it any further, now that Cheseret was well and the doctor had said the sickness would never come back.

"It is sinful and cruel to other people to cover up a deadly disease because you worry about it being known that Cheseret had it. Go home and find out if the woman who circumcised Cheseret has this sickness, and then stop her from giving it to more children," said Chebii.

When they got home, they sent word to where Cheseret had been circumcised to ask if there was anyone with the sickness to come forward, but everyone denied having it. On hearing that no one there had it, Cheseret's mother asked that Cheseret's virginity be taken away until she explained how she got the sickness. Mary was immobilized.

Tapchamgoi, who had checked Cheseret at first said, "What a shame her virginity has been taken away. Cheseret *was* a virgin. She must have got *taganet* from the woman who circumcised her. That woman must not have washed her hands after touching herself where she had the sickness."

Kiriswa came and told Cheseret, "I know you have not gone with anyone, but I don't know how it happened."

All Cheseret could say was, "I don't know."

Arap Temoet finally gave way, "She is all yours," he said. "Now that you have made her sick, there is no one else who wants her." He asked for bridewealth of four goats, four sheep, six cows, and five hundred shillings to be paid in the next two weeks. He did not want to wait for his clan elders to say how much he should be paid and took more than usual. Cheseret was denied the honour of being proclaimed a virgin, and her father never allowed her back home because no one in the history of his family had ever had such a debasing sickness. Nowadays, when it is known that penicillin can cure any kind of infection, it can be safely said that the women who operated on her were not expert, and she received poor care after the circumcision. A chronic infection resulted and confused people because it remained for so long.

CHAPTER TWELVE

*C*heseret was taken back to Mary's. Now that she knew she would never go back to her mother's house, she learned to be happy with what she had. She paid attention to supporting Chepsisei during the last stages of her pregnancy. One day Chepsisei was sick, the next day she was better. Taptamus said that for the first child, some people could be in labour for days and days, even for a month. She told Mary that Chepsisei should not be left alone with Cheseret. She would not be able to help her because of Chepsisei's inability to understand what to do. For two weeks, Cheseret got to see her mother every other day. When Mary was away, Tapsalng'ot came to keep an eye on Chepsisei until her sister came back.

Chepsisei moaned, sweated and cried when the baby came out of her womb. She spoke with real words for the first time in her life. She watched the women washing the baby, and then she extended her hands. She said, "My baby, give me." Tears poured down from the women's eyes. They were touched. The baby had opened the mouth of a mother who had not talked since she was born. That answered Mary's question if she was still wondering what to do with the baby. She got the answer. Chepsisei wanted her baby.

The happiness that showed on Chepsisei's face was mystifying. No one would ever have imagined her changing this way. The blankness that had been on her face ever since she was born was gone, replaced with a look of complete serenity. Her heart was full with love for her baby daughter. She did not say much, but her eyes alone spoke more than words, laughing and twinkling like midnight stars. The feeling that emanated from her could only be understood by women who had endured the pain of labour and the relief after a baby was born.

When Taptamus and Tapchamgoi had finished cleaning the baby, everybody came to sit around and have fun choosing a name. Since the Nandi named children according to the time they were born, Tapchamgoi suggested the name Chepkorir, 'Dawn'. The others tried it out, then Taptamus asked, "Is it really dawn?"

People usually used animals to tell time, since there were no clocks. Mary spoke. "Listen, all the animals are quiet. It must be midnight. Even the crickets have stopped chirping, and the frogs are no longer croaking. We should name her Chepkemboi 'Midnight'. Chepkemboi Lydia Cheptarus."

"Lydia? What kind of name is that?" asked Taptamus.

"It's a name I picked up in Chepterit Church," said Mary. Everybody stared at her.

"Who is she?" asked Cheseret's mother.

"It's just a name I heard in church."

"I thought it was like you. You told us you were reincarnated as Mary the mother of Jesus, didn't you?" said Tapsalng'ot.

"No, I was not reincarnated. I was baptized as Mary Magdalene, not Mary the mother of Jesus."

"Is Lydia at all related to Mary Magdalene?" asked Taptamus. The women were confused. A central tenet of Nandi belief was that nothing was done without a reason or a meaning. Mary alone was "educated" in the ways of the outside world. She had lived with her husband when he was in the police, and then, later, going to the Catholic church had widened her horizons. She knew that things could be done without reason or meaning.

"I like the name Lydia because it sounds musical to me," she said.

"Yes, I think the name is attractive," said Cheseret.

Chepsisei was given cold milk to drink and asked to take two steps forward and backward to straighten her hips. In the meantime, the women discussed how to go about introducing the baby to her. Tapchamgoi suggested that she or Taptamus pretend to give the baby the breast for Chepsisei to get some idea of what she should do.

"Let us warm her breast first before the baby sucks," said Taptamus. Mary warmed some water, and Taptamus washed Chepsisei's breasts. Then she set the baby gently on her lap. A second layer of radiance came over her face as though she was glad she had finally got to hold her baby. Taptamus took Chepsisei's breast and placed the nipple in the baby's mouth. She felt Chepsisei's body stiffen and then relax.

For days and days, Chepsisei clung to the baby. She looked at her baby's hands, feet and eyes. Nothing could make her take her eyes off it. She got upset when the baby was asleep and tried to force it to stay awake. Her temper rose when Mary told her to leave the baby alone to sleep. She shouted, cried, picked the baby up, and would not put her down again for the rest of the day.

Mary and Cheseret did as much for the baby as Chepsisei would allow them to do. Things were not simple at night. Mary had to sleep with Chepsisei and the baby to make sure that Chepsisei didn't roll on it. When Chepsisei's spirits were high, she put Lydia in the middle and allowed her mother to touch the baby. When she was upset with Mary and she felt as though her mother should not touch the baby, she turned her back on Mary, and put her baby on the other side. Then she slipped into a stubborn silence. No matter what her mother did, she would not respond.

This went on for some days. Finally, when Tapchamgoi came to visit Mary and saw Chepsisei's behaviour, she suggested that Sukunwa be brought over during the daytime.

"It might encourage Chepsisei to let people hold her baby when she sees people holding Sukunwa," said Tapchamgoi. Taptamus brought Sukunwa to Cheseret every morning with a gourd of milk, and Chepsisei was happy. Cheseret had a baby, and she had one too. Sukunwa was seven months. She could smile and crawl to Mary when Mary called her. When Cheseret fed Sukunwa, Chepsisei fed Lydia. When Cheseret put Sukunwa down for a nap, Chepsisei put Lydia down too. From that moment on, the two children were raised together. When Taptamus came to take Sukunwa in the evening, she cried, wanting to stay. When Lydia began to notice things around her, she wanted to follow Sukunwa home too.

Ever since she had returned from Chepterit, Taptamus had been aware that Kilel was edgy and refusing to talk to her. Walking home with Sukunwa, she wondered what he was planning to do now that the Metuk family had rejected all of their attempts to speak with them. Kilel came home early one evening and spent almost half an hour twisting his moustache. It was an effort to get a word out of him. He just kept on nodding at everything she said and twisting his moustache.

"What happened today? You're not talking?"

"I have this unbearable pain in my head."

"Did you talk with Kiriswa about what to do with Kap Metuk?"

"Kiriswa was about to start, but I cut him short. Kap Metuk! I am disgusted with Kap Metuk. If everything were up to me, I would let them do what they want with their daughter."

"You've made your point. I'm unhappy with them too, but we don't want to be like them. We will do what is expected of us if they don't budge," said Taptamus.

"Do you want us to go forward to ask Kap Metuk for their daughter's hand?"

"Yes, I think we should even though they have made it clear they don't want us at their door."

This made Kilel pause. He sympathized with Taptamus. She was desperate, while he was only exasperated. She felt it was necessary to work to save their name, to work hard so that people would not say, "You see, her son kidnapped Kap Metuk's daughter, but it ended in disappointment. The mother failed to work hard to gain their respect." Kilel remembered there was only one family Kap Metuk would listen to. He decided he would go to see them in the morning. He told Taptamus he was too tired to talk anymore about it that evening.

"Let us talk again about it tomorrow." He went to Tapchamgoi's where he slept. Tapchamgoi had dinner ready when he arrived, and afterward they drank home-brewed beer as usual and went to bed.

He left the house at sunrise for Kap Kilach, Tolony's parents and the only family in the neighbourhood Kap Metuk would speak to. They were in-laws — Kap Metuk's son had married Kap Kilach's daughter, Tolony. Kilel spoke to Arap Kilach about the interminable difficulties they were having with Kap Metuk.

"What can we do for you?" asked Arap Kilach. He was not known to talk in circles. He liked coming right to the point.

"We need some help from you and your family. Take us to Kap Metuk. I know this way is backwards. We are not supposed to go until after we have heard from them, but I have been in Kamasai for a long time, and I would like to put Taptamus' mind at ease before I return home."

"Yes, as you say, it is backwards. This is how I see it. You should let Kap Metuk cool down. The time will come. Their daughter has to come out of seclusion, and then they will have to let her get married. You people should be ready then. It's not easy to marry off a daughter who has already been engaged to another man. Who would want her?" asked Arap Kilach.

"Taptamus doesn't know it is backward, or she knows and just wants people to see she is making the first move."

"What are you suggesting?"

"We should take her to see for herself because she would be devastated if I left before we went to Kap Metuk."

"I have spoken my thoughts, but we can take you if it is important for Taptamus."

"Yes, we don't have anything to lose," said Kilel.

The next day, Taptamus took Sukunwa to Mary's early in the morning and came back. Kilel, Arap Kilach and his wife had arrived in the meantime. They did not talk about Kap Metuk because it was believed to be bad luck to talk about what you were going to do before it was done. On their way, each of them broke off a sprig of *korosek* — a special bush which one carried when going to ask for the hand of a girl in marriage. The two men walked ahead, and the women followed. Traditionally they were supposed to go by the back door to the part of the house reserved for sheep and goats. There, under normal circumstances, they would have remained until the relatives

213

and the parents of the girl came to listen to what they had to say. Arap Metuk did not allow this to happen. He was outside. He stood and watched them come. When they were about 100 yards away, he walked away without showing any sign of having seen them. He walked past the house, and Arap Kilach had to move quickly to catch him. This was a bad sign. It was extremely rude to refuse to listen to visitors coming as a delegation.

"We've come, and it seems as though you are leaving," Arap Kilach said.

"I have somewhere to go, and I hope you don't mind. I'm not taking the house and the wife. If you want something, go in and ask her," Arap Metuk said. Taptamus stood meekly, but her heart sank to the bottom of her stomach. Kilel and Arap Kilach's wife were silent. They wished Arap Metuk would have it in his heart to listen to them. Arap Metuk stood with his face lowered for a few seconds, and then he lifted up his head to face where Taptamus was standing.

"Unfortunately, I don't seem to get through to these people. I told this woman's daughter Cheptabut where we stood. I would have thought she would have passed this message to her mother. They spend a good deal of time together. Don't they discuss things? I don't ever want to see them on my door," he said. "I'm glad you came. You may help them to understand what I'm saying. I have nothing to discuss with them," he added.

"People forgive. Can't you forgive them?" asked Arap Kilach.

"I have spoken and I will not allow you to question me. Either you leave or I leave," said Arap Metuk.

"If I were you I would leave," said Tabaes peeping out from inside the house. "What my husband has just given you is important advice. Leave our family alone. There will never be any communication between us," she said before returning to what she had been doing.

The men led the way back home again. They pulled away from the women. Arap Kilach's wife, Tamutwol, trying to be helpful, told Taptamus to give them time.

"They will come around. Who would have known my husband would ever talk to me again after our Tolony got herself pregnant."

214

Taptamus was watching the men ahead and trying to listen attentively in the hope they were talking about what to do next. But she could not hear what they were saying. The animal skin clothes the two women wore were noisy as the women walked, and Taptamus could only hear the men's laughter. She could have run after them to hear what they were talking about, but in order to prevent the scandal of an affair, it was a custom that married women not walk intermingled with men. Taptamus turned to Tamutwol.

"I wonder if Chelamai noticed that we were outside?" she asked ignoring what Tamutwol had been saying.

"I suppose so. Her mother knew we were there, and if she didn't, I'm sure she heard her mother talking to us. "Don't worry, Taptamus. Even Chelamai knows you have tried. I was lucky. I went there yesterday after Kilel left our place. Arap Metuk was not at home when I got there, and Tabaes had gone to the river to fetch some water. As you may guess Chelamai and her sister-in-law Tolony were at home. I got to talk to Chelamai. She is quiet, but believe me she cannot be intimidated easily. You know, I was feeling sorry for her at first, but when I had finished talking, I knew she did not need to be pitied. She had made up her mind. She knew what she wanted to do. I told her that I hoped her parents would find a soft spot for Kiriswa because he would feel bad if her parents were to marry her to someone else. Taptamus, you could not imagine what she said. She said that nothing, nothing in the world could make her marry someone she didn't like. And she was so self-assured when she said that! I could not imagine her speaking like that? I hope that after you hear how confident Chelamai is, you will be confident too," said Tamutwol.

"I have the feeling that both Chelamai and Kiriswa think they will be together in the end no matter what, but I don't want them to run away again. We want to do it right this time."

"That's not your problem. I'm sure Kap Metuk knows this will happen if they don't sit down and talk. It would not be your shame if they ran away again."

The men went by way of Kap Walei, and Tamutwol took Taptamus to her place for a cup of tea. Taptamus was still feeling down.

"Now, let's try to talk about something else," said Tamutwol. She set a teapot and two cups on the floor and then sat on the clay bench near the fireplace. She poured the tea. "How are Chepsisei and the baby?" she asked.

"Both the mother and the baby are doing wonderfully," said Taptamus.

"I managed to pass by there yesterday, but I didn't get to see the baby. She was in bed."

"She is a lovely little thing."

"What do the family think about Musimba, the father of the baby?"

Taptamus hesitated a moment. "I have no idea. I never heard anyone discussing him."

"I'm sorry. Are you surprised I knew Musimba was the baby's father? The family did not talk about it, but this is Kamasai. People do know, believe me," said Tamutwol.

"I was not trying to conceal it from you, Tamutwol. It is just that in my present situation, I have not bothered with anyone else's problems."

"If Mary has not discussed him with you, that means they are trying to sweep him out of their lives. Some say Mary arranged for him to have the baby with her daughter, and some say it was a rape. I have no idea which one is right, rape or arrangement."

"It doesn't matter really how it was conceived. Chepsisei is so happy with the baby, we should be happy for her too and let her parents worry about the rest."

"I'm sure they are glad either way. They should be in debt to Musimba the rest of their lives. I'm sure she would never have had one otherwise. She is so handicapped."

"I have to leave. Kibet is coming home for lunch," said Taptamus. She felt that this was too much talking about Kap Walei. She wondered what else Tamutwol knew. I'm sure she knew about Cheseret's sickness as long as Tapchamgoi knew about it, thought Taptamus. She went by Mary's to see Sukunwa before going home.

216

Kilel slept at his sister-in-law, Taptamus', that night, so they could talk. He was leaving the next day.

"I think I must leave for home tomorrow, Taptamus. I feel that my staying will not do anything to bring Kap Metuk into any agreement with us. I suggest we let them come to tell us what they want when they are ready. In the meantime, I should go home to help my wife weed the crops. I don't have anything to do here. We were kicked away when we went there, and what else is there to tell them?"

"Nothing at all. It's going to take me a long time to recover from today's rejection."

"I have also told Kiriswa not to be so insensible as to think he can run away again with Chelamai because he is afraid her parents will never let them be married."

"Did he agree to that?"

"You shouldn't worry whether he agreed or not. He knows what to do. I won't go for long — I will be back in two months."

"There is no need for you to come back in two months. I suggest you wait until I hear Chelamai is coming out of seclusion. Then I will send a child to call you." Kilel was grateful for Taptamus' thoughtfulness.

"And of course this does not mean that if you need me any time in between, you should not send for me," Kilel added.

CHAPTER THIRTEEN

The weeks and months went by. Taptamus took Sukunwa to Mary's every morning and brought her back home in the evening. Every two months she took Cheseret, Chepsisei and the children for a week or two to give Mary a rest. Lydia was now a handful. Sukunwa was taking a few steps and could not be kept still. When she walked away, Lydia crawled after her, and Chepsisei did not like it. She was uncomfortable when Lydia moved away from her, and she detested Sukunwa for this. The baby liked Sukunwa more than it liked her. It came to the point that when Sukunwa touched Chepsisei, she brushed her away.

Cheseret was the first one who noticed Chepsisei's reaction and she told Mary, but Mary would not hear of it. Cheseret also had some trouble explaining exactly what it was.

"I have seen Chepsisei eye Sukunwa with devilish eyes. I think she hates her," she told Mary.

"You cannot know what someone like Chepsisei is thinking. Don't be suspicious. You have to see her doing it first," said Mary.

"I have seen that if Sukunwa happens to wander outside in front of Chepsisei, Chepsisei rushes after her and shuts the door behind her. Isn't that something I should tell you?"

"I will keep an eye on her."

Just as they were talking, Lydia went crawling after Sukunwa. Chepsisei waddled up and took Sukunwa by one arm. She opened the door, dropped her outside, and then closed the door. Cheseret was there as the door closed. She opened it and brought Sukunwa back in. Chepsisei snatched Lydia up, went to her room, and closed the door, muttering incomprehensibly. Mary was embarrassed. Cheseret stood there, her eyes daring Mary to say something.

"Leave her alone. I will deal with her later," Mary said.

Cheseret went to feed Sukunwa. She did not want to hear Mary say that. Cheseret knew that since Chepsisei had given birth, Mary had lost her control over her. Chepsisei was behaving like a wildcat. Cheseret was tired of being in seclusion. She was worn out living under the same roof with Mary and her daughter. They were deadly boring people who went to bed every night at eight, and their sole preoccupation in the home was Lydia.

"If I rot in this home for one more month, I will go out of my mind," she told her mother once.

"Cheseret, my sister is not dull and boring. You just don't like her, and if you can't put up with being in seclusion for one or two years, you will never make it in married life. Seclusion is a test, but even if you pass it, there is no guarantee that your marriage will be successful. Staying married is for longer than one year, and many times things go wrong and marriages become boring. Then you start living day by day. You don't know if you're going to last until the next day," her mother said.

Cheseret listened to her mother. It was the only thing she could do for her. She knew her mother would not say things she didn't believe just for her own selfish interests. She thought her mother was the greatest. If only my mother knew what Kiriswa was like as a man, Cheseret thought, she would understand why I want to get out of this dull place.

"Cheseret!" called Mary at the door.

"Mary is calling, mother," said Cheseret to her mother.

"Go and see what she wants."

"I don't see why she always calls me and not Chepsisei."

"Don't be ridiculous! You're not like Chepsisei," Tapsalng'ot said as she went to see what her sister wanted.

"Do you need some help?" Tapsalng'ot asked her sister. Mary was seated, leaning against a load of firewood.

"Yes! Undo this firewood for me."

"You are silly, Mary. Why did you carry so much firewood?"

"I carried this much so I wouldn't have to go back tomorrow for more."

"I was about to leave before you arrived. Do you mind?" asked Tapsalng'ot as she released the firewood from Mary's back.

"Have you made some tea for yourself?" asked Mary.

"No, I forgot. I was playing with Lydia and talking to the girls. I will have some another day."

"Would you help me to take this firewood in? In the meantime I will tell you something I heard from the people I was gathering firewood with."

"Oh Mary, do I have to help you first before you tell me? I'm late," said Tapsalng'ot. She started carrying the firewood in. "Start talking now."

"I was invited to go for firewood with Tolony, Taptamus and Cheptabut. I can't remember now how the whole thing started. I was about fifty yards away when I heard Tolony saying that the family were getting ready to have Chelamai come out of seclusion. Maybe in two months from now. Tolony said they have been gathering firewood for the last four days," said Mary.

"Are they going to prepare everything by themselves? I mean don't Tolony and her mother-in-law, Tabaes, want to invite us to help them with the firewood?" asked Tapsalng'ot.

"Don't ask me. I have no idea. Mind you I would not be shocked if her husband is like your husband."

"Do you think he told his wife to do the whole thing by herself?"

"It's not against the law for a man to make his wife do things alone, is it?"

"Can I leave now, sister dear? You can do the rest for yourself," said Tapsalng'ot.

"Why are you always in a hurry even when your husband is not at home? Have you been conditioned into hurrying always? Be happy when he's not at home. Have fun! Live! Wait for me to make you tea."

"I can't. Maybe he will arrive while you are making me late."

"Where is he anyway? I haven't seen him for three days. I'm not missing him, mind you."

"No one is asking you. I don't know where he went. He never tells anyone where he's going or when he will return when he leaves, but I hope he comes back soon because I'm beginning to worry."

"Are you really? Do you miss him? Please don't make me cry. The only time you are like a human being is when he is away. You should be glad."

"I'm not glad. I will see you tomorrow, Mary."

"Aren't you telling Cheseret and Chepsisei good-bye?"

"They are singing. Tell them I'm gone."

Arap Walei and a guest Tapsalng'ot did not know were sitting on the knoll a little ways from the house where the men made their evening fire and sat and talked. They both said "How are you?" to Tapsalng'ot who returned the greeting and stayed awhile to talk to her brother-in-law. He asked her if Mary was fixing something for dinner, and Tapsalng'ot said she hadn't started when she left.

"I think we should go up to the house. That would make her start dinner," said Arap Walei.

"Is the guest mine or yours?" asked Tapsalng'ot.

"He is ours for today," said Arap Walei.

"Do I know him? I don't seem to recognize him."

"I came here four years ago at night. You couldn't see me as it was a little dark," said the guest.

"Have you ever heard the name Kipsugut?" asked Arap Walei.

"Yes, I have heard my husband mention it. He is not at home today. He left a few days ago and didn't say when he was coming back," said Tapsalng'ot.

"Bamuru, we are leaving you. Let Kipsugut and I go to see what Mary is doing," said Arap Walei to his sister-in-law.

"Can you come tomorrow? Maybe my husband will arrive tonight. He will be upset with me if I tell him you were here and I did not ask you to stay for dinner," said Tapsalng'ot.

"We will come," said Arap Walei.

They went up to the house. Mary was at home. "Is the food ready?"

"Almost," Mary said.

"Look after the guest. I will be back," her husband said. Mary was able to ask the guest his name but nothing more before Arap Walei came back. The guest was hungry, and he ate well, but Arap Walei barely touched his food. Mary noticed this when she went out to bring in the dishes they had used. The men did not stay, but hurried away. Something is going on, Mary thought. The men are in a hurry with everything. She remembered seeing the face of the guest before, but could not recall where or when. She went to her sister's and asked her if she had noticed anything wrong with the man. Mary kept repeating his name, Kipsugut Arap Mirmir. There was something bad about that name. Finally she remembered.

"This man is feared more than malaria. He's like a cat. He never dies. He still raids when nobody else does anymore. The police beat him, tied his testicles, and jailed him for two years. After he came out, in one week he was out raiding again. The last I heard, he was caught by the people he raided from. We thought he was killed. But here he is," said Mary. "Oh god, I don't know what he's up to," she added.

"I don't think Arap Walei would want to do anything like raid with him," said Tapsalng'ot.

"I'm not afraid my husband would go raiding with him. He's smarter than that. I'm afraid he's brought some stolen cows here. You know what it means to be caught with stolen cattle."

"Men are something else. They know raiding now is like committing suicide, and they still do it."

"I will let you know what he's up to tomorrow," said Mary. When she got home, she waited for the men to come back. When they didn't come, she went to bed. She knew they would spend the night in their guest house anyway. Arap Walei came to wake Mary at the main house before sunrise and she went out. Taptamus and Cheptabut were with her husband.

"Mary, I beg you on account of the initiates! Contain your grief even though it's hard, I know," said Taptamus. Mary felt her knees weaken.

"What is it?" She turned to her husband.

"A death has occurred."

"Oh, poor Taptamus," she said. She had thought of Kiriswa first.

"No, no. Cheseret's father had an accident, and he,…well, there is nothing to say. He is finished," said Arap Walei.

"Has my sister been told?" asked Mary.

"Not yet," said Arap Walei. "Taptamus, arrange things here. I have a lot to do." Arap Walei left. Taptamus knew everything; she had been told what had happened. Arap Temoet had been speared returning from a cattle raid a thousand yards from his house along the Cheboiywa River, the boundary between the Kabarasi and the Nandi. The raiding party let the cattle drink and graze. After they had come sixty miles, they thought they were safe, and Arap Temoet had announced to Kipsugut, the organizer of the raid, that he was going to take a nap. Kipsugut told him it was not a good idea, but he did not insist they move on. He realized Arap Temoet was too tired to go any further, and everyone was beginning to relax anyway since they were on the border.

Arap Temoet took his nap. He laid his shield on the left, his spear on the right, and lay down on his back in case he should have to get up in a hurry. In what he thought was a dream he heard a voice that said, "Help yourself now. I can't do anything. We have been surrounded by the enemy." Two enemies had cut Kipsugut and Arap Temoet off from the rest of their party. Kipsugut had already thrown his spear at one of them and missed. Now he had only his shield and a short sheath-knife which was no help, but he was swift with his shield. The two enemies threw their spears, and he deflected them away. When his enemies shouted, "Let's run! We've lost our weapons," the yelling woke Arap Temoet. He got up and saw that another enemy was approaching him. From behind, Kipsugut threw a knife at the one in front of Arap Temoet. He went down, and Kipsugut felt relieved, but as Arap Temoet lifted up his spear and shield, a spear flew out of nowhere into his back. Kipsugut's eyes searched the area, and he saw a man running away. He finished off the one he had thrown the knife at, threw his body in the river, and carried the bleeding Arap Temoet home.

Arap Temoet said, "I'm sorry, I heard you in my dream. You were asking me to get up. If I had, I would have killed them all." Those were the last words he spoke.

Mary could not believe it. It took a long time before anything at all registered on her face. Finally she burst into tears.

"I hated him, but I didn't wish him to die in the forest without his family," said Mary. She cried and cried.

Taptamus hugged her and said, "I have cried all night, too. It would have been easier if he had been sick. It would not be as much of a shock as this."

"Who is going to do it? Who is going to tell Cheseret?" asked Mary.

"Cheptabut has to arrange them first, and we should have Tapchamgoi present to help with changing the initiates' clothes," said Taptamus.

Tapchamgoi came, and they went in. Cheseret and Chepsisei were told not to wear the clothes they wore in seclusion. They were given everyday clothing, and they were told they were not in seclusion any more and not to cover their faces. Mary stood in the middle of the house silently.

"What is this for?" Cheseret asked her.

"We have to take you some place together with Chepsisei."

They were taken to Cheseret's home. Cheseret thought something was wrong, but she could not imagine what it was. Mary went in first to stand beside her sister. Arap Walei, Kiptai, and Arap Metuk also came in to give support. When Tapsalng'ot saw her daughter she said, "Tell me! I can take it! Tell me! Tell me! I have not seen my son since yesterday, and my husband for four days. Which one is dead?"

"Kimaiyo Arap Temoet met with an accident and passed away yesterday afternoon," said Arap Walei.

Cheseret and her mother hugged each other and cried on one another's shoulder. Chepsisei cried and Taptamus held her in her arms with Lydia on her shoulder. Arap Walei and the other men went out. They sat and talked in low voices. Nandi men did not show emotion or sorrow. By the time a man came out of seclusion, he had been taught that men carried death. When they went raiding, they knew they would either die or come back. When wild animals were numerous, they knew also they could die anytime protecting the family from an elephant or a buffalo or a lion. Or they could be killed in war. Either way, those who were the survivors would not display the emotion they felt inside.

Tapsalng'ot asked if her son had been notified his father was dead.

"Yes," Arap Walei said, "he's in isolation with Kipsugut." Kiptarus Arap Maiyo knew ahead of everybody. His father had been brought in with a spear in his spine, and was still alive but paralyzed. His mouth was dry, and his eyes were white. There was almost no blood left in his body. Kipsugut left him in Arap Walei's hut and tried to find someone to help. He found Arap Walei and Arap Kilach. He told them the news, and they rushed back with him. Arap Temoet's eyes fixed on them. He didn't blink. Arap Kilach suggested his spine be cut to remove the spear although none of them had any hope. Arap Metuk was called along with Kiptarus. Arap Walei's cow hide was taken and laid out in the bushes behind the hut. His son held his father's shoulders down while Arap Metuk cut his spine to remove the spear. Arap Temoet did not even twitch when the broken spear was pulled out, but there was a look of relief in his eyes. When Arap Walei saw this, he went to Kap Temoet to tell Tapsalng'ot about the accident. He called into the house for Tapsalng'ot when he arrived, but nobody answered. As he turned around to leave, he saw Kipsugut coming. "Arap Temoet is dead," Kipsugut said "and Arap Metuk thought Tapsalng'ot should be told."

"Let us ask Taptamus what should be done in this situation with the initiates in seclusion," said Arap Walei. Taptamus said not to tell Tapsalng'ot until the initiates' clothing had been changed.

At night fall, Kiptarus stood and watched while his father's body was taken west to his last resting place. He was laid down with his

226

head pointing west for his spirit to follow the setting sun. Then when the sun rose, his new spirit would rise along with it.

The people who touched his body went to the river, shaved their heads, and washed the shadow of death away. Then they were given a sacred oil to anoint their bodies. When this was done, they returned to the hut where the death had taken place. They would stay there for four days and not eat with their hands or drink milk. They would eat vegetables until the ceremony of the Slaughtering of a Goat had been done to purify them.

The rest of the brothers and sisters and close relatives stayed at Arap Temoet's home mourning for twelve days. Then their hair was shaved. Tapsalng'ot, who was now a widow, put away all the things she had worn when her husband was alive. All her ornaments, earrings, necklaces and the beaded animal skin skirts married women wore were all laid away until they could be purified and given to close relatives. Tapsalng'ot would wear her widow's clothing for the rest of her life. Cheseret had to wait. Her mother could not attend her daughter's wedding until she had gone through the purification ceremonies to take her out of mourning.

In the meantime, Chelamai was taken out of seclusion. The people in the neighbourhood were invited, but the members of Taptamus' family were not. The relatives from both sides were invited: Arap Metuk's brothers and their wives; Tabaes' brothers and their wives; the grandparents; second, third and fourth cousins. Taptamus' family stayed close by, hoping to learn what was going to happen when Chelamai was out of seclusion.

"I'm at your mercy. Tell me what they are saying," Taptamus told Tamutwol. Mary was present along with Tapchamgoi.

"I have heard some people whispering," said Tapchamgoi, who then turned and said, "Isn't that true, Tamutwol?"

"Yes," agreed Tamutwol. Mary rolled her eyes in disapproval at the way Tapchamgoi was always the first one to know everything.

"I think Kiriswa and Chelamai should go away and not come back until they have two children," Tapchamgoi proposed.

"Stop putting your good-for-nothing ideas into other peoples' minds. Explain what you said you heard people whispering about first," demanded Mary.

"I was there, Mary, and you were not. And besides, I'm not talking to you. I'm telling Taptamus. I know everything that is going on there. Tamutwol can back me up on this. Wasn't Chelamai's maternal uncle so upset that he wanted to leave because he didn't like the way the man who had been brought to marry Chelamai was being pampered?" asked Tapchamgoi.

"Yes," answered Tamutwol. "All the women and one of Chelamai's maternal uncles want her to marry Kiriswa. The women only think and whisper around. They dare not speak out. Who would pay attention to what they said or take any account of it? When Chelamai's uncle pointed out that it was right to let Chelamai marry the man she had chosen, the women tried to support him. 'Don't give us your opinions. No one wants to know what you think,' Arap Metuk told them. 'The women are right because they know what Chelamai wants, and you don't know,' said Chelamai's uncle. 'I said they don't have any say here. Someday you will be in my position and I want to see how right you think they are then,' said Arap Metuk. Chelamai's uncle was so upset he wanted to leave yesterday," said Tamutwol.

"Has Arap Metuk said who he wants to marry his daughter?" asked Taptamus.

"I don't think Arap Metuk himself has anyone he wants, but his brother has brought along a man from Siwa. His wife told us yesterday that the man stank," said Tamutwol.

"How?" asked Taptamus.

"Both he and Arap Metuk's brother are alcoholics."

"Why do they want to marry Chelamai to a drunken man? To help him stop drinking?" asked Mary.

"No, Arap Metuk's brother is helping himself. The man doesn't need any help — he is married. Arap Metuk's sister-in-law said her husband brought him to marry Chelamai so he wouldn't have to repay the money he had borrowed from him to support his drinking habit," said Tapchamgoi.

"Don't forget the man not only has another wife. They have six children and he is quite a bit older," said Tamutwol.

"What a mess!" said Taptamus.

The festivities connected with the ceremonies went on for a week. The ceremony of Crossing the Bridge of Youth to Adulthood was held on Sunday. At dawn on the following Monday the women had concluded the ceremonies inside the house and gone to a sacred, woman-made dam to complete the ritual. It was all new for Chelamai. By the time they reached the dam, she was chilled to the bone. The wind emptying out of the gorge between the mountains was bitterly cold. She stood and shivered. When she saw the sacred dam and the icy water, she said, "I hope we don't have to go into the water."

"Don't speak anything negative. Do as you are told and follow the leader," her mother said. Four women submerged themselves in the water, and Chelamai watched. Later she was guided into the water herself. After an hour they were finished, and everybody put their clothes back on and went back to the house chanting on the way. That afternoon a goat was slaughtered and its entrails read to see Chelamai's future. The stomach of the goat augured well. Her marriage would be good, she would have children, there would be no hunger, and no war would occur in her lifetime.

In the afternoon the women started the song sung only for virgin girls, in which the father and the daughter jumped together. Each jumped straight up into the air, trying to outdo the other, for twenty minutes. When it was finished, Chelamai was given a virgin's headdress of ivory and cowry shells to wear on her head. The headdress had a long tailpiece ornamented with shells and at the end there was a small bell which jingled as she moved. Afterwards the men, who had come out to watch Arap Metuk and his daughter jump, went back into the guest house to continue celebrating. The women finished decorating Chelamai.

Now Chelamai was out of seclusion, and she was asked what she wanted to do. She said she wanted to go for a walk. Her mother said she could not allow that unless her father agreed.

229

"It's not difficult to go and ask him, is it?" asked Chelamai's aunt, Langok.

Everyone said, "Not me. I don't want the responsibility."

"All right, I'll ask him myself," said Chelamai's aunt.

"'It's your responsibility,'he said," she announced when she returned. Tabaes called her aside and told her not to take Chelamai anywhere near Taptamus' place if she wanted to avoid any problems.

"I don't see that it is necessary to tell me. I know why her father made me responsible for her," said Chelamai's aunt. Tabaes told her younger daughter to go with them anyway. She did not trust her sister. She knew she liked Kiriswa very much.

The women walked down to the river and sat on the stones and looked at each other. Chelamai hoped she would meet someone from Taptamus' family. Her aunt knew how she felt, but there was nothing she could say or do to help her now. "Your mother said..." She was about to describe what Chelamai's mother had told her even though she had told Chelamai when they left the house.

"I know what mother told you," said Chelamai. "I'm not supposed to go near Taptamus' place and you have told me."

"We probably should go back home if we want your father to let us out again," said Langok. She had a lot to tell Chelamai, but it was hard now that Chelamai's sister was with them.

That evening, Langok knew she had to move quickly. She asked Tolony, "You know what I'm up to, don't you?"

"Yes, I think I do," said Tolony.

"We have to move fast. We are not going to let her marry that drunken old man tomorrow."

That evening they took Chelamai's things one by one. Soon everything was gone. There was a chain of women to get Chelamai out of the house. Inside were Langok and Tolony. Outside were Tamutwol and Cheseret, who had been brought in to help. Everything happened quickly. Kiriswa was waiting at Tamutwol's as the women arrived. They left Chelamai in Kiriswa's hands, and Tamutwol took Cheseret back home. Then she rushed back to Kap Metuk to fix up her own alibi.

Tamutwol went to the house where the reception was being held. A lot of women were there cheering for the men as they sang their praise songs. The other women, who were tired, were in the main house. Some were chatting and drinking home-made beer, and some were fast asleep around the fireplace.

Later in the evening, Chelamai's grandmother came back from the reception to the main house.

"I'm going to bed," she said as she entered the house. She went into the bedroom she shared with Chelamai.

"Lamaiya! Are you asleep?" She called Chelamai by her nickname. "Lamaiya!" she called again. "Is Chelamai out there?" she asked the women in the sitting room.

"No! Isn't she in her room?" asked Tolony.

"No! She is not," said the grandmother.

"Oh well, maybe she's out, but it's weird. She has not passed by here since I came in," said Tolony.

The women ran around in search for her in the places they suspected she might be before telling her mother. Tabaes was at the reception, and Tolony went to call her to help. They ran from house to house searching, but a little before midnight they admitted she was gone.

"I don't want anyone ruining my sleep. The men can wait until tomorrow to be told. They are drunk anyway. The two brothers can be unpleasant. I know — they are my sons," said the grandmother and went back to bed.

Tabaes went to look for her sister, Langok. She hasn't come back from the reception, she thought. "When did Chelamai leave?" she asked.

"What are you talking about. You are insulting me. You had better apologize. Are you suggesting I know where your daughter is?" asked Langok.

"Come on, surrender, Langok. I'm not suggesting anything. I know you arranged for Chelamai to leave. You are not that smart you know. I hope for your sake Arap Metuk doesn't even point a finger at me. If he touches me, I will kill you. You'd better deal with him. I don't think that will be very difficult for you if you can smuggle Chelamai under the noses of all of these guests," said Tabaes and walked back toward the main house.

"You can't drop the whole problem in my lap. She's your daughter. She wanted to go," said Langok and went back into the reception. She took Tamutwol aside, "I'm ruined. My sister knows I'm responsible for Chelamai's leaving."

"Did she mention anyone else?" asked Tamutwol.

"No, everyone is safe but me."

"She doesn't know then. She's only guessing."

"Guessing or not, she guessed right," said Langok. "She may guess about you later. I wouldn't look so carefree if I were you."

Arap Metuk's mother got up at six. She wanted to be the one who took the news to her son.

"Where in the hell were you all when she left?" Arap Metuk inquired bitterly when his mother told him the news.

"Don't go hysterical. You weren't so far from the house. Why didn't you come and watch your daughter yourself?" his mother asked him.

"Call my wife here, mother," said Arap Metuk angrily.

"You're not going to suggest your wife should have watched over her, are you? She was watching you at the reception. Kipsoimo, don't make a fool of yourself. Chelamai is a woman. You cannot watch a woman. We couldn't control her every move even if we wanted to. She had to be let out to go to the outhouse. I must say, Kipsoimo, your daughter is much smarter than you. She's chosen a better man than that old drunk your brother has brought with him. She's outsmarted us all. Let her go and be happy," said grandmother Kap Metuk.

Tabaes' sister left that morning, and some of the people who were not happy with the news, like Arap Metuk's brother, left in the afternoon. He had refused even to have lunch. Tapchamgoi heard the news at noon through her friend Tamutwol, but it was old news by then. Taptamus had heard already. Kiriswa had sent someone to tell his mother that he and Chelamai had slipped away to get married that night.

232

"Ohh! They got married on the same night they left here?" asked Tapchamgoi.

"Yes," answered Taptamus. "I'm so glad, and no one can make this day unpleasant for me," she added.

"One to go and everything will be done," said Tapchamgoi, meaning Cheseret. The news spread out through the neighbourhood that Chelamai and Kiriswa were married, and people were happy. All the eyes and ears were on Kap Metuk to hear and see how they were responding to what had happened. They were ready to step in if necessary, but there was no reaction from Kap Metuk.

CHAPTER FOURTEEN

*I*t had been almost two years from the first elopement to Chelamai and Kiriswa's wedding. A month after the wedding, Taptamus visited Chelamai and Kiriswa, partly to inform them of what was happening at home and partly to ask them to come back to the mountain for Cheseret's ceremony.

"Would it be rude if I don't come with you now?" Kiriswa had asked his mother when she told him she had come to invite them back to the mountain.

"No, but it would be better if you did come."

"I don't see any particular reason why I should come right now, but it is essential for one of my wives to go with you to help with the preparations."

Taptamus looked at her son sideways and said, "Think about it and come with me now or later, as long as you don't make Cheseret wait any more."

Taptamus enjoyed the visit. For the first time in two years, she had actually sat down with her son and made pleasant conversation. Kiriswa lived in Kipkarren where he worked for a settler milking his cows. He got up at four in the morning and came home at seven. After breakfast he puttered around with his wives, talked to friends and looked after his own cattle. At one o'clock he went down to the river for a bath. This was his normal life — working for the settler everything ran by the clock. Today Kiriswa took his mother and one wife, Chelamai, to Turbo to buy a few things at the shops for Taptamus to take home for the wedding day. Turbo was just a small stop along the railway line with two shops and one dispensary. There wasn't much to see, and even less to see on the way. One followed the railroad line along the bottom of the gorge to Turbo and back. The track twisted and turned, and you had to keep an ear open for a coming train in order to climb up the cliff to get out of its way. There wasn't an inch to spare alongside the track.

The two wives, Chelamai and Senge, got along well. They looked healthy. They laughed together. Senge and Kiriswa's little girls liked Chelamai. At night they fought, because each of them wanted to sleep with Chelamai. Kiriswa was the way his mother wished him to be. He did not show any more love for one wife than for the other. Taptamus went back with Senge and the younger daughter to arrange the ceremony. Chelamai and Kiriswa stayed with the older daughter. Two weeks later, Kiriswa came after them. Some of the relatives had arrived including Kilel and his wife. Others were still arriving: uncles, aunts, and cousins. Kilel rose when Kiriswa arrived, partly to indicate his respect for what Kiriswa had achieved. Kiriswa welcomed his uncle's acknowledgement. He smiled and shook his hand.

"Taptamus!" Kilel called, but the women inside couldn't hear. Kilel turned to Kiriswa and said, "I was on my way to Kap Temoet myself. I suggest you go in and show yourself or come with me. With four women in the house, they couldn't hear me if I shouted."

"Is my mother-in-law inside with them?" asked Kiriswa.

"No, I haven't seen Tapchamgoi today. I think they are your aunt's sisters and your mother," said Kilel.

"They should be able to hear then. I will go in and wake them up," said Kiriswa, and Kilel left.

"Father, father," said Kiriswa's daughter and ran to him. Her father greeted her.

"What is grandmother doing?" asked Kiriswa, standing in the sitting room.

"She is making beer, father. My mother said there will be a ceremony soon, father, and the women have to make lots of beer. Do you know what else, father? I have to go every morning to play with Sukunwa in Lydia's house. Mother said that is a good idea so I won't bother them while they are making the beer."

"Call your mother. Tell her I want to see her," said Kiriswa.

"No, father, mother isn't here. She went to another ceremony."

"Call your grandmother then." The child ran into the other room.

"Gogo! Gogo! Father is here," the child called Taptamus. The house went silent.

"How long has he been here, I wonder?" Taptamus whispered to Cheptabut. Chemutai and Kilel's wife were known to talk about anything from sex to who was having an affair with whom. I don't know how much my child has heard, thought Taptamus. She went into the sitting room and everyone followed her. Chemutai, Kiriswa's older sister, went to hug him, and his aunt did the same.

"How long have you been here?" asked Cheptabut.

"I just came in," said Kiriswa.

"Cheptabut, look for something for your brother to eat," said Taptamus, who went back to the other room to allow Kiriswa to talk to his aunt and his older sister. Kiriswa said he didn't want anything to eat, only some milk to drink. Cheptabut went to the kitchen, and her sister Chemutai followed her. Their mother was setting a pot on the fire to cook some food for Kiriswa. Cheptabut said that Kiriswa didn't want anything to eat, just milk.

"He looks run-down," said Chemutai.

"You would look run-down too, if you had to get up very early every morning to milk thirty cows," said Taptamus.

"Don't forget to mention the two young wives," said Chemutai and looked at Cheptabut.

"He's going to marry another tomorrow," said Cheptabut and smiled shyly.

"I hope he can survive this one," said Chemutai.

"Stop it! Take the milk to your brother and have some self-control. You're not saying anything I like to hear," said Taptamus. Kiriswa drank the milk and left to look for his cousin Kibet who was looking after the cattle in the meadow.

"He looks so tired," his aunt said after he left.

"He milks the settler's thirty cows every morning," Chemutai was in a hurry to say. "And I bet he gets milked plenty himself," she murmured to Cheptabut who went about doing what she was doing. My sister doesn't know when to stop, Cheptabut thought.

Cheseret's circumstances were complicated. After the ceremony of passing from youth into womanhood had been completed, she had to be purified from everything that had happened while she had been in seclusion, including her father's death. First, a sheep was killed for her purification. The Kap Temoet elders prayed and blessed her. They rubbed the contents of the stomach of the animal on her body to remove the pollution. The next day they slaughtered a goat to read her future. There was one small thing which was disturbing about it — the left ovary had a red growth. However, all of the signs for Cheseret's future were excellent. Both of her uncles analysed the stomach contents and one asked the other if they should slaughter another goat. But they realized that it would be highly unlikely that they would find another animal with such good signs. They showed Cheseret the growth, and the elder uncle suggested they cut it out because apart from the growth, nothing could read better. Cheseret accepted and was told not to talk about it, or it would be bad luck later. Her uncle spent an hour moving the parts around and pointing out the long red arteries and veins that covered the surface of the organs.

"Do you see this? This means your life is happy. This one means you will be surrounded by love, and have lots of cattle, sheep and goats and people to help you. You will live a long life." She was shown a lot, but she didn't understand what it was she was learning. Later all she could remember was that the entrails were very white and intact with red veins everywhere.

The reading of the stomach was done in the morning, and in the afternoon there was another feast. The older men and women drank beer. The men sang and danced, and the women punctuated their singing by calling out their praise names. In the evening Cheseret was taken to Taptamus' place from her mother's house. She spent the night and the next day in Taptamus' house. After sunset, she was dressed for the wedding ceremony, which was going to be held in Kiriswa's old house. Kiriswa had been married before. He knew what to do, but both of them had to go through the same teaching nevertheless. An older couple gave them counsel. The wife took Cheseret and her husband took Kiriswa.

Two children were also chosen to be in the ceremony, a boy and a girl. The boy was a shepherd, and the girl a babysitter. Cheseret chose Sukunwa for her babysitter and one of her younger brothers for her shepherd. Cheseret and her bridesmaid/counsellor got ready in Taptamus' house, while Kiriswa and his best man/counsellor waited at the back door of the other house for Cheseret to be brought and handed over to Kiriswa. The wedding procession took a long time, and Kiriswa and his best man began to shiver with the cold of the mountain. Kiriswa called his sister, Cheptabut, to find out what was keeping them.

"They have to move with great care. No one wants to cause the bride to stumble going to her own wedding," said Cheptabut.

"What is going to make her stumble from that close? I can spit from here to the house where they are," said Kiriswa.

"You can wait a little. Don't talk like that on your wedding," said Cheptabut and turned to go back in.

"Hey! Don't go in. Go see what is holding them."

They were not ready when Cheptabut got there. Tabutich, Kiriswa's aunt, was gathering the things Cheseret was to carry and handing them to Senge and the other women. The articles were things a family would need in its daily life and they were also symbolic. Special arrows used for bleeding cattle symbolized the work that Cheseret's husband would do and also meant that she would have sons to carry on the work of men. A small gourd of milk symbolized the wish that she would have children, and also the wish that she would have girls to continue women's work. Cheptabut joined the preparations. Cheseret wore a cloth toga suspended from her right shoulder and closed with a belt around her waist. The special articles were tied to her back like a baby. Over her shoulders an animal skin cloak was draped and tied at the front with a drawstring.

The formal procession set off. Tabutich, Kiriswa's aunt, led the way followed by Cheseret's bridesmaid, Cheseret's little brother, Cheseret, Sukunwa, Cheptabut and Senge last. The night was extraor-

239

dinary. The sky was a clean, silky blue, and a full, tranquil moon shone overhead giving an almost arrogant beauty to Mt. Kamasai, the mountain they all took for granted. Senge, Kiriswa's first wife, took a deep sigh and remarked, "This wedding ceremony is going so well! The moon is relaxed; the grass, the stones, even the leaves are standing motionless alongside the path."

Cheseret shook as they drew up to the house and she saw Kiriswa standing at the back door waiting for her. She remembered that every eye in the house, her relatives and Kiriswa's, were going to be watching her and Kiriswa get married that night. Kiriswa was dressed in a toga like an old man. In a wedding, everything had to be done in an old-fashioned way. Cheseret stood two feet from Kiriswa and trembled as though the ground was shaking under her. Her bridesmaid held on to her. She took her aside to talk to her. "Don't be nervous. You must have confidence to get everything going your way. I will look after you. Follow me, and I will tell you what to do. We will enter by the back door, but we will have to follow the men."

Cheptabut, Senge and Tabutich had nothing more to do. Their jobs ended when they had conveyed Cheseret safely to Kiriswa. The men went in first. Cheseret, the children and her bridesmaid followed. The whole party stood in the middle of the section of the house where the sheep and goats slept and the sacred oil was handed to them to anoint the children. The children were then taken away to bed. Kiriswa and his best man led the way into the sitting room where the wedding would take place. Cheseret was about to follow them, but her bridesmaid pulled her back.

"Don't follow them. Wait until they call you. And when they call you, don't rush. Trust me. If you don't let them beg you, you shouldn't expect anything after you have been married. Ask for whatever you want. Ask for a cow. Do you hear me?" Cheseret nodded yes. "Demand it! Don't you dare go into the other room to get married before you get what you want. And make sure everything is explicit."

Kiriswa called Cheseret from the sitting room.

"I want a cow before I come," Cheseret said. Kiriswa promised the cow as was customary.

"Ask him how old the cow is. Get a complete description of it."
Cheseret did this.

"She's a white cow with amber horns and black on both sides of her stomach," said Kiriswa.

"Don't accept a promise from Kiriswa alone. That cow will turn out not to exist after you are married."

"What do you want him to do? Bring the cow here for me to see it?" asked Cheseret.

"No, I want you to ask someone else for something. Ask one of his uncles. Trust me. I know what I'm doing. I've been married for eighteen years and was promised a cow by my husband that I never got."

Cheseret's face showed irritation. Her bridesmaid noticed. She stuck her head into the sitting room and said, "Cheseret wants to ask one more person."

"Who?" asked Kiriswa.

"She is asking Kiriswa's uncle for a sheep."

"I'm giving her a whole cow. Come out now Cheseret," said Kilel.

"A complete description first," the bridesmaid said, holding on so that Cheseret would not go in before the deal was made. Kilel described the second cow.

"How is the cow going to get to Cheseret?"

"The cow is here at a friend's house. She can have it tomorrow if she wants," said Kilel. "Come on in now."

They went into the sitting room. The people were seated around the beer pot drinking and singing to welcome the ceremony. Kiriswa stood when Cheseret entered. Cheseret was embarrassed — she felt her bridesmaid had made her sound like a greedy woman — but when she entered, the women burst into ululation and restored her good feelings. The bridesmaid removed the articles from her back and together they set them down gently against the wall. Taptamus rose to do her part. She took the ceremonial horn with both hands and handed it to the best man. The master of the ceremony rose to his feet. He asked the congregation to join him in blessing the opening of the ceremony. He took a sip of beer from a small, spherical gourd used

241

by men in ceremonial blessing. Then he held the gourd for Kiriswa and Cheseret to drink from, to symbolize the life they would share together. Taking it back, he took another sip himself and sprayed them with the beer to unite them.

"I'm uniting you," he said. Then he told the congregation, "Say after me, they are getting married."

"They are getting married."

"We acknowledge their marriage."

"We acknowledge their marriage."

"They will always be surrounded by happiness."

"They will always be surrounded by happiness."

"The wife will care for her children and husband, and the husband will care for her and the children."

"The wife will care for her children and husband, and the husband will care for her and the children."

"Take out the rings now."

The best man reached into the horn, and pulled out two braided lengths of *segutiet* grass. He handed one to his wife to give to Cheseret, and one to Kiriswa.

"I marry you."

"I'm married to you."

Kiriswa and Cheseret coiled the grass around one another's wrists, and then they walked around the beer pot four times. They danced, drank from the same gourd and ate from the same basket as part of the ritual. The young married women went home as soon as the actual ceremonies had ended, but the older people stayed up to celebrate. For them, the feasting would go on with everyone indulging themselves as much as they wanted. Some sang, some danced, and some talked with their childhood sweethearts. This went on all night.

Cheseret and Kiriswa were instructed by the husband and wife who were their best man and bridesmaid to go to bed in the next room. The bridesmaid made the bed. Her husband stayed in the other room to celebrate. Cheseret, Kiriswa and the bridesmaid went to bed together. Cheseret and Kiriswa must sleep in the same bed, but must not do anything else. Cheseret slept in the middle between Kiriswa and the bridesmaid.

"He can wait one more day. Don't let him touch you," the bridesmaid said to Cheseret. She snuggled close to Cheseret so that her body was touching Cheseret's. She put her arm across Cheseret to make sure Kiriswa wouldn't move too close. Kiriswa faced the wall and slept until they were all awakened in the morning to complete the ceremony.

Kilel went out with Taptamus to arrange for food for the guests. When the guests first arrived, Taptamus had given a *tesimiet* or young he-goat to be slaughtered to serve as food for the guests. The neighbours would bring other food. Today she was going to select the best ram to be sacrificed. She and Kilel selected the healthiest animal. Taptamus anointed the ram with milk to make its spirit happy before it was slaughtered. In the meantime, the guests congregated in the house were praying for Kiriswa and Cheseret that their marriage might be a happy one. When the prayers were concluded the two were brought out to have their heads shaved. Kiriswa was shaved a little bit above his left ear because Cheseret was not his first wife, and Cheseret's whole head was shaved because Kiriswa was her first husband. The rings they had worn last night were taken off and put in a horn, which was given to Taptamus. The ram had been skinned. The men roasted the meat for all the guests, men and women, to eat. The women rapidly dehaired and dried the skin over the fire to make a dress for Cheseret to wear. A ring and a bracelet were also cut from the skin of the hind leg. Kiriswa wore the ring on the middle of his right finger, and Cheseret the bracelet on her left wrist.

The rest of the day people spent feasting. Kiriswa joined the men, and the women took over to prepare Cheseret for married life. Her bridesmaid, and Senge, Kiriswa's first wife, took her to bring some water.

"You must take a bath every morning after having sex. Never hand food to men when you are having your period. Blood is unclean." They told Cheseret everything they knew about married life. Then they went back to the house to teach her about the fireplace. She was helped to cook a mock meal for her husband Kiriswa, his friends and the two children, her brother Kipchogei and Sukunwa. She was instructed to give the food to the children to eat first and then to take a stool to her husband. Kiriswa took the stool and sat. Cheseret held water for him to wash his hands. Then she went in to bring the food for him. Kiriswa refused to eat. His best man had told him he could get back at Cheseret today because if he didn't eat, she would have to stand there until he did. Cheseret stood for a minute. Her bridesmaid came and told her to promise Kiriswa a cow. Cheseret promised him a cow that her brother had given her. Kiriswa asked her what colour it was and smiled.

When the men finished eating, Cheseret was taken to milk the cows. Finally her bridesmaid had accomplished all of her duties with her. They wished each other good luck, and then the bridesmaid and her husband left. They lived ten miles away. Little by little people began leaving. By evening, everyone was gone, the couple were alone, and Cheseret didn't know what to do or say. Two years of being apart and the reality that she was actually his wife made her shy. They sat at the fireplace. Kiriswa looked at her more than she looked at him. He whistled and whistled. Cheseret wished he would stop.

"The fire is going out. Would you light the lamp?" asked Kiriswa. She had forgotten where the lamp was. She looked at Kiriswa and smiled.

"Would you light the lamp?" Kiriswa asked again laughing.

"Where is it?"

Kiriswa pointed to where the lamp hung from a peg on the wall. Cheseret walked over to it and stood. She couldn't reach it. Kiriswa went and brought it down for her. She lit it and set it down. They sat by the fireplace again.

"Bed?" asked Kiriswa. Cheseret got up to make the bed. Kiriswa went to help. "Are you afraid of me?" he asked.

"No," said Cheseret. When the bed was made, Cheseret went to make another for herself.

"Why?" asked Kiriswa. "Did your bridesmaid tell you to sleep alone again?"

"No."

"So what are you doing?"

When there was no answer, he moved to her bed. Their honeymoon went on for the usual four days, and for the whole four days, Senge waited on them hand and foot. The three of them spent time together in the afternoons, but Senge slept at her mother-in-law Taptamus' place. Not, however, with the blessing of her mother, Tapchamgoi. Her mother said to her, "Senge, you are so tired. You have been used too much. Leave and come to stay at home. Let Taptamus and her daughter worry about Kiriswa and Cheseret. You're not their housekeeper."

"No, my wife stays where I stay. We came together to mother's, and we stay there together," Kiriswa had replied to this remark.

Kiriswa had only one week to spare. The man who helped to milk the cows had told him he would do it for a week. Taptamus wanted Kiriswa to leave Cheseret behind to be with her.

"No, mother, I'm taking both wives with me because we have to think of building a second house."

"You can stay in one house until Cheseret and Chelamai get used to housework," said Taptamus.

"Senge knows what to do, mother. She looks after things. Don't worry, mother."

They reached home just as the sun was going down. Chelamai had food ready for them.

The three wives had little to do. The house was small — two bedrooms, one for Kiriswa, and the other for the children and wives — and there was little to clean. Kiriswa was visited by each wife once a week. The wives had a good time doing things together. If Chelamai and Senge went to look for wild vegetables and firewood, Cheseret would take over the children, telling the babysitter when to wash them, when to take them out and when to feed them. If she finished before Senge and Chelamai returned, she went to visit the wife of the overseer and her daughter, Jenny, downriver where all of the women in the neighbourhood went to chitchat about the settler and the settlement. The overseer's wife knew a lot because her husband talked to the settler every day.

"My Dad said Kiriswa was getting ready to build another house, but he told him to wait," said Jenny.

"We haven't been told that," said Cheseret.

"Kiriswa was talking about it this morning. He has not had time to tell you," said the overseer's wife.

"Yes, we were thinking of building another house," said Cheseret.

"You will be building soon. My husband just told Kiriswa to be cautious until relations between the settler and the Nandi workers improve."

Cheseret returned home. Chelamai and Senge had settled down for a cup of afternoon tea when she arrived. She stood in the middle of the kitchen looking surprised.

"What are you standing there for? Come join us for tea," said Chelamai.

Cheseret laughed, "What happened to you. It looks as though you haven't seen water for ages."

"What do you mean?" asked Chelamai. Senge turned around to see what Cheseret was talking about.

"I don't believe it. I hadn't noticed myself. You must have gone through a spider web when we were looking for firewood," said Senge.

"Don't laugh then. Pick it off me," said Chelamai.

"Here, point your head at me," said Cheseret. "Hmm," she sighed.

"What was that about?" asked Senge.

"Chelamai, go wash your head," said Cheseret.

"No, I don't want to. Pick it off for me please."

"Chelamai, are you afraid of water?"

"No!"

"Wash your head then. I will boil the water for you," said Senge and poured some water into a pot and put it on the fire.

"Cheseret, can you share with us what you are sighing about?" asked Senge again.

"Yes, I'm about to tell you. I went to visit Jenny and her mother today. In the middle of our conversation, Jenny said, 'I heard Kiriswa telling my dad you were thinking of building a house, but my dad told him to wait.' She just said it out of the blue; I don't know why," said Cheseret.

"I'm worried. I don't like the sound of this," said Senge. "Has Kiriswa been home since we left this morning?"

"No, but maybe he came when I was away at Jenny's place."

"The babysitter would have said something about it," said Chelamai.

"Go wash your hair Chelamai, the water is warm enough," said Senge. "I don't think either of you know that we're living here illegally. Kiriswa has no job. The European asked the overseer to fire him two years ago. He didn't, but he told the settler that he had. The settler must have found out that Kiriswa is still in the settlement," she added.

Nandi never did what the settlers told them to do. They were ungovernable. They had refused to do domestic work for the British and said they would look after the cows and milk them. The overseer had to be Nandi, the cattlemen had to be Nandi, and the milking men had to be Nandi. That way, they could live their life the way they wanted to and trust themselves first. The money they made from working for the settler had no significance for them. They came to work so their own cattle could get grass on the settlers' lands. Kiriswa had been a milker for three years, but the total time he had spent milking might have been two months out of those three years. People had come from as far away as Mt. Kamasai to take over for him because he had better things to do than milk cows.

Kiriswa arrived home at six. He seemed happy and didn't look any different than usual. "Where is Senge?" he asked.

"She went to get some water," answered Cheseret. "The food is ready. Do you want to eat now?"

"Yes," Kiriswa answered. Chelamai took water to him to wash his hands, and Cheseret brought the food. "What did you people do today," he asked.

Cheseret told him what they had done. Chelamai was quiet as usual, and talked to the children. Kiriswa looked at her. She looked down.

"Aren't you well, Chelamai?"

"No."

"Why aren't you talking?"

Chelamai smiled and looked back at the fire again.

"Can you make the bed for me then? I'm tired, and I want to lie down."

Chelamai got up to go make the bed. Cheseret came to take the dishes away, and Senge arrived too.

"I had to wait for the water to be clean. Some one must have let the cows walk in it," she said.

"You know what happens in the evening, Senge. Why do you bother to go at this time?" asked Kiriswa.

"I never learn," said Senge laughing.

Chelamai finished making the bed and walked into the kitchen. Senge remained standing in the sitting room talking to Kiriswa.

"Does she stay quiet like that all day?" asked Kiriswa.

"Chelamai? No, only when she gets up in the morning and in the evening."

"What's wrong with her?"

"Chelamai has been like that ever since she was a little girl. Don't worry. Your daughters will get her talking in a little while. They know how to make her talk. By the way, what is happening with the settler? I heard that the overseer told you to wait on building our house," asked Senge.

"The waiting has nothing to do with the settler. Our cattle are dying in this arid land. Nothing ever grows on it."

"What is going to happen? Are we going to move again?" asked Senge.

"That is the problem. The people who went west to check what it was like came back today. They say it is good for cattle. The people there don't keep cows. They are willing to put you up on their farms just to have milk, but the country is not good for people. It's full of mosquitoes."

"It sounds like the place my aunt moved to," said Chelamai from the kitchen. "They want to move back because they can't take the blood-sucking flies anymore."

"Yes, what your aunt called the blood-sucking flies are mosquitoes," said Kiriswa.

There had been a time in Nandi history when the area around Turbo was regarded as having the most pleasing landscape and the best grazing land in the country. At the beginning of the rainy season, the flowers used to bloom all at once. Once a year, the people moved the cattle away to Kapkeimur and burned off the land. Then, when the rains came, everything would bloom again. But since the British had taken over, they had stopped people from burning the land, and Turbo had become barren. The only thing that blossomed was the flame tree, which was fertilized by its own leaves. Whether it rained or the sun shone, the grass lay broken down and brown forever. The English used fertilizer on the land, which they planted with wheat, and they allowed their cattle to feed on the stubble after the harvest. They also grew fodder for their cattle and fed it to them. Initially, the Nandi grazed their cattle along the Kipkarren River. After a few years, the land along the river become barren also.

One year was both lucky and unlucky. A passenger on a train dropped a cigarette and burned the land along with half of the settler's cows. The settler asked every man and child in the settlement to come to fight the fire. Everybody went except for the Nandi people, who went to rescue their own cattle and take their families to safety across the Kipkarren River. The ones who put in an appearance to fight the fire, like the overseer, arrived late when the fire was about to be brought under control around the settler. When the fire was finally put out, the settler made an attendance list, and the overseer was told to sack all of the Nandi men on the settlement who hadn't heeded the call to come and fight the fire. The settler would bring new people. Because only the Nandi knew how to look after cattle, the new people who were hired were Nandi, and of course all of the ones who were supposed to have been fired didn't really leave, but stayed to do the same job. Because there was now a surplus of workers, individual Nandi were free to come and go pretty much as they always had done. They could go and explore for new land, visit relatives or whatever. The overseer always reported the same people.

But it was becoming increasingly clear as the days passed that they would have to move. The Nandi cattle were starving and not producing enough milk, the Nandi's main dietary item. Kiriswa went west to see the land for himself and, if he liked it, to arrange for a place for he and the families to stay. Kiriswa's wives were alone again for a month.

"When did Kiriswa say he was coming back?" asked Cheseret looking at Chelamai while she was handing a wooden spoon to Senge to stir vegetables. Chelamai and Senge looked at each other in surprise. Cheseret smiled, "Don't look so surprised. I just thought you might know more about it since you visited him the night before he left."

"He didn't tell me any more than he told us all together the morning he left," said Chelamai.

"Of course," said Senge. "If there was something important, Kiriswa would tell us all."

Cheseret did not understand why Kiriswa had called Chelamai to visit him when it was her turn that night. Why? she thought. Senge knew Kiriswa had invited Chelamai because he had wanted to find out if she was being bothered by anything. Her quietness worried him.

Kiriswa returned home one night. He told his wives that they would be moving west. He had found a deserted house. They discussed the living arrangements they would have when they got there. In fact all of the Nandi on the settlement were packing to move. Before dawn, the women were all at Kiriswa's door to be taken to the train station. Kiriswa took them to their new homes. Then he came back himself by the evening train. At midnight he and the other Nandi men left with the livestock. The trip had taken only half a day by train, but it took four days with the cattle, sheep and goats. Some of the animals gave birth on the way.

In their new home, Kiriswa discovered after a time that Chelamai and Senge were a good match. He built Cheseret her own house, and his and Senge's six year old daughter moved in with Cheseret so she would have someone to talk to at night when Kiriswa was at the other house. By tradition, every wife was permitted to take an extended leave for a month or two every few years, whatever the family agreed on, to visit her own family or whoever she wanted to visit. Taptamus sent word to Kiriswa for Chelamai to come to visit her and Sukunwa. This happened because Taptamus had heard that Chelamai was six months pregnant, and she had wanted to make sure that Chelamai had first choice to return home. Kiriswa came with her, stayed for two weeks, and then went back. Taptamus told Kiriswa that she wanted Chelamai to have her baby in Mt. Kamasai.

"With me around. And I hope her parents will have a change of heart now that their daughter is going to have a baby," she said. Chelamai had a little boy, but when Taptamus invited her parents along with all the other relatives and neighbours to celebrate the birth, Chelamai's mother came alone.

"Be happy her mother came. That is good for a start," Mary said to Taptamus.

When the baby was three months old, Chelamai went back home. The following day, Mary received a message that her oldest daughter, Tabarbuch, was sick and wanted her mother to come to see her.

"I suggest you let me look after Lydia and Chepsisei when you go to see her. I assure you I will manage fine," said Taptamus.

"No, I would not leave without Lydia," said Mary.

"Why what is wrong with that? I have people to help me, and besides Lydia can play with Sukunwa."

"I will take Lydia. Sometimes it is hard even for me to deal with Chepsisei and her child. Women have been cursed never to rest as long as they live."

It was not easy to take Lydia from her mother. Chepsisei cried, and she fought with Mary to get her baby back. She was small with a wiry body and a strong grip. She got a hold of her mother's clothing from behind, and it took Cheptabut nearly five minutes before she

251

could loosen her grip to separate her from her mother. Taptamus shut her eyes and ears throughout the ordeal. She hated what Mary was doing to her daughter. For days and days Chepsisei cried. She threw herself to the ground and writhed as though she was in terrible pain. Mary was gone for a month and a half. By then Chepsisei was only pointing to the path Mary had taken with her daughter and cradling and rocking her arms together in her sign for "baby."

The day of Mary's arrival was appalling. Chepsisei went to greet her mother with a hug, and Lydia ran to hug her. But Chepsisei gave no sign that she even knew her daughter. Mary immediately tried to explain to her that she was reunited with her daughter now, and that they would not be separated again, but Chepsisei did not change. As the days went by she segregated herself farther and farther from her daughter. Elders in the family were asked to speak with her, but they fared no better. And yet, Chepsisei continued to say in signs that she had a baby who had gone away. She remembered the path Mary and Lydia had taken when they left and pointed it out time and time again.

The elders told Mary, "Give her time. She will soon come to recognize that this is the same child you took." But she never did. Lydia and Sukunwa came thus to be raised as though they were twins, now that Chepsisei was no longer over-protective of Lydia. Mary took them in the morning, and in the afternoon they went to Taptamus' place.

CHAPTER FIFTEEN

*B*y the age of six, Sukunwa and Lydia were capable of playing outside by themselves. In the morning they sat around the fireplace with cups in their hands waiting for tea. Mary took them to the cattle kraal in mid-morning to teach them how to milk. After the lesson, Mary went with them to take the sheep, goats and calves out to graze. Taptamus brought her own small stock to them also.

"Lydia and Sukunwa!! These are the sheep and goats and the calves. Don't let the calves nurse from their mothers. And I don't want to see any of them missing when I come back to get you!"

"Yes, yes" the girls squeaked assurances, but they never liked herding at the places Mary or Taptamus took them to. They waited until the grown-ups were out of sight, and then they took the animals to the meadow and played. They climbed up in tall trees for big leaves to use as dishes when they played at cooking. The herd was quickly forgotten as Sukunwa dug a hole in the ground for a fireplace and Lydia looked for clay-like soil to make porridge. They ran half a mile to the river to bring water in their mouths and spat it into the hole. When it wasn't enough, one would squat over it and pee into it. By the time the cooking was finished, the goats were nowhere to be seen, and when Mary or Taptamus arrived to tell them to bring the animals home, the children looked up in shocked disbelief at their loss. Sometimes the goats just wandered home on their own. Many times, however, the neighbour children would bring them over after they had strayed far away, and Sukunwa and Lydia would be given a stern lecture by Mary.

The children played many different games. If Mary told them not to play at cooking again because the goats would stray, they took

253

maize-cobs with them and made dolls, dressing them with big leaves or with rags from their old clothes. Sukunwa was fond of building huts. She went to the river to bring sand for the building. When she was done with this, she skinned the bark off the *silipchet* tree and wove necklaces and bracelets for the dolls.

Lydia was fond of collecting grasshoppers, beetles, snails and baby birds. She climbed into trees where the birds made their nests and when she found fledglings, she brought them down. The snails became cattle, the beetles were sheep, and the grasshoppers were goats. She brought everything in a small bag, and set it on the ground. Then she and Sukunwa sat down and divided the contents so that they each had the same amount. By the end of the afternoon, the grasshoppers and beetles had been fed to the birds. The birds were taken back to their nests, and the snails were covered carefully with leaves for the next day's play.

When Sukunwa was seven, Cheptabut had a brother for her.

"Sukunwa, you must go to your mother to learn how to babysit," her grandmother told her.

"No, grandmother, you forgot! I learn things with Lydia."

"I know, but you can learn some things by yourself. You won't have Lydia with you when you are old and married like Chelamai," said Taptamus. Sukunwa gave her a scathing look.

"I'm not going to be married alone. I will be married with Lydia. We already have the same play husband."

"Who is that?" Taptamus asked smiling.

"No grandmother, you don't know him! He lives in the meadow. He's made of a maize-cob!" Sukunwa laughed.

"Let us go to your mother's. I promised her I would send you there today," said Taptamus.

"Will I go to Lydia's later?"

"Yes."

Sukunwa liked her baby brother because she was told he was her very own. She promised her mother to come every day with Lydia. She did, but Cheptabut fell ill when the baby was six months old. She developed a headache and couldn't stand the slightest sound when she had it. Taptamus took the baby from her. The elders thought the headache was due to the anger of deceased ancestor spirits. The senior elder in Kiptai's family was called in to investigate to see if there were any ancestors who were upset. The result of his investigation was negative. Taptamus begged Kiptai to have Cheptabut taken to where Kiriswa lived.

"She listens to her brother, and there are more people around there to take turns keeping an eye on her," she said.

"I would rather have her here with me, because if I take her there and stay here myself, I will be worrying constantly about her condition," said Kiptai.

"I can't say it has been easy for me, either, with the baby. I only think it would be better for both you and me," said Taptamus. Kiptai made no reply.

"I will discuss this arrangement with Cheptabut," continued Taptamus and left. She had made her suggestion with the best interests of both Kiptai and Cheptabut in mind. She thought Kiptai was hurting far more than anyone else in the family. He had not moved from Cheptabut's side since she had taken sick, except when he went for medicine for her. Cheptabut was not taking the medicine correctly. She was taking advantage of the fact that Kiptai couldn't be strict with her and force her to take medicine the way she was supposed to. In two weeks, the house was full of medicine from bark, leaves and roots, but Taptamus thought the medicine was killing Cheptabut faster than the sickness, because of the way she was mixing it.

"Cheptabut, at least take one kind of medicine for four days before changing. The medicine won't work if you take one kind in the morning, another for lunch, and then a different one in the evening," she said.

"I'm sick, mother. I'm in pain. You don't know how I feel."

"I would like to take you to Kiriswa's place. What do you think of that idea?"

"Ask Kiptai. What he says is what I will do."

"I already have. He wants you here with him, but I think you should go understanding you would be helping him more than anything else." This was too much for Cheptabut. If she said no, she was not going, that would mean she was being selfish in everyone's eyes.

"I would like to be taken to my brother's to get better there. Maybe the change of place will help," she told Kiptai that evening.

Kiptai knew that was not what Cheptabut really wanted, but he said, "I will take you wherever you want to go and stay there with you until you get better."

"Yes, yes, I like that way better," agreed Cheptabut. That evening Kiptai told Taptamus what they had decided. But after a week at Kiriswa's, there was still no sign that Cheptabut was improving. Kiriswa's new neighbours told them they had seen many people with headaches taken to the hospital where they got better. Kiptai wanted to know if he could meet someone who had been there. Three people met with him. They told him that they would have to take food with them —because the food in the hospital was horrible — and dishes, a cup, a bowl and a plate. Tororo Hospital was on the border between Kenya and Uganda. The doctors were English, but they only came once a week. The African people were looked after by other Africans. Neither Kiptai nor Cheptabut spoke Swahili, and they were helpless without Kiriswa. No one spoke Nandi at the hospital or in Uganda.

They packed food in the morning and went to the bus stop in Bungoma. At ten o'clock they reached Tororo. Cheptabut was taken to the hospital and admitted. To Kiptai's shock, he was told he could not stay there. It was hard for Kiriswa to get him to leave. He said he was going to stay outside Cheptabut's window. The people in the hospital told Kiriswa that the English doctors didn't want to see anyone around the hospital grounds after five o'clock. The woman who shared a room with Cheptabut promised Kiriswa she would talk to her even if they did not understand each other. Kiptai and Kiriswa went there every day from Bungoma. They had one bicycle. Kiriswa rode Kiptai going, and Kiptai rode Kiriswa returning. When Taptamus saw that Kiptai didn't come back to the mountain, she left everything for the neighbours to look after and followed them. Arap Walei took her and Cheptabut's children to Bungoma, and the next day they all went to Tororo. Cheptabut told them she was not feeling too bad. She asked about her children three times.

"I brought them with me. Sukunwa would have liked to see you, but they don't let children in here," said Taptamus.

"I can't believe she left Lydia and came with you unless you told her you were going back the same day," said Cheptabut.

The hospital food was brought in while Taptamus and Arap Walei were still there.

"You'd better leave now, the patient has to eat," Taptamus and Arap Walei were told, but Cheptabut said she didn't want to eat.

"You should eat it, you may not see meat again until you leave," the woman who shared the room with Cheptabut told her. "There is a little meat in it today," she added glancing at Cheptabut. Cheptabut fished out and handed the single piece of meat she was talking about to her. Cheptabut had not eaten the hospital food since she had come. Her brother and her husband always brought her yoghurt from home, and Cheptabut gave her room-mate some of this as well. In fact, the room-mate was gaining weight on Cheptabut's diet. Arap Walei and Taptamus left at three-thirty.

For two days, no one went to the hospital. They didn't have money to pay for the bus, and Taptamus could not sit on a bicycle. When a goat was sold and they finally got money, Kiptai and Taptamus went. Cheptabut was much better. She wanted to come home with them that same day, but Kiriswa, the only one who could release her, hadn't come. They left a little food and carried the bottle of African medicine Taptamus had been smuggling in for her. Kiriswa and Kiptai returned two days later. Cheptabut's clothes were hung by the side of her bed. But, she had vanished. The same night Taptamus and Kiptai had been there, her room-mate saw two hospital people wearing long white gowns with gloves walk her out of the room. She never came back. The English doctors would not talk to them. The hospital workers avoided them and refused to say what had happened. Cheptabut's room-mate cried and said she would be next.

"She's dead. I've seen many people walk out of this room and never come back. I'm next if I don't leave this place," she said.

Kiriswa and Kiptai stood numb in the middle of the room. Confusion reigned together with emptiness, dismay, worthlessness, and humiliation brought on by their helplessness. All the feelings that human beings go through when things have reached a dead end went rushing through them. Cheptabut was their loved one. To the English doctors she was just another dead African. They walked out of the room into the corridor. It was empty. There were only the echoes of sick people moaning for help. Kiptai couldn't contain his emotions. He cried a painful cry. Kiriswa could see the swollen blood vessels on his face, but did nothing to comfort him. He was overwhelmed himself with his own helplessness. He could not call the police because they worked for the British. What would he tell them when the doctors told the police she died? They walked out of the door in silence. An African nurse ran after them with Cheptabut's clothes.

"Take them! She will never come here to wear them. She is dead," she said. She set them on the ground and left.

The family mourned but a little hope remained just the same. Taptamus got up at night when the wind ruffled the leaves thinking maybe it could be Cheptabut. She got up when the dogs barked. She got up when the cattle made noises. Kiptai went back to the hospital every day hoping for the impossible until he was kicked out. So as not to shock them while the adults were confronting their loss, Cheptabut's and Kiriswa's children were taken to Cheseret's house. Sukunwa did not know her mother was dead, but it did not take long before she put the pieces together.

When she asked, "Why are we not allowed to go to our grandmother's?" Cheseret would answer, "She is not feeling well and she wants the children to stay with me until she is better."

"Is mother home from the hospital?"

"No," answered Cheseret getting up. "Sukunwa, go play with your cousins. I have to wash the dishes," or "I have to make a fire."

But sometimes Sukunwa followed her after hearing these fabrications. She saw tears running down her cheeks and knew something was wrong. Even after the children had been allowed to return to their grandmother, Sukunwa saw Taptamus looking extremely sad when she thought the children were not around, and Senge would put her arm around Taptamus and they would cry together. Sukunwa knew they were crying because of her mother's death, but she did not tell anyone she knew this. She kept it inside her to make it easier for the grown-ups. She only cried on her own. She cried herself to sleep silently at night, but during the day she played with the other children as usual and kept her pain to herself.

Kiptai reached up and down for answers. He sold a cow and went to seers. They cast their pebbles and all said that Cheptabut was dead and that she had died by human hands. Eventually he was convinced by them and accepted the fact of her death. Before the new moon, the family was purified. Cheptabut's children, Taptamus and Kiriswa's family were shaved, and then their hair was thrown toward the setting sun — what they believed was now Cheptabut's resting place. After the family had taken baths, Taptamus spent the entire afternoon with the clay of purification and protection from unhappiness. Kiriswa was sent to tell the close relatives to purify themselves. Kiptai would mourn for a year before he would be made clean.

Taptamus said they had to go back to the mountain. "I think the neighbours have been more than kind," she suggested. Kiriswa would have suggested they leave Cheptabut's baby behind, but he saw that Kiptai's heart was in his children. It was as though they were the only reason he had for living. Chelamai was sent back with Taptamus to stay with them until they got used to being on their own.

"I will come to the mountain every other week. If that doesn't work out, I may move the whole family back," Kiriswa told her.

When the party arrived at the mountain, the rain was forming at the peak, humming like a moving beehive. The countryside grew dark until it rained and the skies turned from the darkness into a greyish-white with silver rays of sunlight against the steel-blue clouds. When they got home, Taptamus suggested to Sukunwa that she go to visit Lydia.

"That will make her happy," said Chelamai.

"Yes, you saw how her attitude changed when I told her to go," said Taptamus.

Mary and Lydia were coming towards the house, and Sukunwa ran back.

"They are coming here, Grandma!" she said and ran back out to meet them.

"Oh, for heaven's sake! You're back. When did you arrive?" asked Mary smiling at Sukunwa.

"About an hour ago."

"Why didn't your grandmother send someone to let me know you were back?"

Sukunwa didn't reply. She and Lydia were measuring each other by eye. Presumably to see who has grown taller thought Mary as she turned to walk away.

"I'm going in, girls. Don't go far — play around here," Mary interrupted their concentration.

"What should we do now?" inquired Sukunwa.

"Probably chase the butterflies. I usually chase them after the rain," said Lydia.

"Oh no, people will think we are crazy chasing butterflies in the wet grass."

"They will think we are even crazier if we stand here without doing anything," said Lydia. "Let's go look for mushrooms. I found two yesterday on the hill near Ketele's house, and I've told everyone not to go there. It is *my* mushroom hill, but I'll share it with you." They went to tell their grandparents they were going mushroom hunting.

But when they reached the hill, they found footprints all around and no mushrooms. Lydia asked Sukunwa to walk cautiously and not step on the footprints because she had to track down the stupid person who had come to her area and picked her mushrooms.

"Maybe it was Ketele himself," said Sukunwa. "Tapchamgoi says he is ridiculous. He takes children's things," she added. She looked across the ground and saw two white buttons on the ground. She rushed over to look at them. "Lydia! Lydia!"

"What? What?"

"Mushrooms!"

"We'd better take back what we said about Ketele," said Lydia.

"Why? He didn't see these, or he would have taken them," said Sukunwa.

"Maybe he's blind, not stupid. Do they have mushrooms where Kiriswa lives?"

"Yes, a lot, but they are red. My aunt says you have to show them to grown-ups before you pick them because they can be poison," said Sukunwa.

"What is life like there?"

"There is a lot of grass, trees with fruit and a beautiful river with a sandy bottom. In the morning my cousin and I take the sheep, goats and calves to the meadow to graze and we hunt for all kinds of fruit. Then we share these with the other children. My little brother likes black strawberries, and my two younger cousins like *motongoek*."

"What are *motongoek*?"

"Large fruits like oranges. They grow at the base of a low shrub with long green leaves."

"Do you peel them to eat them?"

"No, you break one open and then eat the yellow fruit inside."

"You had a really good time there didn't you. I wish I had gone with you," said Lydia.

"No, we were chased all over by the children from there. They didn't like us because we were Nandi. We had to take them food almost every day to get them to leave us alone. We couldn't go out at night because you could get killed. This woman who lived next to our house told us a lot of stories. She said big holes had been dug in all of the paths. During the daytime they were covered with boards, and soil was put on top so no one would know. At night the people opened the holes and put grass on top. Then they went and waited in the bush. When strangers walked by, they didn't know. They thought it was just grass. They walked on it and fell in. The people in the bush rushed out to cover the hole with the boards and soil. They came back at midnight to dig the person out..." Sukunwa hesitated a moment. She thought that to say the last part would really scare Lydia, and if Lydia could be scared, she would be scared too.

"What do they do to him after they take him home?" asked Lydia with terror in her eyes.

"They boil him alive and eat him!"

"Oh! Let's go home. I'm scared." They walked in silence for a few minutes. Lydia stopped. "Weren't you afraid?" she asked.

"Yes I was," said Sukunwa.

"Your Aunt Cheseret told Mary about the English people she used to babysit for. The husband used to kill people at night. She said he worked in Eldoret Hospital and at night he dressed in white clothes and went out to wait for people. Your aunt said that after he got one, he tied his neck with a rope until the veins stuck out like a cow about to be bled. Then he took a long needle and stuck it in his neck right where the vein came out and sucked the blood until the person dropped dead. He left the body there and took the blood with him," said Lydia. "Your aunt said she was caught one day. When he was about to put the rope around her, he discovered it was your aunt. He told her to go home and pack and leave. Never to come back to work for them."

"Did you know my little brother and I don't have a mother any more?" asked Sukunwa.

"No, what happened?" asked Lydia now shaking with apprehension.

"I think she died in the hospital. My aunt and my grandmother cried and nobody talked about my mother anymore."

"Did you cry, too?"

"I cried at night a lot, and I still cry when my brother cries."

"Sukunwa! Lydia!" Mary's voice called from the distance.

"Oh dear me. I think we are being called," said Lydia.

"We had better run. We were told to play near the house," said Sukunwa. They each pulled up their dresses so they wouldn't trail on the wet grass. Gathering them just above their knees, they tore across the meadow like wind ripping through the jungle.

Kiptai and Arap Walei were in the sitting room when Lydia and Sukunwa came in. Arap Walei cleared his throat, "Did you get any rabbits?" he asked.

262

Lydia turned to Sukunwa and laughed, "Women don't hunt, Grandpa," she said.

"Who says so? They eat meat. They should hunt," said Arap Walei.

Sukunwa and Lydia looked at each other. They were speechless.

"Your grandfather is joking, you two," said Mary. Lydia looked relieved. She had been sure her grandfather had wanted rabbit for real.

"Well, do you want to come home with me or stay with Sukunwa for the night?" asked Mary.

"I will stay with Sukunwa," said Lydia.

"I'm going home then," said Mary.

"Here, take this mushroom to my mother," said Lydia. "And tell her Lydia and Sukunwa found it," she added.

Chepsisei didn't show the slightest indication that she cared about Lydia, but she worried all the same when it got dark without seeing her. When Mary got back home, she asked about Lydia by making a cradle with her arms and rocking it back and forth. Mary told her that she was spending the night with Sukunwa. Chepsisei slowly changed. She pulled away from Mary and walked around the house talking to herself and watching at the door. Her temper got shorter, until Mary suggested she go to Taptamus'. Mary had been terrified of Chepsisei's temper ever since she had taken Lydia away from her.

People appeared at Taptamus' place every day. They didn't let her be depressed once. Everyone was afraid Taptamus and Kiptai would fall apart. Chelamai was more than a daughter-in-law. She had something special. Any place she touched was surrounded with people's love because of her sweetness and beauty. People admired her and acknowledged her genuine patience and tenderness.

Six months after Cheptabut's death, Taptamus' daughter Kikwai, who was married to a family from the Nandi Escarpment, moved to Nchebichep, a five-day journey with cattle southeast of Mt. Kamasai, and strangled herself shortly afterwards. Taptamus was in the attic where she always took a nap after lunch when the news arrived. No one knew she was in. When she heard people talking about Kikwai's death, she rushed down from the attic. Her foot missed a rung on the ladder. She fell head first, flat onto the ground.

Tapatmus remained in a delirium for two days. Mt. Kamasai was like a haunted place. It rained on the mountain day and night. Wind and hail flattened the crops in the fields. It was a nightmare of nightmares. Kap Metuk had taken Cheptabut's children and their daughter Chelamai's child to their place when Taptamus had fallen and lost consciousness. When she came out of her delirium, her first wish was to see the children. Mary told her that the children would wear her out, "Wait for a day, at least."

"No, I want to see them. I'm fine," said Taptamus. She struggled to her feet when the children arrived. Oh, how she loved those children. The two little ones ran to hug her. Sukunwa stood away from her grandmother. It was hard to ignore the pain that came through her eyes. She remembered being told that her grandmother did not feel well at the time of her mother's death. Now she felt if her grandmother wasn't well, someone else was dead or about to die. Her grandmother extended her arm to her to come. She was shivering when Taptamus put her arm around her.

"Nobody will love me if you are sick, Grandma," she whispered with tears in her eyes.

"I'm better now. I'm only tired."

"Tomorrow will be another day. The children should leave now, Taptamus. You need a lot of sleep," said Mary.

Taptamus died that night, quietly in her sleep. She could not live forever, and her heart gave out. Chelamai woke up at four in the morning and made a fire before going outside. She discovered that Taptamus was not moving and went to the guest house to wake Kiriswa. Arap Walei was called. She must have just died, for her body was not yet cold. Arap Walei gave Taptamus her last food, pouring milk into her dying breath. She was taken out into the darkness before the children were awake. Her body was put in the guest house, and Kiriswa stayed with it until the evening, when she was taken to be buried.

Sukunwa was taken to Mary's house to be with Lydia until her grandmother had been buried. Then she was taken to her uncle Kiriswa to be told. Kiriswa had said she had to know her grandmother was gone. It would mean breaking custom for him to tell her for she was still very young, but he had to.

"I will make her understand," he said.

There were some wonders in Mt. Kamasai that day. No one could have explained how the trees and the flowers that surrounded the community, the grasses, the cattle, and the birds in the bushes all looked sad and unhappy. It rained for a week after Taptamus' death. For days and nights, everything in Mt. Kamasai looked dead. Even the moon, encased in a veil of haze, seemed dimmed for the occasion. Arap Walei said heaven was mourning the death of Taptamus, too.

Six months passed with Sukunwa living happily with Kiriswa's family. Then, as one year had gone by since his wife's death, people insisted Kiptai get married, and he was given a wife. Kiriswa wanted to keep his sister's children, Sukunwa and her brother. Kiptai said, "No I want my children. They are mine and mine alone. I will be both their father and their mother."

People told Kiriswa not to fight for the children, to let Kiptai have them. Sukunwa's brother, Kipchamtany, was a year and a half. Sukunwa was eight. Kiptai's new wife loved the little boy; she could not love her own child more than him. But she could not stand Sukunwa. Sukunwa talked about her grandmother constantly. If her stepmother woke her at six in the morning to make a fire for breakfast, she would say in all innocence, "No, I don't make the fire. My grandmother used to make the fire." If the stepmother asked Sukunwa to clean the house, the reply was the same, "No, I can't. My grandma didn't ask me to do it. She did it on her own."

"What did you do when you were with your grandmother?" her stepmother asked.

"She woke me after she had made tea. I went out and washed my face in the dew and came in and drank tea with a little left-over *kimiet*. Then I went to Mary's to learn how to milk with Lydia. Sometimes I played with my brother."

"Look at me! I'm not your grandmother. You do what I say and don't play with Lydia until later in the evening when there is no more work."

Kiptai did not see this. When he was around, his wife did all the work. Sukunwa quickly learned to disappear when he was home. She ran to Lydia to tell her about her stepmother. They lay down lined up on the top of a hill and then rolled down the slope to the soft grass at the bottom.

"I can't stand her," declared Sukunwa at the bottom of the hill. She lay on her back looking up. "I hate her. I hope she dies like...like my mother," she said and covered her face. "I hate her. I hate her. When she asks me to make a fire, I leave a long stick sticking out, hoping she will trip over it and fall into the fire, but she never does."

"Have you tried putting mud beside her bed? She may trip over that and break her leg."

"Oh, Lydia! Can you come to sleep over tonight to help me do that?"

"To do what?" asked Mary from behind them.

"Nothing," whispered Sukunwa. Wearing a guilty smile, Lydia turned her eyes on her grandmother, wondering how much she had heard.

"Nothing, Grandma," Lydia affirmed nervously.

"You know children should not trip grown-ups. It is a big sin." The two girls hung their heads, motionless like pond water.

It was at this point that Mary became actively curious about Sukunwa's life. She told Chelamai to keep an eye on her, and that she would too. She thought it was wrong to let Sukunwa go to live with her stepmother, because she had never lived with her mother when she was alive, and besides, Kiptai's new wife was practically a child herself. In the evenings, Mary sent Lydia to sleep over, so she could help Sukunwa with evening chores and with looking after Sukunwa's brother. Chelamai asked Kiptai and his wife to let Sukunwa and her brother come to spend days with her. That would help her, she said, because then her own little boy would have someone to play with. This arrangement was more than a pleasure for Sukunwa. She left her house early to go to her aunt Chelamai's place. Kiriswa always waited for her to come and have breakfast with him when he was in Kamasai. By mid-morning, Sukunwa was finished with her chores and went out to play with Lydia. Chelamai's babysitter looked after the two little boys.

Sukunwa's stepmother didn't like this arrangement. She thought Sukunwa was not doing anything. Her aunt let her wander around. "If they don't need her," she told Kiptai, "they should let her come help here with the fire, the house-cleaning, and bringing the water, for she's surely old enough to do that much!" Kiriswa and Chelamai could not oppose this because, by law, Kiptai had the right to do what he wanted with his children. So Sukunwa was taken back again.

Then, Chemutai, Taptamus' daughter, came from the city to visit her sister-in-law Chelamai. She quickly learned that Kiptai's wife couldn't stand Sukunwa. "My heart fell down to the bottom of my stomach. I don't like to see how my Cheptabut's children are being treated, Sukunwa in particular. I'm going to take her with me. She does more work than a child twice her age," Chemutai told Chelemai.

"No one can say I haven't tried. I have, but they don't let her out of their sight," said Chelamai.

"Don't tell my child she's being abused," said Kiptai. Chemutai had told him she wanted to take Sukunwa, because she did not like the way she was being made to work like a grown woman at eight years old.

"My child won't go to the city to watch you bring one man into the house after another," said Kiptai. "Never!"

Chemutai did not reply. Mary had told her that if the father became impossible they would arrange something. Mary thought anything would be better for Sukunwa than where she was. Lydia was shown how to get Sukunwa to come to spend the night with her, and told not to say that Mary or her aunt Chemutai wanted her. The two girls had one night together before Sukunwa left. They talked until Mary told them to sleep. Then they went to bed and whispered instead.

"Can we be sisters?" whispered Lydia.

"Yes, we could imagine we are," Sukunwa whispered back.

"We don't have to imagine. If we break a red bead, we'll be like real sisters."

"How? Where did you hear that?"

"Well, my grandmother was talking to Tamutwol, and they said that the reason Tolony didn't marry her boyfriend was that they broke a red bead and that made them be brothers and sisters. So I think if we break a red bead, too, then we'll be sisters.

"But I don't have a red bead," Sukunwa replied.

"I have some in my necklace."

"How are we going to find a red one in the darkness?"

"Let's go outside. We can see by the moonlight," said Lydia.

"Where are you going?" asked Mary.

"We're going to wee-wee," said Lydia.

"Are you afraid? Should I take you?" asked Mary.

"No, we are not afraid, the moon is shining" said Lydia. She was eight months younger than Sukunwa, but she knew more than Sukunwa. Mary was careless, and she talked without checking if Lydia was around. Taptamus had been careful — when she was talking about adult matters she had always asked Sukunwa to leave. "Don't sit around when grown-ups are talking," she had said. "Go out and play."

Once outside, Lydia quickly located a red bead on her necklace and told Sukunwa she had found it.

"Let's break it and go in," said Sukunwa.

"Oh no, we have to do a little ceremony first," said Lydia. The ceremony was more trouble than it was worth. Lydia insisted they must kneel and both hold the bead together before breaking it, and say some Nandi prayers. Sukunwa knelt, although she hated getting down on the muddy ground, and together they held onto the bead.

"Let us feel as though we are sisters from now on. Repeat after me, 'From now on we are sisters.' My sister, together we will own these mountains of Kamasai. Sukunwa takes Mt. Kabiyet, the smoky mountain, I take Mt. Kaigat, the long-necked mountain, and we share Mt. Kamasai. Here let's break it!" Lydia took a bite out of the bead and gave Sukunwa half to bite."

268

"What are you two doing outside? Aren't you done yet?" called Mary.

"We have finished, Grandma," said Lydia.

"Come in then," said Mary.

"Coming," Lydia answered. "Have you bitten it," she lowered her voice and asked Sukunwa.

"I have," said Sukunwa.

The next morning Sukunwa and her aunt Chemutai quietly left Mt. Kamasai for the city.

CHAPTER SIXTEEN

Sukunwa hated life in the city. There was no Lydia, and there were no other Nandi children. Her aunt worked for an English family as a babysitter and lived in a one-room cottage behind the family's house. She got up at five in the morning, made tea, sliced the bread, spread Bluebonnet margarine on it, and set it aside for Sukunwa to eat when she got up. She left at six for work. Sukunwa got up and stirred the charcoal fire on the stove, added more charcoal and heated up her tea. When she had finished her breakfast, she went to stand at the window and wait for the family to leave. Sukunwa had been told never to go outside until she had seen the English family going out with their car. It didn't take long. They took the older daughter to school early in the morning. Sukunwa thought their daughter was her age and that she was exquisite. She liked the way her clothes looked. Once the family were gone, Sukunwa could get out. She took her blanket and went behind the cottage. Her aunt had shown her where it was safe to stay, if the family arrived unexpectedly, they wouldn't see her there.

Sukunwa spread her blanket out on the ground in the tall grass, and a world of fantasy sprang into her mind like magic. She was a dreamer. She blinked and let her mind and eyes travel a thousand miles up into the sky. She saw the clouds move and make the shape of a man with a long beard looking after sheep, cattle and something wandering, like children without anyone to love them. She imagined those children were her and her brother, and bitterness rushed into her heart and she cried. Suddenly she heard the sound of the car. The family had returned for lunch. She snapped out of her reverie. Through the tall grass she watched them get out of their car. The joy of being alive rushed back into her heart. She loved all their clothes, but she liked the daughter's best, because she could imagine dressing like her. The daughter wore a green school uniform with a white blouse, white shoes, a white ribbon in her hair and white stockings. When she came home, she changed into a blue and white checkered dress, black shoes and white stockings. When she came out to play, Sukunwa undressed her in her mind and pretended she was wearing the clothes herself.

At one o'clock her aunt came for lunch. The family had retired for an after-lunch nap. If Sukunwa was not in, Chemutai knew where she would be. She either smuggled Sukunwa's food out of the house to her or smuggled Sukunwa in to eat it. She had one day a week off, from Saturday afternoon through Sunday morning, and at two she would again smuggle Sukunwa out with her and go to visit friends in Eldoret town. There, women without jobs lived with their half-husbands, men who left their real wives at home on small pieces of land to come to the city to look for jobs. When the men found work, their bosses, who were always European, told them that they didn't want them to bring their wives and children to where they worked. So all the men in the city found themselves city women whose only work was to please men to get money to live on.

On their way to the city, Sukunwa was taken to a shop which sold ready-made clothing and shown some dresses. Her aunt asked her to choose one. She broke into a big smile, but thought she didn't see anything she liked.

"Aunt Chemutai, do they have a green short-sleeved dress with a white blouse, white socks and a white ribbon?" she asked.

"No, those are school uniforms, Sukunwa. Choose something else. I like this black skirt with the white stripe around the middle."

"Yes," agreed Sukunwa.

"Buy it for now. I will buy you the green and white outfit when you start school."

"Oh auntie, you are so nice! You will send me to school! I only wish Lydia could come to school with me."

In addition to the skirt, Sukunwa's aunt bought her a white hat, a red scarf and some black shoes. "Let's carry the clothes in the bag,

272

but wear the shoes," she said. A light drizzle was falling. Leaving the shops, Sukunwa and her aunt walked past the police station. The houses of the African police were round, of white-washed mud, with conical, thatched roofs. A circle of bare earth surrounded each house, and the grounds were well-kept grass lawns. Here and there, yellow flowers were planted. Fifty yards beyond the police station they encountered an unkempt assemblage of tiny brick houses with small rectangular windows. The houses were built in rows right next to one another along narrow, dirt alleys.

Sumuni ran to meet them. "Is this the Sukunwa you have been talking about?" she asked.

"Yes," said Chemutai.

"I'm Sumuni," Sumuni said.

Sukunwa was surprised. People at home had said that it was very clean in the city, but she thought Mt. Kamasai was a paradise compared to this place. Not a blade of grass was to be seen, only dirty stones. Here and there some people passed wheeling charcoal and shouting, "Charcoal! Charcoal! Buy some charcoal! One shilling, mother."

Everyone's eyes flashed. They looked as though they knew everything there was to know in the world. The alleys were noisy and full of people walking quickly with jubilant, sure-of-themselves expressions on their faces. Others shouted from their windows to anyone they knew walking by in the alleys. "Did you hear? Finally, we are going to be independent. The radio said everyone should go out to vote." Still others sat on their door stoops, weariness on their faces said they had seen it all before.

Sukunwa went in with Sumuni. Her aunt was in already. Sukunwa greeted Sumuni's mother, Awa, with a bow. She was sitting on a big bed covered with a beautifully embroidered white bedsheet. The chairs in the room were covered with white cloth embroidered with little beads, like tiny pearls. Sumuni's mother looked liked no one Sukunwa had ever seen. Sukunwa stood in the middle of the room staring at her creamy face and her dazzling smile. She was heavily made up with powder, penciled eyebrows and eyelids, and she had a black dot on her forehead. One of her teeth was capped with gold and sparkled whenever she smiled. I would run for my life if I met her outside at night, Sukunwa thought.

"Let's go to my room," said Sumuni.

"You should go out. I don't like children in when grown-ups are talking," said Sumuni's mother. But Sumuni showed Sukunwa her beaded bracelet and clothes, and soon everyone forgot they were still inside.

More women came when Chemutai came. They liked to hear talk about how the English people were so inferior, about how immoral they were. They, the Nandi, felt they were far superior to them in such matters. One of them said, "I used to work for one who went to bed with his wife when she had her period, and then he would turn around and kiss his mother-in-law the next morning. Her bedroom was right next to theirs!"

"That one didn't do anything. The one I work for does something even more horrid. He follows his daughter into the bathroom, and one day, when I heard the child crying and went in, I caught him with his hand in her private place," said Chemutai.

"That isn't bad for them. It is considered shameful for a father if his daughter is a virgin," said Awa.

"How bizarre! How do you know this?"

"My aunt married an Englishman. I babysit their son Kimunai."

"And her husband told you such an intimate things as this?"

"There is nothing intimate about this to them. It is their custom. My aunt's husband found it ridiculous that Nandi girls worry about being killed by their fathers if they lose their virginity."

"This explains something I've been puzzled by. I tried unsuccessfully to teach the girls I babysat not to climb on their father, but they did it again and again even in front of their mother. The daughters wiggled on their father's lap until I could see the father's erection."

"What was the mother doing?" asked Awa.

"Laughing and jumping all over him, too."

"You should have known it was their custom then if the mother was participating, too."

"I thought it was my responsibility as a babysitter," said Chemutai. Although in Nandi women's law it was stated clearly that girls should show respect for their fathers from a distance, mothers were still responsible for ensuring that their daughters behaved with propriety. Chemutai had assumed that every woman in the world taught her daughters the same thing. That was how much those Nandi knew about the Europeans in Africa. European customs were what they saw happen in front of them.

Sukunwa was somewhat embarrassed about her aunt's outspokenness about sex. She must have thought Sumuni and I had left the house, Sukunwa thought. "What would your mother and my aunt say if they found out we were here all the time?" she asked.

Sumuni pointed to the window in her room. They crawled out through it. Sumuni led the way and then turned to help Sukunwa down. Then the two girls went around the house and went back in by the front door.

"Did you have fun with Sumuni outside?" Chemutai asked Sukunwa. Sukunwa blushed a dark red, but Sumuni jumped right in.

"We sat down on the doorstep, and the sun started to sink behind the mountain. Then we watched the stars appear, and ..."

"Never mind," her mother cut her off, "put the charcoal on the stove."

"Sukunwa can help," said Chemutai. "I haven't told you, Sukunwa, we are going to spend the night here," she added.

"Sukunwet," Sumuni's mother called.

"I like being called just 'Gold,' not 'Goldie,'" Sukunwa murmured softly.

"Oh, you made a mistake. I'll never forgive myself. Sukunwa likes her name as just Sukunwa for 'gold,'" said Chemutai.

"I will call her 'Gold' only from now on. Sukunwa, come sit beside me. I would like to talk with you." Sukunwa came to sit beside her, and Sumuni followed to listen to what her mother told Sukunwa.

"Sumuni, you are practising bad manners. You never do something when you are told to. Go put the charcoal on the stove! For the last time! I don't want to tell you again," her mother told her.

"But mother, Chemutai said Sukunwa was going to help," said Sumuni.

"I want to talk to Sukunwa. Didn't you hear me?

"I will help you," said Chemutai.

"She can do it alone. She is ten years old and not a baby," Awa said. Sumuni left.

"Did your aunt tell you your mother, Cheptabut, was a very good friend of mine?" Awa asked Sukunwa.

"She hasn't told me yet," answered Sukunwa.

"I will tell you now that she was, and I want you to feel at home here. Your aunt and I have talked about your staying here with us to go to school. Don't be afraid — every child here goes to school, and you will go with Sumuni." Sukunwa looked at her aunt.

"I agree. You can't stay with me and go to school. But I will make sure I come every other evening to see you and bring you whatever you want."

"I know Sukunwa will not be disappointed. I will do everything to make her happy, said Awa.

"Go see what Sumuni is doing," Chemutai said to Sukunwa.

"I think she is a very pleasant young girl," said Awa.

"Oh yes, very pleasant. She does not like it where I work because I have to make her sit inside alone," said Chemutai.

"I think she is really quite beautiful — just like her mother."

Sumuni was listening behind the door. "Did my mother say you will go to school with me?" she asked.

"Yes," answered Sukunwa.

"Oh you will be very happy. I will share some of my friends with you, although I dare say some of them have crazy mothers," sighed Sumuni. "You will see some of them..." There was a little hesitation in her statement. "You are going to see for yourself today. Muna is nice, and so is Marta, but the rest are neither here nor there."

"Are they coming here?" asked Sukunwa.

"No, we are going there because your aunt and her..." Sumuni stopped. "Because your aunt will sleep on our bed," she said. Chemutai had a boyfriend who came to meet her every Saturday and who slept over. They had to use Sumuni's bed, but Sumuni had been told not to talk about what grown-ups did.

"You are going to Tonti's today, Sumuni. I'm sure she will want to talk to Sukunwa about the mountains. She comes from Mt. Kamasai herself," said Awa.

"Honestly, mother! Must you ask people to go to Tonti's house?" asked Sumuni.

"Yes I must, for the reason I've already told you, and it's close to us."

"I'm not going to Tonti's place for all the treasure on earth and all the glory in paradise!"

"Watch your mouth! Don't make promises you won't keep!"

"It's the truth, mother. I would rather sleep in the alley."

"Sorry Sumuni. You've run out of luck. You may end up in the alley as you wish because you only have two choices. Go to Tonti's or you WILL sleep in the alley tonight."

"Listen mother, we are going to Marta's. I told Sukunwa she would meet her tonight."

"Sumuni, for the hundredth time I have told you, you can't go to Marta's house on Saturdays. Her mother's husband will be home, and he is a strange man. I would not want Sukunwa there. I don't care what you say, and I don't want to hear any more from you."

"Tonti's husband is home on Saturday too, and he's worse than the other. He never sleeps when he's drunk. He wakes people up and swears at them. The other one does all sorts of strange things, like dancing naked or peeing through the window," said Sumuni smiling.

"And asking for you-know-what in front of the children," said Awa, looking knowingly at Chemutai.

Muna and Marta saved the night. They arrived, and the whole group ended up at Tonti's house, after going by Marta's house for Marta to tell her mother that she was going to Tonti's. Marta's city stepfather was holding Marta's baby sister. Maybe he's drunk, thought Sukunwa. He was tossing the baby high in the air. As it came down, it was making very frightened noises. The man did this again and again. Sukunwa closed her eyes.

"Sukunwa, you haven't said much at all. Do you feel well?" asked Marta.

"She is new here, Marta. I think you city children talk so much you cannot imagine or understand that some people are simply gentle and quiet," Marta's mother said.

"Oh yes, mother, I'm quite aware of that. 'Everyone is gentler than us city children.' You always say that," Marta replied with a smile.

"We had better go," said Muna.

"Help," yelled Sumuni as she opened the door.

"What is it?" asked Marta.

"It's dark in the alley. Ask your father to take us," said Sumuni.

"Why? Did you only come here to make trouble? Ask your mother to take you," he answered when they asked.

"Have some compassion and take them. They asked you," said Marta's mother.

"No, I'm not their night watchman."

"He's afraid of the dark. Let's go," said Sumuni.

At breakfast the next morning Chemutai asked, "Did you have fun last night with the other children, Sukunwa?"

"Yes, but Marta's father, or perhaps her grandfather, appears rough, as though he hates children," said Sukunwa.

"He's not a grandfather. He is a city husband. He looks bad to you because you're new, but he's better by far than Tonti's husband," said Sumuni, getting to her feet. She never said anything without worrying about what her hypersensitive mother would say.

"I have given up on you, Sumuni. I hope you will borrow some manners from Sukunwa while she's staying with us," said Awa.

"I'm going home this afternoon. Are you staying or going with me now and coming back next week?" Chemutai asked Sukunwa.

"I'm coming with you," Sukunwa said with a sigh of relief.

"I should ask Awa to let Sumuni come with us. Then you can return with her to stay," said Chemutai.

"Oh yes! I will thank you forever. I will give anything to get out of this vile place. I would thank god if I never came back to this dusty no-good alley. No grass, no trees, no fruit, no water and everyone is drunk by four. It's an absolutely disgusting place!" said Sumuni.

"Don't swear at this place too much, Sumuni! Chemutai only asked you to go with them for four days. You have to come back here," said her mother.

"Mother, it would be a pleasure even if I only went for one day," said Sumuni on her way to her bedroom to pack her belongings.

"Remember now, Chemutai, I did not ask you to take Sumuni. If she causes you to get the sack, don't blame me," said Awa.

"Leave her to me," said Chemutai.

The next morning Chemutai was back at work in the European's house. Sukunwa got up to add more charcoal to the stove as she had been instructed by Chemutai. The stove was small, and it was intended to be carried outside until the charcoal had stopped smoking.

"Sukunwa can you take the stove outside until the smoke is gone?" asked Sumuni.

"No I can't. We have to open the window a little. The English family are still home," said Sukunwa.

"So what if they're home? Take the smoke out," Sumuni insisted, coughing for good measure as she spoke.

"I can't. They will see me," Sukunwa said.

"That's their problem, but this is a matter of principle. No one is asking them to be considerate of us. I'm going to do what I can within my power to remain alive. No one, not even a European, is going to force me to die from smoke inhalation. Do you know how painful it is to be killed by smoke?" Sumuni asked as she got to her feet and took her nightdress off to use as a pot holder. She carried the stove outside in her underwear in the morning chill of Eldoret, and then used her nightdress to fan the charcoal into flame.

The Englishman stood at the kitchen window, half-smiling at Sumuni's antics as she fanned the stove and half-angry that an African child had been brought onto his property. "Liona, come here," he called his wife.

"Well, well! What have we here. Chemutai, whose child is that?" she asked.

"My sister's child," said Chemutai looking down at her feet in shame over Sumuni's near-nakedness.

"Why isn't she at home with her parents? This is not an African camp. Remember we are not Africans. We don't want African children here."

"When my sister died, I brought her children back with me," said Chemutai half-lying because she couldn't bring herself to say that one child wasn't even related to her.

"Children? How many children?" Liona asked.

"Two," said Chemutai. Liona rushed to her bedroom, and her husband followed her. Chemutai stood in the kitchen waiting to be kicked out. She heard the husband say, "No, no." After a few minutes he came out.

"Chemutai, you take those children back on Saturday. We don't want African children here," he repeated.

At lunch time, Chemutai was furious with Sumuni. "Sumuni! I don't know where to begin. You defeat us all. Why did you go out without any clothes on?" she asked.

"I had to use my nightgown to hold the stove with, and it didn't bother me. I hope you didn't mind. I didn't see your boss hating it. He laughed and waved to me out of the window." said Sumuni.

"He didn't wave to you. Maybe you waved to him. An animal would wave to you before he would. He does not like Africans."

"I know they don't like Africans. That is why I did not let Sukunwa take the stove out. I didn't want to cause a problem."

Sukunwa shook her head and wondered at the way Sumuni was lying. Sumuni had asked her to take the stove out first.

"Too bad! They failed to notice you aren't African, and you were alone out there, so they couldn't have confused you with someone else," Chemutai said.

"He is a mean, unkind man! How dare he think I am an African? Did he see me with knotted hair? Go tell him my grandfather was Asian, and my father was Somali," said Sumuni, sobbing and feeling degraded.

"Don't cry! Maybe they knew your grandmother was Nandi."

"Well tell them I'm not Nandi, and I don't speak Nandi."

"I will tell them you're Asian, not Black. But don't try any more stunts. Even Asians put clothes on when they go out," said Chemutai.

In those colonial days, to be called African meant one was Black and less than human, nothing but an empty-headed, walking lump. Mixed children of African mothers were ashamed to be called African. Although the name African simply referred to the continent Africa, being colonized by Europeans had changed the meaning in people's minds. It now meant everything that was evil. It meant that your colour was black and that you were poor, primitive, stupid, and beneath everything else on earth. The name African was contaminated for those of mixed descent and even for some who weren't mixed. The members of the Somali community in the city somehow thought they weren't African.

Only those of mixed European-African descent accepted to be called African. The others hated everything African — the mud houses, the animal skin beds, the skin clothing, even the food, despite its many nourishing qualities. They hated everything that they thought black skin stood for. In the eyes of black Africans, however, these mixed peoples were considered the children of prostitutes and everyone was ashamed of them.

Two weeks later, Kiriswa and Kiptai arrived to take Sukunwa back home. Kiptai had said, "I want my child back home with me. Chemutai can bring her own children to the city." But when he saw how his daughter was, he said that her body agreed with city life and changed his mind. Sukunwa was disappointed. She wished her father had insisted on taking her back home so she could see Lydia. Her uncle and father left without her.

The next Saturday it rained all morning, but by noon it had stopped. Soft blue sky shone through motionless, ash-coloured clouds.

"Oh, Sukunwa!" Sumuni sighed. Chemutai glanced at her.

"What?" asked Sukunwa.

"Look outside! Not even the leaves are murmuring after the rain, and the clouds are standing still. Can we go out there? I'm sure the English family are taking a nap and wouldn't see us?" asked Sumuni.

"No, we have to leave in half an hour," said Chemutai.

"That is even more reason to go out — to bid the trees farewell," said Sumuni.

"You will tell them good-bye on your way out. Pack your clothes," said Chemutai.

"You are forgetting to tell the trees bye-bye," Sukunwa pointed out to Sumuni when they left. She had liked Sumuni's idea of saying good-bye to the trees.

"I have waved to them already," Sumuni said. "What about you?"

"Oh, I will do it now then," said Sukunwa looking at her aunt for her approval.

"Don't mind me. You can do what you want," said Chemutai.

Sukunwa went and stood beside the trees, silently touching the leaves. "Good-bye trees and grass. I feel miserable to leave you. My feet tremble and my heart aches at the thought of leaving you. I will come back to see you." The speech she gave was borrowed. Sukunwa had overheard Kiriswa tell it to Chelamai once when he left Mt. Kamasai.

CHAPTER SEVENTEEN

*C*hemutai was not happy leaving Sukunwa alone with a family in the city. The city children spoke sharply, and Sukunwa was very gentle, but it was necessary if she was to go to school. Chemutai told Sukunwa to hurry home after school and to put her mind into her books. "I don't want to hear you are running around with your mind on boys," she told her. Chemutai had discovered education through babysitting for the English family, and she liked it. Putting Sukunwa through school was, for her, a dream come true.

Sukunwa was very clever. She started in Standard One and jumped to Standard Four, where her age-mates were, in one year. She was calmer than the city children, and her teachers liked her for this. She had fewer excuses in class, she did her homework, and she handed it in on time. Joshua, one of her teachers, discovered that she liked books. She was eager to know everything in any book she came across. Africans did not have many books to read for pleasure. They only had a few textbooks which had been provided by missionaries. Joshua had a bible and read it to her every day for half an hour after school. Joshua told Chemutai that Sukunwa had a great natural love for books.

"It is so disappointing, finally to have a student who makes the teachers feel like they are good teachers, and then not to have any books for her to read to develop good learning skills," he said.

There was no place to buy books, and even if there had been such a place, Chemutai would not have known where it was. However, the children she babysat had many books. Chemutai wished they could spare some. Finally, she helped herself to two of them. Both were about science, one about the scientific study of the ocean, and the

283

other about the science of things above. Joshua told Sukunwa that the people who studied the stars long ago thought that the sky was a big balloon and the stars were inside it.

"These people were called astronomers, but modern astronomers think that space goes forever without an end," Joshua said to Sukunwa after she had read the book.

"What do you call the people who study the ocean?"

"Oceanographers."

Sukunwa had always been a happy child and, at home, she had been outgoing among children her own age. In the city, however, she became quieter than the children her own age. She could not keep up with the city children. They talked big, shameful words of sex, lying and smoking. Sumuni, Muna and Marta were always around. Though she did not have much to talk to them about, they liked her. They went to school in a group of four. Sukunwa and Sumuni got up at six o'clock to help each other with the morning chores. They made tea and pancakes for breakfast and then boiled water and took it to the house for Awa to take a bath. At seven-thirty they left for school.

Everyone took an umbrella, for Eldoret was a rainy city. The sun rose at seven o'clock and shone gently until eleven. Then thick clouds moved in with a wind that blew strongly from east to west, mixing the clouds with rain to darken the city by twelve o'clock. People in the city never walked. They ran in sunshine to make it to their destinations before it rained, and when it rained, they ran to find shelter.

"I hate it raining every day so! I like leaving a little early so I can walk, but oh no, I can't," Sumuni complained, "because I have to boil water for my mother. She has as much energy as spinach in a cooking pot! She can't even move a cup on the table. She takes a bath and goes to bed. She never sets her feet outside. I wonder what she washes. I will get married as soon as I get out of school and leave her to boil her own water." Sumuni turned to see if Sukunwa had anything to say about it. Sukunwa looked at her blankly.

"Well, don't you agree with me?"

"Well, she hasn't caused me any trouble," Sukunwa said shyly.

She had nothing to say, and she now had far worse problems of her own. She was depressed and confused, and she couldn't tell anyone what was happening. School had become a nightmare for her. Not one boy in her class liked her and, although she liked learning, she dreaded being in the classroom. When she was passed three times in a year, the word got around that she was showing off and that she wouldn't talk to anyone. Who did she think she was? Anytime the teacher asked a question, she was the first one to put her hand up.

"You'd better be careful," she was warned. "Don't ask questions, and don't answer any," the city boys told her. "You are a woman. Let us men answer. Don't show off because you're not going anywhere. You're just taking up a space that a man could have. Start thinking about something else, like a husband and children," the older boys told her and pulled her ears. Sukunwa looked down and let her tears drop.

Sumuni, Muna and Marta came by Sukunwa's classroom that afternoon. They waited for her to come out at the path they took to go home to lunch. When she didn't come, they went looking for her. There were four boys around Sukunwa. They had torn her notebook, and she was crying, her hands on her face. Sumuni ran to hug her and picked up her shredded notebook.

"Look what you have done to her book, you sonofabitch, you mother's cunt, you thief like your father!" she shrieked, staring fiercely at them.

"Tell your friend we are not dazzled by her intelligence," one of the boys said with a laugh. "We know where her intelligence is going to end. Everything she thought she knew will disappear into a cooking pot."

"Look! You've ruined her book and now she is crying," Sumuni said.

"We wanted to see if she was as strong as she is intelligent," one of the boys said.

"Let's go, man," another said.

"How can you expect a little child to stand up to you? You cowards! You screaming mules! You bastards! You sons of bitches!"

said Sumuni, trembling. She had picked up a stone, and so had the other two girls, waiting for the boys to move towards them.

"You call us sons of bitches?" one of the boys asked. "You're going to wish you hadn't." He turned. "Come this way!" But the others were pulling back.

"Leave her, man. She's a crazy loud-mouth," they said.

"She called us names," he said.

"Forget it," they said and ran. They had seen Joshua approaching.

"I will call you the same again, you numb-brains," said Sumuni, who had not seen Joshua.

"Sumuni, you are provoking the boys," said Joshua.

"I did not. They tore Sukunwa's book."

"Sukunwa, you should stay away from the boys. Unlike boys in the country, they fight girls and have no morals. They will beat you up and call you unbelievable things," said Joshua calmly as he walked to the classroom.

At home, the girls did not talk about the problems they had had at school. Sumuni said to Sukunwa, "Please don't tell Awa we had trouble with the boys. She will say my loud mouth caused it."

Sukunwa spent the rest of the afternoon in her bedroom, reading her two science books and watching out of the window for her aunt to come. She realized it would be dark in a little while and Chemutai might not come. She stopped watching and went back to bed to read. Not very long after, Chemutai arrived. Just as she entered, there was a scream from the alley. Someone was calling for help.

Awa and Chemutai exchanged glances. Chemutai remained standing at the entrance.

"Strange. I didn't see anyone on my way here," she said.

"Forget it. Come and sit. The children in the neighbourhood, I tell you, have an unpleasant habit of scaring each other in the dark. You shouldn't think they haven't been told not to scream in the night. Oh no, they've been told a thousand times. They just don't listen," said Awa.

"Help! This dreadful son of a sinner is strangling me!" The screaming voice was clearer this time, and it belonged to Sumuni.

"Let's run!" A second voice — Marta's — cried out.

"It's Sumuni for god's sake!" Awa said, rushing to get a flashlight. Both she and Chemutai ran outside.

"Sukunwa, don't come out! Stay inside!" Chemutai yelled on her way out.

Sumuni, Marta and Muna were all beating someone on the ground.

"What is the matter with you Sumuni?" said Awa with a little more feeling than usual. "You are hurting him."

"I should have known you would be on his side instead of mine. How dare you say I was hurting him when he almost strangled me," Sumuni said getting up and running into the house past her mother and Chemutai.

"Jeremiah! What are you doing with the girls?" Jeremiah got up and ran wordlessly away.

Sukunwa had her eyes in her book when Sumuni burst in crying. She was not reading, but she thought that was the safest place for her eyes to be at that point.

"My mother is the greatest evil of all evil. Do you know what she did?" asked Sumuni sobbing, her faced buried in the pillow. "She accused me of beating this boy up, I swear to god, without making any attempt to find out who started it." She turned to lie on her back so she could see Sukunwa's reaction. Sukunwa was still looking at her book. She didn't know what had happened with Sumuni outside, and there were too many people arguing about it at the same time. She also didn't want her aunt to find her talking about things she knew nothing about.

"Was your mother like mine?" asked Sumuni grabbing Sukunwa's book out of her hand so Sukunwa could no longer evade her.

"No, I was with my grandmother," Sukunwa said sitting on the corner of the bed.

"Didn't you have a mother?" Sumuni asked, drying her eyes now.

"I used to have both, but I don't have them any more."

"I know that. I mean, was your mother like Awa and full of hate?"

"No, I used to live with my grandmother. Mothers in Mt. Kamasai like children, and we don't have alleys to go through in Mt. Kamasai,

287

and nobody beats people up on the path going to Lydia's house. We are only afraid of monkeys there, not people," said Sukunwa.

"Did I hear anyone mention Lydia's name?" Chemutai called as she entered the room. "Sukunwa, you know you haven't hugged me, and you haven't either, Sumuni."

Sukunwa went to hug her, and Sumuni turned back on her stomach and buried her face again in the pillow. "Nobody cares for me! Why should I care for anyone at all!" she stammered.

"How long is this wound going to go on festering on me for heaven's sake?" yelled Awa as she came into the room with Muna and Marta. "Are you determined to make everybody miserable tonight? You'd better quit! You know I hate a brush fire that refuses to go out, and you're being a nuisance. What were you doing with Jeremiah in the alley anyhow? You explain yourself, and explain it well!"

Chemutai felt Sukunwa twitch with shock. Jeremiah was exactly the boy who had torn her exercise book that afternoon. Maybe he was coming for me, she thought. She burst into tears.

"What's happening with the children?" asked Chemutai.

"Come on, all of you sit down here and explain what you were fighting about," Awa said. "Chemutai, don't you think we're entitled to an explanation at least?"

Sumuni didn't move from her bed. Marta and Muna sat beside Sukunwa. "Jeremiah hates me putting my hand up in class," said Sukunwa.

"Did you hear that, mother? I did not start it," said Sumuni scrambling to her feet to explain what had happened. "If you don't believe me, ask Muna. I didn't say anything to him. I went to help Sukunwa after they had torn her book. I think he didn't like it at all. That is why he wanted to kill me, and you didn't even ask who had started the whole thing before you accused me when you found him beating me up."

"He wasn't beating you, Sumuni! You were beating him!" interjected Awa.

"Everybody knows Jeremiah's brain is dead. He has been in the same class with his other friends for the last three years, and now they are blaming Sukunwa for their unimprovable brains," said Sumuni.

"Are you finished?" asked Awa.

"You don't believe me?" asked Sumuni.

"That is the end of the discussion Sumuni. I will take Sukunwa to school tomorrow personally," said Awa.

"I will go with you. We have to make sure they never do this again," said Chemutai.

Chemutai didn't go to work the next day. They came back from school at eleven and felt lazy. Tonti invited them to lunch and to drink. After that they went back to Awa's place, and Chemutai spent the afternoon in bed.

When Chemutai arrived at work the next day, it was a disaster. No one spoke to her. Peter, the Luyia cook, was extremely happy, whistling as he washed the dishes, and Chemutai knew that was the end of her job. All the Africans working as cooks for the English expected the babysitters to go to bed with them, because they didn't have their wives with them. Chemutai would have no part of this. She hated Peter. Peter hated her and was always unhappy around her. At midday she went to her house for lunch. She returned to work and as she entered the kitchen Peter told her that Liona wanted to see her. "What for?" she asked.

"Go and ask her," said Peter and left the room.

Chemutai went through the doors into the sitting room. The floor and chairs were covered with black paint. Then and there Chemutai knew there were big problems.

"Yes, memsahib," she said.

"Chemutai, go and see my husband," said Liona. Chemutai walked out of the room and into the husband's office.

"Sorry Chemutai," he said and handed her some money. "You are dismissed. No job."

"Why?" Chemutai asked.

"No questions, Chemutai. You know why. Leave."

Peter was at the kitchen door waiting for her to leave. He smiled to himself and tried not to look at Chemutai. Chemutai walked half-way to her house, then turned around.

"I want to ask you for curiosity's sake. I know it will be easy to clean the paint you poured on the floor, but how are you going to clean the paint you smeared on the chairs?"

"What are you talking about? You left the paint lying around. Didn't you know the children would pour it out?" said Peter smiling.

"I should know you are too selfish to give away your cleaning recipes. I was only asking in case I run into another cook who pours paint on floors and chairs and I'm asked to clean the mess up," Chemutai said as she walked toward her house to pack. Peter passed by while Chemutai was packing. At three o'clock he came back with a short, stocky woman. Chemutai ran in front of the house to see a face that was instantly familiar.

"Oh for heaven's sake, it's you Agnes! How nice to see you! If I had known it was you who was going to have my job, I wouldn't have been so shocked when I discovered what Peter had done. Good luck with the job," said Chemutai.

"Thank you, but I don't know if I'm going to get it," Agnes said.

"Oh you will get it. You know what to do with Peter, and I hope he doesn't wear you out," said Chemutai going into her house. She felt better. She had said what she had set out to say.

For two weeks, everybody crowded into Awa's place. Fortunately, the cramped feeling was ameliorated by the fact that Chemutai and Awa both thought alike about a lot of things. Sukunwa gave no opinion; she observed, but never disagreed. Sometimes she lay back and giggled at the way Sumuni never stopped to listen to anyone, but just let the words run out of her mouth.

Chemutai tried to find another job. Awa suggested she look for a house nearby and go into the homemade beer business. Chemutai gave up job-hunting, found a house a block from Awa, and did not regret Awa's recommendation. The house was never empty, especially on Saturdays. All kinds of people came by — policemen and prison guards, young and old alike — to buy the beer. Since Chemutai liked to cook, the people often left their own houses without eating.

"I've got flour, but no vegetables," Chemutai would say, and the people would contribute money for meat or vegetables. There was always something good cooking on the stove.

Sukunwa's education was going well. She was in the same class now with Sumuni. Sumuni didn't pay the least bit of attention to her own education, but this didn't change Sukunwa. She learned never to put her hand up when the teacher asked questions. She let the boys do it. The teacher knew Sukunwa was smart. He called her name when asking a question, but Sukunwa would say that she didn't know the answer even when she did. The boys would laugh and answer the question. Many times Sumuni would not know the answer, but when she did know, she would reply. She paid no attention to the boys. When one sneered at her, she would say, "Why are you staring at me? If you don't like me replying, go stick your head in the outhouse hole." She would say this out loud, and then war would start in class. This way, no one dared to look at her when she was giving an answer. Sukunwa wished she had this power herself, but she never dared to try it out. When she got her tests back, she hid them. She wouldn't even talk about them to Sumuni. Sumuni might say that Sukunwa had gotten high marks, and then Sukunwa would suffer the consequences later from the boys.

In the evening, Sukunwa went into her bedroom before the other children arrived and sat and shared her life with a dream she had inside her. This dream was her closest friend, the only friend she had except for Lydia. She sat on the corner of her bed and felt terrible. She felt like a thief and a sinner, and was disgusted with herself because, although people thought her a wonderful child, she dreamt like a man. She was not good, she knew, because she dreamed the dreams of men. If my grandmother were alive and knew what was going on in my mind, oh how angry she would be with me, she thought. She hated herself and tried to break the habit, but she couldn't.

Sukunwa had been raised traditionally. Ever since she had learned to walk and talk, she was taught, like Nandi girls, that a woman should not talk like a man, swear like a man, or wish to do what a man did. When she discovered the world of books, she became confused. The books were about men and science, and she liked the feeling of their life of discovery. She did not know how to read well, but when Joshua read to her every day after school, she memorized what he said and then read to herself the way he had read to her. She was glad for the occasional times when Sumuni did not come home, because she was sleeping over with friends. Then, she could read on her own.

"Sukunwa, we have to shut the lights off by eight o'clock, and then you must use the lantern," her aunt said, interrupting her dream. "It is better to buy paraffin than to pay for electricity."

"Yes," said Sukunwa, going into her room to light her lantern. She took out her two books and set them on the bed so she would know where they were when she came back. Her aunt had told her always to wash her feet before going to bed and then to oil them. She did this and then went to her little bed. She picked up one of the books and read it. It said "First Science Course for Oceanographers." The word oceanographer sent her back into her dream. She dreamt of being the best oceanographer in the world, and she was a man!

But how? She was a woman! She turned the page and saw two men under the water with four little salmon hatchlings in their hands. Sukunwa found this fascinating and frustrating at the same time. She could not imagine herself in a long dress under the deep sea. Then she told herself this was her dream, and she could wish anything she wanted to for herself. Who will ever know I am a man in my dream, she thought.

"I wonder if I made a mistake getting you those books? You never sit and talk to me after dinner. What is in this one?" asked Chemutai as she came and sat at the edge of the bed and lifted up the other book. "What does this say?" she asked as she opened a page. "Can you read it?"

"Not very well," answered Sukunwa.

"Can you try to read it here?" asked Chemutai as she pointed out the page. Sukunwa took the book.

The people who lived in Babylon many, many years

ago thought that the blue bowl of the sky touched the
Earth at its rim.

"What do people think today?" asked Chemutai.

"This is a book about the history of astronomy, Aunt Chemutai. I
would have to read to the end of the book to find out what people
think about the sky nowadays," said Sukunwa, against her principles.
She liked to read a few lines a week out of her books and then
elaborate them into rich dreams of her own future.

"Can you read this bit again?"

"Yes, aunt."

> The Hebrew people who lived long, long ago thought
> that when good people died, they went above the sky
> to Heaven, and when bad people died, they went to
> Hell.

"Well, did they really go to heaven or hell?" asked Chemutai.

"I don't know. You can ask Joshua."

"Joshua!"

"Yes, he can read better."

"Yes, he knows how to read, and he is also extraordinarily stupid
and boring. Never mention to him that I want him to read to me. I tell
you, make no mistake, he is impossible. For after you let him — I
remember he used to come to Awa's place and spend innumerable
hours even after no one wanted to listen to him."

"What did you do to have him leave?"

"Awa had to show him to the door. He's your friend, isn't he?"
asked Chemutai.

"Yes, he reads to me after school, but he mostly talks to me about
god."

"That's his trouble. He doesn't talk about anything else but god.
Sukunwa, you must think of something else besides what's in your
books," said Chemutai. "You're going to be like him."

"What else can I think of?" asked Sukunwa.

293

"Lydia. What if I tell you she is coming here this week?"

"I know she would not come, but if she would come, I would stay home with her and give her my other shoes to wear. I know she would like that. I wonder what she would say if you took us to that shop. Oh Aunt Chemutai, she would be quite astonished. But I know she can't come."

"Sukunwa, if you would stop talking, I would tell you more. Lydia and Mary are coming the day after tomorrow. I was keeping it as a surprise for you. Mary sent a message to let me know they are coming."

Two days later, Sukunwa did not go to school. She got up in the morning and put on her best clothes.

"Should I wear my necklace, Aunt Chemutai?" she asked.

"Of course, if you want to."

"I thought I would never see Lydia again, Aunt Chemutai. Should I wear my hat and belt?"

"Yes, Sukunwa, wear whatever you want."

"Lydia will be absolutely dumbfounded to see me like this. I hope she will recognize me. She will be astonished. I know because I remember how I felt the first time I saw European children dressed like this."

"Are you going to eat anything today, Sukunwa? You haven't eaten breakfast."

"I'm waiting for Lydia."

"They may arrive late. Eat a little and then wait."

Sukunwa ate, combed her hair, brushed her teeth and came to sit in her aunt's room, which had a big window that allowed her to watch the path outside. Chemutai looked at her and smiled to herself. My sister's daughter is beautiful, she thought. What a shame her mother did not live to see her grow.

"Here they are!" cried Sukunwa, as she rushed out to meet them.

In half an hour, the parties had separated — Mary and Chemutai were alone in the sitting room, and Sukunwa and Lydia had gone to Sukunwa's bedroom. Sukunwa asked about her brother and her cousins in Mt. Kamasai. Lydia, however, was speechless and sat on the bed nodding her head and mumbling, "Yes, they are fine."

She had never seen a bed in her life, let alone sat on one. Sukunwa had a basket that she used as a wardrobe, and Lydia's eyes fell upon this now.

"Sukunwa!" she exclaimed. "Are all these clothes yours?"

"Yes," replied Sukunwa as she went to bring the basket of clothes. She poured them out on the bed for Lydia to see. Lydia went through all the clothes one by one smelling each as she picked it up and set it aside. "Oh, this one is so beautiful," she said as she picked up a red dress trimmed with black along the bottom.

"Would you like to try it on?"

"Oh, would I!" Lydia tried on all of the clothes, and at last Sukunwa asked her if she wanted to keep them on. Lydia said yes, but also said she would like to try on the dress Sukunwa had on. Sukunwa took it off and handed it to her.

"Could I wear this for a while?"

"Yes, you can." Sukunwa wore another one.

Each day she was there, Sukunwa got out of school and ran home to be with Lydia. Lydia wanted to go to Sumuni's to play, but Sukunwa always said, "No, we shouldn't. I have a lot to tell you." She read to her as soon as she finished changing out of her school uniform and explained her dreams to her.

"I can dream like a man, but don't tell anyone I have done it! And when I am a man, I can imagine doing anything I want. I'm going to be an oceanographer," she said.

"Can you really do it, Sukunwa?"

"Yes, in a dream you're capable of doing anything you want."

"I would like to be the one in the other book."

"Which one? The astronomer?"

"Yes, but what does an astronomer do?"

"They study the universe — the sun, the moon, the planets and the stars."

"I don't think I can."

"Imagine Lydia! Don't give up! Our planet is the Earth. It takes one year to go around the sun. Pluto is the farthest away. It takes 248 years to go around the sun. And if you imagine, Lydia, you can go there and come back now."

Lydia thought that was hard to imagine, but she tried it nevertheless. "What does it look like?" Sukunwa asked, looking into Lydia's eyes.

"I didn't see any people, but it was a mountainous country. The sun was bigger than the moon and more brilliant. The moon was bigger than the stars, but the stars were more brilliant than the moon," said Lydia.

"I must go and see for myself," said Sukunwa, closing her eyes.

"You were there for a long time. What did you see?"

"I saw a big house with many, many children. The moon is the mother of the stars, and the sun is the father."

"I think the ones I saw were the Mt. Kamasai moon and sun," said Lydia.

"Sukunwa!" Chemutai called.

"Are they in?" asked Mary.

"Yes. When they are together, they won't hear you."

"I'm glad their love for each other hasn't worn out. What are you calling them for? Let them stay in their room."

"I thought I should excite them. I'm taking them out tomorrow."

"They don't sound gloomy to me," said Mary.

"I know. Sukunwa and Lydia! Come here!" called Chemutai.

"Yes, Aunt Chemutai," answered Sukunwa.

"Listen! I'm going to take you downtown tomorrow, but I think you should help with the housework in the morning so we can leave early."

"Yes! Yes! We will. We will," said Sukunwa.

The sky was clear, calm and warm the next day. Downtown was packed with people — Africans walking and cheering in all of the places that were for whites only. They had been reassured by political activists that the country was theirs and were urged to get out and show their happiness. Chemutai had forgotten that in three days,

Kenya was going to become independent. They joined the crowd, cheering. "At last, at last! We are going to get our country back!"

The weather cooperated and it did not rain. A little past noon they left the crowd in the city and went to the Eldoret Club to watch the English people swim. When they got to the club some more Africans there were watching and chanting, "Swim in our water now! It may be the last time for you to do it!" They chanted a little and left for the city.

Chemutai bought presents for her sisters-in-law — Kiriswa's wives —and clothes for Sukunwa's brother. Two days later, the girls parted. Chemutai told Lydia, who wanted Sukunwa to go with them or she herself to stay, that two months from then, she, Chemutai, and Sukunwa would visit them.

When Lydia got back to the mountain, she became more unhappy. She told her grandmother Mary that she wanted to go to school like Sukunwa, hoping she would be taken back to Eldoret to go to Sukunwa's school. Instead she was taken to Chepterit to Mary's sister, Chebii, and there she was put into the Catholic girls' school.

The girls were twelve when they saw each other again. Sukunwa was taken to Chepterit. At twelve, they thought they were grown up and talked about what they would be doing in the future.

"I know I will never be married because I'm an only child, and I must look after my mother," Lydia told Sukunwa.

"I will always help you to look after your mother, Lydia."

"What if you get married to a bad husband?"

"I will leave him and come help you."

Sukunwa was with her for three days. The day of her departure, she and Lydia held a little ceremony to renew their sisterhood.

CHAPTER EIGHTEEN

Sukunwa went back to Eldoret. Now that the country was independent, more children were in school. However, except for city girls, nearly all of the newcomers were boys. Sukunwa made no new friends. Sumuni dropped out of school two years later, at fourteen and married a man who was visiting from Nairobi for the weekend. Sumuni said, "Do you know what it means to be married to a man from Nairobi? He is more sophisticated than these vile farmers who think they are city men but who arrive at school with dust and cobwebs in their hair because they oil it and don't wash it for months at a time."

Muna quit school and followed Sumuni to Nairobi, hoping to find a city man for herself. Marta just faded away. Later, she became pregnant through a man from the neighbourhood. Tonti's daughters were at home helping their mother to cook for the five boys going to school. There were no girls Sukunwa's age in school, and no girls at home. Coming from school, the boys made remarks, "Hey smart woman! No man wants to marry you. Are you going to rot here? You're getting old!"

Sukunwa shrugged her shoulders. "You can say all you like," she said as she walked away.

Sukunwa had Tonti, too, running after her on her way home from school to invite her to visit her daughters. Sukunwa hated her invitation because she always added at the end of it, "I would tell my daughters to visit you, but it would be embarrassing for people like us to be seen where you live. I wouldn't go there even if I was paid to. You know, people think every woman from those houses is a prostitute — even the girls there. I wouldn't let them into my house."

Sukunwa had been to Tonti's house many times with Sumuni,

Muna and Marta, and she wondered which girls Tonti meant. She never went to Tonti's willingly herself, only when she was dragged into it or begged to come. She liked Tonti's middle daughter, and didn't care for the rest, although they all wanted to be with her. They were mixed children, and they didn't go around with African girls. Tonti made it clear to Sukunwa that it was something big for her children to be with her. But when Sukunwa told her aunt this, Chemutai said it was the other way around. "They should be glad you even set foot in their house; you're worth more than all of them put together," she said. "If Tonti isn't a prostitute, why isn't she at home and married to a Nandi?"

Everyone agreed that Sukunwa was a beautiful child and that no other girl even came close to her in looks. But Sukunwa herself wasn't aware of this, and all of the other girls liked her and said she was their friend. Tonti's children invited her to a Christmas party. It was excellent, and she had a good time dancing the twist. Before leaving, she mentioned that she was departing the next day for Mt. Kamasai, and Suiyeta, Tonti's middle daughter, cried to her mother.

"Oh mother! Can we take her? I would like to see the mountains and all the children. Say yes, mother! We want to see the countryside."

Tonti agreed. "You and Kimibei can take her with Kitoi and Kimunai."

"If you decide not to go in the morning, let me know because I must go anyway," said Sukunwa. It was dark outside as she opened the door, and she drew back, shivering, because of the darkness. Tonti asked Kimibei, her older son, to take Sukunwa home. When they got there, Chemutai was still at Awa's. Sukunwa opened the door, and Kimibei followed her in. She turned on the light and offered him a chair. "Can you drink a cup of tea with me?" she asked.

"No, I don't drink tea at night; let's sit and talk," he said.

"What should we talk about?"

"School. Are you going to nursing school when you finish?" he asked.

"I haven't thought about it yet. Maybe I will and maybe I won't."

"I'm going to be a captain on a boat. My mother wants me to."

"Kimibei!" Tonti called from outside. But instead of answering her, Kimibei spoke to Sukunwa.

"That's my mother! She's followed us. Tell her I've gone. Is there another door?" he whispered.

"No," Sukunwa whispered back.

"Sukunwa! Open the door! Otherwise I'm going to break it down," said Tonti.

"Open the door and tell her I've gone," said Kimibei and ran into Sukunwa's room.

"How can I say you..."

"Just do it," he cut in before Sukunwa could finish.

Sukunwa had no idea what this was about. She opened the door. "Kimibei has gone," she said, standing at the door to stop them from coming in.

"I heard you talking to him," said Tonti, maneuvering herself around Sukunwa. Her oldest daughter followed. They were determined to find him. "Kimibei come out! Otherwise we will embarrass ourselves here if I have to turn the house upside-down to find you." They looked under Chemutai's bed, and then they went into Sukunwa's bedroom. Sukunwa closed her eyes. She was so miserable. What will happen if they find him in my bedroom, she thought. Tonti came back.

"Where is he? You were talking with him, and we heard you. Where is he?"

"He's not here I told you," replied Sukunwa.

"I've always thought you were better than the rest, but apparently I was wrong. But watch out! I won't stand around and watch you ruin my son. He's a school boy. I will destroy you personally."

"Please leave. I must close the door now," said Sukunwa.

"Leave and don't worry. You are going to remain with your sons as long you live. No one would even look at them — not because they're ugly. Oh no, it's because everyone fears you the way they fear poison and snakes," said Chemutai coming in behind.

"She must have stood outside when she heard us talking and listened to the whole thing," said Tonti.

Chemutai went straight to her bed and lay down. "Close the door Sukunwa and come sit beside me. I will tell you what we did at Awa's."

"I can't close it. They are standing in the way."

"Tonti, get out! Or do you want me to show you how!"

"Oh well. Do you think I would like anyone to see me in your house?" Tonti said as she left.

"Sorry Sukunwa! You had a bad time on Christmas day. Why didn't you come to Awa's house? You knew where I was. Kitoi, Kimunai and their mother came too, and we really had fun," said Chemutai.

"I had fun until just now," said Sukunwa as she walked to her room. She couldn't understand why Kimibei wasn't found in her room when he was there. She looked under the bed and shook her blanket out, but he wasn't in it. The room was small, and there was no way he could still be there. It was a complete mystery.

"Sukunwa!"

"Yes."

Chemutai hesitated a moment. What had gone on that day? "I told you Kimunai and his brother and mother have arrived, and you didn't say anything."

"Have they left?"

"No, Kimunai said he would take you to Mt. Kamasai tomorrow."

"I will see them tomorrow then."

"Yes. Are you going to bed now? I hope what Tonti said is not bothering you — everybody knows she is a witch."

"Oh no, it doesn't bother me, but I am ready to go to bed. Should I get up at any particular time?" Sukunwa asked standing beside her aunt's bed where she had come to wish her goodnight.

"I will wake you up. I know Kimunai and his brother Kitoi are going to sleep at Tonti's house, and no one will let them out until noon. Tonti is working hard to have her girls seen by Tapsirorei's children, but I'm afraid Kitoi has been taken. His father sent him to school in

England before he died, and last year he came home with a beautiful English girl. His father was on his death-bed, but he was extremely happy his son was with a white girl. I'm sure he gave them his blessing even though Tapsirorei was not agreeable to it. She has always wished her two sons to marry girls from home," said Chemutai.

Sukunwa didn't offer any opinion. She had seen Tapsirorei's sons, and didn't think there was anything extraordinary about them. She thought that Kitoi was handsomer and had better manners than Kimunai. Now that she heard Tonti wanted them, she thought Kimunai and Tonti deserved each other. She didn't sleep well that night, and she had a nightmare about Kimibei being found in her bedroom. At sunrise she got up and packed her clothes.

"Sukunwa, you are overdoing it! I told you they may arrive here before noon," said Chemutai, awakened by the noise Sukunwa made dragging her basket of clothes out from under the bed to pack.

"I know, but I would like to go on my own."

"Be reasonable, Sukunwa. Why spend money you've saved when someone is willing to give you a ride? That money will come in useful sometime. You can buy something you like for your brother."

Anger swept across Sukunwa's face. "I'm trying very hard to stay away from anyone who is connected with Tonti."

"Well, they are not connected with them. Tapsirorei is a close friend of mine, and I don't know what I will tell them."

"I will go with them, Aunt Chemutai. I had no idea they thought they had to take me."

"Do you want to go back to bed then?"

"No, I must take a bath and make breakfast and then dress to look good. They have to notice me too," Sukunwa said with a smile on her face. Lately she had developed a habit of gently teasing her aunt.

"You don't need to do anything to be noticed," said Chemutai.

Kitoi arrived earlier than Chemutai had predicted. He met Sukunwa at the entrance just as she was coming back from taking her bath. Sukunwa knew Kitoi, but she had been a little girl when Kitoi last saw her, and he hadn't taken much notice of her. Now he wasn't sure it was her. She greeted him warmly, but Kitoi returned her greeting without a sign of recognition. "Who is this?" he asked Chemutai.

"You don't know her? Try to remember if you've seen her before," said Chemutai.

"I don't know her."

"It's Sukunwa."

"I'll be damned! I would have passed her if I had met her in the street. Sukunwa, do you remember me?"

"Yes, I remember you well."

"Your uncle Kiriswa and I used to babysit you. Now you've grown up."

"Children grow up so fast, especially girls," said Chemutai. "Is Kimunai coming?"

"I don't know. I got up and left. I wanted to have breakfast with Sukunwa and you, but I must say I was thinking of a ten-year old Sukunwa," Kitoi said.

"I hope you're not too disappointed," Sukunwa smiled.

"No, I'm not."

At nine o'clock, a child was sent from Tonti's to ask Kitoi to come for breakfast. Kitoi said that if Sukunwa wanted to come with him, he would come.

"No, I'm not coming. I have a lot to do before leaving," Sukunwa said.

"I'll wait for you then. Tell your mother to make breakfast for two tomorrow. I'll bring Sukunwa with me," Kitoi jokingly said to the child.

Kimunai, Suiyeta and Kimibei arrived at ten and they all left a half-hour later. The party went by Awa's place where their mother had spent the night. Kitoi and Kimunai never went anywhere without letting their mother know. "Kitoi, I expect you to do the driving on the mountain, and if it rains, spend the night there. And watch your brother not to make a fool of himself. He doesn't know how to stop when he gets a drink, and..."

"I know mother..."

"Also, don't let Kimunai touch the car after he has had a drink," Kimunai added, to make a joke out of his mother's list.

"If I'm going to be driving, Sukunwa should sit in front with me, and you young people sit in the back," said Kitoi.

"Let Sukunwa choose herself," said Kimunai.

"I have chosen. I would like to sit in front," said Sukunwa, who was glad Kitoi had solved her problem. She had been dreading sitting with Kimunai in the back of the Landrover. He touched too much. He had already touched her once. Poor Suiyeta, she was going to be touched to death, Sukunwa thought. Kimunai sat in the middle between the brother and the sister. He leaned on Suiyeta with his hand behind her neck as though he were in love with her. What a nerve! thought Sukunwa. His voice was so gentle as he talked to Suiyeta, completely neglecting her brother. He smiled lovingly as his eyes met Sukunwa's. Sukunwa smiled back at him with a look of polite disapproval and turned around, shaking her head.

"You are so quiet! What class are you in at school?" asked Kitoi.

"Form One," answered Sukunwa.

"That's a lot of education. Aren't your parents afraid you may not get anyone to marry you?"

"I don't know. They haven't told me yet."

"There was a girl I went to England with, and a year later her brother came. He is at Oxford, but she left England and went to America. Last year she came home, hoping to find a man to marry her, but she couldn't."

"Couldn't she get a job?"

"She did, but she wanted a man too, to have children," said Kimunai.

"I don't think I want to get married anyway."

"Don't worry Sukunwa. I'm sure that when you are ready to get married, everyone will want to marry you. You are very beautiful — and I will be the first one at your parents' door," said Kimunai.

"Sukunwa will do what her aunt is doing," said Suiyeta.

"Sell home-made beer?" asked Sukunwa.

"Yes. Is that so bad?"

"Please," said Sukunwa, lying back and closing her eyes.

"Do you want to lie down?" asked Kitoi.

"No, I'm not sleepy."

"Nonsense! I can see you are! Put your head on my lap," said Kitoi.

"No, I couldn't sleep in a moving car," said Sukunwa.

"Talk to me then."

"Tell me about England then."

"What do you want to know? They don't live in grass houses. They don't eat *kimiet* like us, and they don't make maize beer."

"I know about their food and their houses. I want to know about the people and the country. Do they have grass, trees, and mountains? What do the women and the girls do?"

"The women stay home to cook, and the girls go to school."

"Do the girls have boyfriends?"

"They have boyfriends, and they love men."

"They love sex, but they don't know how to do it!" said Kimunai.

"I asked about boyfriends, not about making love," said Sukunwa.

"Listen, Kimunai has a good story to tell," said Kitoi.

"It's not a story. I had this girlfriend when we lived in Molo. She was not really a girlfriend, but I worked for her parents as a stable-boy when I was not in school. I used to play with her when her parents went to Nairobi. She was beautiful — I couldn't stop looking at her. Eventually I knew she wanted me as much as I wanted her, and I couldn't sleep at night thinking of how exciting it would be. However, when the day finally came, my weapon died and I almost cried. She was too soft, too cold and didn't know how to move. I had to put the light back on and hope that seeing her beauty would bring my weapon back to life."

"Ask him how many English girls he has gone with," said Kitoi.

"No, I don't want to ask him — he might tell me more. But if I had been ready to be a woman, I would never have done it with him," said Sukunwa.

"Anyway, you can't prove that every white girl is cold in bed by just having one," said Kitoi.

"You know what you said, Sukunwa. You said if you were ready to be a woman, but you are a woman," said Suiyeta.

"You know what I mean. I'm not a woman. I'm a child — I haven't been circumcised," said Sukunwa.

The conversation from Eldoret all the way to Mt. Kamasai was about women and men, and Kimunai was by far the winner. It sounded to Sukunwa as though the only woman he hadn't gone to bed with was his mother. Sukunwa was outraged at the way he talked about them as though they were rubbish. She hated him.

When they arrived, Taptamus' house looked deserted, but as soon as Sukunwa got out of the Landrover, Chelamai came out from a bush behind the house laughing.

"I was scared. I thought everybody had moved out of my grandmother's house," said Sukunwa.

"The children heard your car, and ran and told everyone that a car was coming. I tell you, people were climbing all over each other trying to escape."

"Why?"

"Alcohol has become a crime here since independence. The government wants home distilling banned completely, and of course nobody wants to part with it. As a result, when people hear a car is coming, they disappear. They think the police are coming to get them. Whose car is that?"

"MacKenzie's son's," replied Sukunwa.

"Oh, Kitoi and Kimunai. Tapsirorei and the Englishman's sons. I know them."

"Yes, Suiyeta and her brother are with us, too."

"Who are they?" asked Chelamai.

"Tonti Cherotich's children. She comes from Mt. Kamasai."

"Oh, then I do know them. Cherotich comes from here. Their father is an Asian, isn't he?"

"Yes."

"Ask them to come out. What a shame your uncle Kiriswa didn't know you were coming. He left here yesterday, you know," said Chelamai.

"Do come out of the car, please," Sukunwa said smiling sweetly. She led the party into the living room where an enormous clay chair lay to one side. They all sat on this in complete silence for two minutes, with Sukunwa half-praying that Kimunai wouldn't open his mouth about women in front of Chelamai.

Chelamai, who felt extremely shy in front of the city people, stayed in the kitchen. She didn't even come in to say hello.

"Is Lydia home from school?" asked Sukunwa, going into the kitchen after her.

"Yes, she arrived yesterday. If she had known you would be arriving, she would have been here. It's too bad we don't have anyone to send to call her. Everyone must be hungry," said Chelamai with the typical hospitality of people from home.

"We just left Eldoret an hour and a half ago, I don't see how they can be, but I can ask them."

"What language do they speak? It doesn't sound like anything I know." asked Chelamai.

"They are speaking Swahili. Kitoi and Kimunai can speak Nandi, but the other two don't speak it."

"Sukunwa, we want to see the mountainside," Kimunai said as he came into the kitchen. "I'm Kimunai McKenzie, Tapsirorei's son. Who are you?" he asked while he leaned forward to whisper in Sukunwa's ear as though he had been her friend for many years.

"I'm Sukunwa's aunt," said Chelamai.

"Kiriswa's wife?" asked Kimunai.

"Yes."

"I hope you are not trying to make something to eat because we have some food in the car. We would like to see the mountainside," Kimunai said and left to join the others in the sitting room.

The party went on their way. Sukunwa suggested they go by Lydia's to pick her up. By three o'clock, they had reached the top of the mountain. Kimunai took Suiyeta by the hand and led her aside. They talked for a minute, and then Suiyeta came over to Sukunwa. "Kimunai says that if you would ask him to stay overnight, he would stay."

"Tell him I wouldn't ask."

"Why don't you want him to stay?" asked Lydia, who was rather enjoying listening to Kimunai. There were no dull moments around him.

"He's obnoxious. That's why you think he's fun."

"Don't pay any attention to him," said Suiyeta.

"Yes, Sukunwa. Why do you care what he says?" asked Lydia.

"Go tell him I didn't ask him to stay, but that Lydia would like him to stay," said Sukunwa.

"I don't want him, please," said Lydia.

"Just say one thing. What should I tell him?" asked Suiyeta.

"Do you want one thing to say? Go tell him I didn't ask him to ask, but if his brother Kitoi and Kimunai want to stay, they are welcome to," said Sukunwa.

The group ate dinner at Kilel's house and Lydia took them to her home for tea. Then they went back to Chelamai's. It was the first time Sukunwa had ever slept in the same bed with a man. Suiyeta and Lydia knew that Sukunwa would not take Kimunai for any amount of money. Suiyeta ended up with him, Sukunwa with Kitoi, and Lydia with Kimibei.

"Don't try anything! Everybody sleep with their clothes on because we are not women," said Sukunwa.

"Speak for yourself," said Kimunai.

"That goes for me, too. Don't try anything," said Suiyeta.

"Me too. I'm going to bed with my clothes on," said Lydia.

"I don't want anyone with clothes in bed with me," said Kitoi. "Take them off. I won't try anything — I'm too sleepy," he added.

"I don't mind if they sleep with their clothes on, but we should change partners," said Kimunai.

"I'm happy with mine. I don't want to change with anybody," said Sukunwa.

"I think it's a good idea to change," said Suiyeta.

"I do, too," said Lydia.

"Kimibei, what do you think?" asked Kimunai.

"I would like to, but if Sukunwa doesn't, then we shouldn't do it."

Kitoi knew his brother wanted Sukunwa badly. "I suggest we change partners starting from now, but only for half an hour," he said.

"Yes," agreed Suiyeta, hopping into Kitoi's bed. Sukunwa and Lydia glanced at each other. Lydia went to Kimunai, and Sukunwa ended up with Kimibei. The light was put out so people could talk and hug with no fear of being watched.

"I beg your pardon for what my mother did to you last night. Can you forgive me?" asked Kimibei.

"I only wondered why you hid when your mother came. Why didn't you stay? What was so bad that it made you run? And how in the world did you get out anyway?" asked Sukunwa.

"I didn't want to talk to her while she was drunk, and the window bar was loose. I pulled it out, climbed outside, and then put it back in place," said Kimibei.

"I've never seen anyone like your mother. Don't tell her about us today."

"You don't know what is in my heart, and my mother doesn't either, but I say sorry about yesterday."

"What is in your heart?"

"I'll tell you when we have more time."

"If you can't tell me now, don't dream of saying it some other time."

"Why shouldn't I?" asked Kimibei as he smiled with pleasure and moved closer to Sukunwa. His mouth was almost touching hers. Sukunwa had heard that boys and girls in the city kissed. This was something they had learned from the English — watching them at a distance, kissing. Sukunwa wished she was kissed so she could feel what it was like.

"Tell me now, please. Otherwise you may never get to tell me after you leave here tomorrow. Your mother said that if she saw us together, she would destroy me," said Sukunwa.

"Don't be silly! Who gave her the right to destroy you?"

"I guess she did herself."

"And I say she doesn't have any right. We will see," said Kimibei.

"No, we won't see. Count me out."

"Stop sliding your hand down beneath my breasts, please! I don't like it," yelled Lydia.

"I'm only trying to warm my fingers," said Kimunai.

"Can you stand Kimunai?" Sukunwa whispered in Kimibei's ear.

"I'm not a girl. I wouldn't know how bad he is."

"You heard him."

"Don't take him seriously, and anyway, let us talk about us."

"What about us?"

"Do you know something called a 'kiss'?"

"Yes."

"Do you like kissing?"

"I don't know. I saw the English people kissing in the swimming pool in Eldoret, but I've never done it."

"There is nothing hard about it. You do it like this." Kimibei kissed her. "Did you like it?" he asked.

"No, what is there to like? Just a wet mouth," said Sukunwa.

"I'm afraid the half-hour is up," said Lydia. She wanted to come back to Kimibei.

"Oh, don't you want to stay there a little more?" Sukunwa asked.

"No, I don't," said Lydia.

"Suiyeta, go back to Kimibei. The time is up," said Sukunwa.

"Not yet," said Kimunai. "You come here first."

"Oh, I'm sleepy," said Sukunwa, almost pleading with Kimunai.

"If you promise to come in the morning, I'll let you go."

"Oh no. Let me come now to get it over with, or he'll wake me up in the morning and beg again," Sukunwa muttered.

"I want to ask you something first," whispered Kimibei to Sukunwa.

"What?"

"How long are you going to be in Mt. Kamasai?"

"One week. Why are you asking?"

"Because I didn't know," said Kimibei.

"Sukunwa, get up. I have to sleep," said Lydia.

Sukunwa had nothing to talk to Kimunai about. "You see there's nothing wrong with me. I keep my hands to myself," said Kimunai.

"Yes, thank you."

"I wish you weren't afraid of me, Sukunwa. I have loved you ever since I saw you."

"Which is today, isn't it?"

"It shouldn't take forever before you love someone should it?"

"Time is up," called Kitoi. "All the birds should return to their nests."

"What is happening. Are you having problems?" snapped Kimunai.

"I would like to talk to my girl before I sleep," said Kitoi.

"I want to sleep, too. You must let me go," said Sukunwa.

"Please stay a little, or at least tell me to come next time without Kitoi. He's going to get married anyway," said Kimunai.

"Good for him! Can you let me go now, or I will get up and go, because I'm not your property," said Sukunwa. The Nandi had a custom that if a girl was old enough to have had her period, she should not get out of a bed before the man she was sharing the bed with did.

"Why don't you get up Sukunwa? In church we were taught that Nandi customs were the work of the devil," said Lydia.

"Let the child go, Kimunai. You are eighteen, and she is fourteen," said Kitoi.

"Is she fourteen, or is she twenty? She has a sharp mouth like a twenty-year old," said Kimunai. "Go, then," he said to Sukunwa. Sukunwa was happy with his remark because she didn't want anyone to think she was speaking like a child.

"You don't get along with my brother? Suppose he marries you? How will you deal with him then? He likes you a lot," Kitoi whispered to Sukunwa.

"He won't marry me."

CHAPTER NINETEEN

*I*n the morning, Chelamai had breakfast ready for everyone.

"I enjoyed this visit very much," said Kitoi, as Sukunwa bade them farewell. "I hope I will see you before I leave for England." Kimunai left the impression that he would see Sukunwa soon.

"The two brothers want you, don't they?" Lydia remarked after they had left.

"And it just so happens I don't care for either of them, said Sukunwa. "Do you have a boyfriend yourself?"

"Yes, and I'm in love. What about you?"

"I don't have any one. The boys in Eldoret hate me for being smarter than them in school."

"What about Kimibei?"

"The truth is, last night was only the second time I talked to him."

"I think he's charming."

"I'll pass your message on to him."

"I don't need him. As I told you, I'm in love."

"What does it feel like to be in love?"

"It's something inside. It comes like a wave. When you are sad about something else, love appears and makes you happy."

"Makes you happy like when you get a new dress?" Sukunwa asked again. She wanted to know because when she had left Eldoret yesterday she had felt as though she would love Kitoi, and at night she had felt as though she would love Kimibei, and now that they weren't there, she didn't care for either of them. "Do you love him even if he is not here?"

"Yes, I do. I can tell you what it feels like a little bit. You know when you are sick and you don't like tea?"

"Yes."

"Well, it is like that except this is a sickness of happiness. You don't care about food because you are happy. Nothing else matters."

"What is his name?" asked Sukunwa.

"Kiptoigor Arap Siembui."

"Will you marry him?"

"I can't. You know I have to look after my mother. Have you forgotten?"

"No, I have not, but I wanted to know if you had changed your mind. I suppose you want him to be your boyfriend forever?"

"I'm a child. I don't know. Maybe when he gets married, he won't think of me, but you will be there, Sukunwa, with me. We will see." That made Sukunwa feel a little better. She worried that the man might make Lydia forget her.

"He's coming tomorrow, and I'm sure you will like him. He's very tall, and he dresses very nicely. He has a watch, wears a white shirt, black pants, shoes, belt, sun glasses, and a tie. He is so good-looking, you cannot imagine he's my boyfriend! You'll see for yourself."

"I'm dying to see him," said Sukunwa.

"You two have been lying down on this hill for so long you are going to skin the grass off it. Get up! You have to go to the river to wash the clothes," said Chelamai. They took Chelamai's children, and Mary's clothes to wash, and took a bath in the river.

Since Independence brewing beer and selling it had become the business of Mt. Kamasai women, and the next day was another busy one. Kiptoigor arrived when Sukunwa and Lydia were on their way to the river to bring some water for Mary, who was selling homemade beer. Kiptoigor was left to wait inside Mary's house. Since Sukunwa and he were not yet old enough to drink in front of elders, when they returned from the river, Mary asked Lydia to take three chairs to the back of the house and set them in the shade of a big tree. Kiptoigor asked Sukunwa about school, but he didn't listen to her. He talked about his family, how both he and his brother's school marks ranged from sixty-five to seventy, and how his brother was going to specialize in mathematics and he in English. Sukunwa had thought when she

314

first saw him that maybe he was a little bit stupid, but it was obvious now. She didn't bother to tell him about her marks. Her lowest mark was eighty-five, and here this man thought to specialize in something with a mark of seventy. What a sin, she thought.

Lydia stayed inside to help her grandmother wash beer glasses and only came out for a few minutes at a time. When she saw her two best friends seemed to be enjoying themselves, she was happy. Each time she came out, however, Sukunwa pleaded with her to let her go in to help Mary. Lydia was unwilling to let Sukunwa go in. She wanted Sukunwa to have fun with Kiptoigor. Kiptoigor supported her by saying, "Sukunwa, you and I are both guests here. If Lydia tells us to sit, we sit." He placed his hand on Sukunwa's lap. Lydia was hoping Sukunwa would like Kiptoigor as much as she did, and fortunately she didn't see the odd look on Sukunwa's face.

Sukunwa was fourteen years old and did not drink. Kiptoigor was eighteen and, in Sukunwa's eyes, already an alcoholic. He insisted Sukunwa be given a glass to drink with him. Sukunwa was ashamed even holding a glass of beer and hated that people might think she drank when she didn't. She struggled to keep the conversation going. As the day went by, Kiptoigor became more and more drunk, touching, hugging and lying on her lap. Finally Sukunwa got up and in a stony silence picked up a big bucket of beer, poured it over Kiptoigor's head and left.

"The bitch has poured beer all over me. I'm giving her two minutes to leave Mt. Kamasai, and if she doesn't I'm going to rip her apart in front of her mother," were the last words Sukunwa heard him say. She ran home worrying more that she had lost Lydia than about being beaten by Kiptoigor. "What was I doing? I wish I had put up with him," she told Chelamai.

"Don't worry! I know you did the right thing. He shouldn't have touched you as much as he did," Chelamai said.

"I have lost the only friend I have," said Sukunwa.

"Give her time. She will come."

Sukunwa didn't have the courage to go and ask to be forgiven.

She spent the next couple of days with her brother worrying about Lydia. Three days before she left, she wrote a note to her.

Dear Lydia,
I don't mind so much that I have spent the whole week without seeing you, but I am leaving Mt. Kamasai in three days, and I would love to see you before I leave — even if just for you to wave good-bye to me because I don't know if I'm ever coming back here. There is nothing to come back to if the one you love cannot stand you. Please do come even for one minute.
Love,
Sukunwa

Lydia came, but their conversation was lackluster. They talked, but they were not talking about anything. Their spirits were not close. Sukunwa felt it was necessary to explain herself to Lydia.

"Lydia, I admit I should never have poured beer over him."

"I think we shouldn't talk about it."

"You are upset, Lydia, but I had no choice. Kiptoigor's hands were crawling all over me like safari ants. I don't like being pawed like that."

"He was playing with you Sukunwa. Don't you know when people are playing with you?"

"He nearly attacked me, Lydia. He was bad! I sat with him for I don't know how long, and he made me feel as though I had been put in a cage with a slimy snake and had to free myself from it."

"You misunderstood him completely. He is nice. He wondered afterward if you were crazy. Mary said men play with girls like that, and she thought you should learn to be with men because if Kiptoigor hadn't been a good person, he would have come after you."

"What is there to learn? Do men play with girls even if they have been asked to stop? I told Kiptoigor for the tenth time to stop touching me, but he didn't. So am I to blame for everything that happened, or should he be blamed too?"

"Oh how much more do you want to talk about it? I was not there when it happened. I'm surprised you don't remember. You should have tried not to get upset when he touched you."

"Oh well, I thought we had promised each other no one would ever break our friendship. I thought I should have been nicer to him, though he was impossible, just for you. Well, if I had to do it over again, I wouldn't change anything. I would do the same thing to him."

"Wait a minute!" said Lydia rising to her feet. "Who said our friendship was broken, because I'm not ranting and raving like you? How many more times do you want me to say I was not there with you?" said Lydia, now upset.

"This dispute should end, you two. I need you both to help me go to the river to wash these clothes," said Chelamai.

"Sukunwa is mad at me," said Lydia near tears.

"I'm not. I just don't want you saying I should have put up with him."

"Maybe it wouldn't have been so bad to put up with him for exercise. When you get married, you will put up with far more shocking things than touching and hugging," said Chelamai. "On the other hand, I think fourteen-year-old girls should not be put with eighteen-year-old men. It is not nice."

There was silence between Sukunwa and Lydia as they picked up the clothes and went to the river. Each would have liked to say more and then apologize to the other, but no one was willing to be the first.

Next day, Sukunwa got up to pack. In the middle of it, her brother came to announce that they had seen a man coming on a big bicycle that made a noise like a car. Sukunwa didn't pay any attention, but in a few minutes, the noise grew louder. She went out to see. The machine went to Mary's, and she thought maybe Kiptoigor had a motorcycle. She went back in. Half an hour later, the bicycle approached her way. Chelamai was getting ready to go to Mary's, but Sukunwa asked her to stay. She thought Lydia was bringing her boyfriend for her to make an apology, and she didn't want to. Her aunt's presence would help her to refuse she thought. The motorbike came to a stop.

"Kimibei has come!" Lydia announced as she dismounted and removed the crash helmet she had been loaned.

"Why did you come?" Sukunwa asked Kimibei in relief.

"I've been in Kisumu, and I remembered you are going home tomorrow. So I've come by to take you," said Kimibei.

Sukunwa, Lydia and Kimibei spent the night in the guest house at Chelamai's. The next day, Sukunwa and Kimibei loaded Sukunwa's suitcase on the motorcycle. Sukunwa had to cling to Kimibei all the way. Desire, fear and hate all rushed into her heart. She liked Kimibei. He was quiet, very calm, and he talked to her as though she were not just someone whose breasts could be fondled, but a person worth talking with. She feared her aunt. What would Chemutai say if she found out that Sukunwa had Tonti's son for a boy-friend? She hated Tonti, and wondered why she even thought of being with someone who was related to her.

They stopped for lunch in the outskirts of Eldoret. No matter how careful she was not to let Kimibei know, she was beginning to like him. They ate and sat in the corner of the restaurant, skirting around their feelings until seven. Sukunwa asked Kimibei not to take her home. He dropped her off a block from home. They stood for half an hour before they parted.

The following day, coming from school, Kimibei was waiting for Sukunwa on his motorcycle, and they took a long way home. It did not take long before news of the time they were spending together leaked out.

One day, Chemutai noticed that Sukunwa was later than usual coming home from school. She went to Awa's to see if Sukunwa had gone there.

"Has Sukunwa come here?" she asked as she entered.

Awa looked at her blankly. "Sit and have some tea with me."

"I asked you if you had seen Sukunwa around," repeated Chemutai.

"I heard you the first time, Chemutai. What do you want me to tell you? Everybody knows where Sukunwa goes after school. Today she was seen in the city."

318

"Doing what?"

"This is not the first time she has been out late, Chemutai."

"What do you mean? What have you been cooking with the neighbours?"

"Nonsense! I haven't been cooking anything with the neighbours. Everybody knows Sukunwa has been brought home late by Kimibei for at least a month. I'm surprised you didn't ask her yourself when she came home late every day."

Chemutai went home silently. Sukunwa had arrived when she got there and was making a fire. "I have heard some disturbing news and want to find out from you. Tell me why you have been coming home late."

Sukunwa didn't answer.

"You can't answer? I will tell you. People have seen you with that, that — you must not spend time with Kimibei," Chemutai finally said, finally putting words to her thoughts. "You must part with him at once. I don't know what you see in him after his mother made it clear that she couldn't stand the sight of you with her son. What is the matter with you? Are you desperate? You are lucky you are beautiful. Why do you go for rubbish like them? There are better ones available." Sukunwa bowed her head. "You can go and finish what you were doing."

Sukunwa finished making the fire and then made dinner. There was a silence to end all silences. It was the first time Sukunwa had ever been accused of anything. She thought of telling her aunt she was in love, but she restrained herself. What is love? she thought. Does this kind of love have any result? Probably not with the kind of mother he has, she answered herself. She ate enough dinner not to make her aunt suspicious about her feelings for Kimibei. Immediately after dinner, she went to bed with a painful expression on her face. She could not convince her aunt that she and Kimibei were not doing anything wrong, because she knew Chemutai would only believe what everyone else believed — that city girls would not just date, that the first thing they did when they met a boy was to make women out of themselves.

In bed, Sukunwa thought she wouldn't be able to sleep that night, but she fell asleep immediately after she got underneath the blanket. She was awakened by voices around eleven at night.

"There is a very disturbing thing you don't know about that family. You must know there is a young lady with a baby in the house who poses as a housekeeper. Not many people know who she is, but I know everything that is going on there," Awa said.

"I don't care to know very much about that family. Knowing Tonti is enough to make up my mind. I don't want Sukunwa to get mixed up with them," said Chemutai.

"Chemutai, wait until you finish hearing what I have to tell you. That girl who works for them is a daughter of a close friend of theirs. The family died a year ago in a car accident — two children were killed along with the parents. Only the one daughter was left. She was staying with her grandmother. Last year Tonti brought her here. After two months the girl was made pregnant by her son Kimibei. When Tonti discovered this, she sent her back. When the grandmother learned the girl was pregnant, she brought her back to Tonti. We don't quite know what happened. All we know is that after she had her baby, Tonti and her daughter took it over and turned the girl into a housekeeper. When she holds the baby, they snatch it away as though it's not hers."

"I'm not a bit surprised what a sinner like Tonti can do, but she won't do it to my sister's daughter," said Chemutai.

Sukunwa cried and cried. They were lying, she thought, as she cried herself to sleep. She got up in the morning, and with artificial happiness in front of her aunt, made breakfast and ate it. As she was going out to school, her aunt said they might go downtown when she came back from school. After school, Kimibei was waiting as always.

"I have someplace to take you to today," he said.

"No, I cannot go. I'm wanted at home immediately after school," said Sukunwa.

"We will go there tomorrow, then."

"No, you come and find my letter here under the grass tomorrow," said Sukunwa bending down and clearing out a little nest underneath the thick grass that grew alongside the path. She walked away.

"I hope you will be better tomorrow," Kimibei said after her.

Sukunwa came home and went straight to bed.

"Can we go shopping?" asked Chemutai.

"No, I cannot," answered Sukunwa sounding as though she was crying.

"It not your fault, Sukunwa. Don't cry for them. They are nothing. How were you to know that the family of the person you wanted to love were beneath anything on this earth," said Chemutai.

The next day, Sukunwa put her letter under the grass where she had shown Kimibei. After writing "Dear Kimibei," she had drawn a red line across the page, the sign for fire or trouble. The blank white page that followed meant that her mind was empty, that she didn't know what to do. A black line across the bottom meant "I don't see the light at the end of the tunnel."

That evening when she arrived home after school, her aunt was extremely happy. "Oh Sukunwa, what good news! We are moving to Kisumu. Tapsirorei has found me another babysitting job there."

"When are we leaving?" asked Sukunwa as she rose to her feet.

"We should leave immediately. The family wants someone right away."

Sukunwa stood at the window looking outside. Her face showed anguish and trepidation.

"Do you worry about leaving here?" asked Chemutai.

"I don't, but what about my school?"

"There is a better school in Kisumu, and better people, too. You are going to make new friends in no time. You will discover that the Luo girls are very friendly."

"Are we moving into Tapsirorei's place?"

"No, they live in Chemase. Kimunai will come to move us."

"The people in Mt. Kamasai would like to know we have moved, wouldn't they?"

"We will write to them."

The next day after school Sukunwa waited on the path for Kimibei to come, but he didn't. She went to their "mailbox" — the hollowed-out nest they had made under the grass — to check if he had left a note for her. She found a two-page letter, the first page with a drawing of an idyllic scene — rain, green grass, flowers blooming, blue sky, and trees with birds singing above. The second page was written on:

Dear Sukunwa,

I've heard everything. Tapsirorei has asked your aunt to leave Eldoret because of the scandal about you and me. Don't worry because I know that is only hypocrisy on their part. They should understand I will come after you regardless of what scandal there may be. You must know that Tapsirorei is pretending to help your aunt, but in fact she is looking after her own interest and of course assuming no one will discover what she is doing. I won't try to see you soon because my mother is going after me, too. You are leaving on Sunday. I've heard that Kimunai is coming to move you, but don't worry about him. I will make sure he stays with us that night. When you get to Kisumu, look for the Nyanza Cinema and go there next Friday at three o'clock. I will be waiting for you where they sell popcorn, and I'll explain everything you've heard about me. I was never in love with that girl. She had the baby because she wanted me to marry her. Until then,

Yours,
Kimibei

Sukunwa was smiling when she got home. She wore no make-up, but she looked absolutely lovely. Her eyes sparkled like the water in Lake Victoria when the sun shone on it. She had long eyelashes under which her eyes twinkled like stars.

"Why are you so happy?" asked Chemutai.

"I've changed my mind. I'm looking forward to the move — to see the lake. I've never seen a ship, or live lake fish, or Luo people."

"There is a letter from Lydia. Can you read it?"

"Yes, do you want me to read it out loud?"

"It doesn't matter, just tell me what it says."

Sukunwa read the letter silently, and then she said, "Something really big is going to happen to them. Lydia's grandfather is going to buy a car from an English teacher who is going back to England, and they are moving soon to Mosoriot."

"I can't believe it. What are they going to do with the car. I mean who will drive them around? And where did they get the money for it?" asked Chemutai.

"Arap Walei drove a police car when he was a policeman," Sukunwa said. "But I have no idea about the money."

"I wouldn't have thought Arap Walei would want anything like a car. What changed him? I really don't understand this. Read it again — maybe you didn't read it well the first time."

"I read it well. I think he has changed. You know he is going to church nowadays. Maybe he wants the car to take Mary to church."

CHAPTER TWENTY

*C*hemutai and Sukunwa moved to Kisumu on Saturday. Kimunai and his mother came to help them. Sukunwa and Kimunai sat in the front seat of the car and Tapsirorei and Chemutai sat in back. Tapsirorei made critical remarks about Tonti all the way to Kisumu, which was a blessing, Sukunwa felt, since it meant she didn't have to listen to Kimunai.

"Tonti has always been very envious of me and of my children's good fortune," she said, adding that the reason Tonti was so proud and such a show-off today was entirely due to her and her late husband. "We introduced her to that 'old man.' Otherwise Tonti would have ended up like her sister — a drunk who let one man after another into her house," she said.

Chemutai did not get a house right away. She and Sukunwa stayed with Tapsirorei's friends — other city women who made a living selling beer. Many of them had city husbands, just as in Eldoret. That was city life — if one did not have a job, one found a "city" husband with a job. When you got a job, you got rid of him if he was bad. Like Eldoret, school was a catastrophe for girls. No matter how hard they tried to be good students, nobody had high expectations for girls. Their lives were like those of North Americans of African descent. The only girls who made it did so because luck had fallen on them. A missionary had helped them because their parents went to church, or a father had liked the idea of having his daughters educated, and so put them in a private school.

But Sukunwa liked Kisumu. It only rained once a week, and when the rain ceased, the sun came out again. People walked about outside under the street lights until midnight, and some who did not have jobs walked all night. Sukunwa made a few friends with girls there; she found out later that the only basis for friendship among them was gossiping about their family life and exchanging secrets about boyfriends. She trusted one girl in the group, Saidaa, and told her to cover for her whenever she went to meet Kimibei. Sukunwa did not know that Saidaa was a traitor until Chemutai asked her one day to read a letter that she had received from Tapsirorei. The letter told her aunt to do "anything in her power to prevent the catastrophe" that was about to happen. Sukunwa became embarrassed reading the letter. Everything she had ever told Saidaa about herself and Kimibei was in it.

From that moment on, Chemutai was bitter towards Sukunwa. The next day, Sukunwa was about to leave to go school as usual, but her aunt called her back.

"Sukunwa, I disapprove of your continuing relationship with Kimibei. You must stop school. I believe you are ready for circumcision and then to get married, if that is what you want, because I'm tired of telling you to stop seeing Kimibei."

Sukunwa cried all day. Everything was coming to an end. And so quickly, she thought, and did not know what to do. At that moment she had no way of seeing Kimibei. He will never know what has happened, she thought. In the evening, she was cooking outdoors where people cooked food when it was too hot inside the house. Chemutai and everyone else were inside. A little pebble dropped onto the plate she was about to put a chapati on. She turned around. Another pebble was dropped.

"Ssss," a hissing sound came from the shadows around the house. Sukunwa hesitated a moment. She hoped it was Kimibei, but she was afraid to look because her aunt might see her. She looked quickly at the door and the windows.

"Come on! Don't waste time," said Kimibei. He dashed out of the shadows, took Sukunwa by the hand, and quickly led her away.

"What are you doing?"

"We must leave this place and these people. We are old enough to get married, and then our troubles will be over."

"No we can't. We have to think about it."

"You won't regret it Sukunwa. Let us go now."

"Come back next week. We'll talk about it then. If I go now, I would be unhappy."

"How are we going to meet again? Can't you see how difficult it is already?"

"I don't know."

"Ask for permission, then, to go to Mt. Kamasai on Friday for the weekend. I will meet you at the bus station at eleven o'clock, and if you aren't there, I will come to see you at night and we will arrange something else."

Kimibei returned Sukunwa quietly to her cooking place. She wondered if anyone had noticed she was away. As she arranged to sit herself down, her aunt called, looking out of the window.

"Where have you been? I just called you a minute ago."

"I was in the out-house."

"I went there, and you weren't there, Sukunwa."

"Someone was at this one, and I went to the other one."

Although Chemutai felt there was more to it, she accepted this explanation.

Sukunwa talked to herself for the whole week. In the 1960s, every Nandi girl had to be circumcised, but Kimibei, being half-Asian and half-Nandi, did not understand the custom. He didn't know that if they ran away and stayed together for two years it would not matter. No one would count that as a marriage.

On Thursday, Sukunwa told her aunt she would like to go to Mt. Kamasai for the weekend to see her family. Chemutai approved and told her to bring back some maize flour if there was any. Sukunwa made a decision before leaving that she would not run away with Kimibei, but what was she going to tell him? Would she tell him that the feeling she had for him was not enough for her to disregard the custom and live with him without having been circumcised? She could not say that without losing him, she thought. Should I go and blurt out, "I cannot marry you until I get circumcised first?" She reached the bus stop without finding an answer. Kimibei was waiting.

"I was afraid. I didn't think you would come," he said.

Quietly, Sukunwa looked down. She was worn out from trying to solve her problem.

"Are you sad?"

"No, I'm not. I'm happy to see you, but..."

"Let us go and talk when we get away from here," Kimibei cut in before she could finish.

"Where are we going?"

"Kericho."

"No, we cannot. I have to be back on Monday. I'm sorry."

"Too late. We have to go to Kericho because I have arranged a place for us there tonight."

"But I must come back by Monday."

"Kericho is a one-hour trip. If we must come back, we will."

They went to Kericho. It was just like Nandi. It rained and rained. The Tea Hotel was the best hotel in the town. Sukunwa was taken in by the back door. She had never seen such a beautiful place in her life. Everything was brought to them in their room. Sukunwa had never seen as much money as she saw when Kimibei paid for the food.

"What should we do now?" she asked after lunch.

"We will lie down and talk," said Kimibei. He was handsome, slim and well-shaped, with a dark mustache and silver-rimmed glasses. In those days, dating a man with glasses was itself the best thing that could happen to any girl. Glasses showed that you had been to school and were very smart.

"Can we talk? I have a friend in Arusha, and I think that if we leave here tomorrow, we can be there in four days," said Kimibei as he lay down next to Sukunwa in bed. His voice was sincere and affectionate. Sukunwa felt that his voice was the sweetest thing she had ever heard on the earth.

"I love you very much. I would love to be with you forever," she said.

"You can have me. Please be mine. I have given myself to you. Have me please," said Kimibei.

"I can't now. I have to be circumcised first."

328

"Why should you want to be circumcised when I want you the way you are?"

"I'm not doing it for myself alone. I'm doing it for my family, and if I don't, I won't be a Nandi any more."

For the rest of the day, they nearly drove each other crazy. At the end, it was obvious it was not going to work. Kimibei came to terms with the fact that he would have to wait until Sukunwa had gone through the whole Nandi ritual. At five they went downtown to see an Asian movie. Now all thought of their future was pushed aside. Sukunwa thought of suggesting that they find two old people who would perform the *ratisiet* ceremony for the two of them and keep it a secret until she had been circumcised. That way, their future would be guaranteed. No other marriage could take place afterwards. Sukunwa thought all this, but knew nothing could come out of it because Kimibei wouldn't understand it. He would not know where to go since he had not been raised as a Nandi, and Sukunwa could not bring it up directly because marrying was a man's work.

They went back to the Tea Hotel. At nine o'clock they called for food. At ten they bathed together. The darkness about their future drew them closer together. They washed each other. Sukunwa dried Kimibei, and he dried her. In bed, their feelings were beyond words. Sukunwa was convinced she was never going to have Kimibei. She gave herself to him, going only by the feeling she had for him, not knowing how good she was supposed to feel. Kimibei was almost blind with desire. He went in at high speed. Sukunwa let out a yell, and Kimibei was done. He collapsed on her.

It must have been bad for both of them, thought Sukunwa who was burning. She wished Kimibei would get off her so she could go to sit in cool water. Kimibei turned and lay on his back. His arm pulled Sukunwa closer to him.

"Why didn't you tell me?" he asked.

"I wanted you to be the one." Sukunwa shivered as though she were coming down with a cold.

"Do you want me to ask someone to make a fire? Are you shivering?"

"No, I want to go to the bathroom."

Sukunwa ran cool water into the bathtub to sit in to dull the pain. The water turned blood red — she had bled. She let it drain, then refilled the tub with fresh water. Kimibei turned on the light to check the wet bedsheet. When he saw the blood, he panicked, and with his pocket knife he cut out the bloodstained part. He wrapped it in newspaper, put it in his suitcase, and went into the bathroom to see if Sukunwa was all right.

"What happened?" he asked.

"I don't know."

"Should I take you to a doctor?"

"No." She could not imagine the possibility of being asked what had happened to her and then having to explain.

The next day, Kimibei put a sign outside the door. "No interruption please." He tipped a maid to take the soiled bedsheets away and bring clean ones for them. Then they were left alone. Kimibei went out to bring breakfast, lunch and dinner. Sukunwa stayed in all day. She was even embarrassed to face the sun. Kimibei gave her all the time and attention he had. They left Kericho on Monday afternoon for Mt. Kamasai. They stayed with the family for two hours and then went back to Kisumu. They didn't even go by Chepterit School to see Lydia. They arrived at six o'clock and went to a movie so they could kiss again. They cried, not knowing if they would ever have another opportunity to be together, and parted at midnight.

Four months passed. Sukunwa had been taking a course in sewing with other girls in the neighbourhood. Chemutai was about to send a message to Mt. Kamasai to the family to get ready for Sukunwa's circumcision, but suddenly she discovered that Sukunwa was pregnant. She noticed that her breasts looked very large, and she asked her when her last period had been. When Sukunwa told her four months ago, Chemutai almost fainted.

"Who did this to you? Why didn't you wait one more year? Why did you let me go to all this trouble for you? Putting you to school and making beer and selling it to have food to keep us alive. Did you also know I sold myself? The clothes we have on our bodies are from

330

the money I got by selling myself. And yet you had a man whom you gave it to for nothing. What will your father think? How many fingers will point at me? 'Look at that woman! She took her sister's daughter to the city and sold her to men to feed herself!' And how will I deny it when this is the evidence?" asked Chemutai. They both cried.

"Who is he? You must tell me so we know what to do," Chemutai said that evening before going to bed.

"Kimibei."

"Let this be the last day you mention his name or mention that he made you pregnant. We have to leave here at four o'clock in the morning. I will take you to a friend's place until the baby is born and then give it away for adoption."

"I'll marry him, and we will keep our baby."

Chemutai could not control her temper. She slapped Sukunwa twice across the face. "Shut up, you whore! What caused you to open yourself up for him when I provided everything for you? It is a nightmare! I will be buried like my sister Cheptabut and our mother Taptamus before you marry that, that...oohh!" she screamed. "Don't mention his name in my presence again, and get up and pack. We have to leave now. We can't wait until tomorrow."

They got an eleven p.m. bus to Eldoret, got off at Chepterit and walked four miles west to Baraton. They went to an old woman who lived alone. There was no smoke coming out of the house, and it looked sad and lonely. The woman was staring into the dead fireplace and talking to herself. Maybe she was hard of hearing, too, or nasty, thought Sukunwa. Chemutai called at the door to announce their entrance into the house, but the old woman did not turn around.

"So what if you have come. Look for a chair if you can find it in the dark," she said waving a small tin lantern without a chimney. It sounded as though she resented their presence.

"Who is it anyway?" she asked.

"Why don't you turn around and see for yourself?"

"Oh, Chemutai! What has brought you all the way here before daybreak? Don't you live in Eldoret any more?"

"No, I don't live in Eldoret any more. I've moved to Kisumu, but

I don't have time to talk now because I have to return to work. I have brought you a child of mine to look after for me. I will be back on the weekend, and then we'll have more time to talk."

"I don't have time to look after other people's children." The old woman turned around now and searched the room with her eyes. "Where is the child you are talking about?" she asked.

"This one," said Chemutai.

"She is a grown-up. Is she running away from her husband?"

"No, she is not. I will tell you. Come walk me back." Chemutai turned to Sukunwa. "Make yourself at home. She will be back in a moment." She gave Sukunwa a hundred shillings. Sukunwa sat on the stool beside the fire her eyes going around the lonely house. How do people get pregnant, she wondered. Was it that easy? Does one catch it like a cold? Don't you have to do it more than once? She hadn't even done it for a long time, she thought. Did Kimibei realize I was going to have a baby and not want to tell me? Deep inside her she hated that night they had spent together, but she erased the thought when the memory of it came to her mind. She loved Kimibei, and she was not prepared to think anything else about him but love. She would find her way back to him, no matter how long it would take.

"You are Taptamus' daughter, Cheptabut's child," said the old woman when she came back.

"Yes, I am," agreed Sukunwa.

"Why did you do this to yourself?"

Sukunwa shrugged her shoulders. "I have no idea, but I don't want to talk about it, and I don't have any reasons to give for why I did it," she said angrily. She could not stand being asked why, why. She didn't know how it happened, and she did not want to be asked any more.

The old woman told everyone around about Sukunwa's situation. People whispered and pointed behind her back, and she was an outcast. No one knew her torment but herself. The house itself was haunted. Before Sukunwa went to bed, the spirit of a beautiful woman appeared to her. "You will have a baby boy, but you must leave four days after his birth," it said. Chemutai came every two weeks for months, then she suddenly stopped. But the spirit continued to come every day saying the same thing, "Leave this place four days after your baby boy is born."

Sukunwa was in labour all night. After she gave birth to her baby boy, the spirit came three days later to remind her to leave. The next day when the old woman had gone to get water from the stream, Sukunwa knew that would give her time enough. The trip would take the old woman an hour and a half, as it was far and she walked slowly. Sukunwa threw her belongings in her small suitcase, wrapped the baby up with a bedsheet and took off with little thought of what would happen. Going to her aunt was not going to be any more pleasant than being with the old woman. My aunt's temper awaits me, she thought. But she had nowhere else to go.

Words do not exist that can express Sukunwa's feelings that day. She sat alone at the road waiting for the bus and cried. She thought of laying the baby down and going to follow the sun in the west. When it set, she would kill herself. When she thought this, she looked at her baby's face, and the baby looked as though he understood his mother was about to abandon him. Sukunwa decided to go to face her aunt's bitterness. She got to Kisumu at twelve o'clock noon. The sun was already hot. Upon entering the house, she dropped the suitcase at the door and sat on it. She was holding the baby against her chest as though it was a piece of clothing wrapped up. To her surprise, she heard a voice with happiness and exclamations of affection welcoming her from the other room.

"Oh, Sukunwa! Thank goodness you have come." It was Lydia. She came to hug her. "What is this, Sukunwa?" she asked.

"The baby," said Sukunwa in a surprised voice. She thought Lydia knew.

"A baby? Whose is it?"

An expression of shame flashed across Sukunwa's face.

"It is your baby? I'm sorry. I didn't know," said Lydia.

"Don't be. What a surprise and what a pleasure to have found you here because I couldn't bear to see my aunt on my own."

"The baby should be unwrapped. It is too hot to let her be in clothes," said Lydia and took the baby. "He is a boy! What is his name?"

"Kimoru," said Sukunwa. "Where is my aunt?"

Lydia rose quickly to her feet and answered awkwardly. "Oh, you haven't heard about it," she said, struggling to keep her tears from coming. "Oh, Sukunwa! I was hoping you had heard about it. I have lost my grandparents! Both in the same day," said Lydia, holding the tears back.

"Don't tell me Mary and Arap Walei are gone for good?" said Sukunwa.

"I'm afraid they are. They left us last week, and today Chemutai is to go to the police station to bring some of the things the police found in the car after their deaths."

"What happened?"

"For the last six months, my grandma had been asking my grandpa to take us to Kisumu to see you. Two weeks ago, I came home from school. Mary told Grandpa that they didn't have any charcoal and that he should take us to look for some when he had time. Grandpa didn't say we were going to Kisumu — he just said why didn't we all jump in the car and go look for charcoal. My grandma made breakfast for us, and we took off. When we got to Kaimosi, Grandpa said that we could go on to Kisumu since it wasn't far from there. It was broad daylight. No rain, no wind. Everything was still, not even rustling of the leaves could be heard. We were coming down the Nandi Escarpment at Kiboswa when the car went out of control. It rolled and tumbled three times. The doors opened and everyone was thrown out. We were all thrown in a pile. My grandma on the bottom, my grandpa on top of her, and then me. I watched the car roll further. I got up feeling so small, like a fragment of matter, but my grandparents lay there immobile.

"I was not hurt, but I was afraid to look down where they lay. For what seemed like ages I stood staring at the heat waves coming up from the Kano Valley at the bottom of the escarpment. I felt a tingling in my feet as though water was running over them. Then I heard my grandpa. 'Mary! Mary! Are you dead? I'm dying too,' he said as he rolled off her. He lay down next to her and closed his eyes. My feet refused to move from where I was standing. I leaned over to lend him my hand. I was too far away. Then I remembered I had feet and could move. I looked down at my feet and saw that blood had run over them. I traced the line of blood with my eyes up to my grandma, and my eyes passed over to my grandpa. He looked at me with a little smile. It faded away, and he was gone. I stood there for half an hour. The shock and pain I felt was too great for tears. The tears came after the police came to remove Grandma and Grandpa," Lydia said looking down, her hands covering her eyes.

She and Sukunwa hugged each other and cried for a long time.

"Why are the only people who matter for us all gone? My grandmother Taptamus, and my mother Cheptabut, and now your grandparents," said Sukunwa.

"What is becoming of us, I wonder?" said Lydia. "Do you see darkness ahead?" she asked.

"No, Lydia, we have each other," said Sukunwa. "When did Chemutai leave here?"

"Half an hour before you arrived. She said she was going to hurry back because Kimunai was to come later."

"She said Kimunai was coming today?" asked Sukunwa with terror in her voice.

"What is wrong, Sukunwa? You sound frightened?"

"Don't ask. It won't take long for you to know. You will see my aunt today. She does not know I am back, or she would have returned by now," said Sukunwa as she got up and walked to her room. On the way, she saw a letter addressed to her on the table beside Chemutai's bed. The letter was open, and she suspected it had been read. She took it to her room and read it. It was from Kimibei and was full of hate. When she had finished, what stuck in her mind and hurt her most was a line in which Kimibei said he didn't know Sukunwa was that cheap. Why did you pretend that night in Kericho that I was special to you? Sukunwa crumpled the letter and put it in her pocket. Lydia suspected something bad was in it.

"I guess that letter is really bad. Can I read it?" she asked and extended her hand to Sukunwa for the letter. Sukunwa shook her head, her big brown eyes swimming in tears. The golden irises of her eyes shimmered through the tears.

"No, you don't want to read it. It is so aggravating, humiliating and degrading to know my aunt read it," said Sukunwa, her hands on her face. Lydia hugged her.

"Please! Everything has an end. Cry, but don't forget tomorrow is another day," she said.

"Can you forgive me? You have been through more than I have," said Sukunwa.

"Let us not cry any more. The baby will cry, too," said Lydia as she attempted a smile and went to pick up Kimoru while Sukunwa lay down. At three o'clock, Chemutai arrived with Kimunai. She came in first. Lydia had the baby on her lap.

"Whose baby is this?" she asked.

"Sukunwa's baby," replied Lydia. Immediately, Chemutai told Lydia to go into the other room with the baby and followed her. Sukunwa was sound asleep.

"When she wakes up, do not come into the sitting room. Stay with the baby and do not come out with it," Chemutai said. She made tea and brought some to Lydia. Kimunai asked why Lydia was staying in the other room alone.

"She is not alone. She has a baby," said Chemutai.

"Whose baby is it?" asked Kimunai.

"Hers, of course. That's not very intelligent. Do you think I can still have children?" said Chemutai.

"Of course not, but you didn't mention before that Lydia had a baby."

"It is very sinful to sit here and listen to her say the baby is yours," whispered Sukunwa.

"I don't mind, and why should you mind?" said Lydia.

"Lydia! Can I see the baby?" asked Kimunai.

"No, it is too little to show men," said Chemutai. She then rushed Kimunai into leaving with her to visit some friends. Lydia and

Sukunwa were left wondering who they should say the baby belonged to if someone else visited.

"Dear god, I hope..." Sukunwa stopped. She was going to say, I hope she won't make everyone believe the baby is yours.

Chemutai returned quickly without Kimunai. "Sukunwa!" she called impatiently at the door.

"Hush!" Sukunwa said to Lydia when she heard Chemutai's voice. "Yes," she answered Chemutai's call with forbearance.

"When did you have the baby?"

"Four days ago." Sukunwa's once happy face now was dead, and tears were beginning to float in her eyes. Her low voice sounded distant.

"Why did you come before I came to get you?" Chemutai was still standing at the door. Sukunwa did not answer.

"Sukunwa, there is no point in being stupid and stubborn! Were you kicked out by Tapteger?"

"No, I came alone. I didn't tell her."

"Sukunwa, you cannot use a tree for shade and then when it is cool, cut the tree down because you no longer need it. You should have thanked her before you left. But there is no point in talking to you. Now I have to go let her know you are in Kisumu. In the meantime you had better stay in the house until I get back from Mt. Kamasai. I'm going to spend one night in Baraton and then leave for Mt. Kamasai the next day. I shouldn't have to worry about you two. If you can have a baby, you are old enough to look after it. You must also remember that Kimunai thinks the baby is Lydia's. And from now until I get back, it is Lydia's baby until Sukunwa comes up with what to do with it," Chemutai said. Before leaving, she gave Lydia two hundred shillings for food. "Here is some money for food. And you should know that it represents two night's solid work for me! I sold myself. Heaven knows how many men I went to bed with to get that much." Chemutai's last remark made Sukunwa feel as though she were something less than human.

"What should I do with this money now? Should I throw it after her?" asked Lydia when Chemutai had left the house.

"No, you can't. We have to eat," said Sukunwa.

"I have money — five hundred shillings — given to me by my grandfather for school fees. We can use that."

"No, save your money. You may go back to school at home."

"I know I won't go back to school again. I'll have to look after my mother."

"Who is she with now?"

"With Cheseret's mother."

"She doesn't know now that her parents are dead, does she?"

"She will know when Chemutai gets to Mt. Kamasai."

"Will she understand?"

"I don't think she knows what not being alive means, but she feels when people are sad, and she looks sad too. I know that when Tapsalng'ot finds out about her sister's death, she will cry, and my mother will cry too."

"Poor her," said Sukunwa.

Under normal circumstances, Lydia would have cried talking about her mother and the death of her grandparents. Today she was too flabbergasted. Poor Lydia! She had never heard anyone say she had sold herself for food. Sukunwa, however, was sad inside. On the outside, she looked tranquil while Lydia looked agitated. Sukunwa made an effort to shift the conversation to Lydia's family, but Lydia did not want to go on talking about that.

"What are you going to do with the baby now that your aunt doesn't want anyone to know you have had a child?" asked Lydia.

"What can I do? I don't have any say. You know that. But after I get circumcised and get married, I will ask her to give me my baby back, and then I will never see her again as long as I live."

"She will be the loneliest woman in the world when she can't sell herself for food and has no friends or a family that needs her. And you should never, never feel guilty when that day arrives!"

"She doesn't sell herself for food. There are other people who sell themselves, but not her. She only says that to me so I can feel guilty. She thinks I had the baby to punish her. Why, I don't know. She will never be lonely either. She is the most nasty, vicious, selfish and unforgiving woman I have ever seen, but nobody dares to criticize her. She cares for only two people in her life — Awa and Mother Kimunai, Tapsirorei. The rest of us tolerate her horrid manners for her money only."

"I like Awa. I saw her once and thought she was nice, but Tapsirorei is just like Chemutai."

"Yes, I lived with Awa for almost a year. She is a very humble person," said Sukunwa.

Neighbourhood women came from time to time while Chemutai was away, to express their sympathy to Lydia for the deaths of her grandparents. The more the neighbours came to visit them, the more the baby was associated with Lydia and the more Sukunwa became confused. How was she going to get her baby back? Sukunwa thanked Lydia for being with her. The small talk she provided was therapeutic during this crisis with Chemutai. But now, in everyone's eyes, the baby was Lydia's. Never in her wildest imagination had Sukunwa ever thought that one night with Kimibei in Kericho would result in so much pain and confusion.

Chemutai returned saying she had made arrangements for Sukunwa to go for her circumcision in two months. Chemutai and Lydia and the baby would go later. Sukunwa was dismayed by her aunt's quick decision to make Lydia, who was still crying over her grandparents, an instant mother. She wanted to explode inside, but she could not say anything, she had to do what her elders asked of her. Lydia interrupted Chemutai, "Where Sukunwa goes, I go."

Lydia did not mind the baby. She found it rather funny that it had come to her as though it had dropped from the sky. She told everybody with pride that she had a baby, and she took the whole thing as a joke. Sukunwa nursed the baby for a month, but her aunt asked her to stop before the baby got used to her.

The first week, she washed her breasts every morning with warm water and then milked the milk out of them. She repeated this in the evening. In the afternoon she was told to rub the nipple of her breast if the milk came out by itself, and the milk would stop coming. Sukunwa did this, and in three weeks it had dried up altogether.

"You know now that I will be going to Mt. Kamasai. What will you do if my aunt really insists you are not coming with me?" Sukunwa asked Lydia.

"I'm still going to come with you. I don't see why I should stay to endure your aunt. I don't care for her money, and the ones I care for are dead. I love the baby a lot, and I hope you don't worry about him. Because if you want him back after you are out of circumcision, you can. You won't have to do what your aunt wants after you have been circumcised."

"I don't mind if you have the baby, but you are a child too. People will make fun of you."

"I will fight them off."

"I will help you fight them off, and we will raise the baby together," said Sukunwa who was now relieved that the baby was going to be with her as long as Lydia had it and that she would never have to face her father, Kiptai, over becoming pregnant before she was initiated.

When the time came for Sukunwa to leave, Lydia packed the baby's things to leave with Sukunwa. "I should advise you, Sukunwa, not to let Lydia come because the baby won't get along with the dirt at home. He is used to the cleanliness of the city, and remember, if he gets sick, traditional medicines won't work," Chemutai said.

"I will go. If the baby gets sick, I will bring him back," said Lydia.

"I won't want a sick baby," said Chemutai. Lydia didn't stop packing.

Kimunai arrived at eleven. Obviously, Chemutai had asked him to take Sukunwa to Mt. Kamasai. "Women, women! You are not ready yet! I thought the luggage would be waiting at the door for me to load into the car," he said in his usual frenzied manner.

"Kimunai, you had better talk to these children. A small infant who is used to a clean place should not be taken to a dirty place where no one washes baby clothes or baby bottles," said Chemutai.

"That is nonsense, Chemutai. The baby won't be sick. People have children in Mt.Kamasai, and Lydia will make sure the baby's things are clean. Let's go," said Kimunai.

"I have to go, then, to make sure the baby is settled," said Chemutai. On their way Chemutai asked Kimunai to take them shopping. She bought the baby clothes, canned milk, more bottles, and three big baskets, one for the baby's bed, another to store clothes in, and a third to store the baby bottles and canned milk in. Chemutai would stay in Mt. Kamasai long enough to make sure everyone knew the baby was Lydia's, even those who didn't ask.

CHAPTER TWENTY-ONE

*I*n Mt. Kamasai, everybody gathered at Taptamus' house, which was occupied by Chelamai and her youngest son John Taptamus, who was the spirit reincarnation of Taptamus. Taptamus was a man in her second life. Chelamai's oldest son was the reincarnation of Taptamus' husband, Arap Mararsoi.

Kiriswa arrived the day before Chemutai left. They spent the whole day discussing with Kiptai how many people to invite to Sukunwa's circumcision festival. Kiptai wanted to have every relative come, but Chemutai said she wanted a small ceremony with few relatives. Chelamai and her husband agreed with Kiptai. Because he was the father, he could do what he wanted.

"She is fifteen years old, and she is an orphan. There is no reason to make her work hard going around inviting all of the relatives. And for what? Her mother is dead, her grandparents are dead," said Chemutai.

"She doesn't have to go around. I will go to the distant relatives," said Kiriswa.

A week before the event took place, Sukunwa and Lydia went to invite the near relatives and also went to Eldoret to invite Awa. Sukunwa tried to find Kimibei to let him know he had a son, but she was told he had a job with a bank in Nairobi and had moved there. They returned home. When they got there, Lydia's aunt, Tapsalng'ot had come to Kiriswa and Chelamai and asked them to help have Lydia circumcised because there was no reason to have her wait when she already had a baby. Sukunwa was happy to learn this. It meant they would raise the baby together.

When Chemutai learned Lydia was to be circumcised with Sukunwa she panicked. Suppose Lydia was a virgin, she thought. What

343

about the baby? Before the women proceeded to the head shaving ceremony, Chemutai took Tapsalng'ot aside. They went inside the guest house for a long time. In the meantime, all of the women at the house of the ceremony were waiting for them. The women were getting frustrated. Chelamai asked to go to find out what was holding Tapsalng'ot and Chemutai up. She was accompanied by her co-wife Senge. Before they went in, they heard Chemutai pleading.

"Please, I beg you. Don't mention it to any one. I was desperate after Sukunwa had the baby and didn't give it away. She arrived with it when Lydia was there and you know the rest. I gave it to her with love. She can make him a brother or son if..." Chelamai went in before Chemutai finished her sentence.

"Everybody is waiting for you before shaving the girls," said Chelamai, who knew everything now, but neither she nor Senge gave any sign that they had heard anything. They both went out in mute silence. Each of them was trying to recover from what Chemutai had revealed. Before the shaving of the hair, Tapsalng'ot announced that Lydia's virginity should not be checked because it was not important nowadays. Chemutai proposed the same thing for Sukunwa. Senge and her co-wife Chelamai gave sighs of relief. Cheseret had no idea what was going on, but she liked it. Why should anyone let a stranger look at one's virginity anyhow, she thought.

Because Lydia and Sukunwa were not pure — Lydia because she had given birth illegitimately and Sukunwa because she was an orphan — Cheseret was asked to apply anaesthetic for the girls' night ceremony even though, as Chepsisei's first cousin, she was called "mother" by Lydia. She had to check them again and again to see if the anaesthetic was working, and later she told her co-wives, Chelamai and Senge, "I could have sworn that Lydia, who has had a baby, looked like a virgin, and Sukunwa, who has not had a baby, her vagina was like a woman who has had children. Her labia were shredded like a woman with children."

Senge and Chelamai could only glance at each other in silence. Later Senge said to Chelamai, "Chemutai is a sinner — the day of her death she will die miserably, and this secret will haunt us forever.

344

I don't see any way to let Cheseret know what we have heard and tell her not to bring it out in the open."

"It would have been easier to tell her if her mother had not accepted having the shame of an illegitimate birth put on to Lydia," said Chelamai.

"There would be war between Cheseret and her mother, not to mention Kiptai and Kiriswa. They would kill Chemutai with their bare hands, and her death will bring a curse upon us and our offspring forever," said Senge.

The girls were very brave at their operation, and all the relatives enjoyed the party which was held in Kiptai's house. The two girls were brought to Taptamus' house and all the distant female relatives and neighbours were asked to leave because Sukunwa was in danger. Anyone of them who had a son or a male relative could tie a grass engagement bracelet on her wrist, and that would have been as good as if the man himself had engaged her. And although such a method of engagement was illegitimate, there was no way to undo it once it was done.

The girls were tired after the operation, and they fell fast asleep once they were in Taptamus' house. Kiriswa's wives were looking after the guests with food and beer and watching the young neighbourhood men and girls dancing outside after the circumcision. Chemutai stayed long enough to slip Kimunai's engagement ring over Sukunwa's wrist and left. What Chemutai had done was discovered at noon, and people ran around outside screaming, "Why did she do this?" Even Lydia had no idea, but Sukunwa knew who she had done it for.

"She is your mother. I know that much. Who did she marry you to?" asked Lydia, referring to Chemutai.

But it was more than mere disappointment for Sukunwa. She collapsed before she could answer the question. She trembled for a minute and then jerked and lay rigid. Kiriswa's wives ran around aimlessly, one saying, "Open her mouth to give her milk!" Another said, "No! Pour cold water on her!"

345

"Go call her father and her uncle. We can't do much. She is foaming at the mouth, and that is a bad sign," said Chelamai.

Kiptai and Kiriswa came. Kiptai's aunt, Taptigisei, the only older woman in the family, arrived shortly after. Kiptai and Kiriswa, who were kneeling beside Sukunwa, rose to their feet. Taptigisei went past them, knelt beside Sukunwa, touched her forehead, and said a few calming words to her. She rose to her feet again and turned to Kiriswa and Kiptai.

"Don't be afraid. She will be fine. I know her. She takes after her spirit reincarnation, your mother, Kiptai. She could be upset like that. Go call all of the close relatives to anoint her with sacred oil and then make a peace offering to the ancestor spirits."

Sukunwa's uncle Kiriswa anointed her first. "Oh spirits! I anoint her with sacred oil! I pray to you to let her be happy, and may God give her health and love!"

Her father, Kiptai, anointed her, "Oh spirits! I am anointing her with sacred oil! May you guard us all together with our children and bring happiness to the family!"

Taptigisei gave Kiptai milk to give to the spirits with prayers and then beer. When they had finished, Kiriswa and Kiptai sprayed the milk and beer on both girls, and everyone took a sip of what was left over.

Lydia lay watching Sukunwa. At four o'clock, Sukunwa recovered consciousness.

"What happened to me?" she asked. She turned around, and saw Chelamai sitting beside her.

"You fell ill," said Chelamai.

"Now I remember. I was dead, and I should die again. I have been married to Kimunai. I can't stand him."

"You mustn't talk like that. You are in seclusion. You must learn to speak a different language, the gentle language of seclusion, and you must not raise your voice," said Chelamai.

"Where is Lydia?"

"I'm here," answered Lydia.

346

"Why, and why again? Why did you let them revive me when you know I can't stand Kimunai?"

"I had no idea you were married to Kimunai. Besides, I wouldn't have let you die anyhow."

"May you have sin because you betrayed me. There is nothing for me to live for," said Sukunwa.

"Sukunwa, you might as well learn right now seclusion is a time of trial. You can't talk that kind of language in seclusion. We will have a hard time finding women to help with the ceremonies when you are coming out. You will have become an unclean person, and no woman will want to be associated with you," said Chelamai. "You have people who love you — leave everything to them. Your uncle Kiriswa is mad at his sister Chemutai for what she has done to you. I know he would like to slap that witch across the face."

"We say not to do anything for show unless you derive some benefit from your action, and believe me, Kiriswa will not let Chemutai get away with this," said Cheseret from the other room where she had heard Chelamai talking to Sukunwa. "However clever she is, Kiriswa will get to the bottom of it."

Two weeks passed. All of Lydia's relatives gathered to arrange her future. She, her mother, and the baby Kimoru would stay with Mary's sister, Tapsalng'ot, who was Cheseret's mother. Kimunai's mother, Tapsirorei, had come with her son to complete Sukunwa and Kimunai's engagement, but no one wanted to talk to them. "Bring Chemutai to negotiate with; we don't know you," said Kiriswa. Chemutai knew her brother was upset and she was afraid to come. She sent a letter with Tapsirorei. The letter said, "Whatever I did was only to ensure a good future for my sister's daughter, and I know all of you will thank me some day." When the letter was read to Kiriswa, he was outraged, and he told the Kitoi family to go and drag Chemutai back with them. Chelamai told Kiriswa to go bring Chemutai by himself. "Otherwise this will take forever, having them come and go," she concluded. It was upsetting Sukunwa to see them every other day.

Kiriswa was blunt with Chemutai after she was back. "If the

marriage does not work out," he said. "You will be responsible for Sukunwa's well-being for life. You chose those people."

"I have washed my hands of the whole affair," said Kiptai. "My daughter's life lies on your head, Chemutai."

Kimunai came every week to visit, now that Sukunwa was his wife, each time bringing presents for the baby. He thought he was helping Lydia, and Lydia thought maybe the baby was his. She had never dared to ask Sukunwa about the baby's father, and never once had Sukunwa said anything to make it easier for Lydia to ask.

Eight months passed and Sukunwa and Lydia came out of seclusion. Chelamai, who was in charge of looking after them, was glad. She had had a hard time with them. Lydia did not want to have anything to do with learning Nandi traditions because of the teaching of the church. She prayed every night on her own, and she told Chelamai she would go to hell for agreeing to be circumcised.

Sukunwa had her own problems. She did not even know basic things such as how a woman should behave when she was menstruating. Chemutai hadn't taught her that when women or girls were having their periods, they could not cook food because they were unclean. For the same reason, they also could not shake anyone by the hand. If they were married to men who were wife-beaters, the law stated that they could not be struck while they were having their period. They should seclude themselves, not mix with men, and not use ordinary words referring to having a period. They should say that they have been killed by the enemy, or if they were talking to other women, they should say they had "the things of the hands" or that they "had the moon," and the most important thing was never to hand food to a man until it had ended. Sukunwa knew none of these simple customs, and Chelamai found herself covering for a lot of Sukunwa's mistakes when they were visited by the women of the neighbourhood. In the end, Chelamai was glad herself that Sukunwa had been married to a man from the city because it would never have worked with a traditional Nandi man.

Kiptai almost refused to go to his daughter's wedding. It cost too much money to get there, and he would rather pay school fees for his only son, Sukunwa's brother.

"I've given them my daughter. Chemutai can act like a mother and a father if she wants to," he said.

Kiriswa demanded he go. "I won't allow my sister's daughter to be humiliated any more. Her mother would have gone to her wedding if she was alive."

Sukunwa, Lydia and their baby were taken to Tapsirorei's house in Chemase two weeks ahead of the wedding. Kiriswa, Kiptai and Chelamai, who was acting now as Sukunwa's mother, arrived two days before the wedding started. The westernized appearance of the house maddened Kiptai on their arrival. "I never thought I would find myself in one of these square, brick houses built by our enemies," he said.

"Don't look at the house. You know Kimunai's father was an Englishman, and that is his mother's house. Kimunai and Sukunwa will build their own traditional house later," said Kiriswa trying to be as positive as possible, although he had no idea what kind of house Kimunai and Sukunwa would build.

Chelamai was thrilled. She had never been in a city, and this square house was the only "city" she had ever been in. The interior of the house upset Kiptai even more. As he stood in the sitting room looking down the hallway at the doors leading from it, he was reminded of the maze of runways that mice built in the fields of maize stubble at home. And he was even more disgusted later, when after Kimunai had taken Kiriswa aside for what appeared to be a serious discussion, Kiriswa explained he had just been informed that the bathroom and the toilet were inside the house.

Sitting was confusing even to Chelamai. When they were welcomed in, the city women who were sitting got up to make room for them. Kiptai could not imagine women sitting on chairs. And then the men came in and were expected to sit right where the women's bottoms had been. Kiptai had never seen a woman sitting in a chair like a man. He thought the family were rubbish. Sumuni, who was hostess, pointed out the chairs to Kiptai as he stood in the middle of the room.

"Do you have any men's chairs?" Kiptai asked.

"Those are men's chairs too," said Sumuni. Kiptai walked out of the room.

Kiriswa was sitting already. He didn't like the idea of women using men's chairs, but he knew that in the city women did, and he didn't care as long as it was not *his* wife on a man's chair. Sumuni went into the kitchen to relate Kiptai's opinion of the chairs. A different chair was brought to Kiptai from another room.

Dinnertime brought yet another crisis. To begin with, at home in the country, no one owned unessential things like knives, forks, spoons, dining tables and chairs and — worst of all — radios. People owned very few items — mugs, glasses, pots and pans, a lamp, bowls, plates, and one kitchen knife. Kiptai refused to use a knife and fork.

"Why am I given a fork and a knife? I'm not unclean, and I'm not in seclusion," he said. He didn't want to sit at the table to eat. Sitting on a chair to eat made him feel as though he was squatting while he ate. And if he couldn't eat by hand, he would not eat at all.

Kimunai asked his mother to feed the city people in a different room, so the country people could eat in their own room. "Let them sit on animal skins and give them water to wash their hands like home," he said.

"What is wrong if men eat with forks?" asked Sumuni.

"Women use a fork when they have a period or a baby, and this makes forks into women's utensils," said Tapsirorei.

"What about the chairs?"

"Chairs elevate one above the ground, and men should rise above women in Nandi custom," said Tapsirorei. "And that means, you know, stay off the chairs until the men of the country have left," she added.

Chelamai had fun. Ever since she had been married, she had looked after others. Here someone was making her sit and looking after her.

The two days were hard for both the people from Mt. Kamasai

and the city people working to please them. Kiptai, in particular, was difficult to please. He said he was beginning to smell like onions, and unlike Kiriswa, was not enjoying the beer. Kiptai did not like bottled beer. He said it tasted like cow's urine. "And the women and men are driving me crazy. The men seem less intellectual. They sit around the house debating with women all day long and waving their arms like women. Never in my life have I had to sit on a chair in a house all day listening to a bunch of women whining," he told Kiriswa.

"Only one day to go," Kiriswa said, with a bottle of beer in his hand.

Men at home got up early in the morning and went to let the cows out to graze. After lunch, a man left home and descended the slopes of the mountain to relive events of the past with other men and to talk about their cattle and where to find home-brewed beer. Talking about the future was for city people. The Nandi lived in the past and day by day. The future was only mentioned in prayers, "if the sun shines on us, we will have three more milk cows next year, maybe four with a good crop."

CHAPTER TWENTY-TWO

*S*ukunwa and Kimunai were married. But Sukunwa's feelings did not change. After six months, the marriage of Sukunwa and Kimunai was one-way. Kimunai showed his affection, but Sukunwa neither gave anything back, nor took anything. Kimunai was neither here nor there for her.

After a year Sukunwa tried to show a little love for Kimunai, because people were beginning to talk about her, saying that she wasn't worthy of him. By the time a girl was married, she should know her duties towards her husband. Kimunai was still doing the work of an unmarried man, making breakfast for himself and pressing his own clothes.

The respected elder women of the neighbourhood suggested to Tapsirorei that Kimunai and his wife move out of her house so they could observe Sukunwa. That way, the women in the neighbourhood could critize Sukunwa for being a bad wife without arousing Sukunwa's ire towards Tapsirorei. Tapsirorei thanked the elders for the suggestion and for noticing the problem. She had noticed it too, but could do nothing for fear of being called a bad mother-in-law.

Sukunwa hadn't changed since her marriage. She did what she wanted, as though she were still single. She left without notifying her husband. When told by Tapsirorei that a married woman didn't walk out without her husband's consent, Sukunwa said, "Those are old-fashioned ways, and besides, I'm not in prison, I'm married."

Tapsirorei kept chickens, and every morning the eggs had to be picked up. Sukunwa never offered to help. When Tapsirorei requested her help, she said, "I wasn't told I would have to collect eggs after I had been married."

At the elder women's suggestion they moved to Nakuru. The

situation worsened. Kimunai behaved like a wild animal who had been trapped in a cage and now was set free. He left the house at seven in the morning for work, returned for lunch, and then left the house, sometimes not to return until three in the morning.

Tapsirorei, moreover, was worried that Sukunwa was not becomming pregnant. She said in a letter sent to her son, "If your wife doesn't have a baby soon, your marriage may not last. What is happening? Take her to a doctor or to me, and I will take her to wise women."

When Kimunai read the letter to Sukunwa, she thought a long time before she replied. "There is nothing wrong with me. If I wanted to have a baby, I would have had one."

"Why aren't you having one then?" Kimunai demanded, but he got no answer.

After they moved to Nakuru, Sukunwa wrote to Lydia that she had made up her mind what to do with her life.

> Dear Lydia,
> Nothing has changed between me and Kimunai. I continue to be unhappy. Besides being crazy, he also lacks sympathy. After we moved to Nakuru, I realized our marriage had become a social habit to him, and the situation is getting worse. Sadly, the tension between us has increased. I have been sick since we came to Nakuru, and Kimunai has been irresponsible. He leaves the house at seven and comes back in the evening, pretending to worry. Then he asks for food. If I haven't cooked, he leaves. After one of his mistresses has made dinner for him, he comes back. If he's not doing this, he is bringing little girls and asking me to make friends with them, instead of saying, 'Lure them for me.' I don't know how long I will last with him. I have accepted him, but I can't condone his behaviour. He is asking me now to have a baby because his mother wants us to. I think I'll have to

leave because I would not want to have his child. I'm afraid I would kill it if it was like him.

Greetings to your mother, Chepsisei and to Kimoru.

Love,
Sukunwa

After two years the marriage of Sukunwa and Kimunai ended. Sukunwa went home to Mt. Kamasai to her uncle Kiriswa and aunt Chelamai's home. Lydia alone knew Sukunwa was leaving Kimunai, until Tapsirorei came looking for her. According to custom, a mother-in-law was required to go after a daughter-in-law to find out what her son had done to her. It was determined that Kimunai had behaved irresponsibly towards Sukunwa after the elders had heard from both sides. Tapsirorei asked for forgiveness from the elders for her son and to be given permission to take Sukunwa back with her.

Kiriswa's wives, Senge and Chelamai, said no. "You and your son's neglect of Sukunwa has been too great to let her go with you. We want Kimunai to come and promise us that he is never going to leave Sukunwa alone and ill in the house," they said. "We love her dearly, and her uncle is still young enough to provide for all of us," added Chelamai, pausing to hear what Kiriswa would say.

Kiriswa agreed with his wives. "You have heard what my wives say, Tapsirorei. There is nothing more to add," he said.

Tapsirorei left that afternoon. Sukunwa was so happy that she cried and cried because of the happiness. That evening Chelamai asked her if she agreed with them that Kimunai should come first for them to hear what he said. Sukunwa said yes she was very glad for that.

Sukunwa slept at Lydia's and they talked all night. She told Lydia, "I'm going to leave and go so far that no one will ever hear from me again because I cannot bear to return to Kimunai and his family again."

Lydia tried to talk Sukunwa into staying, but Sukunwa had made up her mind. The next day, when every one was out clearing land for cultivation, she left Mt. Kamasai.

The next thing people heard was that she was in Kisumu looking for a job. Kiriswa said he was going to bring her now that he knew where she was. But in Nandi, it took time to organize a trip to the city, and after two months, Kiriswa still had not gone for Sukunwa. Kimunai came to accuse him of losing his wife.

Half a year later, while her uncle was still preparing to go to Kisumu, word arrived that Sukunwa had disappeared. Gradually, her name faded away. Stories began to be circulated about her. Some said she had left Kisumu for Nairobi, some said Mombasa, and others said Zanzibar. Some said she had met a road engineer from Malawi. When he was transferred to Zanzibar, she went with him. People who claimed to have seen her there said she had been abused. "She's changed completely; you would not recognize her when you met her."

These stories were told and retold in the years of Sukunwa's absence, by well-meaning people trying to keep her spirit alive and spare themselves from grief. But the guessing and the hoping only came to an end deacdes later, when Sukunwa arrived from Canada — a place distant beyond their guesses — with two beautiful children. All the city people and all the young, educated people were curious to hear her tell her own story. In Mt. Kamasai, however, where Sukunwa's father and her uncle and his wives lived, no questions were asked that might remind Sukunwa of Canada. They all hoped she would never leave Africa again.

THE CHARACTERS

Sukunwa's Family:

Sukunwa	Nandi, married to Speedo
Speedo	Canadian, married to Sukunwa
Chepkiyeny	Sukunwa's daughter
Kibet	Sukunwa's son
Taptamus	Sukunwa's grandmother
Arap Mararsoi	Sukunwa's grandfather, Taptamus' husband
Cheptabut	Sukunwa's mother, Taptamus' daughter
Kiptai	Sukunwa's father, Cheptabut's husband
Taptigisei	Kiptai's aunt
Chemengech	Sukunwa's aunt, Taptamus' daughter
Tilinkwai	Chemengech's daughter
Chemutai	Sukunwa's aunt, Taptamus' daughter
Kiriswa	Sukunwa's uncle, Taptamus' only son,
Kibet	Taptamus' nephew
Tapchamgoi	Kiriswa's mother-in-law, mother of Senge
Senge	Tapchamgoi's daughter, Kiriswa's wife
Senge	Taptamus' deceased sister

Lydia's Family:

Lydia	Sukunwa's friend
Kimoru	Lydia's older son
Kimosbei	Lydia's younger son
Mary	Taptamus friend, Lydia's grandmother
Arap Walei	Mary's husband
Chepsisei	Lydia's mother, Mary's daughter
Musimba	Lydia's father
Lydia	Chepsisei's daughter, Mary's granddaughter

The Rest of Mt. Kamasai:

Arap Metuk	Chelamai's father
Tabaes	Chelamai's mother, Arap Metuk's wife
Chelamai	daughter of Arap Metuk and Tabaes
Arap Temoet	Cheseret's father, husband of Tapsalng'ot
Tapsalng'ot	Cheseret's mother, Mary's sister
Chebii	Cheseret's aunt
Chepkurgat	Chebii's daughter
Lawrence	Chepkurgat's boyfriend
Cheseret	Sukunwa's babysitter, daughter of Tapsalng'ot
Kiptarus Arap Maiyo	Cheseret's brother
Arap Kilach	Tamutwol's husband, Tapchamgoi's cousin
Tamutwol	Tolony's mother, Arap Mibei's wife
Tolony	Tamutwol's daughter

JANE TAPSUBEI CREIDER was born and raised in Kapseret, near Eldoret, Kenya. Her mother started her in elementary school, but her father later removed her, saying it was not good for girls to be educated. She was initiated and while in seclusion for the following four years received instruction in the ethical principles, laws and traditions of her people. After coming out of seclusion, she went to Kisumu to live with her mother and attended school there where she first heard of North America. Later she worked in Kisumu before leaving Africa. She now lives in Canada where she has worked as a potter, clay sculptor and writer. She is the author of several scholarly papers about her people, the Nandi, and has also written *A Grammar of Nandi* (1989). *Two Lives: My Spirit and I*, an autobiography, was published in 1986. She is married and has two children.